MARK HOLLOWAY

The Soul's Aspect

MARK HOLLOWAY

Copyright © 2021 by Mark Holloway

All rights reserved. No part of this publication may be reproduced, stored or transmitted in any form or by any means, electronic, mechanical, photocopying, recording, scanning, or otherwise without written permission from the publisher. It is illegal to copy this book, post it to a website, or distribute it by any other means without permission.

This novel is entirely a work of fiction. The names, characters and incidents portrayed in it are the work of the author's imagination. Any resemblance to actual persons, living or dead, events or localities is entirely coincidental.

Mark Holloway asserts the moral right to be identified as the author of this work.

Cover figure design and creation by Decky Yuriadi (available on Fiverr)

Cover design and composition by Mark Holloway

First edition

*This book was professionally typeset on Reedsy.
Find out more at reedsy.com*

For

My Dad, who taught me to love reading,

My Mum, who taught me to love people and the world around me,

And

My wife, who gives me love in such abundance, spills and nurtures stories like this, which is a testament to the love we share.

Contents

1	Felling	1
2	Broken Things	9
3	Return	16
4	Cider and Ale	24
5	Smoke and Lavender	32
6	Bitter	44
7	Wooden Whispers	55
8	Catalyst	65
9	Fury	74
10	Tethers that bind us	79
11	Forest Fire	83
12	Sweet	88
13	Patterns	95
14	Precipice	104
15	Isale	113
16	Pattern Trial	123
17	Kin and Kith	132
18	Aberration	141
19	To See	150
20	Break	166
21	The Scribe	175
22	A Burning Soul	191
23	To Rend a Heart	204
24	Waterfel	216
25	Forest	225
26	Trail	233

27	Aspector	239
28	Fruits of labour	250
29	The Altar	257
30	The Aspect	266
31	The Square	273
32	The road less trod	286
33	Winterwhail	290
34	Epilogue	301
Thank you for reading		304
About the Author		305
Also by Mark Holloway		306

1

Felling

"Tema!"

The panicked call pierced through the lazy silence of the afternoon. I jumped to my feet, tossing the book I'd been studying to the kitchen floor.

"Kehlem!"

The shrill voice called again, louder now as I ran to the front door. I knew that voice. I yanked the door open to see Bill, red-faced and panting on my doorstep.

"Kehlem! Thank the Martyr you're in, boy," Bill panted. "I wasn't sure if you'd already be at the festival."

"What's going on?" I asked, my eyes darting from Bill to the crude sledge behind him. Laid atop was the writhing form of his friend, Job. A tattered blanket covered him up to his shoulders. I stepped out into the cold autumn air and peeled the blanket back. Job let out a soft whimper.

"We were out collecting wood for the pyre," Bill babbled. "The stupid ejit tried to cut down a yew. The tree had rotted to the core and toppled straight onto his leg." Wide-eyed, pale face. Bill was in shock.

With the blanket lifted, I could see the mangled remains of Job's leg. It was bent and twisted at grotesque angles. Muscle and bone, which up until now I had only seen in our anatomy books, lay open to the elements.

I turned to Bill. "I'll get him inside, you look exhausted." I grabbed a fist full of the rough hemp rope tied to the sledge. "Go get my father, he'll be in his study."

A wave of relief washed over Bill's face and he pushed past me, racing inside. I could hear him shouting my father's name as he went.

Job was dropping in and out of consciousness. Bill had enough sense to tie a tourniquet on his thigh, but he looked like he'd lost a lot of blood.

Bracing myself, I heaved the sledge inside. I was half the height and a quarter the age of Bill, who had years of sinewy muscle gained only from a life lived outdoors. I managed to get the sledge into our kitchen, scoring and scratching our wooden floors on the way, by the time Bill and my father joined us.

Father stood a full head taller than Bill but was of a slighter build. He had a cropped mass of grey hair which had at one point matched the auburn colour of my own. Despite his willowy frame, he radiated an aura of certainty that people of the town gravitated towards like a leading stone.

Father's gaze shifted from Job's leg to Bill. "Let's get him on the table."

The three of us lifted Job. My father used the blanket as a makeshift sling to hold his ruined leg in place as we lifted him carefully onto our kitchen table. The movement woke Job and he cried out.

Bill grabbed Job's hand. "Can you set it, Tema?"

"No," my father said.

I turned to him, shocked. Job, understanding the significance, wailed louder, while Bill tried to hush him with a steady, whispering mantra "It'll be alright, it'll be alright…"

I wasn't certain if it was for Job's or his own benefit.

"Kehlem," my father's voice rang clear through Job's wails. "Get me poppy milk."

I rushed to our store cupboard, grabbed the dark brown bottle, and passed it to my father.

"You may as well kill me Tema," Job cried, "I'm never gonna work again! Oh, please let the Martyr take me, I can't do it, I can't —"

"Hush now, drink this." Father interrupted Job's steady stream of worry with a cup of the white, thick fluid. "Bill, can you pass that bottle of whiskey down from over there? Yes, that one."

Once he'd finished helping Job with the poppy milk, he uncorked the whiskey bottle and poured out three glasses. Giving the tallest glass to Job, who looked at it with dismay, shooting it back as quickly as possible. Father then passed a glass each to me and Bill.

"For the nerves," he explained. "I will need your help with this."

Bill followed Job's lead, shooting the drink to the back of his throat. Having never had a taste before, I imitated Job and Bill, and immediately regretted it. The burning, peaty liquid ran through me like liquid fire. I coughed, spluttering as I wiped tears away from my eyes. Despite himself, Bill gave me a brief smile. The warmness of the whiskey washed through me, rising from my chest, spreading up my neck, and laying warm hands across my cheeks.

The whimpering coming from Job slowed to a quiet sob. Without being asked, I fetched a leather strap and slid it gently into Job's mouth. Poppy would only take so much of the edge off, and it's better to bite through leather than tongue.

Father looked at me with a raised eyebrow. "Assessment?"

This was our routine.

Where was the issue? How do we treat it? What should the patient do? What shouldn't the patient do?

Usually, it was simple things like wrapping a sprained ankle, or stitching closed a slight cut. A small town like Barrowheld doesn't see that much in the way of serious maladies.

His tone and question did more to soothe my nerves than the whiskey.

What's the plan? No different from the other patients we've seen and treated. We can do this.

I calmed my mind and tried to assess the situation dispassionately, as he had taught me.

I cleared my throat. "The tourniquet has already cut the blood supply to the lower thigh. With the time this has been laid open and exposed, infection is likely here," I indicated the area just above the kneecap where the bone had splintered through Job's thigh muscle. "We should amputate here," I moved my finger higher, pointing to a section of the thigh that was mostly undisrupted.

"Good," my father said. "And how?"

I paused, trying to think back to a book I'd studied.

"Fish mouth incision, saw and then file the bone smooth, sew any remaining usable muscle to bone, stitch closed the fish mouth and bandage."

My father just nodded, apparently pleased. "We also need to strap Job down. Him moving around won't do him any good," he added.

I nodded and started fetching straps around Job's now unconscious body.

"Hands," my father commanded. He tied my hair back out of my face, and we pulled our sleeves above our elbows.

As we got to the sink and scrubbed our hands with lyesic soap, Bill got his cue and joined us.

"Right." My father took a deep breath. "Let us begin."

We only realised how much damage had been done to Job's leg after we had cut away his trousers. The bones in his lower leg had splintered, his knee was shattered, and his thigh muscle had been torn open, either by the force of the tree felling or, more likely, from Bill pulling him out from underneath. We would have to amputate higher than expected, as the lower flesh was already sallow and waxy, too ruined to survive.

My father and I had finished the incisions and were working on stripping and lifting back the muscle to expose the remaining intact femur when I heard a stifled sob coming from the other end of the table. I peered over the table. Job was still unconscious, Bill, however, was staring at the exposed bone, mouth clamped shut. Father had asked him to keep an eye on Job, to make sure he didn't stir too much and to mop and cool his brow while we worked.

"You okay there Bill?" I asked, trying to keep my voice level.

Bill said nothing, eyes fixed on his friend's ruined leg. I caught my father's eye, and he nodded to me. I gently let go of the flesh and grabbed a chair. Bill was swaying a little, sweat beading on his forehead.

"I'm just bringing you a chair, Bill. That's right, just here. If you just stand away from the table a little…" I kept up the even tone, talking the way you would to a spooked horse. Before I could get to him, however, Bill's eyes rolled back and his legs gave way. He fell to the floor unconscious, banging his head on the corner of the table as he went.

"Everything ok?" Father called.

"Bill just managed to knock himself unconscious," I sighed, reaching down to check his pulse and pull an eyelid up. "He isn't bleeding, I think he's alright."

"Just make sure he won't choke on his own vomit. We need to finish this before Job wakes up."

I rolled Bill onto his side where he lay underneath the table and walked back over to the other side of the table.

"Kehlem," my father scolded. "Hands."

Shit. I stood up and ran back to the sink, scrubbing my hands again.

"Right," my father said. "You hold the leg still, I will saw the bone."

Stealing myself, I grabbed whatever I could, bone, tissue, skin, and squeezed tight. The soft *squelch* of flesh in my grip hit me in my stomach, and I struggled to swallow the rising bile.

"Ready?" Father asked, picking up a large, square saw from his leather wrap of instruments.

I swallowed, taking a deep breath. I nodded once.

Father gripped one side of Job's leg and began to saw. A loud squeaky, grating sound rang through the air, and I could feel the vibration of the saw against bone through the flesh I gripped. My legs buckled slightly, and a cold sweat beaded out on my face. I tightened my grip, forcing myself to ignore the sounds.

The table shook as Job struggled into consciousness, woken by the pain. He thrashed against the straps we'd set. I craned my neck to see his eyes wide, staring up to the ceiling, jaw clamped on the leather strap. Despite his struggling, my father held an iron grip around the femur and finished sawing, the weight of the leg in my hands coming free of the ruined lower portion.

"Wrap that up, and place it on the counter over there, would you?" My father pointed to the now excised leg.

Gulping down bile once more, I again set myself and tried to clear my mind. I used the blankets we had placed underneath the leg and wrapped the remains. I lifted it, surprised by how weighty it was, and dropped it carefully on the counter behind us, unnerved at the sight of a toe pointing out from beneath the blanket. Job had passed out again by the time I sat back down.

"What will we do with the leg?" I asked.

"I imagine the priest will want to burn it on the pyre after tonight's activities. Make an offering to the Martyr or something stupid like that."

It would be generous to say Father and the town's priest did not get along especially well. He called him a 'frivolous middle man' and had little patience for him.

Father began filing the bone, filling the room with a scraping sound that made me long for the sound of the saw. Worse than the sound, the filing created a dust that settled in the air, accentuating the pale sunbeams from the late afternoon sun that were streaming into the kitchen. I held my breath, desperate to not breathe it in.

The vibration woke Job again, this time screaming as he spat out the leather bite. Perhaps too tired to fight against the bindings, he lay still, just screaming and crying out for his Ma', pleading for the Martyr to take him. Nothing he said seemed to reach the ears of my father, who kept the file going at an incessant tattoo.

I stood to fetch the leather bite for Job, hoping to offer him some small comfort as we finished. At some point during the procedure, he'd pissed himself, and the smell of urine added to the cacophony of blood, sweat, and bone. I mopped his head, wiping the sweat and tears from his face, and he slowly drifted back into unconsciousness, his mind retreating from the horrors of his reality.

I would like to say I went back afterwards, sat back down and helped my father suture muscle to bone, and sew closed the remains of his leg. I would like to say that, unlike Bill, I had a constitution that kept me calm and dispassionate, and I remained unaffected by such trivial things as a mere amputation. I was the son of Barrowheld's physician, after all.

That, however, would not be an honest account. In truth, I stayed by Job and Bill, making myself look busy by checking straps and washing Job's face. Job's pleading for his dead Ma' had been the final straw for me. I'd never known my mother, but to hear a grown man sobbing for his, cracked my heart.

The sun dipped below the horizon as my father tied off the final bandage. Together we lifted Job to a spare bed and placed the still unconscious Bill in a chair next to him. We then spent the next few hours cleaning down our kitchen as best we could, despite our exhaustion.

Taking one look at our kitchen table, we made an unspoken decision to throw it out front, leaving it for the town pyre. With Job and Bill sound asleep, and the kitchen as clean as we could make it, we retreated to the study, collapsing into two armchairs facing our fireplace.

"Well done today," Father said, turning to me, bloodstains drying on his linen shirt. "The first time I assisted with an amputation, I puked all over my master."

I held my head in my hands, too exhausted to really process what had happened.

"It was…" I paused, trying to think of the right words, "different to how the books explain it."

My father smiled. "Most things are. Everyone reacts differently. A book can't prepare you for that. It can't prepare you for the feel of gripping a man's femur in one hand and a saw in the other while he begs you to stop."

Desperate not to relive that moment so soon, I tried to change the subject. "What do you think will happen to Job?"

"He won't be any good as a farmhand anymore, that's for sure," Father sighed. "A shame too, I know he and Bill have worked together for a long time." He saw my worried look. "He'll get by. He's lucky he wasn't killed."

The only time I'd seen another amputee before was in Mercy. Draped in tattered cloth and emaciated, he'd been sitting on the street, calling out to anyone who would hear for food or spare change. Not one soul turned to even look at him. I wasn't sure I could describe Job as lucky.

"Was there anything we could have done to save it?" I asked

My father rubbed his face. He looked very tired. "Us? No. Possibly an Aspector could have."

"An Aspector?" I asked, incredulous. "I thought they were all soldiers."

"Most of them are now, thanks to Vin Irudur. Before the war, before the Vins, the Casere had the right to train our own Aspectors." His next sigh grew into a yawn. "I knew an Aspector once," he mused quietly. "She could have willed the leg together without a second thought."

I turned to him, stunned. Every child knew the tale of the Caserean Aspectors, and the crater left in Narrowmarsh at the end of the war. They were heroes of legends, canonized saints who'd died for Casere and the Martyr. They weren't the people your father casually claims he once knew.

"You knew an Aspector?" I said, aghast. My tone seemed to jolt my father from whatever stupor he had fallen in.

"Hmm? No. That's not what I meant. I knew *of* an Aspector. *Of.*" His voice had changed from slow and sleepy, suddenly sharp and alert.

I tried to interrupt.

"It isn't important, Kehlem," he said, holding his hand up. "The point is, we couldn't save his leg. And even if an Aspector could, Mercy is miles away and Job wouldn't have survived the journey. Don't waste your time questioning yourself. It doesn't do you or your patient any good."

Before I could respond, he was on his feet, walking out of the study and leaving me alone by the fire. Confused by his sudden sharp rebuke but too exhausted to care I watched the flames in the fireplace dance.

Did my father really know an Aspector? Would a Vin Irudur Aspector have cared enough to save a Casere farmhand's leg?

My eyes closed slowly, and a heavy weight dropped on my consciousness. As I slept that night, the screeching of file on bone accompanying the cries of Job's pleading tormented my dreams.

2

Broken Things

"I can get you another fluid ounce of the laudanum, perhaps two, but we're all out of buckthorn." The apothecary shrugged his shoulders at us. He knew as well as we did that our options were limited. He was Barrowheld's only apothecary so if he didn't have what we needed, our next best option was a day and a half's ride away.

My father sighed. "Fine, an ounce of the poppy milk then. How much, Anick?"

Anick sucked his teeth, eyeing my father. "Twelve pennies even."

Even my eyebrows raised at that. I looked over to my father, who was still staring at the man evenly.

"I'll give you eight." He counted the coins from his purse and slid them over the counter.

Anick made no move to take them. "Tema, you're a good man, and normally I'd be happy to dither, but twelve is the best I can do for you. The Vin's raised the tax on its import —"

As he spoke, my father slid two more silver coins across the counter.

Anick let out a long sigh. "Fine, have it your way!" he exclaimed, sweeping the coins up, and pushing an amber bottle across the counter. "When you're riding to Rethersford to get a few scruples of nightshade, you'll regret having run me out of town."

"Always a pleasure, my friend," my father smiled. No trip to Anick's was complete without him complaining that we were putting him out of business.

Together Father and I left the warm, spicy air of the apothecary for the chill wind of the town square. It was mid-day, and the square was filled with people bustling to and fro as they attended their errands of the day. With the partial restock of our stores taken care of, next up were some home visits. I drew my cloak closer around my body to stave off a sudden blast of the winter wind.

"Are the taxes really getting worse, or was Anick exaggerating?" I asked as we made our way south.

My father nodded to a passer-by in greeting and then turned to me. "Knowing Anick? Probably a little bit of both. He'd never turn down an opportunity to thumb the scale if the opportunity presented it."

There was an unspoken 'but' there. I nodded to myself in silent agreement. Twelve silvers was a lot to ask. Even Anick wouldn't be that brazen without justification. We rounded a corner, and the road turned from smooth flagstone to dirt as we left the town centre.

My father cleared his throat. "I noticed this morning that there's still a fair amount of your tincture left…" He left the question unspoken.

I cursed to myself silently as my face flushed, betraying me in an instant. I knew this question had been coming.

"Umhm" I grunted, non-commitment. No need to implicate myself any more than was needed.

Father drew to a halt, placing a hand on my shoulder. "Have you stopped taking your medicine?"

I hadn't expected him to be so direct so quickly. It caught me off guard. I forced myself to meet his eyes. "No," I said honestly.

His gaze didn't falter. He wasn't dropping it. He kept quiet, letting the silence drag on between us.

"Not stopped," I hedged, if only to fill the silence.

He raised a single eyebrow

"It's just, I haven't had a seizure in years! Since I was a baby!" I tried to sound confident, all the practiced words tumbling out from my cluttered mouth. I persevered, "I'm so sick of how the medicine makes me feel. It's so hard to concentrate!" My voice sounded whiney even to my own ears.

I took a deep breath and cleared my throat.

"About a month ago, I titrated my dose down, just enough so that I could think clearly again. It's been so much easier to study since. And," I continued, "I've not had any incidents! No seizures, no fainting, nothing! Maybe this dose is strong enough." I shrugged my shoulders, and my eyes fell to the floor. In my heart of hearts, I knew it was stupid to interfere with my dosage without telling my father first, but I knew what he'd say. I figured it'd be easier to show him I didn't need the medication rather than asking to come off it completely. He was still watching me, but a slight frown had touched his brow.

His hand slid off my shoulder and he let out a long sigh as he rubbed his eyes with thumb and forefinger. "I'm not happy about this, Kehlem," he said after a long moment. "You can't just change your medication without telling me. What would have happened if you'd had an attack and I wasn't home?"

His voice wasn't angry. Not exactly. It wasn't raised, his tone was level, but regardless, it cut through any of my prepared arguments as deftly as a scalpel.

I had no response, and was barely able to offer up a mumbled 'I don't know'.

The tension deflated out of him. He put his arm over my shoulder and pulled me into a quick, one arm hug, before setting us off walking again.

"I won't lose you Kehlem. You're all I have. Just promise not to do something so thoughtless again."

"Does this mean I'm going back up to the higher dose?" I asked, dismayed.

He glanced at me, eyes flitting from left to right as they searched my own. "No."

My heart raced and warmth ran through me as muscles I hadn't even realised had tensed, relaxed.

"As you say, you've had no incidents with the lower dose, so I can't see a justification to put you back on the higher dose." He glanced over to me, looking at the grin which had spread across my face. "However," he said slowly, "that comes with two expectations," he said, fixing me in his gaze.

I nodded eagerly.

"Firstly, no more experimenting with your dose. When I let you make up your own tincture it came with a certain level of trust. You broke that by not coming to me first, and so for the foreseeable future, I will be preparing your medication going forward. Second, and most importantly, if you have any symptoms, any at all, you will go back up to the higher dose. Is that understood?"

"I understand," I said, abashed.

"Good. Right, enough of this." He pulled his cloak around himself tight. "Let's get to Job's and get those stitches out. I'm bloody freezing."

The sun was fully set by the time we'd left Job's. Mercifully the wind had died down, but the clear skies above harboured a promise of a sharp cold snap. Father and I were the only ones braving the evening, most others safely tucked away in their homes, or more likely in the amber embrace of the tavern in the town square. Normally the sound of distant music and frivolity would make me long for the alehouse, but Job's visit had left me feeling dour.

He'd recovered well from his surgery, physically at least. But mentally, he had a long way to go. He communicated to us in monosyllables and grunts, and there was a substantial lack of vitality behind his eyes. He sat on a rocking chair, staring out into space as we worked on cleaning and checking his stump. No complaints, no idle chat, nothing.

It must have affected my father as well, as we strode home in total silence.

"I noticed Maggie's limp was back today," father said, looking up from his bowl of stew.

"What?" I asked, through my mouthful of potato and rutabaga.

We sat in the kitchen, cross-legged on the floor next to the fire. We still hadn't got around to replacing the table after Job's surgery.

"Maggie. She was limping when we walked past her by the butchers. You should go around tomorrow and check in on her."

I grunted an acknowledgement and carried on eating. Maggie was one of our regulars, the town chandler and the mother to one of my closest friends.

"You spoken to Eva recently?" Father asked.

"She's still in Mercy," I shrugged. "Her Uncle's still trying to help her get an apprenticeship."

"Mhmm," he grunted. "I can't say I blame Maggie trying to get Eva out of Barrowheld. There's not a great deal of jobs left here."

I nodded to myself. Barrowheld had never been a thriving town, but things had certainly seemed to have gotten worse in recent years. Thankfully there was always work for a physician. Physicians, levy men, priests and gravediggers. Quell in fear all ye at Casere's mighty industry. Not that I was pleased with the thought of my best friend moving to a new city, leaving me alone, stuck in Barrowheld.

We continued our meal in silence, with only the occasional crack of the fire, or slurping of stew to puncture the woollen quiet of the evening.

"Go on," my father said, interrupting the stillness.

"Go on what?"

"There's a question heavy on your lips. Ask it."

"How did you know?" I smiled, putting my bowl down and stretching my legs out.

My father shrugged his shoulders. "Well, I did have my part in making you," he said.

An unwelcome mental image sped through my mind.

"Gross," I said, pulling a face.

My father laughed, deep and rich. "Go ahead, ask whatever it is you've been holding on to."

"Could an Aspector truly have saved Job's leg?" Ever since the surgery, I hadn't stopped thinking about it. To save Job's leg, they would have to regrow flesh. Not just the muscle and bone, but nerves and cartilage, ligaments and tendons. It was beyond anything I had heard of. I wanted to know more. Any scrap, any morsel of information.

Father eyed me, and then lifted his bowl to his lips before setting it aside on the floor next to mine.

"When I was a lad, a little younger than yourself, the Casereans were not bound by the accords. Aspectors were still rare of course, but they were around. More importantly, they did more than fight. Back when I was an apprentice, my master took me to the capital. There was an Aspector at the university who taught anatomy. Not just to Aspectors mind, it was open to the public. Occasionally a patient would arrive who would agree to be treated in the amphitheatre."

My father stretched his own legs out, pushing his feet closer to the fireplace.

"On the second day of my visit, a tradesman arrived at the university, sweaty, running a high fever and walking with a limp. On closer inspection, the physicians found an infested wound that had eaten into his calf muscle, from which a sweet-smelling fluid was leaking. The Aspector explained all of this to us in the audience, and many of us being trainee physicians knew the prognosis. Amputation, and even then, the man would be lucky to survive.

"But the Aspector was a showman, through and through. She used it as a teaching moment, explaining the course the injury has taken through the various muscles, ligaments and bones of the leg. She explained the various methods for treatment, including herbal and surgery. She had even laid out a tray of bone saws, scalpels and sutures. But then, at the end of the lecture, without hesitation, she laid one hand on the man's leg and drew a single, intricate symbol in the air with the other. There was a bright light, and several moments later, the leg was healed. No scar. No mottling or bruising. No fever."

I sat quietly, desperately absorbing the information. "It sounds too good to be true," I said.

Father looked at me and smiled slightly. "You'd be quite right, I think. There's always a payoff. Besides," he sighed, "even when Aspectors were more common, you'd be lucky to find a healer like that within fifty miles of a town like Barrowheld. There's a reason why I was still learning to be a physician without being an Aspector."

"Do you think they could have healed me?" I asked. The question had spilt unbidden from my lips.

My father leaned forwards and grabbed my hand firmly. He held my gaze within eyes with such a sudden, deep sadness that I struggled to catch my breath.

"There is nothing in you that is broken, my boy."

3

Return

"I don't suppose either of you knows what tonight's meeting's about do you?" A burly man with forearms that would not look amiss hanging from a butcher's meat hook called over to us from the bar. It was Risa, a carpenter and neighbour, although, in a town as small as Barrowheld, the latter was hardly a unique delineator.

"Haven't the foggiest," father called back to him.

It had been a couple of weeks since we'd last visited Job, and winter had fallen in earnest. The days were dark and the nights were long, so more often than not, the townsfolk found themselves at The Rosen Pyre. If you've ever visited a town in Casere, you've visited a Rosen Pyre or a tavern just like it. Windows that were bought cheap, warped and were in a constant state of condensation. A single hearth in its centre, above which an enormous iron pot hung with the day's meal. Of course, the floor would be filled with more tables and chairs than what was good for it, and the room was always thick with the heady concoction of ale, spilt wine and candle smoke. In summer the innkeeper would throw open the doors and set the tables and chairs out into the town square, and in the winter the tavern would be so packed with bodies, laughing and shouting that the patrons would often stand outside in the freezing temperatures just to cool off.

I loved it, and for many in Barrowheld, including myself, it was a second home.

My father nudged me with his elbow as he noticed Risa making his way through the jumble of chairs from the bar over towards us. I stood up from my stool to make room and shifted to the other side of our table.

"How we doing lads?" Risa asked, mostly rhetorically. "Mind if I join ye?" again, rhetorically.

"Middling to well, and yourself?" Father responded, and so the call and response were complete. He nodded his head to the spare chair, and Risa sat his bulky figure down with a grunt, setting three tankards down with him. He pushed one each over to me and Father.

I eyed it, not sure if I should take it. I could already feel the warm glow from my first drink, and we had strict rules about drinking. I glanced at my father.

"Go on," he smiled, "I'm sure one more won't hurt."

I grinned, and thanked Risa for the drink, taking a long sip.

"You got a good lad there, Tema," Risa said, approvingly.

"Oh, I know, he won't let me forget," my father smiled.

Risa laughed, his red cheeks glowing and glistening with sweat. He slapped me on the arm, causing me to spill my tankard over the table, which only sent him howling even more.

"Sorry, don't know my own strength! You need to get some more meat on your bones boy!"

I nodded, more than a little embarrassed, and hid my face in my drink.

"What have you heard about the meeting then?" Father asked, blessedly changing the topic.

That was, of course, the other reason the tavern was so busy tonight. The Mayor had called a town meeting, and by unspoken tradition, the town would often have an impromptu meeting at the tavern first. On reflection, it probably spoke volumes about the town's opinion of the mayor that imbibing alcohol before listening to him was not only expected but strictly encouraged.

"Buggered if I know," Risa said, wiping the beer that had dribbled down his gnarled beard. "If it's to announce more taxes, he'll have a hell of a time explaining it though. Folks have bled enough this year. There's only so far good folks can be pushed."

"You think there'll be trouble?" I asked, surprised.

"Aye lad. Not tonight. Not tomorrow. But the more they keep pushing us, the closer we'll get to the edge. You can only back up an animal into a corner so much, 'fore you leave him no choice but to bite."

"I doubt it'll come to that," father said. "The Vin's aren't stupid."

"No, they 'ent. And if that isn't half the problem."

Half an hour later, and ever so slightly unsteady on my feet, father and I made our way to the town hall, along with the rest of the tavern. The cold wind and gentle patter of rain was a relief after the sweltering tavern, but thankfully the hall was only on the other side of the square, so before we got too cold, we were once more embraced by the more modest, dryer warmth of the hall. It was a simple building, one that would double up as a function room for town fairs. Tonight, its wooden floors had row after row of benches laid out on it, all facing towards a lectern at the opposite end of the hall.

"Quiet!" the Mayor called out as the townsfolk made their way to their seats. He was a thin, well-kept fellow with a ring of grey hair by his ears, sharp chin and an impressively bushy moustache. The townsfolk, slowly and begrudgingly, complied. The noise dimmed until it was just a few voices pattering between the most stubborn of folk. Or the drunkest.

"Before we start tonight's meeting," the Mayor said, "I thought I'd ask Father Jed to lead us in a blessing."

I stifled a groan as the Mayor stepped aside and the cowled figure of Father Jed took to the lectern. It's not that I disliked the church, or even that I didn't have faith in the Martyr. Jed just really liked the sound of his own voice, which had this incredible, soporific quality associated with it. In my modestly merry state, I would be lucky to escape even a short prayer without drifting off. I bowed my head along with everyone else.

"...thers and sisters, let the Martyr gaze down upon us to grant us her blessed and holy vision, may the pyre..."

Bloody hell this man was dull.

I wondered idly if the priesthood required their clergy to be as close to the human embodiment of grey as possible. His words had already lost all meaning and were reaching my ears only as unintelligible sounds. My head suddenly grew very heavy, and there was a curious tugging at the fingers of my left hand. Then a sudden sharp pain blossomed in the meat of my left arm. My head shot up, eyes flying open to see my father smirking at me, dropping his elbow back down. Jed had just stepped down from the plinth. I must have dozed off. And from the way Jed was staring at me, disapproval etched on his face, he'd noticed. I sat up straight, flushed with embarrassment.

A soft voice whispered behind me, close to my ear, "Don't worry, I think only half the town heard your snore."

The horror of realising I'd actually snored during the priest's prayer fought hard against the rising recognition of that voice. I spun around on my bench and spotted the smirking figure of a girl with jet black hair. Her amber eyes danced like candlelight as she stifled a giggle.

"Eva!" I whispered, "When did you get back?"

She laughed again, brushing the hair that had untucked itself from behind her ears back out of her eyes, and nodded towards the front. I turned around to see the Mayor standing ready at the pulpit, staring at me.

"If you are quite done, young master Kehlem?"

A deep rosy wave of embarrassment flushed my cheeks. "Apologies, Mayor Dane, please continue," I called back, mortified.

"Well, since I have your kind permission," he rolled his eyes, and then mercifully turned his attention to the rest of the room. "I gathered you here today to share with you some news I received earlier in the week. I have been informed by the Eastern Garrison that we are to play host to a Vin Irudur Aspector."

At the mention of 'Vin Irudur', harsh whispers erupted amongst the crowd. The words 'taxes', 'thief' and 'brazen bastards' were loud enough to be picked out. Of course, my ears pricked mostly to the fact they were an Aspector. A real Aspector. I strained my ears to try and make out what the mayor was saying above the audience's muttering.

"They are expected to arrive towards the end of this month and will be staying for at least two months. It goes without saying that the town will make every accommodation to them, and any interference of their duties," at this last he raised his voice well above the rising volume of the crowd, "will be dealt with immediately and swiftly."

The Mayor surveyed the townsfolk, who were now in open, heated conversation with one another. With a look of resignation, he called out, "Any questions?"

Several came at once.

"What right do they have?"

"What do they want with Barrowheld?"

"Are they a Hunter or what?"

"We best be bloody charging them Dane, I swear to the Martyr."

Dane held up his hands at the barrage of noise. "All I know is that they aren't a Hunter. I've no idea what they want with Barrowheld, and frankly, I don't care to know either."

That raised a much louder furore.

It was easy for me to forget sometimes, but most of the townsfolk were old enough to remember the war. Old enough even to have taken part, or known loved ones who never returned.

The Mayor raised his voice once more. "If any of you know what's good for you, you'll do the same as me. Keep your head down, and don't draw attention to yourself. The Aspector's are precious to the empire, and they have its ear. The last thing this town needs is to draw the attention of the Vins. I think we all pay enough tax already."

The audience quieted at that. Levies were an easier, tangible thing to complain about. It's simpler to talk to your neighbour about bleeding taxes than how much you'd like to shiv a Vin if you had the chance.

"That is all. Please share the news with anyone unable to make today's meeting." And as simple as that, the mayor strode away, and out the door.

That had to be a record for Dane. I'd never seen him close a meeting so quickly. Clearly, he was eager not to get caught up in the inevitable slew of questions, demands and expressions of outrage.

I turned back to Eva. "Glad to be back?" I asked, gesturing around to the hall which had now broken out into groups of people.

"Oh absolutely. There's a certain quality of nonsense that you can only get in Barrowheld," Eva said, standing up. "I'd love to catch up with you, but I'd better get back to Ma'. I'm free tomorrow if you want to call in?"

"I'll be there," I promised.

She flashed me a bright smile and nodded her head at father, and strode to the exit.

"I guess we should be heading home too," I turned to Father. "What?" I asked, realising he was smiling at me.

"Oh, nothing," he said. "You just seem happy."

I looked at him confused for a moment, before putting two and two together. "I'm just glad she's back!" I protested, "there are loads we have to catch up on."

"Of course," he said, waving his hand. "Hey, maybe you should take the day off from the practice tomorrow. Go spend some time with your friend."

"Are you sure?" I asked, excited at the prospect of a day off. I hadn't had many days to myself recently, especially not in the past year. Times being tight, father needed all the help he could get.

"I'm certain. It'll be good for you to get away. Besides, there's something else I want to talk about on the way home."

We said our goodbyes to Risa, who, along with most of the townsfolk, had decided to head back into the tavern, and instead made our way back home. The road home was cobbled and lit with the occasional street lamp. The town couldn't afford their own lamplighter, and we certainly couldn't afford any of the fancier clockwork lamps like they had in a few cities. We made do with tallow lamps that would get lit occasionally, usually only on nights when events were being held.

"I think it's time you start thinking about a journeyman project," Father said.

I turned to look at him, surprised. Completing a journeyman project was one of the last steps of an apprenticeship. Completing that would give me the rights to start my own practice. My mind was racing. I could move, start somewhere new. Maybe I could move to Mercy? I'd always known I wouldn't be an apprentice forever, but like most things in a child's life, they seem impossibly far off, right up until you're stood upon the precipice.

"I think it's the right time," my father continued. "I realised back during Job's surgery. You know a lot more than I did when I was a journeyman myself. It's not fair to keep you as an apprentice forever when you're capable of so much more. I..." he paused, looking up to the night sky for a moment, "I don't want to hold you back, to smother you. But you have to understand, without your mother, you're all I have in this world."

A flash of guilt ripped through me at the thought of moving to Mercy. How could I leave my father alone? I gripped his shoulder. "I understand," I said.

He gave me a soft smile. "I know you do."

"So what kind of project have you got in mind?" I asked

"That's half the fun, isn't it? I want you to decide. Come up with your own project. Dazzle me with your ingenuity, and I'll let you know if I approve."

That surprised me. Usually, a journeyman project was assigned by the master. I suddenly felt very overwhelmed by the scope of the task.

My father must have sensed what I was thinking. "You don't need to think of something right now," he laughed, "you've got plenty of time."

After the revelation about an Aspector coming to town, and finding out Eva was home, my mind was already too full to even start grasping at what type of project I could do. The ale was making my eyes droopy and I was glad to see our home at the far end of the street.

"What do you think about the Aspector coming to town?" I asked, yawning.

Even in the dark, I could see my father frowning. "It's going to cause trouble. A lot of folks still remember the war."

It was rare to hear father talk about it. From what I'd pieced together, he had served as a medic during the war, but other than that, he refused to talk about his involvement. I knew not to press it.

"Do you think there will be violence?" I asked, thinking back to what Risa had said.

"With an Aspector? Hah," he barked. "Only from the terminally stupid.

There is not one person in this place that could pose any threat to a fully trained Aspector. You may as well kick a wasp nest for all the trouble it'd cause not just them, but this whole damn town." He looked at me and sighed. "I wouldn't worry about it too much Kehlem. Look around," he held his hands wide, pointing to the nearby houses. "Vin tiles, clear glass, wrought iron. The Vins have done a marvellous job of working their way into our lives like an insidious vine. A balance has been struck, and even if it does weigh heavily for the Vins, there are few who would be willing to disturb it."

We spent the rest of the walk home placing bets on whether we'd be getting a request to see Risa tomorrow for treating acute drunkenness. Father offered me three pennies. I knew better than to take those odds.

4

Cider and Ale

The next day I woke up excited, and for the first time, oddly nervous at seeing Eva. We'd been close friends as long as I could remember, being the only two in the small town of a similar age. But she had been away for a long time, leaving at the end of summer last year. Part of me had worried that she would be somehow different when she returned, not interested in spending any time with me. Still. She was the one who asked me to meet her, and with the announcement of the Aspector yesterday, Father wanting me to take on a journeyman project, and with all the things that undoubtedly happened to her in Mercy, we should have plenty to catch each other up on.

"Good, you're awake!" Father said cheerily as I walked into the kitchen, rubbing the sleep out of my eyes. "I thought I'd prepare a picnic for you to take with you. There's some cheese, some apples. Oh, and there's a bottle of ale for you and a cider for Eva. I know she's not got a taste for ale."

I paused, trying to blink out my bleariness. Father stood proudly next to a waxen sack that he'd tied to a close.

"You made me a picnic?" I asked, taken aback.

He grinned at me, "It's the least I could do, you've been working so much recently. A boy your age should be out in the sun more. It's good to get out now and then! Any idea where you might take her?"

"Maybe the old woods past Aldridge farm," I said, testing the heft of the sack. There was a distinctive 'clink' of glass.

"That's quite a way away," father said, hesitating.

"There's a patch of waelig trees there, I figured I could gather some bark while I'm out there, bring it back with me. Save us a trip to the apothecary."

His expression softened. We didn't really talk about the family finances often, but I could guess it wasn't out of laziness that we hadn't replaced the kitchen table yet.

"Alright then," he said. "Just be careful."

I smiled at him. "I'll be fine. Anything else you need while I'm out?"

"If you could get a bundle of candles from Maggie, that'd be great. We're running low. I better be off anyway, I've got some errands of my own to run. I'll see you home for dinner?"

"See you then," I promised.

I grabbed a cloak and hefted the sack over my shoulder with a grunt, and stepped out into the crisp morning air.

The winter day held a distant promise of spring. The trees lay dormant, the wind carried a sharp chill and the hedgerows were silent. But the blue sky held nothing but the bright sun which lay a kiss of warmth that held whispers of longer days, warmer nights and the smell of blossom. There was a sense of preparation in the air, and the townsfolk around me seemed to notice it as well. They bustled and laughed, bought hot cider from market stalls and haggled over the price of salt, meat and grains. It wouldn't last of course. Spring was still months away, and the worst of winter was yet to fall. But today's brief reprieve graced the town like a held breath before a long, deep plunge into an icy ocean. So, they made the most of the hesitation.

Eva's cottage was on the outskirts of town, towards the east. It was a wonderful amalgamation of workshop, outhouse and home. Her mother, Maggie, was well known for her use of herbs and oils in her candles, the smells of which permeated through the house leaving a distinct, yet soft aroma of spice and freshness.

Like me, Eva was also the child of a widow, and like me, she never spoke of it. It was another factor that drew us together as children, an unspoken bondage of broken families. That's not to say she ever seemed to lack because of it. Maggie was the strongest person I'd met. Furiously protective of her family, she'd carved out her business by herself without help from anyone else to ensure there was always food on the table for the two of them. Not to mention her haggling would crumple even the likes of Anick.

"I suspected I might be seeing you today."

I heard Maggie's voice before I saw her as I strode into the front garden.

"Morning!" I called back and headed over to Maggie who was in the process of hanging pairs of candles out onto a line. "How did you know it was me?"

"No one else walks as quiet as you do." She placed a hand on her hip, breathing hard. "You couldn't give me a hand, could you?"

I smiled and strode over, grabbing a handful of candles from the box at her feet and draped them over the line by their shared wick. While I worked, Maggie leaned against the wall and caught her breath. She was a short, stocky woman with a messy bundle of dark hair. I knew from working with my father that she suffered a lot from pains in her joints, so I didn't mind helping her with these menial tasks.

"I assume you're here to see our Eva?" She asked as I finished wrapping the last candle on the line. As she asked, she nodded her head to the sack I'd set down on the floor.

"If she's free?" I asked. "I thought I'd bring some lunch and we could catch up."

"Aye, I'm sure she'd love that," Maggie said, with a warm smile. "Thanks for your help," she said as I wiped my hands on my trousers.

"It's no bother. Father also mentioned he wanted to buy a bundle of candles."

"I've got a box full of bad dips in the workshop. They ain't pretty but you can have them for free if you'd like," she suggested.

"They'd be perfect," I said. "You sure you won't take any coin?"

"Don't be daft," she waved her hand, impatient. "I'll be popping around tomorrow anyway to see your Pa', I'll bring 'em with me."

"Thanks, Maggie," I said, earnest.

"Think nothing of it lad. Now, where's that girl?" She took a deep breath.

"Eva!" she yelled.

Eva's head popped out one of the many windows of the cottage. "Yes?" she called and then spotted me next to her mother. "Oh! Kehlem!" she withdrew and slammed the window shut. A few seconds later she burst through the front door.

"Well, don't you look pretty," Maggie said, eyeing her daughter.

Eva flashed her mum a quick smile.

Her dark hair had been tied back into a single dark braid tied off at the end with a dark red ribbon. It had been so long since I'd seen her last, I gaped a little. Of course, I'd stolen a glance here and there in the dim light of the town hall last night, but in the cold light of day, I realised how much she'd changed since last year. I couldn't exactly pinpoint it, but it was as if she'd become more solid. More confident.

Having a friend like Eva, it becomes easy to take them for granted. You get used to seeing them day in and day out, and like the smell of home, you become almost blind to them. But by her absence, my mind saw her quite clearly once more. And for reasons I couldn't explain, my heart was racing.

Maggie coughed, breaking the silence I hadn't realised had sprouted between us. "Young Kehlem here has packed you a lunch," she said.

Eva turned to me, smiling. "Has he now?"

That was my cue. I latched on. "If you're hungry that is?"

Eva rolled her eyes. "You sure you don't mind?" She looked to her mother.

"Don't be daft! Get ye gone girl, go have some fun. I've got work to be getting on with." She then turned to me, "I'll bring those candles tomorrow, Kehlem." She grabbed her empty crate and walked inside, leaving Eva and me alone.

"Shall we then?" I asked, grabbing the picnic sack.

"Was that glass I heard?" Eva asked, walking in step next to me.

"That," I said, "would be telling."

She rolled her eyes and wrapped a hand around my elbow. My heart quickened once more. "It's so nice to see you again, Kehlem. I missed you."

I turned to look at her. "I missed you too."

Emotions are messy, complicated things, no more so than when you're on the bridge between child and adulthood. If you're stupid, you hide them from those you care about. If you're really stupid, you hide them from even yourself. But with them being messy and chaotic, they are quite incapable of staying buried, and will inevitably find a way out. Those four words of mine were just the escape mine had been looking for, bubbling out of my clumsy mouth with such earnestness that I almost halted mid-step. If Eva noticed, she didn't let on, but I turned back to the path ahead, certain that my face was beet red.

"How was Mercy? How's your uncle?" I asked quickly, trying to move on.

"Still a hopeless bachelor. I think he's chased just about half the male population of Mercy. But," she gasped, suddenly excited, "I have some good news. I've got a scribing apprenticeship lined up! It starts in spring." She jumped ahead of me, cloak swirling in the winter wind, grinning.

"Eva, that's..." I tried to think of the right word. Amazing. Awful. "Congratulations," I finished. "I'm really happy for you." That at least was honest. "You really deserve it."

She flushed brightly and gave me a toothy smile. "You're sweet. What about you? What did I miss?"

So, I filled her in on all the comings and goings of the town while we walked arm in arm to the old woods. I told her about Job, of course, and the surgery. In return, she filled me in about Mercy.

I'd visited a couple of times but didn't know the city that well. She told me about the morning market and the harbour. She spoke of the ocean and spices, bakeries and libraries, and I felt very foolish for having grown envious of a city. Just hearing her talk about her favourite places to visit and her daily routine of walking the seafront with her uncle before browsing the market was enough to lift my mood. It was easy to imagine her fitting in there. She deserved to escape and be happy, and I knew I wouldn't be the one to hold her back.

By the time we made it to the woods, the sun had reached its apex, and we were both ready to eat.

"Oh, this is pretty," Eva said, admiring the rolling forest floor. Even in winter, verdant moss-covered almost every nook and cranny with a lush green carpet of life, in stark contrast to the swaying empty canopy above.

"You've never been here?" I turned to Eva, surprised. "It's one of my favourite places. Come on!" I grabbed her hand and darted off down a familiar trail, deeper into the shelter of the ancient woods.

The place I had in mind was a small clearing I'd discovered a few summers back, one I'd often come to on days off to explore. A small brook babbled through one side and a few boulders peaked through the mossy carpet, providing a most excellent bench. Even better, the tightly woven trees provided much-needed shelter from the wind. When we reached the outskirts, I stepped aside so Eva could see the place for herself.

"This place is amazing." she spun around trying to take it all in. "We've got to come back here in spring, I bet it's even better when the blossom is in!"

I would love to give an account of the clearing, and how it truly looked in winter. But in all honesty, all I can remember is Eva. Recalling the clearing while Eva stood in it, would be like lighting a candle in broad daylight and describing the shadow it cast. Eva outshone the clearing, and my mind was full of her. The way she darted to the stream and touched the moss. The swirl of the hem of her cloak as she danced back to me, pulling me into the clearing. The bright bubble of her laugh that shamed the brook into silence. There was a fluttering, leaping feeling in my chest and stomach, and all I wanted was to talk and listen and just exist next to her.

Eva pulled me down to sit next to her by the brook. "You're awfully quiet. Penny for your thoughts?"

My mind raced. I needed to tell her. I needed to translate the urgency of my heart, the racing of my mind into words. "I need to tell you something." Too fast. She doesn't feel the same way. Don't do it. Don't spoil your friendship. She's leaving soon. Enjoy what time you have left.

She arched an eyebrow, "Oh?"

"I…" My eyes darted, looking for an escape, and fell on the picnic sack. "I'm not sure exactly what's in there."

"So, my Prince Chivalry didn't prepare my meal?" she sighed. "I like it better this way," she shrugged. "We both can be surprised. Let's find out!"

She grabbed the bag and untied it, letting the sides fall down to reveal a boule of dark bread, a small truckle of cheese, three rosy apples and two dark glass bottles.

"A feast!" She proclaimed, delighted. Without hesitation, she grabbed the bread and started tearing it into chunks.

Relieved, and perhaps disappointed that the moment had passed, I grabbed the two bottles, uncorking them with my teeth. I gave them both a sniff. "I think this one is yours," I said, passing her the cider.

"Well thank you kindly, sir," she said, and we both took long gulps. My ale tasted slightly stale but nevertheless, I was thirsty enough to drink half it down.

For a moment, we sat in silence, and a hidden tension that had been bobbing beneath the surface the whole day popped up like flotsam.

"I didn't tell you, Father wants me to start my journeyman soon," I said, desperately trying to quell the silence.

Eva's eyes widened, "That's amazing!" she managed, between mouthfuls of bread.

I smiled at her muffled words. "He wants me to pick the project myself. I've got no bloody idea what I'm going to do."

"Don't look at me. I hate your tinctures. Solutions, lotions and potions. They all taste horrible. Ick."

"Ah," I said, lowering the octave of my voice, "that's how you know they work!"

"Oh," she laughed, "Martyr you sound just like Tema when you do that! That's really good news though. You'll be able to start your own practice before you know it."

I shrugged my shoulders, still uneasy at the thought of leaving my father alone. "What about you?" I asked, taking another deep drink from my bottle. "Now that you've got your apprentice sorted, what do you want to do when it's done?"

"I'm being 'prenticed at the church in Mercy. I expect it'll mostly be transcribing old books to new parchment. I guess I'll see how that turns out first. It'd be interesting to read some of the old Mysteries though. Usually, it's only the clergy that gets to read them."

"Funny, I can't imagine you in a stuffy church," I smiled. I felt an odd, tugging sensation on my lip.

Eva looked at me, dropping her food to the floor. "Kehlem? What's wrong?" her eyes were wide. Panicked.

"What do you mean?" It took a moment for my ears to catch up. My words were slurred. Something was terribly wrong. I looked around, confused. The sun in the sky had become but a small pinprick of light, and darkness seemed to centre around my vision. A deep, primal fear struck me to my quick, and I tried to stand up.

"Kehlem!" Eva shouted. She sounded terrified.

I grabbed her shoulder and felt a pang of guilt at the situation I'd put her in. A blinding headache struck me like a thunderclap, and the world went dark, filled with pain, and terror.

5

Smoke and Lavender

I was somewhere between waking and sleeping, the limbo before the mind decides it's had enough sleep, but my body was full of protest. Everything hurt. Every inch of me had fallen beneath the blacksmith's hammer. I needed more rest. More darkness, please. Hazy memories from the walk to the woods filtered through my mind like candle smoke. Just glimpses. A damp hem. Pale skin framed by black hair that had escaped a plait. Dark ale, and brown bread. Someone was running their fingers through my hair, and I could feel my mind slowly give in, relenting under the pressure to just *rest* some more. I was just falling deeper into the welcoming, undulating arms of sleep when I felt a sharp tug on my scalp, followed by someone whispering, 'Shit' under their breath.

No point trying to sleep now. Slowly, and painfully aware of just how painful light seemed to be, I eased my eyes open. The world around me resolved into the familiar sight of my bedroom and sat on my bed next to me, her hand raised guilty above my head, was Eva.

"Well," I croaked, my throat dry and painful, "I'm not sure you've got a physician's touch."

She looked at me, all colour drained from her face and her mouth a perfect 'o'. She burst into tears.

Several moments later, Eva had regained her composure, her nose running and her eyes puffy, and I had slowly, and very painfully, lifted myself so I was sitting closer to upright in my bed. Eva was gripping my hand with a white-knuckle fury.

"I thought you were dead," she whispered, barely meeting my eyes.

"I don't think I am," I said, stroking the back of her hand with my thumb. "Even though I'm sure I'd be in less pain if I were."

She looked at me, stricken. Too early to make jokes then.

"What happened?" I asked.

"We were just talking, one moment you were fine, the next you were slurring all your words. Your skin. Martyr, your skin! I swear it turned grey!" she sniffed and shuddered at the memory. "In the next breath, you collapsed on the ground, shaking. I think you hit your head pretty hard as you fell and then that was it. You stopped moving. I thought…" she took a wavering breath, and again there were tears in her eyes. "I thought you'd died Kehlem."

I reached over with my other hand to cup hers in both of mine, ignoring the pain. "It's okay," I said quietly, trying to soothe her. "I'm here, I'm safe. Wait, how did I get here?"

"Oh!" she cried even harder. "I had to leave you. I ran to get help. I left you alone, on the forest floor. I'm so sorry Kehlem. I'm so sorry." She sobbed in earnest now. I tried to reach forward to comfort her, but it was no use. Pain radiated across my body like lightning and I fell back, exhausted.

"If you hadn't gotten help, my son would be dead."

Father appeared at the doorway, holding a steaming cup. He strode over and put an arm around Eva, comforting her. "You did the right thing. The only thing, *the only thing*," he stressed, "you could have done, and I will forever owe you for saving my son's life." His voice was strong, level and seemed to cut through into Eva. She buried her face in his shoulder.

"Why don't you go downstairs and take a nap," he suggested, his voice soft, but insistent. "You're exhausted. Come on, let me take you." Father eyed me, and set the cup down next to me, and then helped Eva to her feet, leading her out the room. He returned a few moments later.

"A true friend you've got there," he said, sitting down on the edge of my bed. "She's been awake this whole time, watching you. Poor thing is absolutely drained."

"How long was I out?" I asked

"Just over a day," he said. "Here," he reached for the cup and put it into my hands. "Drink this, it'll help with the pain."

"Waelig?" I asked, sniffing the tea.

He nodded.

"Hah," I laughed, then immediately regretted it as my abdomen cramped. I took a sip of the bitter liquid. "What happened?"

"From what I gather you had one of your episodes, and from what Eva tells me, hit your head as you fell. Luckily Eva bumped into Bill just on the outskirts of the woods. The two of them were able to drag you out of the woods, and Bill carried you the rest of the way home."

"I don't get it," I said, more to myself. "It's been so long since I had an episode. I can't even remember the last time I had one. Why now?"

"If I had to guess, I'd say it was probably triggered by a strong stimulus. Maybe you were feeling some strong emotions at the time?" He glanced at me, knowingly.

I flushed, recalling how I'd felt in the clearing. "Possibly," I said.

Father ruffled my hair. "It's to be expected," he said, smiling at me. "We're going to have to increase your dose I'm afraid."

I nodded, crestfallen.

"Don't worry about that for now though," he said, sensing my disappointment. "Finish your tea and try and get some rest." He eased himself to his feet and planted a kiss on my forehead.

I shuffled back down into the bed and took another gulp of the tea. Already I could feel the soft lull of sleep call me. As I drifted off, I saw my father gripping my door frame for support. At that moment, he looked intensely vulnerable and afraid.

"You ready for some food, Kehlem?"

"Hey," I mumbled, rubbing the sleep out of my eyes. Eva was standing at the foot of the bed, carrying a tray of food and drink. I eased myself against the headboard so I could sit up. "Only if you join me."

She smiled at me, nodded and set the tray down on the bed. She looked a bit better than earlier. "Am I ok to sit next to you?"

"Here," I said, shuffling to make room.

She sat down and rested her head on my shoulder. Her hair smelt of lavender and smoke. I breathed deeply and felt myself relax a little.

"Is it true you stayed up all night?" I asked, taking a piece of bread she offered me.

"Mhmm," she nodded. "You were snoring so loud, there's no way anyone in this house could have slept," she said, earnest.

I nudged her with my shoulder, laughing, and then winced in pain.

"Are you okay?"

"I am now," I said, looking at her. Knowing better than to let the tension resurface, I made the excuse of reaching for the fresh cup of tea to look away. I took a sip, letting the bitter liquid wash down my dry throat.

"What is that?" Eva wrinkled her nose. "It smells awful."

"See for yourself, have a sip." I passed her the cup.

"Eugh!" she said, passing it straight back. "How do you stomach that?"

I smiled, trying not to laugh. "It's a good pain reliever, not as strong as poppy milk, but also not addictive."

"Does it hurt a lot?"

I considered it for a moment. "It feels like I've been hit by a horse."

"How would you know what that feels like?"

"You're right. Maybe that can be my journeyman project! 'Compare and contrast the sensation of seizure to that of equine collision'"

It was her turn to nudge me, laughing. "Be serious. Make better tasting medicine, then I'll be impressed."

"I…" a thought struck me. "I think you might just be a genius."

She shrugged her shoulders. "What can I say?" She stretched out and placed her head on my shoulder again. "I'm glad you're ok. I'm not sure what I'd do without you."

I'm glad she wasn't looking at my face. My heart fluttered. "And I, you," I said simply, and immediately cringed at how lame it sounded out loud.

We snoozed like that for a few hours, heads resting against each other, and our backs leaning against the wall. Despite the pain, and the rising fear of the higher dose of medicine I'd need to take, I was perfectly at peace at that moment, adrift in a sea of lavender and candle smoke.

All in all, it took around a month for me to recover from the seizure. At first, I needed rest and time for my muscles to heal. Not to mention being knocked unconscious isn't something that you can immediately jump back from. For a time, Eva would visit in the evenings to check in on me, but eventually, she was needed back home to work in the chandlery, so I used my abundant spare time to study. We had a small library at home and an armchair that I could curl up into. After my strained muscles healed though, came the second part of the recovery. The higher dose of my medication. After being on a lower dose for so long, I'd forgotten how it felt.

If you've ever been roused during a deep dream, you probably knew something of what I was going through. Whereas before my mind was sharp, alert. Now it was soft like a heavy blanket lay atop my consciousness. Reading for more than an hour at a time became a chore. I'd walk into rooms and forget what I was doing, or lose my train of thought midway through a sentence. Worse still is that my mood was all over the place. I would be studying by myself, content as could be in one moment, and in the next I'd grow frustrated. A hot, furious irritation that made me want to itch my skin off and dive into the nearest lake. The first week of the higher doses were the worst, but eventually, by the end of the third, the effects seemed to calm down a little, with my main complaint being a slight tremble and headache in the evening time, but this was usually resolved with my next dose. And so, with spring getting ready to push winter out the door, I was ready to start my journeyman project.

You're up early," father remarked looking up from his breakfast.

"I wanted to catch you before you head off," I pulled a chair up opposite him. Bill had kindly built us a new kitchen table to replace the one we cut his friend open on. Ironically, that was the only reason he was by the woods the day I had my attack; gathering wood for the table top.

"How are you feeling?" father asked, sliding a plate of toast and a boiled egg over to me.

I grabbed a spoon and took the top of the egg off, and dipped a corner of toast in. "Better," I said, between bites. "Seems to have settled down a bit. I still can't focus for very long on things, but" I shrugged, "I guess it's better than the alternative."

Father nodded, unsurprised. "You wanted something?"

"My journeyman, my project. I've got an idea."

Father's eyes lit up, and he leaned forwards. "Let's hear it then."

"It wasn't my idea actually," I said, "well, Eva gave me the thought. Waelig. I want to try and purify it. That tea is really disgusting. I was thinking if I can make a purer version, maybe crystallise it out, you could swallow the dose whole. Wouldn't have to sip that awful tea for half an hour. What do you think?"

"I think," he said, chewing on his own toast slowly, "that you're lucky to have Eva. I think it's a great idea. Any plans on how you'll get started?"

I ignored his comment about Eva. I didn't 'have' anything. "I'm planning on asking Maggie if I can borrow one of her rendering pans. They're large and shallow enough to at least test it."

"And if Eva is there to lend you a hand, more the better, right?"

I flushed at that.

He laughed and slapped me on the arm. "I'm just teasing you. Sounds like a great idea to me. Now you're back on your feet, I could do with a hand this morning getting some tinctures prepared, but you're free to get started this afternoon."

Four hours later I was walking up the garden path to Eva's house. It was the first time I'd been out of the house since the seizure, and I'd had to stop three times to fight back nausea.

I rapped my knuckles on the front door.

"Kehlem!" Maggie said as she pulled the door open. "Come in, come in! How are you feeling?" She didn't wait for an answer, "Eva! Look who's here!" she lowered her voice, conspiratorially to me, "I expect you're here to see my Eva?"

"Well, actually, I wanted to ask you a favour."

"Kehlem!" Eva said, bursting into the hallway. "What are you doing here?"

"I was just wondering the same thing," Maggie said.

"Well, I'm not sure if Eva told you, but I'm starting my journeyman."
"That she did…"
"Well, to cut a long story short, I was hoping I might borrow one of your rendering pans for the day? And maybe borrow Eva as well?"
"And here I was thinking you were here for my charm alone," Maggie chuckled. "Of course, you can. I should warn you though, they ain't clean. Eva, could you go fetch one from the workhouse?"

Eva nodded and disappeared down one of the many warrens that sprouted off the hallway, leaving her mother and me alone.

"It's good news about her apprenticeship," I said. "I expect you'll miss her though?"

"Oh of course," Maggie sighed, "but I always knew I couldn't keep her here forever, she's a bright girl. Takes after her Ma'" she winked at me. "You both had better make the most of the next few months 'fore she leaves." She gave me a pointed look.

"How do you mean?" I asked, confused.

"Got one!" Eva's voice interrupted the conversation. She reappeared in the hallway carrying a wide, flat pan in front of her. "You ready?" she asked me.

I nodded. "Thanks again Maggie," I said.

She waved us off, holding the front door open, "Any time, have fun you two."

"Where we off to then?" Eva said, passing the pan to carry.

"How would you feel about revisiting the woods? I promise not to faint this time."

She did not look impressed.

"Too soon?" I ventured.

"Too soon," she agreed, wrapping her hand around my arm.

"You look nice," I said, willing myself to be a little bolder than normal. It was true though. Her hair was down, and loose, framing her face in a way that I found very distracting.

She seemed surprised by the compliment but didn't miss a beat. "You don't look too bad yourself. Very pretty."

I rolled my eyes, and she laughed. "So why the pan?" she asked, "What's the project?"

"Well, a friend of mine once complained about how bad my medicine tastes. I took that very personally, and wanted to see if we could rectify that."

"Oh, how exciting. Your friend sounds like a delight. Must be such a burden on you having such an erudite person constantly outshining you."

"Erudite?" I asked, uncertain.

She poked her tongue out at me and tapped the side of her head. "Very knowledgeable."

"I defer to my lady scribe," I smiled.

"Oh, *your* lady, am I?"

I flushed. "Well not *mine*, of course…" I stammered.

"Of course," she said, agreeing, but as she said it, her hand slid down my arm, and she gently grabbed my hand, entwining hers in mine, all the while she fixed her gaze forwards.

I almost froze and was suddenly very conscious of my stride, how gangly and awkward it was. Was I breathing funny? In. Out. Martyr that was a deep breath. Why have I suddenly forgotten how to breathe?

Something was happening, and I had no idea what it was. We'd walked arm in arm before. And we'd hold hands to comfort the other on occasion. But we'd never walked hand in hand, not like this. It seemed so silly a thing to get worked up over. But it felt almost intimate. Like a distance between us had grown just an inch or two smaller. It was thrilling. And terrifying.

We both said nothing, walking in silence, hand in hand. The longer we walked though, the more uncertain I became. My feelings for Eva had been all over the place since she'd come back to Barrowheld, that's why it meant so much to me. But for Eva, maybe holding my hand was just a casual expression of friendship. She was probably just concerned I'd trip or seize again.

Ironically, telling myself that it meant nothing gave my mind room to calm down enough to think coherently to ease some of that silent tension that never seemed to stray too far away recently.

"I don't suppose you know how to lay a fire do you?" I asked.

Eva snorted, turning to look at me with a half incredulous look. "Where did that come from?"

I shrugged, a little embarrassed. "I know how to start one in the hearth, but wasn't sure if it's different if you need to light one outside…?"

She looked me in the eye, and for a moment, I thought I might drown in the amber pools that held my gaze. "You'd be lost without me, huh?"

"I suppose I would," I agreed.

The forest path grew tighter as it wove between the trees, and I reluctantly let go of Eva's hand as she took the lead. It was still too early for the trees to be budding, and there was even snow on the ground in places, but the sun was shining in earnest today, and the forest reflected that warmth with an earnest vitality.

"Just on the left, here," I called to Eva, as I spotted a likely collection of waelig trees. Even without their leaves, their distinctive mottled bark made them easy to spot. I set the pan on the floor leaning it against one of the trees and pulled out a short knife from my belt. "I don't have a spare," I apologised, "but you should be able to tear it in strips where it's already loo—"

"It's alright," she said, interrupting me, pulling out her own knife from somewhere deep in her tunic. "I've got my own."

Dumbfounded, I stared in silence as she happily began stripping pieces of bark off the tree. "Since when did you carry a knife?" I asked.

She looked over her shoulder and raised an eyebrow. "Since, when did you?"

"A…" I started but thought better of it. "Fair enough," I shrugged, and started working on a neighbouring tree.

"I think that should be enough." I tossed the last strip onto the pile and roughly threw that pile into the rendering pan. We'd stripped a few of the trees, careful not to cut too deep. Waelig naturally shed its bark so these ones would regrow over the next month or so.

"You go on ahead to the clearing, I'll meet you there," Eva said, wiping her knife on her cloak. "I'll grab us some firewood."

I nodded and grabbed the pan by both hands, careful not to drop any of the bark we'd just spent the last hour collecting. The clearing wasn't far away, close enough that the brook could be heard, but I was sweating and my arms were rubber by the time I set the pan down by the brook. The awkward way I'd held the pan had given me a numb arm, and I could feel a headache coming on.

While I waited for Eva I gulped some of the fresh brook water and then tipped the bark onto the mossy floor. After filling the pan with river water and setting it aside, I started the backbreaking work of cleaning the strips of bark off in the river.

"Oh, River Maiden, How fair you this morning? I'd kneel down beside you, and spend the day talking…" *Eva's clear voice sang through into the clearing. It was bright and sweet like birdsong.*

I smiled to myself, and sat up from the river, shaking my hands dry. Turning around I saw Eva carrying a bundle of deadwood, wrapped in her cloak. With a huff, she unravelled the sticks at my feet.

"You should sing more," I said, "you've got a pretty voice."

She raised a brow but said nothing. She shook her cloak clean, and then set it on the ground. She was wearing a simple homespun tunic dress, with the sleeves pushed up. At some point, she'd tied her hair back.

Five minutes later she had a fire going, wide and flat enough to set the pan to boil. With the bark brewing, there was little to do but sit, and talk. But with the quiet that came with setting the tea to simmer came that secret, insidious tension between us once more. A thought would pop into my head, a question, but then I'd look over to Eva sat opposite me, hugging her knees and humming to herself as she watched the water boil, and the thought would vanish like a candle flame.

"You've gone quiet again," Eva said softly, looking over to me.

"Just thinking," I lied.

She stretched out, propping herself up with her elbows. "Prey tell."

It was so tempting. I was standing on a precipice and I was egging myself to jump. Do it. Just tell her. I blinked. "It's going to be weird in Barrowheld after you leave."

"Don't," she said, her voice suddenly serious.

"What do you mean?"

"Just…," she paused, and then drew her knees back underneath her. "It's already hard enough leaving this town. Leaving Ma'…" She glanced at me, "and you."

"Sorry," I said. I'd upset her. I flailed, trying to change the subject. "I can't believe an Aspector is coming to town."

"I'd forgotten about that." She rested her chin on her knees. "What do you think it's about?"

"Not sure. Maybe someone is a secret Aspector. Maybe it's you!" I laughed. "All these years, have you been lying to me? You're a secret sorcerer with grand and powerful magics?"

She smiled at me. "I wish. Imagine that. My bet's it's Risa. Or Dane."

We looked at each other for a moment, before we both burst out laughing at the same time.

"I couldn't picture Risa wielding great and ancient magic, can you?" I asked, giggling.

"He'd go to jostle someone and set them on fire," Eva agreed.

"You've noticed that too? He uses his hands like punctuation, I swear."

The conversation devolved from there, with us coming up with stranger and stranger suggestions for who the Aspector could be. It seemed to have worked though. Eva relaxed again, and by the time the fire had burnt down, we were lying side by side watching and naming clouds as they drifted above us.

"We should head back," Eva said, lifting herself up from the ground. "It's getting cold and it'll be dark soon." She held her hand out to pull me up. I took it and grabbed her cloak which we'd been using as a blanket. Instead of taking it from me, she turned around. Taking the hint, I draped it around her shoulders, and in an action of stalwart bravery, I reached around her shoulders and clasped the broach closed. As I did so, she reached up and grabbed my forearm, and turned to look at me. For a moment I thought she was going to push me away, but instead, she held onto my arm and stared into my eyes. She looked like she wanted to say something. I had an indescribable urge to lean forwards and kiss her. We were only inches away, it would be so easy. Easy as breathing.

She smiled at me. "We should get going," her voice was soft, like a starling landing on pine. She let go of my arm, and the moment passed. "What do you want to do about the tea?"

The tea. In all honesty, I hadn't thought about the tea in about four hours. The water had reduced down and was a deep ochre colour. Steam was still coiling off the surface into the cooler afternoon air.

"I'll come back tomorrow," I said. "It's too hot to carry with us anyhow."

"Sorry we didn't make much progress," Eva said, as we left the clearing, making our way into the murkier shadows of the woods.

"I don't know about that," I said, smiling as I followed her lead.

6

Bitter

Father was already out on his rounds by the time I woke up the next morning. There were a couple of slices of cold toast left on the counter for me, so grabbing them, a large, empty jar and my cloak, I made my way back to the forest.

"Morning Master Kehlem!"

I turned and saw Bill jogging to catch up with me. "Bill!" I called, "How have you been?"

"Not half bad, not half bad. Where are you off to, if you don't mind me asking?"

"The woods past Aldridge, need to pick up some stuff I left there yesterday."

"Ah, well I have business that way too, I might walk with you if you have a mind?"

"Be my guest," I said.

For a while we strode in silence, making our way east down the main high street out of town.

Bill was first to break the silence. "So how you been? You know, since the *incident*."

It had totally slipped my mind that Bill had played a role in helping me. "Much better," I said, "I've upped my doses, not had any incidents since."

"Touch wood," Bill reminded me, reaching out to tap lightly on a fence post.

"I should have come to see you after, Bill. I'm not sure what would have happened had you not been nearby."

"Oh, think nothing of it, young sir, think nothing of it. Good thing your Pa' asked me to pick up that wood otherwise I wouldn't have been there."

"For the table?" I asked. I didn't realise my father had put him up to it. Probably wanted to give Bill some coin. Everyone in town knew Bill was supporting Job and was bleeding through the nose for it.

"Aye," Bill nodded. "That Eva lass scared the life out of me though, stumbling out of those woods screaming like that. You've got a good friend there."

"I do," I smiled, thinking about yesterday. Memories of her holding me close fluttered briefly across my mind. "She'll be leaving soon, for Mercy," I said softly.

Bill eyed me carefully. "Is that so?"

"Aye," I sighed. "She's going to be a scribe."

Bill whistled. "Good for her. Not a bad life that 'ent." He put his hand on my shoulder and drew us to a halt. "I'm needed that way," he said, nodding his head down a drystone wall lined path. "Word of advice before I go, if you'll listen. Tell her how you feel. Before she leaves."

Was it really that obvious? From the look on Bill's face, I knew there was no point denying it. "I don't want to ruin what we have," I said. "I don't want her to think I'm asking her to stay."

"And is that what you would want? Would you have her stay in Barrowheld?" His eyebrows furrowed.

"No, of course not," I protested. "I want her to get her apprenticeship. I'd want to join her, eventually, when I'm not a 'prentice anymore. I just don't want to leave my father."

"Now you listen to me. Your father is a good man. A strong man. I know him well enough to know he wouldn't want you chasing around his shadow for the rest of your life. There's nothing for the young here anymore. The Vins," he turned his head, and spat on the ground, "made certain of that. Tell her. Otherwise, you'll regret it."

"I'll…I'll think about it," I promised.

He held my gaze a moment, and then apparently satisfied nodded his head once. "See that you do. Fare you well boy." He turned on his heel, leaving me to mull on his words as I continued on my way to the clearing.

I grew nervous as I walked through the woods that an animal may have disturbed the pan, and either drank from it and poisoned itself or perhaps worse, tipped the entire pan over, wasting the bushel of bark we had harvested yesterday. The concern was unmerited, however, and I was relieved to see that the pan was in the exact same location we had left it by the brook, undisturbed and happily with no dead animals surrounding it.

The liquid looked to have separated. Yesterday the tea was an opaque murky brown, but as I crouched down to get a better look, there now seemed to be sediment at the bottom of the pan, with a clear amber liquid sat atop. That was a very good sign. Grinning to myself, I took out a jar from my sack, and very gently, so as not to disturb the sediment too much, I scooped a mixture of both the liquid and the sediment. I sat down on my haunches and held the jar up to the sunlight.

The liquid and the sediment had mixed during the sampling, but with the sunlight streaming through the liquid, I could already see the particulates falling once more to the bottom of the jar. Now I wasn't a chemist by any means, but on the face of it, it seemed like *something* had crystallised out of the suspension. Not sure what else to do, I dipped a finger into the liquid and touched it to my tongue.

Immediate, burning bitterness spread across my tongue. I spat out the contents onto the ground, and when the bitterness continued, I scooped a handful of water from the brook to rinse my mouth out. Better, but the bitterness persisted. I spat the river water out too and repeated the process. Swill, spit, repeat. It took ten handfuls of water before the bitterness began to fade.

With noticeably less enthusiasm, I pressed my finger to the bottom of the jar and pulled out a few of the particles. Holding my fingertip closer to my eye, I could see that the particles were actually very small brownish crystals. Hoping that the taste couldn't be any worse than the liquid, I touched my finger to my tongue.

At first, it seemed like the crystals had no taste at all. But a few moments later, a numbness spread across my tongue from the point my finger had touched. It was an odd, not quite unpleasant, sensation. Like my tongue had been replaced by meat. I needed to be very careful not to bite it by accident.

"Weirth." I mused aloud, holding the jar up again for closer inspection. "Weirth?" I repeated. "Ha!" I barked, realising what was happening. It seemed without being able to feel my tongue, I couldn't pronounce certain words. "Kehldem. Thema. Thibia. Bugger. Sihd." I listed the first words that came into my head to hear how they would sound. Next, I tried singing, *"Oh River Maithen, How fair you this mornding? I'th kneel thown beside you, and spenth thee thay thalking...."*

I laughed, and jumped, actually jumped into the air. It *worked*. Not only had it worked, but whatever I had done seemed to have concentrated the strength of the waelig entirely. Excited, and desperate to share the news with father, I scooped as much of the remaining crystals as possible, dumped the rest of the liquid in the brook, and raced homewards, jar in one hand, empty pan in the other, and singing all the dirty rhymes I could remember overhearing in the tavern.

"It worked! Pa' it worked!" I shouted as I burst through the front door. Happily, the numbness had worn off just as I ran past the bakery on the outskirts of town. I ran into the kitchen, clutching the jar. "I did it—" I almost tripped over my own feet as I realised my father had company. Stood opposite him in the kitchen was a tall woman with a mane of red hair. She turned to look at me as I entered the room. I'd never seen her face around town before. The fine lines on her face and the strands of grey hair placed her at a similar age to my father to my eyes. She had sharp, angular features, but kind looking eyes. She gave me a quick smile.

"This must be your boy, yes?" She asked, turning back to my father.

She had an accent. It was faint, but it was there. A soft, lilting, almost musical undertone to her words. Vinnish. She must be the Aspector. I looked over to my father, who did not look happy.

"Aye, this is Kehlem. Kehlem, this is Themia. She's newly arrived in

Barrowheld."

If I hadn't been already sure, I was certain now. I'd never seen Father look so fierce. Like a caged animal. Oh, he hid it well, and I doubt Themia would notice. But I knew him well enough to see eyes glimmered like a forge fire.

"And what is this?" Themia asked, nodding to the jar in my hand.

"Oh," I said, surprised at being asked outright. "It's a project I'm working on…"

Themia kept her eyebrows raised, and hesitantly I carried on.

"I'm trying to purify an extract out of some bark. For medicinal purposes," I explained.

Themia held her hand out, and not sure what else to do, I passed her the jar. All the while Father's eyes bored into the two of us.

"And you did this with just evaporation?" She asked, nodding to the pan I had left in the hallway.

I nodded.

"Very impressive. Well. This is most fortuitous. I was just explaining to your father here that I am an Alchemist. I think you will struggle to purify this any further with evaporation alone. It just so happens that I have a distillation set up with me. It would be my pleasure to let you make use of it, especially with your father being kind enough to let me borrow some of your solvents."

I blinked my eyes. An Alchemist? "That's very generous," I said.

"It's settled then!" she said, clapping her hands, making me jump. "Come see me early tomorrow. I'm staying on the south side of town, big house, yellow door?"

I nodded, "I know it."

She turned to father, "Tema, thanks again for the solvent." She nodded her head to us both and strode quickly out of the house.

"What," I asked, turning to my father, "was that all about?"

"That was an Aspector sticking her nose in exactly where it doesn't belong."

"What was she doing here?"

"Bloody stupid Anick told her to come see us. Apparently, she'd lost a bottle of wood alcohol on route here, and Anick didn't have any in stock. Told her to come visit us instead. I could kill him." He turned around and started chucking wood into the empty hearth.

"What am I supposed to do?"

"Hmm?" he asked, not bothering to turn around. "Oh. You're going to have to go. She's just going to come back if you don't."

"I don't get it. Why offer?"

Father sighed. "Who knows? If I had to guess, I imagine she'll ply you with questions about the town. Use you as a way of getting to know the place."

"What should I say?"

Father turned to look at me. "Just be honest, Kehlem. There's no point lying. I doubt there's anything you could tell her that will get anyone into trouble. Of course, if you want to make something up about Anick, I could certainly understand…"

I laughed and chucked a dirty rag at him. "You're awful."

He smiled at me, and some of the tension seemed to leave his body. "So," he said, "tell me more about the waelig."

The next day I woke up early and made my way firstly over to Eva's to return the pan to Maggie. When I knocked on the door, however, it was Eva who greeted me.

"You're up early," I said, surprised.

"Hello to you too." She stifled a yawn. "What are you doing about this time of the morning?"

I gestured to the pan.

"Oh, I forgot!" She took the pan from me and set it down inside the doorway. "Did it work? Do you want to come in?"

"It did," I grinned. "and I do, but I'm supposed to be meeting Themia."

"Who's that?"

"The Aspector. She came around to visit us yesterday."

"Oh wow. What does she want with you?"

I shrugged. "To help with my project apparently."

"Lucky you to catch her eye, I can't imagine others are so pleased."

"Don't get me started," I sighed. "Are you free this evening? We could catch up, and I can fill you in on all the sordid secrets I learn…"

Her eyes lit up, "I'm there."

"Kehlem! Excellent timing!"

I hadn't even knocked on the front door before Themia had pulled it open, and stepped out onto the doorstep. She was dressed in a rich, purple-dyed cloak, the collar of which draped around her shoulders instead of forming a hood. I assumed it to be a variety more common to the Vinnish, having not seen its likeness before.

"I hope you don't mind, but I thought it might be good to have a walk before we get started on your distillation. Better to get to know one another first, no?" Without waiting for an answer, she walked straight past me, out onto the cobbled street.

Hesitating for only a moment, I turned around and caught up with her.

We walked in silence. Was she expecting me to start the conversation?

"How was your journey?" I offered, unsure what else to say.

She turned her head without breaking stride to look at me, with a frank expression on her face. "I am quite sure you can do better than that."

I looked back at her, nonplussed, and tried again. "You're an Aspector?" I asked.

She nodded. "Specifically, an Alchemist."

"What is that?"

"Well, you understand what a chemist is?"

I nodded. "Of course."

"And you understand what an Aspector is?"

"Well, not really," I said, honestly.

"Really?" This time she seemed surprised. She looked at me for a moment, before continuing. "An Aspector, quite simply, is someone who can touch the Aspect," she said as if it were the simplest thing in the world.

"What's the 'Aspect'?"

She snorted. "'What's the Aspect' he asks! Everything!" she threw her arms wide. "It's everything. Every breath of every animal. Every thought of every child. It's the falling of the rain and the heat from the sun." She turned to look at me and then continued when she saw my confused face. "When you play with a ball Kehlem, and you kick it, does the ball roll forever?"

"No," I said, "of course not."

"Good. And until you kicked it, the ball didn't move, correct?"

"Well…" I paused, not understanding how literal she was being, "no?"

"Good answer," she nodded. "So, no energy was made, and no energy was destroyed. It was just converted, like currency from one unit to another."

I'd never really thought about it, but it made sense to me. "I guess so."

"That is a small thing, simple. But what about the big things? Babies are born, grown in the womb of mothers, and they are living, breathing, *thinking* humans. Where did the energy come from?"

"The mother?" I asked, genuinely unsure.

"And when the baby grows to be an old lady and dies, where does the energy go?"

Now I was stumped.

"That," she stressed, "that is the Aspect. Our world, the one we live in is a physical world. The Aspect is a world, one that overlays ours. You cannot see it. But there are some people, Aspectors, who can reach and for the briefest moments, touch the Aspect. All energy lies within the Aspect. In truth, everybody uses the Aspect without knowing it, down to the insects beneath our feet. The only difference is an Aspector can be more direct in their use of it."

It was a lot to take in. The way she explained it, was far more…rational than I was expecting. Don't get me wrong, I still had no idea what it was to be an Aspector, but now that there seemed to be a logic to it, it almost cheapened the mystery of it all.

"So…" I said slowly, trying to piece together what she had explained. "An alchemist is someone who uses the Aspect in chemistry?"

"Just so Kehlem! Just so!" she said, excited. "Aspectors tend to have a certain propensity to a certain discipline."

"Like healing," I said, thinking back to what father had said after Job's surgery.

"Yes, Kehlem, like healing."

We'd been walking in a wide loop around the town, and being so busy talking and listening to Themia, I hadn't noticed until now, but we were attracting some attention from passers-by. Plenty were not so polite in their stares.

"Is there a place where you study all this?" I asked, thinking back to what Father had said about the university.

"Indeed, there are a few such places. I hail from the Isale Academy, just north of the Eastern Garrison."

My curiosity got the better of me. "And do they have healers there?"

She nodded, "Of course, they teach all disciplines at the academy."

"Do they teach non-Aspectors?"

The question seemed to catch her off guard. "No," she said after hesitating for a moment. "Only Aspectors."

"Oh," I said, a little disappointed. Another thought crossed my mind. "Do you know if any of the healers have any experience treating seizures?"

"Perhaps. It's most likely they do. Why do you ask?"

"I'm sick. I have to take a lot of medicine to stop them from happening."

She gave me a sympathetic look. "Is that why you're working on this medical extract?"

"Oh, no. Waelig is a painkiller. I don't actually know what it is I take," I laughed.

"Oh, my apologies, Tema said you were doing your journeyman."

"I am," I said, defensively.

"A journeyman who doesn't know what's in his own medicine? That seems strange to me."

My face grew hot, and I bit back a sharp retort. I never needed to know what was in my medicine. I'd never asked. Why would I?

We continued walking in silence until Themia's house came back into view. "It was perhaps not my place to say," Themia said, uncertain. "No offence was meant."

"No, it's ok," I said, "No offence taken."

"That is good to hear! Come on in, let me show you the distillation set."

Themia's house was littered with wooden crates and travel bags. Most of the furniture still had dust sheets covering them. After much rummaging, Themia found the bag she was looking for and pulled out a set of objects wrapped in cloth. Contained within were intricately hand-blown pieces of glass, craftwork the likes of which I had never seen before.

"The method is very straightforward," she explained, as she fit the pieces of glass together, holding the pieces up with metal clamps. "By passing a heated solvent vapour across the bark, we should be able to extract the volatile essence of the bark and condense the steam here," she pointed to a large glass column. "Then we can evaporate the condensate, and hopefully, be left with a pure extract of the waelig."

"What's that?" I asked, pointing to an etching in one of the lower flasks. It was an intricately carved pattern, swirling around the round flask without care for symmetry or repetition.

"That is a tool to help with Aspecting. Watch." She poured some water into the beaker and placed it into a clamp. She lifted her right hand and closed her eyes concentrating. I held my breath, unsure what was about to come. Without warning, she suddenly moved her right hand, in short, sharp patterns. The pattern was random at first, but then with a start, I realised it was the same pattern that was on the flask. She was tracing it in front of her. What's more, there was a very faint red light between her fingers, as if she were drawing into the air itself with light as her ink. She stopped moving her hand and opened her eyes. Realising I was watching her, she nodded to the flask. The water was boiling.

"Just energy," she said, smiling at me.

I had a million questions for her. A million and one. But there was a familiar tugging at the back of my skull that told me a headache was coming.

As if sensing my tiredness, Themia started breaking down the set-up. "I think we should probably stop here for now. I have a lot of unpacking to do, and I suspect I am taking up too much of your time. If it isn't too much of an issue, would you be able to come back tomorrow? I need someone to show me around. Of course, in return, we shall see if we can get a good distillation going on your bark."

I wasn't sure I could exactly say no. Besides Themia's company had been pleasant, and I'd learned more about Aspecting in one morning than almost sixteen years of overhearing scraps of information and drunken stories.

"Of course," I said. "I'll be there."

It also seemed that the Vins weren't all as inherently evil as some in this town had led me to believe.

On my way home, the headache grew worse, so I stopped by Anick's to pick up some waelig bark to chew to try and take the edge off.

"That'll be a copper. Anything else you need?" Anick said, passing me the strip of bark,

"No," I said, then paused. Themia's voice was ringing in my ears. "Actually, I'm running low on my medicine…" I looked at him, hoping he'd just jump in with what it was I needed.

"What medicine?" He asked, looking at me expectantly.

"You know," I said, "for the seizures?"

"Oh," he said, surprised. "I had no idea you were taking anything for seizures."

7

Wooden Whispers

Father was already home by the time I made it back.

"How did it go?" He called when he heard me step through the door. "Did she offer you gold to sell out Dane?"

I kept quiet as I made my way into our kitchen. I couldn't figure out why Father didn't get my medicine from Anick. Maybe he harvested it himself, but then, why not tell me? Ask me to help? I resolved to ask him about it.

"You're quiet," he said, spotting me as I sat down opposite him at the table.

"Just tired," I said, "Themia and I spoke all morning."

"Oh, did you now? Are you any the wiser what she's doing here?"

I shook my head. "Folk's didn't seem too happy to see us walking around the town."

"What do you expect, Kehlem? Even before the war, Casere and Vin Irudur weren't exactly pally. People here lost family and friends at the hands of them. Thirty years later they tax us up to our eyeballs and then to rub salt in the wound they send an Aspector without cause to rub her nose into our business. You need to be careful."

I looked up, confused at what he meant. "What do you mean?"

He sighed. "If people see you spending time around Themia, they'll get suspicious. They'll wonder what she's telling you, what she's asking you. The last thing we need is people to stop coming to us if they need help. Still, at least it's over for now."

"Actually," I said, picking my words carefully, "I'm supposed to be going back tomorrow."

Father's face was thunder. "What do you mean, 'going back tomorrow'?"

"The distillation," I explained. "We ran out of time, and she asked for my help to show her around."

"Oh, Martyr's ashes," he swore. "I don't like this. Why is she so interested in you?"

"I don't think she is," I said, calmly. "I think she just wants to help."

"I don't remember raising you to be naive," he said, chiding me. "At least do me a favour, don't go walking around town with her this time."

I nodded, pushing myself to my feet. "I'm going to go read for a bit."

Father's reaction had made me rethink bringing up the medicine. If I asked about it now, there's no way he wouldn't immediately think it was Themia who put me up to it. I either needed to wait until after she left town, or try and figure out what it was by myself.

My starting point was to have a look at what our pharmacopoeia had down as a treatment for seizures. It was fairly old, written around two hundred years ago, but it was well used within our household and contained many examples of preparations to treat a variety of illnesses, common and exotic. Flipping through the index, I found the right section, and hefted the book open to the right page, pouring over the small, tightly printed words.

'Maladie of the brain can lead to over-excitation which may in certain circumstances prove fatal. Symptoms often express themselves in the young as they advance to pre-adolescence. Various treatments have been attempted, but no preventative has been identified so far. Focus should instead be on keeping patients calm, in low stimulating environments to lower the risk of an episode. Should one occur, treatment should focus on symptomatic treatment, see section fourteen on anti-inflammatory and pain relievement.'

I re-read the section to make sure I hadn't missed anything. Other than listing a few examples of natural mushroom toxins that were seizurogenic, there was nothing else. I leaned back in the armchair and shut the book with a *thump*. Was that why father didn't go to Anick for the medicine? Had father discovered a new treatment by himself? It was possible, but then surely, he must have published the knowledge somewhere. Granted the pharmacopoeia was somewhat out of date, but if truly no other preventatives had been discovered, then surely my treatment was not only novel but worth something to the world. I was left with more questions than answers.

That evening father and I suppered in the tavern. Many of the patrons gave me a few pointed stares as we found our seats. I caught the edges of a few whispers that made it clear that mine and Themia's conversation earlier that day had been the talk of the town. As the evening drew on though the gossiping seemed to stop, and we were joined by the occasional neighbour stopping by to share news or ask for advice on one complaint or another. All the while the question Themia had given me lay burning in the back of my mind.

Father left early the next morning to call in on Jea and her new babe after being collared by her husband last night who'd mentioned the babe had a fever, leaving me home alone. Feeling more than a little guilty, but at a loss of what else to do, I entered my father's bedroom, hoping to find something, anything that might give me a clue as to what it was he had discovered to treat seizures. Overnight the question had burned bright, searing itself into my mind and left me impatient to find the answer. It had grown so much more than just idle curiosity on the contents of my medicine. The fact that my father appeared to be hiding a novel prophylactic for seizures seemed so at odds with all he had taught me, it left me with an itching curiosity that demanded to be answered.

Father's room was sparse. Bed, nightstand, chest and wardrobe. Even though I'd been in it often to clean and change the linen, I still felt an inexplicable feeling of guilt, like I was betraying his trust just by being here. I suppose in a way I was. But I also knew I was in too deep now to just outright ask him. So, setting the guilt aside, I began carefully searching through his things. His nightstand had a single drawer which was filled, as it always had been, with various knick-knacks. Broken nibs, empty ink pots, torn pieces of parchment and many, many candle stubs. I went through every item, but there was nothing here, not that I really expected anything either. Next, I quickly searched through his wardrobe, which of course only had a few shirts, cloaks and trousers folded neatly onto each shelf. Finally, all that was left was the chest.

Of all the furniture in his room, his chest was the only one I had a vague knowledge of its contents, and I hesitated to open it. I had a hazy childhood memory of being told off for scratching it. Father had yelled at me, told me it contained the only items of mother's he had. He told me never to go near it again. It was one of the only times I remembered him losing his temper with me.

I also knew I couldn't stop here. The question had burned itself too deeply into my mind. So, with a deepening sense of guilt, I lifted the heavy lid.

The contents had been wrapped with a soft paper, and there was a faint smell of lilac. I gently lifted the paper, and found a neatly folded dress, with dried purple flowers scattered atop. I brushed my fingers over the dress and inhaled. This was the first belonging of my mother's I had seen. Pangs of longing for a woman I had never met rippled through me, amplifying the steady waves of guilt that was crashing against me with every item I disturbed. Perhaps the lilac had been her favourite flower, the scent reminding him of her. The shame and guilt were a bucket of ice water thrown over me, quickly dousing the insatiable curiosity I'd felt only moments before. I gently lifted the paper to cover the contents once more. As I pressed the paper down on the folded dress, however, I noticed something. There was something solid, something not made of fabric beneath the dress. Without thinking, I worked my hand beneath the clothing and pulled out the object. It was a small, leather-bound journal. Lost in the moment, I unknotted the leather cord holding it closed, and leafed through the pages. They were filled in the familiar, spidery script of my father. It appeared to be notes from various patient treatments, the doses of various medicines used and the recovery of the patients. I even spotted Job's name, with details of the surgery we performed and the various treatments father had given him to stave off pain and infection. I continued to flick through the book, and towards the front, I spotted what it was that I hadn't known I was looking for. My name.

This page was sparser than the others, no detail of illness, no prognosis or recovery. Instead, it contained two separate lists, with numbers jotted next to each item. One was much smaller than the other. I recognised them immediately, they were tincture ingredients, with shorthand ratios that could be scaled up and down according to dose. Father and I used them all the time as a way to remember how to make the more complex medicines needed by the town. The shorter list contained only three ingredients, none of which I recognised, although one of them, *faeamania,* seemed vaguely familiar to me. The other list was much more complex. Again, filled with ingredients I had no knowledge of. The largest ratio of ingredient was something called *arrowwood*. I'd never heard of it, or seen mention of it anywhere in the pharmacopoeia. Still. I had my answer, even if it was anticlimactic. I wasn't sure which of the lists corresponded to the medicine I was taking now, but at least I had a starting point. It was possible one of the medicines were part of a series of experiments when I was younger, possibly something that only works in babes. Relieved to have some semblance of an answer, I re-tied the leather journal, and placed it back in the chest, restoring the dress and paper to their original places.

A knock on the front door disturbed me from my reading. All morning I'd been pouring over the books in our study as I tried to find more information on the ingredients in my medicines. I found no mention of arrowwood or faeamania. The latter was especially frustrating as the memory of it was on the very tip of my mind. Sighing heavily, I slammed the tome on my lap closed and rose to open the door.

"Themia! What are you doing here?"

"Well, I assumed you might have gotten distracted about our planned meeting today, so I decided to take matters into my own hands," she smiled. She was wearing the same purple cloak, but today it was accompanied by a wide-brimmed hat, to protect her from the drizzling rain.

My face fell. In my hurry to discover the secrets within the journal I had totally forgotten. "I'm so sorry!" I said, "It totally slipped my mind."

"No harm done! I see you were deep in study," she peered over my shoulder. "Should I perhaps come back another time?"

"No, no, today's fine. Let me grab my cloak. Do you want to come inside while you wait?"

She shook her head. "I'm quite fine here, you get ready."

I raced inside to grab a thick woollen cloak and pulled on my boots, and ran back to the front door, pulling it shut behind me.

"So," I said, catching my breath, "where was it you needed me to show you?"

"I've been informed that there is an abandoned farm to the north of the town."

I nodded, walking in step with Themia. "I know it. Blackhouse farm. I don't think anyone has been there in at least ten years."

"I'm to survey it for some potential minerals."

"It's a bit of a walk," I said, not excited about the prospect of a cold, muddy day in the rain.

Themia nodded to a horseless cart at the bottom of the road. "Who said we'd be walking?"

The cart was not of a design I'd ever seen before. The bed of the cart was flat with iron rails around it to stop luggage from falling out, and a simple bench adorned what I assumed was the front of the cart, but most strikingly I could see no hitch for a horse. Perhaps this was some subtle design more common in Vin Irudur? I expected Themia to walk straight past the cart to fetch a horse from a stable, but again, she surprised me by climbing straight onto the front, sitting down on the bench and indicated for me to join her. The whole time she smiled at me, knowing how confused I was, so not wanting to give her the satisfaction of the question she knew I must have, I climbed aboard.

Themia reached behind her and pulled up a folding canopy to protect us from the worst of the gentle rain, and then lifted a lever at her side.

The untethered cart lurched forward. I yelped and gripped the edge in surprise, and Themia let out a hearty chuckle.

Despite the cart being unhitched, the cart was rolling uphill and what's more, it was picking up speed.

"Themia," I said through gritted teeth. "How are we moving?" My hands were white-knuckled gripping the railing next to me.

She held the lever still in her hand, turning it to the left like a rudder, which forced the cart to follow the road's bend.

She kept her eye on the dirt road in front. "This is perhaps a more frivolous use of the Aspect, but a useful one, nevertheless."

I tried to force myself to relax. "You're doing this?"

"Not me specifically. The cart is tethered to a waterwheel at the academy, I can just control it. Is it left here?"

I nodded, and she pushed the lever to the left, and the cart trundled down the worn dirt path as we moved further out of town. "How do you mean, tethered to a waterwheel?"

"As I said yesterday, we cannot create energy. This cart is just borrowing energy from another source."

"Yes, but how?"

"For that," Themia turned to me, smiling, "you would have to go to the academy."

We travelled in silence a little while, and I slowly eased my death grip on the railing.

"What's it like? At the academy?" I asked.

"It's home," Themia said simply. "I lived there since I was eight. The people I met there, Vin and Casere," she gave me a pointed look, "were my family, my friends. For those of us who desire knowledge, it is the only place."

"Are there many Casere at the academy?"

"A few. It's mostly Vins of course, but there is normally a collection of Casere in each class."

The cart continued down the hedgerow lined trail, bobbing up and down with each divot. The rain had slowed, and the clouds were slowly relenting. *A place for those who desire knowledge.* I shouldn't be envious. I knew the life of an Aspector couldn't be easy. Look at Themia. Sent to the other end of the country on the whim of the empire. And for Caserean Aspector's it was even worse. Ripped from their homeland, forced into the academy lest they break the accords. And yet. There was something that hooked me.

Something that had sparked within me when Father spoke of the healers he had known. Themia's stories of the Aspect, her demonstrations of its power only fanned that flame. What it must be like to have the power to heal the unhealable.

We arrived at Blackhouse farm just after midday. The farm itself was unremarkable. A derelict shepherd's hut lay ruined next to the path, and the drystone wall had collapsed at some point. The field itself was entirely overgrown and alone in the centre stood a single oak tree. The earlier rain had turned the trail to a muddy mess, so Themia and I left our cloaks in the cart as we clambered over the broken gate to get a closer look at the field.

"So, what exactly is it you need to do?" I asked, pushing aside a nettle with my shoe.

"Hmm?" Themia was busy surveying the field, looking from west to south. "Oh. Not much today, today I'm just getting to grips with the size of the place. I'll need to return with some equipment to test it properly."

"What is it you think is here?"

"Oh, the usual, copper, probably tin. Hopefully iron." She turned back to look at me. "They're all fairly important metals for the Fabricas."

"…Fabricas?"

"Oh, sorry. Fabricas are to engineers as Alchemists are to chemists. They are the ones responsible for making things such as the cart, and my flask. Well, I think I'm done here, shall we head back?"

"So soon?" I asked, surprised. We'd only just gotten here.

She shrugged her shoulders. "I needed to see how large the field was to know what to bring."

She scraped the mud from her boots with a twig and climbed back onto the cart. I joined her after doing the same. "Could you not have gotten the plans from Mayor Dane?"

"I was told that there were no such things when I asked."

"Ah," I said. There were. I knew there were. Mayor Dane had gone to great lengths to force each and every landowner to draw up plans of the land that they owned a few years back. It had caused an enormous ruckus at the time, as it inevitably meant higher taxes for the landowners the following year. I could think of only one reason why Dane had refused to give Themia the plans.

"'Ah' indeed," Themia nodded to me, a slight smile on her lips. She pulled the cart lever up and the cart moved forwards once more towards a larger patch in the trail big enough to turn about.

"Still. No harm is really done. A day in good company is well spent in my opinion."

"Likewise," I said. And I meant it. There was something honest about Themia. From the stories I'd been told about the Vins, I'd half expected some duplicitous weasel, the kind that earns all the jeers during a bad mummery play, but the reality had been so different. Despite the warnings from my father, I found myself enjoying Themia's company.

"I am afraid that due to our, ahem, later start today, that I won't have time to set up the distillation tonight, so it will perhaps have to wait till a later time. I am sure that I have taken up enough of your time recently, so I suggest we make plans to run the experiment in a few weeks' time. That would also give me time to properly survey this field." She looked to me, looking for my agreement.

"Of course," I said, "I'm sorry again for being late today."

She waved her hand, dismissing my apology. Themia set the cart back towards Barrowheld and hummed a quiet tune beneath her breath.

True to her word Themia didn't call on me again that week, or the week after in fact. While I missed her company, particularly for the morsels of information on Aspecting she had been dropping here and there, I was grateful three times over. Firstly, Father's face darkened whenever her name was spoken over the dinner table. His distaste for her defied reason, and I knew better than to convince him otherwise. I needed Themia's help to distil the waelig, but I didn't want to picture his reaction if I were to visit Themia a third day in a row instead of working at the practice. Secondly, it gave me time with Eva, time that I knew was desperately running out. We were both busy, her in the chandlery and me with patients, but we saw each other as much as our time permitted. While there were no more incidents like that in the woods, she continued to reach for my hand whenever we went walking together late on an evening. Each time she did I heard Bill's advice ringing in my ears, and I egged myself on to just tell her. Each time I'm ashamed to say I failed, the words sticking in my throat. The final reason, and the one most pressing to me, is I needed as much free time as possible to research. I needed to find out what faeanamie and arrowwood were from. I had to be careful doing so, not wanting to have to explain to Father where I had discovered the ingredients, so most evenings, long after father had gone to bed, I was pouring over our many books, one by one, looking for any and all references. By the third week, the books had run out, and still, I couldn't find reference to either.

8

Catalyst

The birds were singing. Those bastards. They sang of spring. Eva would be leaving soon, and still, I hadn't told her how I felt. We were walking around town after bumping into each other during our morning errands. She needed to pick up some bread from the bakery, and while I was finished and the bakery was in the opposite direction to home, I followed along anyway, just happy to have an excuse to spend some more time with her.

"...the rest of the day?"

"Huh?" I asked. I'd been watching her talk, but hadn't heard a word she'd said. I shook the fog from my head.

"Today. What are you doing today?" She looked concerned. This wasn't the first time she'd had to repeat herself.

"Oh, Themia sent a note. She's finished her study so she's got time to run the distillation today. What about you?"

"Oh," she said. "Are you free this evening?"

Was it just me or did she seem disappointed?

"Of course," I said. "meet you at yours?"

"Sounds like a plan."

Clear droplets of colourless liquid collected on the glass column. They beaded together, slowly, before picking up speed as they poured down the angled glass tube like small rivers, falling into the awaiting beaker below.

Themia and I stood at opposite ends of the table the glassware was set up on, watching the experiment complete. The round flask at the bottom was glowing a faint red across the etchings as Themia held some kind of control of the temperature, carefully heating up the solvent, sending steam across a container that held the waelig bark. I watched in silence as the collecting beaker slowly filled with the condensed liquid, not wanting to break Themia's concentration if she required it to control the temperature of the beaker.

Themia must have spotted some indiscernible marker that she had been waiting for, as she nodded to herself satisfied. "I think we can call an end to the test here, Kehlem."

The boiling flask quickly faded to the colour of normal glass as Themia stepped away from the table, with the remaining solvent seemingly cooling down from a rolling boil to totally still almost instantly.

"Let's check for purity, shall we?" she asked, dipping her finger into the collection beaker. With just her finger, she traced a quick pattern in the liquid, and again I could have sworn I saw a faint red glow where her finger traced. The pattern was quick, and she took her finger out of the liquid a moment later. "Just cooling it down," she said, by way of explanation. She then picked up a glass rod from the table, and used it to scratch the inside of the collection beaker, rubbing it backwards and forwards on the base.

"What's that for," I asked.

"It helps to speed up crystallisation," she said. "Look!" she smiled, holding up the beaker for me to see. The colourless liquid had suddenly grown cloudy, and I could see fine, white crystals had begun to form, suspended in the liquid.

"Has it worked?" I asked, excited.

"It would appear so. I would imagine they could perhaps be a little purer if we distilled them a few more times, however, I would think these are suitable for medicinal practices. Here," she picked up the collection beaker, and poured the contents into an empty flask, through a filter, and then used the glass rod to scrape the collected crystals into a small glass vial.

"Thank you so much for your help," I said, taking the vial, marvelling at how white the crystals were. "I would never have been able to have gotten them this pure without it."

"Think nothing of it, Kehlem," she waved her hand. "I would like to show you something though."

I set the vial down on the bench and watched as she pulled out the sodden waelig bark from the glass container and held it in her palm. She looked at it for a moment, as if contemplating it, and then closed her eyes. Once more she traced a pattern in the air in front of her, faint red light glowing wherever her finger traced, and then touched the waelig bark in her palm. For a moment, nothing happened, and then suddenly, the bark appeared to dissolve. I took a sharp intake of breath. As the bark dissolved in her hand, it left behind a fine, pure white powder. She gently tapped the powder into another vial.

"This," she said, passing the new vial over to me, "is about as pure as it could possibly be."

"Incredible," I whispered. The vial which contained the Aspected extract had about three times as much extract as the one we'd spent the whole morning distilling. For the first time, I was beginning to understand the real power that Aspectors had. To be able to refine and distil something so pure, so quickly. I was speechless.

Themia just smiled at me, obviously pleased by my reaction. "So, what is next in your project?" As she spoke, she began rifling through her chests, unpacking various books onto empty spaces on the table.

I looked up, still distracted by what she had just done. "I guess I'll need to figure out its properties. Hopefully, use it next time someone needs pain relief to see how useful it will actually be."

"Well, it seems like you have a long road ahead of you. If you need more extract, feel free to come by anytime."

"Thank you," I said earnestly. A sudden thought crossed my mind as I watched her unpack. "Themia, I don't suppose you have any books on herbology I could borrow?"

She smiled at me and nodded to a chest by the door. "Be my guest."

I was late getting to Eva's. After leaving Themia's I wanted to quickly check something in the Pharmacopoeia at home and had gotten immediately distracted. The sun was almost set by the time I knocked on Eva's door. The sky was lit with brilliant purple hues, and birds could be seen darting across the sky, revelling in the warmth that had returned. My heart hammered in my chest as I waited for the door to open.

"I thought you had forgotten all about me," I heard Eva say as she pulled the door open, but her smile quickly faded as she saw my face. "Kehlem? What's happened?"

I looked at her, Themia's herbology book held at my side. "I think Father has been poisoning me."

Eva stepped out of the door to join me outside. "What are you talking about?" She grabbed my hand and pulled me out of earshot of the house.

I pinched the bridge of my nose, struggling to put words together. "I found something this morning. Father's notes. He listed the ingredients for two different tinctures. One of them, I thought I recognised an ingredient of, but I couldn't remember where from." I was babbling, I knew it, but I couldn't stop the stream. My skin felt hot and itchy, and I just needed to talk to someone. I ploughed on. "And then I was reading a book that Themia lent me. And it clicked. *Faeamania*. A seizurogenic toxin listed in father's pharmacopoeia." I paused, looking at Eva to see if she got it.

She looked at me, her brows furrowed as she tried to follow the point I was making.

I carried on. "It's a mushroom. People always tell you to make sure not to let your dogs near them because they can make them seize. Eva, I think my father poisoned me, to make me have a seizure." The words came tumbling out of me. I heaved as I gasped for air.

Eva's mouth fell open, stunned. "Kehlem...That makes no sense!" She grabbed my hand. "Why would your father poison you? Maybe you misread it. Or maybe he figured out a different way of using the mushroom?"

"I thought that too!" I said, still trying to catch my breath. "I had the same thought, maybe if it causes seizures, maybe Father found out a way to make it treat them as well. Three hundred or so years ago, that's how they thought some medicines work after all, like cures like and all that. But then, I found this," and I passed Eva the herbology book I'd been holding, and opened it at the right page. "This was also listed as an ingredient."

"What am I looking at?" Eva asked, squinting at the book in the failing light. "What's arrowwood?"

I read the passage without looking at it. I had memorized it this afternoon. "'The first use of arrowwood was documented five hundred years ago by Casere. They described its use as a depressant to help keep prisoners compliant, especially during transport. Specifically noted for its ability to restrict and control an Aspectors connection to the Aspect, it was often used on prisoners of war and deserters.'"

Eva looked at me from the book, and I could see her making the same connections I did. "Father always told me I had seizures when I was a baby. When I was too young to remember. Then, I lowered my dose without telling him. I think he was worried I'd figure out I didn't need the medication. That day I had a seizure in the woods. I think he poisoned something in the picnic, to scare me into not only taking my medicine but upping the dose."

Eva had gone very pale. "But then, how come I wasn't poisoned as well?"

I thought for a moment, thinking back to the meal. "The drink," I said suddenly. "He packed me an ale and a cider for you. He knows you don't drink ale. He poisoned the fucking drink." I was shaking now. A blind fury was raging within me.

Eva reached out to hold my hand. "Kehlem, wait a moment. I know Tema. He loves you, he wouldn't put you at risk."

"No, but just enough risk to make me scared," I hissed. "Do you not find it odd that Bill just happened to be in the woods at the same time I had the seizure?"

"He was collecting wood!" Eva protested.

"For a table, Father had paid him to build! Father knew I was there. He made sure someone was close by to bring me back!" I was breathing heavily, and the hot fury was burning through me.

"Kehlem, calm down, please," Eva pleaded. She grabbed both my hands and forced me to look at her. The fear in Eva's eyes made me deflate. In a single breath, the anger burned out of me, and my shoulders sagged, leaving me with burning embers. I fell to the ground. Eva sat down next to me.

For a while I just sat, and breathed, waiting for my body to stop shaking. "Do you believe me?" I asked.

She looked at me, holding my gaze firmly and then nodded once. "I do."

A wave of relief rushed through me. I wasn't going mad. It wasn't all in my head.

"I still don't understand why he'd go to all this effort though," she said. "Why lie about the seizures, why poison you?"

There was a reason, currently lying faceup in Themia's herbology book, and we both glanced towards it.

"Is it possible?"

"I...I don't know," I said.

"You need to speak to someone. If you are an Aspector, you know what the accords say."

I took a deep breath. Everything was happening too fast. I would have to leave Casere

"You need to talk to Themia. You need to speak to Tema."

The thought of confronting my father made me feel sick. "I can't do it, Eva. I can't." I wiped my face, surprised to find I'd started crying at some point.

Eva leaned forwards and wiped my eyes. "You have to. Go speak to Themia tonight. If you are an Aspector, then she will find out sooner or later. Better on your own terms than on hers."

She was right. I knew she was right.

"Kehlem, there's something else," Eva said. She looked uncertain. "I got a letter a couple of weeks back. I'm supposed to be leaving for Mercy tomorrow. I was going to tell you today. I'd made all these plans to make today special, but then you were busy, and now this!" She sniffed.

I pulled her into an embrace, and she sobbed onto my shoulders.

Despite myself, despite the horror of the revelations that the day had given me, for the first time this evening, I felt almost at peace. The day before I had planned to tell Eva how I felt about her this evening. And now it was too late. Given everything, perhaps it was for the best. A clean break for her to focus on becoming a scribe. My life was on a cliff's edge, and I had suddenly no idea which way it would fall. It would be unimaginably cruel for me to tangle her into the mess my life was becoming.

I pulled back out of the embrace and wiped her tears away with my thumb. "It's ok," I smiled earnestly. "You need to go, get out of this place. You're going to do amazing things, and you've already given me so much. You should get back inside," I said, pulling her to her feet. "I bet your Ma' is wondering where you've gotten to. What time do you leave tomorrow?" I asked.

"Midday," she sniffed, clutching onto my sleeve.

"I'll come find you tomorrow before you go. I promise."

Eva nodded to me, and let go of my sleeve. "Kehlem, promise me something?"

"What?"

"Don't do anything stupid." She looked scared.

How unfair of me to burden her with all of this. "I promise," I said.

"Well, this is an unexpected surprise!" Themia said, opening the door.

"You knew, didn't you?" I demanded, my voice calm. During the walk from Eva, something in me had hardened. The fury at my father's betrayal had tempered itself into solid iron.

Themia looked at me for a moment and then stepped aside. "Come on in," she said.

I stepped into the house.

"Can I interest you in some supper?" she asked, stepping past me. "I have some rice boiling. What is it with you people and stew? It wouldn't hurt you to have some spice in your meal now and again."

"Am I the reason you're here?" I demanded, ignoring her question. I thumped the book down on the kitchen table.

Themia turned to look at me. "There were rumours," she said at last, "whispers that there was a hidden Aspector in the area. Usually, a Hunter would be sent of course, but the Seers said something was off. Sometimes it felt like it was a babe Aspector. Sometimes it felt like an adult. They sent me to investigate." She poured some tea from a pot and passed me a mug.

"Seers and Aspectors, we can sense each other. When I first arrived here, I thought for sure you must be hiding your skill on purpose." She sipped her tea, keeping her eye on me all the while. "But as we spoke, I began to realise. You had no idea. It's rare. Very rare. Usually, Aspectors come into their own around puberty. To be untrained, and ignorant almost five years later. It's practically unheard of."

"Why didn't you tell me?" I demanded.

"Tell you what?" She asked. "I had no idea what was happening. All I knew was that you were an Aspector. I had my suspicions of course. I assume I was correct?" she nodded to the book. "Arrowood?"

I nodded, stunned.

"Mhhm. Makes sense, given the circumstances."

The floor was dropping from under me. I gripped a worktop for support. "So, I'm an Aspector?" My ears were ringing.

"Oh, of course. That was never in doubt."

"So, what happens now?"

Themia sighed. "Well, you are aware of the accords?"

I nodded.

"Then you already know. You are to be trained. You cannot stay in Barrowheld, I must take you to the Eastern Garrison, and from there you will be taken to the Isale Academy. You will learn to Aspect, you will find your discipline, and you will earn your tether." She made it sound so simple.

"What about father?" I whispered.

"That," Themia said carefully, "is another matter. He has broken the accords in hiding you. By all rights, he should be arrested."

I looked at Themia sharply. Breaking the accords was treason. He would be executed. Even in the coldest fury, I didn't want my father dead.

"However," she continued, watching my expression, "if your father were to go missing tomorrow, say before sundown, then I could not spare the time to search for him. I doubt the empire would care enough to send Hunters after him."

I nodded slowly, understanding.

"For tonight, however, I suggest you stay here. I am no physician, but I can perhaps give you something to relieve some of the effects of the arrowwood."

I recalled back to how I felt when I had first reduced my dosage. I'd felt so nauseous and dizzy for that first week, and that had only been reducing the dosage. Who knew how bad it would be to come off it completely.

"It's settled then, you will enjoy some Vin cuisine, and tomorrow we shall see what the day brings."

9

Fury

The air was fresh. I'd never noticed it before. It sounds strange to say of course, but the air *smelled*. I inhaled deeply, and let the smell of bread, blossom and earth wash over me. I closed my eyes and revelled in the sensation of the cool wind rushing past my fingertips. I was standing outside of Themia's house, preparing myself for the day ahead. Last night, Themia and I had spoken little after dinner. She gave me a medicine which she said would take most of the edge off the arrowwood, which in fairness it did, but it brought with it the worst night sleep I ever had, although that may not have been entirely the medicine's fault. I had vivid, terrifying dreams all night, ones I struggled to wake from. I dreamt I was aflame, my skin burning. Charring black as I cried out for help, all the while I could smell my own flesh cooking, and my father just stood watching me, arms crossed, unmoving. I'd dreamt I was chained in a basement, pressed up against a rock that whispered hatred into my ear. I dreamt of people falling lifeless around me. If I closed my eyes, their dead eyes were not far behind the engulfing darkness.

Still, I awoke this morning, tired, but alive, and with none of the nausea I was expecting. Themia greeted me with a quiet nod and told me she had plans for the day, but that we should meet back here in the evening to travel to the academy.

As confusing as the whole situation was, I was grateful for her giving me space to deal with things on my own terms. I knew she was letting me confront my father. As surprised as I was last night that she'd be willing to let my father go, it just confirmed once more that some of what I heard about the Vins was perhaps unwarranted.

Still, Father could wait. Eva was leaving today, and she remained the only source of comfort and stability I had in the rapidly eroding mess that my life was turning out to be. I was damned if I wasn't going to say goodbye. And so, a little unsteady on my feet, I followed my feet to find Eva.

When I got close enough, I spotted a horse and wagon outside Eva's house, and an immediate wave of relief that I hadn't missed her flooded through me, followed quickly by surprise that her new masters were rich enough to send a wagon to collect a new scribe. I spotted Eva talking to Maggie as I drew near.

"Morning," I called to them both, drawing to a halt underneath a blossoming willow tree.

Eva jumped, apparently surprised to see me. She looked at her Ma' and I heard her ask her to give her a moment.

Maggie gave her a knowing smile and retreated back into the house, and Eva came walking over towards me.

"I wasn't sure you'd come," Eva said. "How are you feeling?"

"Of course, I came," I said. "I'm…" I paused, trying to think of the right words, and then gave up. "I don't really know, to be honest. Themia gave me something to help get rid of the arrowwood."

"So, it's true then?" she asked, her eyes going wide. "Do you have to leave for Vin Irudur?"

"Today," I said. "They're taking me to Isale academy."

"What about Tema?"

"I haven't spoken to him yet. Themia is letting him escape."

Eva looked surprised. "That's awfully generous."

I nodded, agreeing. I didn't want to talk about my father. Even now, with the horror that my life had become, all I wanted was to take in the sight of Eva. It would be a long time until I saw her again. It was entirely possible I may never even see her again. I just wanted to commit her to memory.

"I'm glad you're going to the academy," Eva said. "When you finish your studies, would you come back to Mercy?" She stepped closer to me. We were almost touching. She looked up at me through her eyelashes. "Will you come find me?"

I was drowning in her eyes. "I will," I promised. I could feel the warmth from her skin.

She reached up, and wrapped her hand around the back of my neck, and pulled my head down, at the same time she reached up, and our lips touched.

There was a breathless, insatiable urgency that coursed through my body as I held her close to me. I lived lifetimes in that kiss. The warmth of knowing that she felt the same way about me spread through my body like gentle lightning. All I could do was hold her, and revel in this one piece of pure, golden joy.

Too soon we drew apart. We stayed close, holding one another beneath the swaying limbs of the willow tree, looking into each other's eyes, and finally, even though there was silence between us, it was a peaceful, satisfied quiet. We looked at each other as if we suddenly perfectly understood the other.

"I'll find you," I promised again. My eyes and cheeks were wet.

She nodded and tiptoed to kiss me on the forehead. "Be well, Kehlem," she said. She turned around.

I knew if I stayed, I wouldn't leave. Accords be damned. I think she knew that as well. She didn't turn back.

I moved my feet. The first step was the hardest, but I pulled them along with me leaving, Eva to start her new life. I headed west back into town. It was time to speak to my father.

The whole walk there I tried to figure out what I would say. There was a simmering anger within me, it seemed to propel me forwards but refused to lend me any clear thoughts. Each step I took fanned the flames, pushing the glowing warmth of Eva's kiss to the side. It was a primal feeling, fed by the kindling of the many, many lies I must have been told by my father.

When someone so close to you betrays you, it doesn't break the relationship. It's a creeping vine that reaches back into all of your happy memories and despoils them, perverts them until they're ashes in your mouth.

The anger was inconsistent. Last night it had been a blinding rage, a wildfire through my being that would consume me. Now, after the bittersweet of saying goodbye to Eva, it had calmed to the steady burning fire of a forge. The words would never come. I opened the front door.

"Kehlem? Oh, thank the Martyr! What happened to you last night? Where were you? I was so worried!" Father came running to me, embracing me, pawing at me.

I didn't return the hug. I swayed, a tree in the wind, as he patted me over checking for injuries. His eyes were puffy and red from lack of sleep. He grabbed my hand, pulling me to a seat in the kitchen.

"Where were you?"

Still, no words would come. I opted for the simpler choice, an honest answer. "Themia's," I said. My voice sounded odd to my ears, hollow.

"Themia's? All night?" He sounded confused. Concerned.

I sighed. I couldn't do this. I needed to be direct. Purposeful. Like sawing through bone.

I looked at him, fixing his eyes in my gaze. "I know," I said simply.

"Know what?" he asked. He smiled at me as if it were a joke.

How could I possibly summarise? I didn't try. I lifted my hands and gestured around to everything. "I know," I repeated.

Like lightning, true fear flickered behind my father's eye.

Up until that point, I hadn't fully accepted the truth. Of course, I understood the logic, I could follow the breadcrumbs of it, but there had been a part of me, the part that loved my father, which had refused to believe he was capable of lying to me so, of poisoning me. That flicker of fear in his eyes, struck that small part of me like lightning to dry bush, and once more I was ablaze.

"You lied. You lied! To me!" I was shouting. I was on my feet. I didn't remember getting to my feet. The chair I was sitting on had tipped over. My throat was raw, and Father had recoiled, actually recoiled at the sound of my fury.

"I did what I had to do!" he shouted back. "I protected you!"

It was too much. Excuses. Weakness. I could hardly breathe for the inferno of hatred that was raging within.

"You need to leave." I managed, through the fire in my throat. "Leave tonight. Otherwise, they will capture you, and put you to death."

There. I had done my part. I'd warned him. I was feeling too much, everything was too new to be here any longer. Whatever it was Themia had given me last night was wearing off, and the nausea was returning. I would gain nothing by staying here. I knew enough.

He was sobbing now, heavy, nose dripping sobs. They were the tears of a man who had been found out. The tears of a toddler caught in a lie. I turned my back on him, disgusted. It was time to leave.

"Kehlem, wait!"

A hand touched my arm.

Something inside me snapped. The air around me felt suddenly thin and warm. As I lifted my hand to push my father away, a current took hold of it, gripped it, guided it. There was a red light. A feeling of rightness. A relief of the torrential hatred within me. And suddenly, there was a bright, golden fire all around. I flew backwards off my feet. The last thing I remember was watching the ceiling falling in.

10

Tethers that bind us

I awoke to the sound of birdsong, and for a moment, I was back in the clearing with Eva. Eva. We kissed. We'd kissed, and held each other, and for a moment, I was at peace. But then other memories came back, memories of hatred, of crying, nausea. Memories of fire. I jerked upright, and immediately regretted it. My body was ablaze with pain. My chest felt as if it had been struck by a hammer. My eyes watered, but as they cleared, I realised I was sitting on the back of a wagon. A moving wagon. I turned around and saw Themia looking back at me.

"You're awake," she said softly.

"I…" I tried to speak, but my body decided to remind me at that very instant just how nauseous I was. I heaved myself to the side of the cart and spilt my stomach contents on the passing road below.

"Come join me upfront, you'll feel better if you can see the road ahead," Themia's voice called.

Slowly, and painfully, I lifted myself over the lip of the wagon and sat down on the bench next to Themia. We were back on her cart.

"What happened?" I asked, after taking a gulp of water.

Themia sighed. "Something I should have seen coming. As I said, you're old to be coming into your Aspecting. With the arrowwood coming out of your system so quickly, I think it overwhelmed you. It sounded like the town had been hit by a thunderclap. I came running, but it was too late.

You Aspected, somehow, and in doing so, levelled your house."

I blinked away tears that fell unwillingly from my eyes. I didn't want to ask the question, but I knew I had to. "What about my father? Did I…" I couldn't speak it.

"Kill him? No, Kehlem. It appears not. By the time I got to the wreckage, he had escaped. You, however, were very close to being dead."

A wave of relief hit me. He escaped. I hated him. I truly, truly hated him. But I loved him also. I didn't want him dead. I just…in that moment I didn't want to even think about him. He'd escaped, and he'd left me for dead. That was enough for me. Enough for now.

"Where are we heading?" I asked, although I already knew the answer.

"The Eastern Garrison, as promised," she gave me a sharp look. "It's now more important than ever that you get your training. To call the Aspect like that, that much energy? You could have killed yourself."

"What do you mean?" I asked, drawing the blanket up closer to my shoulders.

"Remember I told you that energy and the Aspect is like currency?"

I nodded.

"Well, there is a price to be paid. You cannot take from the Aspect without paying it back. When you leave the Academy, you leave with a tether. It ties you to an energy source, one at the academy. As a second-degree Alchemist, I am tethered to one of the minor waterwheels. The waterwheel pays the energy that I use when I Aspect. As a Nascent, you have no tether. So, when you took energy from the Aspect and levelled your house, the Aspect took the energy right back. From you. By all accounts, you should be dead. Frankly, it's a miracle you're not."

Under any other circumstance, I would have greedily eaten this knowledge and spat back out a hundred questions. Instead, I sat in silence.

We rode together on the horseless carriage down unfamiliar roads. Rolling hills of patchwork fields gave way for wilder woods and unkempt land, and the road retreated into dirt tracks. The wagon kicked up clouds of dirt that left a cloying smell and made my throat itch, and each bump in the track sent a jarring bolt of pain through my spine. Eventually, as the sun began to set, Themia pulled on a lever, slowing the cart to a halt.

"We'll camp here for the night. The wagon should be big enough for the two of us," she said, easing herself off the cart.

I followed, sliding myself down to the floor. My knees buckled and I almost fell onto my face, my body protesting the cramp that had set into my buttocks and legs. I gripped a wagon wheel for support.

"Themia?" I called, "What is this?" The underside of the carriage was covered with a metal plate, which had been carved with intricate, spiralling patterns.

"What's what?" She called back.

I hoisted myself to my feet and helped Themia offload a pot stand onto the ground. "The copper beneath the wagon?" I asked, out of breath.

"Those are the inscriptions made by a Fabrica." She kicked out the legs of the stand as she spoke and attached the metal chain. "They're what tie the wagon to one of the waterwheels."

For a while we worked together in silence, setting up the camp ready for dinner.

"Will I be able to learn to be a healer?"

Themia gave me a knowing smile. "I think it's entirely possible Kehlem."

A sudden thought struck me, and I cursed myself for waiting so long to ask. "Eva. Did Eva see the…" I struggled for the right word, "accident? What time did it happen?"

"I believe she had already left, Kehlem. It was close to sundown that I heard the explosion."

I let out a sigh of relief. I didn't want Eva getting caught up in any of it.

"That being said," Themia said cautiously, "I would imagine the town is now fully aware of what happened. You understand I had to speak to Mayor Dane before I could just up and take you."

I understood what she was saying. A small town like Barrowheld, with news like this? It would spread like wildfire.

"I told Eva everything before she left," I said. "She knows I'm an Aspector. She encouraged me to talk to you."

Themia raised her eyebrows, surprised. "Did she now? That's a good friend you have."

I thought back to the taste of her lips. The softness of her skin. 'Will you come find me?'

A soft smile touched my lips.

"Right," Themia said, clapping her hands. "If you are to travel to Vin Irudur, then I must prepare you. Tonight, I shall cook you the king of Vin dishes; curried rabbit. Now, of course, we have no rabbits, so we will make do with vegetables. I have no idea why you and your kin are so averse to spice, but we shall get you used to it if it's the last thing we do. Also!" she threw her arms wide, "tonight, there will be no ale. We Vins prefer wine, and I'm quite sure the young master will find it to his liking. Now, if you wouldn't mind peeling those potatoes, we shall begin tonight's feast."

That evening, Themia cooked us a delicious, spicy meal, the likes of which I'd never had before. It was similar to stew in that it consisted of vegetables and sauce, but there the similarity ended. Where a broth would be rich and savoury, the curry was thick and had a warmth to it that made my eyes water, and my nose run. She accompanied the dish with a wineskin that we passed between the two of us. I was unused to the taste, with Vinnish wine considered a luxury in Barrowheld, but after I got past the dry texture, I found it quite to my liking. Themia peppered me with tales of her time at the academy and sang me traditional Vinnish songs. She laughed quickly and brightly, and she tried her best to distract me from the torment she knew I was feeling. She kept me awake long enough that by the time we settled down, I closed my eyes and drifted into a mercifully dreamless, and peaceful sleep.

11

Forest Fire

I stretched in my seat, massaging the life back into my legs. Today we were arriving at the Eastern Garrison. It had been four days since Themia had rescued me from Barrowheld. She had continued to try and keep me distracted by telling me more stories of her time at Isale academy, perhaps trying to set my mind at ease, but it was hard to give her much attention. My mind was elsewhere, contemplating how my life had so quickly come to ruin. Themia and I sat in silence together as the cart powered on. As we had travelled further north the rough track we had been following gave way to a wild path through a large, ancient wood which took us two full days to travel through. As the trees became sparser and the land flattened out again, a range of mountains could be seen to shadow the distant horizon.

"At the base of that range, you'll find the academy, and the town for which it's named," Themia said, smiling, her long red hair billowing behind her as the wind once again had the freedom to roam without being obscured by the ancient elm trees.

I'd never seen anything like it. How could something still days ahead of us still loom so large against the horizon? I couldn't comprehend the sheer size of those mountains.

"Still," she said, "the garrison awaits us first."

The Eastern Garrison had been built following the end of the war, some thirty years ago. Originally a Vin Irudur encampment, it started off as a collection of tents and wooden walls. After the war ended it slowly evolved into a permanent settlement. Tents were replaced with houses, and rough-hewn wooden walls were replaced with carved blocks of stone. Now it governed the eastern entrance to Vin Irudur, protecting the borders from a non-existent army. Guarding the only bridge across the Dravé river, it was the safest place to cross for many miles.

We arrived at the garrison by sundown, pulling up beside two lit braziers bracketing the only gate into the city. The pale walls towered over us as we approached, the fires behind us projecting our shadows onto them. The gateway held two enormous wooden doors, riveted with pieces of wrought black iron. Themia stopped the wagon, jumped off, and indicated for me to join her. I followed her up to the gate, where she banged hard against the wood. A seam I hadn't noticed in the wood opened, and a smaller — more human-sized — door opened within the gate. A guard stood in the way.

"Business?" He grunted.

"Themia. Second-degree Alchemist," Themia said, nodding towards me, her voice slipping into an officious tone. "Kehlem, to be taken to the Academy. Nascent Aspector."

The guard eyed me up and down. "Bit old 'ent he?"

Themia stared at the guard, ignoring him. "He's to be taken to the Seers. Tonight. Give them this." She passed a tightly wound scroll to the guard.

The guard sighed, taking it. "Come on then. They're only going to get more pissed off the later in the evening we leave it."

I stood rooted in my spot. I didn't realise Themia would be leaving me at the gate.

"A moment, Kehlem." Themia gripped my shoulders. "Learn well at the academy. Do what you can to earn your tether. Show them you can be of use to the empire, and you'll soon get your freedom." She looked me in the eyes, her own searching mine, desperately trying to implore some subtle meaning I was too tired to understand.

"We 'ent got all day," the guard said, impatient.

Themia nodded to the guard.

I looked at Themia, lost for words. "Thank you," I offered. "Thank you for everything."

She gave me an odd smile and pulled me in for a brief embrace. "Now go, quickly now." She me pushed through the door, towards the guard, but not before she palmed a small, heavy pouch into my hands.

I turned back to give my thanks to Themia, to say my goodbyes, but before I could even open my mouth, the guards inside the garrison slammed the door shut, and Themia was gone.

"Come on." The guard shoved me by the shoulder, pushing me back around and forcing me forward.

The inside of the garrison resembled a small town. Houses lined the sides of the cobblestone laid road, some with lit sconces that cast a gentle light into the night. Small flies and midges from the river swarmed over the lights, and occasionally a faint sizzle could be heard as the wind took hold of a flame, sending it into the dancing cloud of insects.

We walked in silence, the guard's hand lay on my right shoulder, gripping it tight enough to make sure I knew I couldn't run anywhere. As we walked, I blindly felt at the pouch Themia had passed me and realised it was heavy with coins. I smiled to myself. She'd given it to me at the last possible moment because she knew I'd try and refuse it. The guard pushed me left through an alleyway I hadn't noticed, which opened into a small square. A single tree lay in the centre, and opposite the alley stood a tall building. The guard marched me to the door and knocked lightly.

A man, hooded in a long brown robe opened the door.

"A nascent Aspector, Do'Seer," the guard said, his voice soft and quiet. He handed the hooded man the scroll Themia had given him. The monk took it, saying nothing, and stepped away from the door. The guard let go of my shoulder, so I stepped inside, the door shutting behind me.

We appeared to be in some kind of temple, stone walls lined with intricate patterns, and the smell of incense in the air. Before I had time to take in more of my surroundings, the monk walked off, the sound of his bare feet on flagstone pattering off down a corridor. Unsure what else to do I followed behind him through the corridor and into a small room. He pointed me to a chair, where I sat, and he turned on his heel and left, shutting the door behind him. Confused, and feeling uncomfortable being left to my own devices in a strange temple, I paced around the room. Besides a small lit fireplace and a desk, the room was bare. Windowless, it had the same intricate patterns carved into the wall as the entrance. I rested my hands against the carved designs, tracing their maddening spirals with my fingertips. I considered trying the door but thought better of it.

With no windows, I had no idea how much time had passed before I heard the sound of the door behind me opening. I hurried back to the chair and sat down, resisting the urge to crane my neck, waiting instead for the newcomer to come into view, as they walked to the opposite side of the desk. The figure was wearing a similar robe to the first, although unlike the first, his hood was down. A thin, old man with greying hair, he had a gentle smile on his face as he sat down and gazed at me. Only, he wasn't actually looking at me. His iris was grey, and even in this dark room, his pupils were small and tight. He was looking to the left of my shoulder. Blind then.

He reached into his robe and placed the now opened scroll Themia had written onto the desk before him.

"Quite the interesting tale," he said, his voice surprisingly rich and syrupy. "If it hadn't been written by one I know and trust, I might not believe it. An adolescent Nascent. How extraordinary."

"You know Themia?" I asked, surprised.

"Oh, quite well, quite well. But I am much more interested in you, Kehlem. Themia is a smart woman, but she is sometimes frustratingly succinct. Tell me about the fire. Tell me about when you Aspected." He leaned forwards in his chair, fingers steepled against one another.

I hesitated. I'd tried my best the whole journey to avoid reliving that moment. The monk waited patiently while I fought to find the words to explain.

"I was angry," I said simply. "No, that's not the right word. I felt something, here." I pointed to my stomach, forgetting the man was blind. "It was like a burning ember touched a dry forest. My body was suddenly ablaze with hate and I felt I would explode with it. When the pressure grew and I feared I had nowhere to relieve it, I felt something. It was like being in the chandlery when both vats are fired, and the sun is streaming through the windows. The heat inside builds and no matter how much your body sweats, you can't cool yourself. But then a window opens, and suddenly the cool air rushes in, and there's respite, for a moment." I took a deep breath, trying to collect my thoughts. I was rambling, talking more to myself than to the monk. "My rage had somewhere to go, and it pulled me along with it. I saw a pattern, traced in fire behind my eyes, and I just understood. I knew what to do. The next thing I remember was waking up on Themia's cart."

The monk leaned back in his chair, tapping the armrests. "It seems Themia was right then," the man said. He raised his voice, "Kit!" he shouted to the door behind me, which opened. "Take Kehlem to the sleeping quarters, ensure he has what he needs for the night."

Before I had a chance to say anything else, a hand touched my shoulder guiding me out of the chair. The blind monk remained seated, eyes still staring vacantly at the space I'd just occupied.

The hand on my shoulder guided me away from the desk and out of the room. The monk, whose name I assumed was Kit, led me to a room on the opposite side of the temple, filled with empty sleeping mats, and pointed me to a small chamber where there was a wooden bath filled with tepid water and a privy. Despite my unease at being in a strange place where I knew no one, the allure of a bath after days on the road was too tempting to ignore. After I finished cleaning, I dried myself off with a cloth that had been presumably left on the side for that purpose and headed back into the main room with the sleeping mats. Next to one of them, a small pile of fresh, new clothes waited for me, alongside a bowl of rice and steamed fish, of a type I did not recognise. Clean and relieved to be eating anything besides stew, I sat on the sleeping mat and tried not to think about what lay ahead tomorrow.

12

Sweet

Must and decay filled the air. A darkness lay thick in the room, and all that could be heard was a constant, unending muttering. I lay face down, on something cold and hard. Trying to move, I panicked, realising I was bound hand and foot.

I woke up, sitting bolt upright and sweating, confused for a moment where I was. It was pitch black, but the smell of incense perfused through the air. The temple. I looked down, relieved to find my hands and feet were unbound and cursed myself for the stupid dream. Just as my eyes began to focus on the room around me, I noticed a shadow, darker than the ambient grey gloom of the room, standing at the foot of my sleeping mat.

Panicking, I scrambled to my feet. "What do you want?" I called, voice tripping over itself.

"It's time to leave," came a quiet, whispered voice from the shadow. "We make for Isale. Get yourself ready and come meet me in the square."

The sound of slapping feet on bare stone confirmed the exit of the monk. I waited for my heart rate to slow a moment, taking deep breaths. How long had the monk been watching me? This whole place was so strange, why were there so many empty sleeping mats here? The sooner I could leave the better. There were no windows in this room, and no candles had been lit, so I shuffled my way carefully back to the antechamber where the privy was. Someone had left a clean towel that had been soaked in warm water. The towel had a strange smell, that of a spice that I did not recognise, but nevertheless it was pleasant, so I took it gratefully and washed my face, trying to wash the grit from my eyes. I still felt groggy and disoriented from waking so abruptly. With no idea what time of day it was, I'd no clue how long I had slept for either.

Eager to be done with the temple, I left the sleeping chambers, opening the door into the dimly lit corridor. I followed the winding path back into the main antechamber, and seeing no one else around, I opened the main door of the temple, back out into the square. The sun had not yet fully risen, giving the sky above an odd purple hue, and there was a cool chill in the air. Over the sound of the river, I could hear birds singing a dawn chorus. In the square, a hooded monk stood next to a horse and cart, tightening straps, and checking saddlebags. Even though I could only make out half of the monk's face, there was a glimmer of recognition.

"Kit, right?" I asked, walking up to the monk.

He turned back to me and just nodded. He climbed onto the front of the enclosed cart, leaving enough room on the bench for me to join him. I peered down the side of the cart for a moment, curious to know what was inside. There was a tiny, sealed window, but nothing else other than smooth wood. No sooner had I climbed up to the cart, then the monk clicked his tongue at the horse, and started us moving. I fell back into my seat, annoyed.

Kit turned to me, with a small smile on his face.

Did he do that on purpose? Caught a little off guard by the joke I just had apparently played on me, I kept quiet as we pulled out of the alley, and back onto the main thoroughfare of the garrison. The streets were still quiet, and the sound of the horse's hooves on cobble sent echoes bouncing off the stone buildings that surrounded us. The sound of the Dravé river grew louder as we approached the edge of the garrison, and two guards greeted us at an opened portcullis.

"Papers."

The monk pulled out a scroll from a satchel next to him, handing it to the guard. He eyed it dutifully.

"Transporting?" the guard said, eyeing me after handing the scroll back to Kit.

"A Nascent. And a rogue."

The guard just nodded, stepping aside. "Safe travels Do'Seer."

Kit clicked his tongue again, and the horse pulled us out of the garrison. No longer protected by the stone walls, the sounds of the river grew louder, and the cobblestone path gave way to smooth flagstone. The bridge ahead of us was ponderous and arched in a way that meant the other side couldn't be seen. It looked to be made of the same stone as the walls of the garrison. Wide enough for two wagons to fit abreast, it was the largest construction I'd ever seen. As we left the banks, I leaned over the side to watch the river flow some twenty meters below us. A sudden wave of vertigo made me sit back up, unpleasant memories of nausea coming back to haunt me. While I had been gawking at the bridge and the river below, Kit had lowered his hood. A tight crop of brown hair sat atop a young face, probably only a few summers older than me. He looked at me and smiled.

"No point trying to keep my hood up when we're crossing a windy bridge," he explained.

I could see his point. Approaching the midway point, the wind had picked up, whipping the loose clothes I was wearing around my body. It carried a familiar scent of sea air. The sun had just crested the horizon and was sending glorious rays of golden light across the sky. "What did you mean earlier?" I asked. "When you spoke to the guard. You said something about a Nascent and a rogue?"

"Well, as a fledgling Aspector, with no tether or experience, that makes you a Nascent."

"And the rogue?"

Kit squirmed in his seat. "Well..." his eyes glanced back to the wagon we were sitting on.

"Is someone in there?" I asked, dumbfounded.

Kit nodded. "He's from the academy. Granted leave, he was due to return back to Isale last month. All I know is the garrison picked him up four days drunk in some backwater tavern on the other side of the Dravé."

I was uncomfortable at the thought of someone else being shut away in the back of the wagon. "Should we check on him?"

"Not here. There's no stopping on the Dravé bridge." Kit turned to me, seeing my unease. I was surprised to see it reflected in his own face too. "We'll stop mid-morning to eat. We can check on him then."

By the time we were over the bridge, the sun had fully risen. When Themia had explained the bridge on the journey to the garrison, I couldn't understand why people wouldn't just use a boat. But it made perfect sense now I'd seen it in person. Not only was the river enormous, as we had travelled over the peak of the bridge, I could see white froth, and sharp, jagged rocks in the centre of the river. I shuddered at the thought of anyone trying to row across it. Once over the bridge, the paved road gave way to dirt, bordered on each side by lush pines. The mountain ridge on the horizon loomed ever closer.

I rapped my knuckle on the side of the wagon and pressed an ear to see if I could hear the man stirring inside. Silence. I looked back to Kit and shrugged my shoulders.

As promised, Kit had pulled us to a stop once we hit mid-morning, letting the horse rest a moment, and giving us the chance to stretch our legs. Kit pulled a set of keys out from under his robe, and I followed him to the rear of the wagon, where he unlocked a hatch set in the back panel. I peered inside. The lone window had been covered, keeping the inside in permanent gloom, but I could make out the crumpled form of a boy, no older than myself laying against the front side of the wagon. The floor had been strewn with hay, and there was a sweet, musky smell in the air.

"Ho there!" Kit called to the boy, trying to wake him. He didn't stir. Kit looked at me concerned.

Not waiting for permission, I crawled inside the box and shuffled over to the boy. The smell was worse inside. I touched the boy lightly on his shoulder and shook him gently. Still nothing. I checked the pulse on his neck. Steady, but slow. More of a concern was how hot his skin felt.

"Kit!" I called out of the wagon. "Help me get him out of here." I picked the boy up around his armpits, and I pulled him carefully to the opening in the back of the wagon.

"Grab his armpits," I said, dropping the boy so his head lolled out of the hatch. I shuffled back around to the other side of the boy and lifted his feet. Kit pulled, and followed him out of the wagon, setting his sleeping form on the ground.

"What's up with him?" Kit asked, panic thick on his voice.

I started checking over the boy's body, rolling up sleeves and trouser legs. "He has a fever, keeping him trapped in that box probably hasn't helped him either," I admonished. I was more annoyed at myself, for sitting and enjoying a pleasant ride while a boy lay in the back, slipping into a coma. Seeing nothing on his arms or legs, I pulled off a boot. The smell of sweet musk grew suddenly stronger.

Kit started gagging, and I heard him throw up behind me. I was too distracted to turn around. The boy's foot was splotched with purple spots and dried, crusty pieces of skin. Angry red lines radiated upwards towards his ankle. A yellow discharge, the source of the smell, dripped down his heel and fell to the floor.

"Mother's mercy," Kit said behind me. "What is that?"

I lifted his foot by his ankle and inspected it. "Here, look," I pointed to a small, almost circular hole in the base of his foot. "Something must have cut his foot a while back, and he let it get infected." I recalled what Kit had said, about how the guards had found him. "He probably wasn't drunk either, just delirious with fever. Martyr's body and we just left him in the back of the wagon." I let his foot down gently on the ground and stepped back trying to get some fresh air away from the smell.

Kit looked at me panicked, his eyes wild. "What do we do?"

"There's no time to take him back to the garrison now. Can you Aspect?"

Kit shook his head, "I'm just a Seer!" he cried.

I groaned. "If that infection spreads, he'll never wake up. We need to take his foot."

"Kehlem, stop, please!" Kit pleaded, pulling on my clothes.

I was pulling items out of the saddlebags, looking for anything we could use for the surgery. A belt, a large leather-bound book and a small cheese knife was all I had found so far. Could I do this? I thought back to Job's amputation, how awful and strenuous that had been. How many times had Job woken up again? That was with actual surgical equipment, and poppy's milk as well. We had no saw, no file, no soap. I tried to put it all from my mind. The boy would be dead by nightfall, and my doubt will kill him just as swiftly as a sour wound.

"Kehlem, please just hold a minute." Kit grabbed hold of my arm.

"We don't have time for this, Kit. The longer we leave it, the more time that infection has to spread."

Kit looked back at the boy, lying where we had left him on the grass. "They'll take my name for this," he whispered. He looked back to me, "What if we didn't have to amputate?"

"Kit, we can't keep going over this. Do you have anything sharper than this knife?" I asked, waving the cheese knife between us, feeling more than a little hysterical. Kit grabbed my hand, lowering the knife.

"You've Aspected before, haven't you?"

"Yes, once," I said. "What of it?" I was getting frustrated with Kit's unwillingness to help. I shook off his hand and started sorting through another bag.

"If I could show you the pattern, do you think you could Aspect again? And save his foot?"

That made me stop dead in my tracks.

"What do you mean, *show me the pattern*?"

Kit picked up the large leather-bound book I'd left on the floor. "The monastery was rebinding this. I was to bring it with me to Isale. It's a Book of Patterns. There are hundreds of volumes used to teach Nascents. There's a pattern of healing in here. I know because it was me that rebound it."

A hundred questions all fought to be fired at once. "Can you seriously teach me? Right here, on the side of the road? I don't have a tether you know."

"You shouldn't need a tether. Healing is only using energy a body would use under normal conditions anyway. If you focus on clearing the infection, you shouldn't use too much. You'll probably just feel a little tired." The monk's face did not look confident. "I've never taught a pattern before. I haven't earned the right, but I think I can show you."

I looked back at the boy, laying still where we had left him. Even if we did amputate now, there's no guarantee he'd survive the surgery. My mind was made up.

"We'd best get started then."

13

Patterns

"The Aspect is a sacred place. Each of us are tied to it, and there are those among us with whom those ties are stronger, binding them to the Aspect, giving them the gift of —"

"Kit, I don't mean to be rude," I interrupted. "But we don't exactly have a lot of time, can you please skip to the bit where you tell me what to do."

Kit's cheeks blushed, "Yes, of course, you're right. Here let me…" he mumbled to himself as he started thumbing through the pages of the book. We sat opposite each other, the book between us and the sleeping body of the boy next to us.

"Ah, here it is." Kit twisted the book so it faced me. Across a double-page spread, inked in red was a delicate, flowing pattern, sprawling top to bottom across both pages.

"What am I looking at here?"

"Did Themia ever Aspect in front of you?"

"A few times, yes."

"And did you ever see her trace her hands in a pattern?"

I nodded again, recalling the odd red light that trailed behind her fingers.

Kit looked relieved. "Well, that's what this is. When you Aspect you have to follow a specific pattern for what you want to do. It's like a language that Aspectors use to speak with the Aspect. It's what directs the energies."

I nodded slowly. Now that he said it, the pattern in the book did look similar, at least in style to what I had seen Themia do. And the more I looked, the more I could see a logic behind the design, a direction. "So how do I touch the Aspect?" I asked, "I've only done it once, and it wasn't intentional."

"Patterns are read from here." He pointed to the top left of the page. "Without a tether, you can just concentrate on the pattern, and try and feel your way to touch the boundary. The Aspect's world overlays ours. Some people describe it like feeling a warm summer breeze on your fingers."

I looked at him nonplussed. "Kit, I don't know if you've noticed, but it's not exactly chilly out today." I was starting to regret listening to Kit. This was taking too long.

"I'm not an Aspector Kehlem," he said sharply. "I can only tell you what others have told me."

I rolled my eyes. Was it too late to try and sharpen that cheese knife?

"What are you waiting for? You're only going to figure this out one way. Try the pattern."

I pulled myself to my feet awkwardly. "Look, when you said you could teach me, I thought you meant you know, *teach* me."

He gave me a withering look. "You were the one a moment ago complaining I was taking too long. Stop delaying."

Feeling more than a little foolish, I lifted my left hand, as I had seen Themia do, and positioned it in front of me. Kit stood up and held the book open, so I could keep an eye on the pattern. Imagining my hand was a brush, I followed the lines of the pattern, this way and that, trying to trace the image in the air in front of me. My hand felt clumsy as it moved through the air, and I was struggling to make it follow the same tight curls as the pattern in the book. I stopped around midway through the pattern.

"I don't feel anything," I said.

"Maybe try going slower," he suggested. "Don't think about the pattern ahead, think about what you're doing now, in the moment."

Nodding, I tried again, and with one eye on the book, I traced the pattern, slower this time, taking more time to mirror the intricate detail reflected more precisely with my hand. I held my breath, waiting to feel something, anything like I had felt back in Barrowheld. I persevered and completed the entire pattern.

My shoulders slumped. "Nothing."

Kit shifted the weight of the book in his hands. "Try again. You're thinking too much."

Well, that was stupid. How can you think too much? I can see now why Kit wasn't supposed to be teaching people, he was useless.

Frustrated, and trying to calm down, I took a deep breath, and let it out slowly. I stared at the pattern in the book, trying through sheer force of will to make it make sense. It wasn't happening. I was getting hot and sweaty standing in the afternoon sun; the back of my neck was starting to itch and I couldn't help but think that each moment that slipped by was giving the infection more time to spread through the boy laid at my feet.

Don't panic, Kehlem. It doesn't help your patient if you're floundering. Assess the situation, make a decision, and execute it with confidence.

I shook my head. I didn't want to hear his voice. Not now. Not ever. I looked back over to the boy, his foot still oozing yellow pus onto the grass. I cleared my mind like I would do if he were just a patient, back in Barrowheld. I looked back at the pattern in the book Kit was holding. He was struggling to keep it steady, the pages shifting this way and that as the monk's hands wobbled. I placed my left hand in front of me, holding my palm open, and shut my eyes, shutting out everything around me.

What if I wasn't thinking too much? What if I wasn't letting myself think at all?

Like a death grip held too long, my mind had been holding back thoughts and memories ever since Barrowheld. Occasionally one would poke through, and I would swat it back, quicker than I had chance to consider it. I slowly eased the clench on my mind, and my first thought was Father. He was there, rubbing my back, comforting me after I had spent twenty minutes staring at our store cupboard, trying to decide what would be best to give to one of our patients.

Trust yourself Kehlem. The only person who can give you confidence is yourself. If you don't back yourself, no one else will.

I moved my hand, tracing the first part of the pattern I remembered from the book.

Her soft lips on my own. Eva was asking me to find her. Her fingers wrap around mine.

My hand twisted and caught a new part of the pattern.

I was back in my kitchen, and Tema was there, crying as he realised his son knew he'd betrayed him. His son raised his hands in anger, a red glowing light emanating between his fingertips. I watched on, and I could only feel a bitter sadness.

My hand moved through the next curve of the pattern, and there was a sudden thrum of vibration that sent pulses throughout my body. There was a tension and then sudden release, like pushing through an unyielding surface of water. Except the surface had a current, and if I just let my hand float, the current would take it. As my hand traced the current, I opened my eyes. Kit had taken a step back; the book having fallen from his hands. In front of me, the pattern I had traced lit a trail of red light, perfectly mirroring the book. My hand continued to move as I followed the pattern the Aspect was showing me. As I reached the end, following instinct, I dropped to my knees, leading the flowing pattern, and finishing it with a touch to the boy's swollen foot.

As I touched his skin, the pattern in the air disappeared, and reappeared underneath the boy's flesh, glowing brighter and brighter. I screwed my eyes closed, trying to shut out the light. The vibration I had felt within me, I could now feel somehow through the boy as well. Except, it wasn't an even pulse-like mine was. There were discordant rhythms fighting against each other. I latched onto the strongest pulse, the one that was similar to mine. In my mind's eye, I then followed the pattern through the boy's body. Each time I discovered a pulse that was out of rhythm with the boy's own, I snuffed it, imagining the pattern was alive and tightening a curl around it. I followed each of the intricate movements of the pattern, clearing out the discordant pulses. With each errant rhythm that I stopped, the boy's pulse grew stronger and louder. I moved through the final turns of the pattern, and confident I could feel only one pulse, I opened my eyes and dragged my hand away from his body.

Kit stood staring at me, wide-eyed. I looked down at the boy's foot. The swelling and discolouration had disappeared, along with the sweet smell of the infection. The puncture wound was still there, but it no longer looked red and inflamed. Exhausted, and dripping in sweat I laughed incredulously. If Father could see me now.

"I take it all back Kit," I said, pulling myself to my feet. "You are an excellent teac —", as I stood up, blackness circled around my vision, and a familiar cold sweat burst onto my forehead. The momentum I carried trying to stand myself up, sent me toppling face first, back to the ground.

I came to with Kit looming over me, wafting a piece of parchment across my face.

"Oh, thank the Mother!" he shouted, as I sat up. "I thought you'd burned too much energy and the Aspect would take you for good."

I looked around, the sun was still high in the sky, and the boy was still laying next to us, unconscious. I must have only just passed out. I took Kit's hand and he pulled me to my feet.

"What happened to *'you shouldn't need a tether'*?" I asked, indignant.

He shrugged his shoulders. "Hey at least you just passed out. I don't think I could have lifted both you and the boy into the wagon."

I laughed. I hadn't met anyone like Kit before. I'd taken him to be this serious devout monk when we'd first met, but he'd seemed to relax a little ever since we left the garrison.

"How is he?" I asked

"You tell me, I'm not a physician."

I walked over to where the boy's head lay and rested the back of my hand against his forehead. "Well, his fever's gone!" I shook his shoulders.

The boy lifted an arm and swatted at my hand. "Piss off," he slurred and rolled over so he was face down to the dirt.

"Well, he sounds fine" Kit called over to me. "Probably just needs some rest."

The two of us lifted the sleeping boy and put him back in the wagon to let him sleep off whatever ordeal he'd been through.

Kit and I sat back down on the front of the wagon, and with a click of his tongue, Kit sent the horse off again, pulling us along steadily down the road.

"How long will it take us to get to Isale?" I asked.

"Another day or so. Give or take."

"Give or take what?"

Kit shifted on the bench. "Give or take another incident of me having to teach you a new pattern."

We both started laughing. It wasn't particularly funny, but the stress and panic of the afternoon needed some way to vent from us both.

"Would you really have cut off the boy's foot?" Kit asked once we both regained our composure.

"Without hesitation," I said, a hint of pride in my voice. "I helped my father with an amputation once, back home. I think I probably could have done it again." It was the first time since I'd left Barrowheld that talking about my father didn't spark a familiar coal of loathing. Instead, I just felt hollow.

"You must be a good physician," Kit said, smiling, "to cut a foot off with a cheese knife."

I smiled, and sat back in silence, trying to process what had happened back there on the roadside. I hadn't noticed before, but I had been holding this tension in my mind, trapping and gripping tight like rigour mortis, these thoughts and feelings. Now that it was gone, there was nowhere to hide. The only blessing was for every thought of my father, Eva was there twice.

Not for the first time since leaving Barrowheld, I wondered how things would have been different if I hadn't stepped away from underneath the willow. If I had instead stayed with Eva. Travelled with her to Mercy. It was wistful nonsense, I knew it, but there was a hollow aching in my heart that seemed to delight in torturing me with the 'what ifs'.

I needed to let go of the life I thought I could have. The plans I had made before drifting to sleep every night, of moving to Mercy, opening my own practice, of Eva. All that was dead. I am here now. I had just *healed* someone. Months and months of daydreaming, half-truths and hidden answers, and

I had just done it. As simple as that. There was a chance here to become something. I could become a healer, I could change people's lives. Who knows, after all of this, maybe I could go back to Barrowheld, and try and help Job. I missed Eva. I think in truth I loved her. I still love her. But I needed to put her away from my mind. There was too much for me to learn that I could miss out on by living within the past.

Before long, the sun fell, and Kit drew the wagon to a halt.

"Would you see if our guest has finished with his beauty sleep? I'll get some food started," Kit asked, passing me the keys to the hatch.

I opened the hatch and pulled myself into the wagon, moving over to the sleeping form of the boy.

"Hey," I whispered. "Wake up, come get some food."

His eyes opened when he heard me mention food. He pushed himself up and rubbed his eyes.

"Who the devil are you?" he asked, voice rich with a northern Caserean accent.

"I'm Kehlem. You're on route back to Isale. You were er…" I paused, not sure how much I should tell him. "Unwell. We managed to break your fever, but you're probably feeling drained."

He let out a petulant groan. "I don't want to go back. I was quite happy drinking my sorrow."

If his accent hadn't been enough of a clue, his demeanour certainly was. Probably the son of some Baron.

"Well, Kit is making food outside if you want to join us, you must be starving," I said.

"No, that's ok, you can just bring it to me in here." He lay back down, staring at the ceiling of the wagon.

I looked back at him, incredulous. "Look. You can either come outside, and help set up for the evening and eat, or, you can stay in here and starve. Your choice."

Even in the darkness of the wagon, I could feel the withering stare he gave me. I left him to sulk, leaving the hatch open in case he decided to dignify us with his presence. Kit stood over a small fire, balancing a hanging pot over a metal frame.

"Still asleep?" he asked.

I rolled my eyes. "Would rather go hungry then spend some time with the common folk."

Kit smiled to himself and started chopping some pieces of root veg. "Could you go fetch us some water? If I remember right there should be a stream not far that way," he said, gesturing through the pines that bracketed the road.

By the time I'd returned with two full water skins, I was surprised to see the Baron boy not only out of the wagon but helping Kit prepare the evening's meal. Now he was awake, I was not sure how I had missed the aristocracy which was plainly carved onto his face. Straight, if slightly large nose, chiselled cheekbones, and a long, plaited head of dark hair. Dark shadows on his cheeks showed he was probably the same age as me. As I joined the two of them back at the fire, he gave me a sheepish look.

"Ah Kehlem, thank you!" Kit said, taking one of the water skins, and pouring it in the pot, which sizzled and sent steam pouring out the top. I gave Kit a questioning look with my eyes, darting them over to the boy.

"Broch will be joining us for dinner," Kit said, by way of introduction and explanation. "While you were fetching water, I thought I would catch Broch up on all he had missed."

Broch hurriedly stood up, wiping his hands on his trousers and offered me a hand. "Do'Seer tells me I'm in your debt," he said, his tone while still pompous by virtue of his accent, was genuine.

I clasped his hand and shook it. "It's the other way around. You should be thanking Kit. I would have had your foot off if not for him."

Broch's face lost all its colour and his hand dropped out my grip.

Kit and I both laughed, and the three of us sat down, any tension between Broch and I dealt with.

Kit dished out three servings of a thick soup and the three of us sat around the fire, eating together quietly.

"How did you hurt your foot, Broch?" I asked, genuinely curious.

His face flushed, and he lowered the spoon he was holding back into the bowl. "Stupid wench didn't tell me she had a husband," he mumbled.

Kit and I both gave him a questioning look.

"He chased me in my all-together out of their house. Must have trod on a nail or something."

There was a brief pause as the mental imagery slowly formed, and to my left Kit burst out guffawing, slapping his legs. I quickly joined in, the thought of him almost losing a foot over toppling with some married woman. Broch flashed us an embarrassed grin and hid his face behind his hands. That night Kit sang an impromptu song he lovingly titled 'Broch the one foot-philander' which had the three of us howling with laughter. That was the first night since Barrowheld I closed my eyes and felt some small amount of peace.

14

Precipice

We set off early the next morning, with Kit determined to arrive at Isale village before dusk. There wasn't enough room for the three of us to sit abreast on the front of the wagon, so while Kit and I sat up front, Broch hoisted himself precariously onto the roof of the wagon behind us, his leg's dangling next to me. I'd barely noticed yesterday, what with all the excitement, but the mountains on the horizon had grown enormous, their peaks shrouded by cloud. The road Kit was taking us on seemed to keep the range parallel to our right, these boundless giants that sat in silent contemplation, watching us like a human considers an ant.

Broch said something to Kit which caught my attention. "Why do you call him that?"

"Call him what?" Broch's voice carried down from the roof.

"Do'Seer."

Kit next to me flushed a little and kept his eyes in front of us.

"Well…that is his name," Broch said.

I ploughed on, not noticing the hint of awkwardness in Broch's response. "I thought that was just a title, like 'Mr' or 'Ma'am'. That blind man back in the temple called you Kit though, didn't he? Is that not your name?"

I heard a scoff from above us, as Broch mocked me. "'*That blind man*' he says."

Kit's eyes were still on the road ahead, and his cheeks had grown brighter. "Well, yes, Kit is my name. But well...so is Do'Seer."

Broch lay down belly first on the roof, so his head hung upside down between us. "Allow me to explain, what our monk friend here is too humble. The Abbot-Seer has the right to name 'Kit' because, in the grand hierarchy, there are few above him. Monk Seers forgo their names when they abscond all earthly ties. Calling a Do'Seer by their given name is effectively saying he is beneath you." Broch said this so matter-of-factly, that I almost ignored the fact his long braid had slipped and was hanging from his upside-down head, making him look like a bizarre apple toffee.

I looked over to Kit, who was still staring off into the distance, trying his absolute best to not look at me.

"Kit...Damn, Do'Seer. I had no idea, I'm sorry. I've made an arse of myself."

"It's fine Kehlem. Honestly. You weren't to know. And besides. It was me that read Themia's scroll to the abbot. I know what you went through. I figured you could have used a friend more than a monk." He flashed me a quick grin and looked back to the road.

A friend. Huh. I'd only known Kit a few days, but I guess he was. Back home, I'd always found it hard making friends with the townsfolk. There always seems to be this immutable distance between us, or so I had always thought. I was beginning to wonder how much of that distance was due to being drugged my whole life. Was it something I had imagined? Nevertheless, I was touched by the small gesture Kit had made. The moment was ruined quickly when Broch made gagging noises, pretending to be sick. I heard a heavy noise indicating he had flopped himself onto his back. I smiled and rolled my eyes. Kit lifted the brake lever sharply, causing the wagon to lurch. We both heard a wooden 'bang' followed by an "Ouch!" as Broch banged his head on the roof.

Kit smirked to himself. "Don't worry about calling me Do'Seer. At least, not until we're at Isale. It's been a nice break if I'm being totally honest."

"Thank you, Kit." I smiled. "What are things like? At Isale, I mean?"

"Well, classes are held by the Seer monks who live at the academy. That's one of the reasons I'm escorting you actually, I'll be joining them to learn how to teach Aspecting. But most of the people at the academy are the Foclir." Kit noticed my look of puzzlement. "Foclir are people like Themia. They have their tethers, and their degree but many of them choose to stay at the academy and study."

"How long will it take to earn my tether?" I asked my thoughts elsewhere.

"Most people do it in three years. Two if you're quick. When are you taking your test Broch?" Kit called to the roof.

I couldn't feel my face. I'd gone numb. Three years.

"...if they don't suspend my teaching. Who knows. This will be my fifth."

Kit nodded unsurprised next to me.

Three years. Three years before I could return to Casere. I heard a ringing in my ears.

"...ok Kehlem?" Kit was looking at me concerned.

"Huh? Oh, yes, I'm fine. It's just, I didn't think it would take that long." I said, distracted.

"I wouldn't worry about it too much. Besides, I know you're a Nascent, but it's not like you'll be starting fro—"

There was a thump, and Broch slid off the roof, and squeezed between us, pushing Kit and I so we were half hanging off the edge of the bench.

"Hold a moment. Did you just say he's a Nascent?" Broch asked.

"Yes, unusual I know, but he is a Nas—"

Broch cut him off again. "But you must be at least sixteen years. That doesn't make any sense."

I sighed and shrugged my shoulders. "I don't know what to tell you." I didn't particularly want to have to tell the lordling the story of my father poisoning me for sixteen years.

"And didn't you say that Kehlem healed me with a pattern of healing?" Broch said, swivelling over to look at Kit.

"Well, yes but it's not like it was his first time Aspecting, he'd done it once before."

"Fuck me," Broch breathed, turning back to face me. "I know third-degree medicas who haven't been able to pull off a pattern like that. I took you for a sabbatical scholar from another academy."

Kit leaned forward in his seat to look at us both. "Hold on, the pattern of healing is taught to Nascent's in their fourth quarter, it's not that complex."

"Martyr, it's a good job you're coming to Isale to learn how to teach Aspecting. Pass me the book," Broch said, exasperated.

Kit reached behind him, pulling the Book of Patterns out of the saddle pack.

"Here," Broch took the book, and quickly rifled through the pages, landing on the now familiar pattern for healing. "This is the pattern you used, right?" he asked, looking at me.

I nodded.

"Well, this," he said, covering the whole of the second page of the pattern with a hand, and the lower half of the first page with another, leaving only a small section of the entire pattern, "is what they teach Nascents. In their fourth quarter. What you used was a full pattern. Something normally taught in second year before a student becomes a fully-fledged Foclir." He closed the book, and handed it back to Kit, who had turned very pale. Broch turned to look at me. "I don't know what you are, but you're no Nascent."

As the day drew on, the road we were taking slowly began to bank towards the mountains, and the trees on the roadside grew sparse, giving way to flat, open land, inset with a large, sluggish river carrying crystal clear water down from the mountains and presumably towards the Dravé and eventually the ocean. Smoke could be seen in the distance, coming from the base of the closest mountain. Isale town. And our destination for the evening. Apparently, the trek from Isale town to the academy wasn't one you would want to do too late in the evening.

On route, Broch unprompted gave us his life's story, which I only half listened to, still distracted from our earlier conversation. Apparently, my guess was right, he was the son of a Baron, who dutifully sent his son to the academy as a child, after he was tested for his connection to the Aspect at age eleven. I learned that this testing was a more formalised routine in the larger north-western cities, and some of the Caserean nobility saw it as a way of currying favour with the ruling Vin Irudur. The young children weren't taught Aspecting right away, usually not starting till they turn thirteen, with the academy using that time to teach children literacy and numbers. So thankfully I wouldn't be joining a class of children five years my junior.

"Still," Broch sighed, lying on his back on the roof of the wagon. "Father's patience is drawing thin I suspect. I think he'd hoped I'd earned my tether by now, and would have an appointment back home in the court." He let out a heavy, dramatic sigh, as if the weight of the world itself lay on him.

"And what of you, Kit?" I asked, part of me looking for an excuse to shut the lord up, well-meaning as he may be.

"Hmm?" he asked, distracted.

"Why did you join the Seers?"

"Oh." He seemed surprised I asked. "Well, I didn't exactly 'join' the seers. I was given to the monks as a child. I'm an orphan," he said, matter of fact.

"Oh, I'm sorry," I said awkwardly. "I just assumed..." I trailed off, not sure what else to say.

He waved his hand, dismissing my apology. "It's fine Kehlem. The Seer's are all I've ever known. And they've been good to me."

"Why are they called that? The 'Seer's'? What does that mean, exactly?" I asked, trying to change the subject.

"Well, Aspectors, like yourself, can touch that boundary between our world and the Aspect. You've been granted the strength to touch and manipulate that boundary. Even if it's the lightest brush of a finger. The monks, we can't Aspect. Not physically anyway. Through meditation, we learn to glance into the Aspect, to understand its mysteries. To See."

I wasn't sure if he was being literal. "But what is there to gain from that? Isn't it just another world? What can you learn from trying to understand it?"

Kit looked over to me, considering me a moment.

"The Aspect isn't just some place, Kehlem. It's the ultimate destination. Everything in this world is made of energy. When we are born, we are born from energy from the Aspect. When we die, that energy returns. Everyone that has ever lived and died, part of them reside now, in the Aspect."

"So, it's like your heaven then?" I asked, trying to make sense of what Kit was telling me. "But what of the Martyr? What of God?"

"You're trying to interpret what I'm saying through a lens of your own beliefs. There is no God, Kehlem. From the Aspect we are born, and to the Aspect you return. That's all there is to it." Kit said simply.

I sat back, quiet in my seat, considering what Kit had said. It's true that I never took the greatest stock in what the priest back in Barrowheld spoke about, but that was more from disinterest rather than disbelief. The thought that the Martyr would sit in judgment of all those who passed, and welcome the good and honest into Her halls had always been a comforting one to me.

"Look," Kit said quietly, "it's okay if you still want to believe in your Martyr. I'm not trying to tell you that you're wrong for believing in Her. But we have been studying the Aspect for centuries, and we have not found any evidence of any kind of higher being, beyond the Aspect itself. If you allow yourself, it may even be a comfort to you."

I kept quiet. I'd never really thought about it before. Believing in the Martyr was just what people did. In the same way you believe the seasons would change. There was no point questioning it, because it was just a fact of nature. Still, I didn't see how emptiness could possibly give me comfort.

We rode on through the afternoon, across grand meadows, frequently crossing the meandering river and mile by mile, the shadows at the foot of the mountain defined themselves into discrete structures. A small smattering of buildings in the distance, with chimney smoke pouring out of many of the rooftops. As we rode closer to Isale town, the road slowly became busier. We hadn't passed a single person the past two days, but now we were passing two, and then four groups with each hour. Occasionally, one of them would give an odd look to our rag-tag group, particularly to the roof where Broch had started snoring. Each of them nodded in greeting as they passed.

Night fell in earnest and we were still a few hours' ride away from Isale town, the distant amber glow of candle light and sconces flickered in the distance. Above the town, a diffuse light cast shadows on the mountain side, the source of which I could only assume was the Academy.

Kit called a stop to the wagon, all of us agreeing it made little sense to keep riding in the dark, although Broch made his disappointment of not staying in one of the town's taverns abundantly clear. Despite the time of year, there was a sharp chill in the air, so after we ate, the three of us slept inside the wagon, top and tailing with one another.

I woke to the sound of Kit's rumbling snoring, and gently shuffled over the sleeping forms of my two friends, and left the carriage to relieve myself before we undertook the final stretch of the journey. It was a brisk spring morning, and the sun was just starting to rise. There was still a cold chill on the wind, which pulled and tightened the skin on my face.

I quickly rinsed my face with some water from our water skins, and then grabbing a blanket, I hoisted myself onto the roof of the wagon to watch the sun rise in peace.

Despite yesterday's commitment to myself, my mind quickly drifted back to Eva. It betrayed me quietly, slyly. It thought of memories, smells and sounds at first, and by the time I realised they were all Eva, it was too late. The familiar fluttering empty feeling in my chest was back. The temptation to wallow was strong. Thinking of Eva was like staring at the sun as it rose. The warmth it brought washed over my body, easing away the chill I felt, yet if I looked too long, the pain it brought soon crashed over any comfort it gave. I blinked my eyes a few times, washing away sun-spots and tears. I closed my eyes. Without thinking I raised my left hand, and immediately felt a familiar warm sensation as I found the border between our world and the Aspect. With no pattern, I just held my hand in place, and reached a single finger to lean against the boundary, pushing, but not breaking the surface.

In my mind's eye I saw Eva, sitting in her uncle's living room, smiling as she spoke to her uncle about something. She was getting ready to head to the church, pulling a cloak over her shoulders and a satchel around her neck. I imagined I reached out, brushing my fingers against her shoulder. She looked up at me, surprised. She looked like she would speak...but the daydream faded, and I dropped my hand away, breaking my touch from the Aspect. I opened my eyes, washed in the light of the morning sun.

It was stupid to let myself get caught up in my imagination. I was torturing myself. Still even if it were just a daydream, I couldn't deny it was good to see her face so clear again. Rustling in the wagon underneath me told me the other two were waking up. I took a deep breath and tried to clear my mind as best I could, ready to arrive at Isale.

In the light of day, we made quick progress and arrived on the outskirts of Isale town by mid-morning. A smallish place, with a single straight road that ran through its centre. It ended in a cobblestone square that sat beneath a stone archway that opened to a pathway up the mountain. Despite the time of the morning, the town was busy with people moving around, loading crates onto carts. A bakery was open for morning trade, so while Kit and I unloaded the wagon and led the horse to some stables, Broch bought the three of us some delicious hot flaky pastries, filled with spicy meat.

"Very kind of you," Kit said, biting into his pastry, steam curling up between his hands into the brisk morning air.

"It's the least I could do, for you know…" he wiggled his foot between us.

"What's the going rate for a foot these days?" I asked, wiping the pastry crumbs off my hands. "Around three to four pastries would you say?"

"That's for peasants," Kit corrected me seriously. "I think it's six pastries and a flagon of wine for a lordling's philandering son," Kit said, once more humming the song he had made up.

I joined in, and Broch rolled his eyes at us. "If you had chopped my foot off, then you'd be the ones having to carry me up to the academy," he said, nodding his head towards the archway.

I looked over to Kit. "My Lord does make a good point."

"Maybe only one pastry and one round of drinks then?" Kit said, hopefully.

"Sold!" Broch said, "a round on me then. Not tonight though. The masters are already going to bollock me for not returning a month ago."

"Well, we would hate to deprive them of that opportunity," Kit said smiling. "Ready?"

The path up to the academy was well worn, and steep. The path was lined with the occasional metal lantern, presumably to guide waylaid students' home on an evening. Stairs had been hewn into the steeper sections, but the stone was smooth, and it would be all too easy to slip off and lose your footing without the light of day to guide you. The path was small and winding, so it wasn't until an hour later that I caught my first glimpse of the academy. If I thought the Dravé bridge was an impressive construction, then the Isale academy was a feat of wonderment.

It lay within a valley, and was carved almost entirely out of the rock face, with grey brickwork towering out of the cliffside, producing a strange blend between the angular, chaotic natural rock face and the straight edges of the manmade towers. Even in the shadow of the peak of the mountain, the tallest spires were enormous, easily twice as large as the spire of the church I'd seen in Mercy. But it wasn't the enormity of the building which took my breath away. Cascading around both sides of the academy, were waterfalls, landing on row after row of stone waterwheels, some of them stationary, some of them turning by the terrifying strength of the water. The waters pooled at the base of the valley, forming a small lake, which undoubtedly fed into the river we had passed on the plains on the way to Isale. The path we were on led over a small arch bridge made of the same grey rock and into an open courtyard.

"Everything okay?" Broch asked.

I tore my eyes away from the vista, and realised I was standing still, Broch and Kit watching me with smiles on their faces.

I looked between them both, a feeling of dread and excitement building within the pit of my stomach. I nodded, and took a step to catch up with them. "Let's go."

15

Isale

The three of us waited anxiously in the courtyard of the academy, waiting to be greeted by the Seer monks, who according to Kit would soon be on their way. It was impossible not to feel anxious, standing in the shadow of the enormous construction. In contrast to the clean build of the academy proper, the courtyard where we stood was surrounded by sundered walls, and eroded columns, forming empty windows looking out on the valley below. Neither Kit nor Broch could explain why the courtyard was in such a state, just that 'it had always been that way'. The entrance to the academy was within the natural rock of the cliff, stories below where the man-built construction began. Heavy wooden doors interrupted the angular cliff face, and three pairs of eyes were watching them nervously.

The wind was starting to pick up, amplified through the broken stone archways of the courtyard. The grey clouds above us were growing darker, with a promise of rain.

"Do you think they know we're here?" Broch hissed to us, leaning from foot to foot. "Only, I really have to take a piss."

"Shush, listen. Someone's coming," Kit said.

There was a slight metallic sound, followed by a wooden 'clunk' that echoed among the courtyard. One of the wooden doors began to move, opening outwards towards us. Two monks strode out of the academy.

Kit nudged both of us, and lifting his own hood back over his face, strode over to meet the newcomers, Broch and I in tow.

As we grew closer, the first thing I noticed was the lead monk whose hood was down was also blind.

Another Blind-Abbot? Occupational hazard or necessity? I wondered to myself.

The second thing I noticed was that the other monk was a woman. I found myself slightly surprised by this. While the Church of the Martyr didn't have any direct equivalents to the Seer monks, it was a fraternal order, one women were not permitted into. It had always been a fact I'd accepted and never questioned, but now seeing a female Seer monk, I began to wonder why the Church of the Martyr would be so finicky about the gender of their order. I'm sure if there was a God they wouldn't give a damn about the gender of their servants. Perhaps that's how the Seer monks saw it with the Aspect. If we all came from the Aspect originally, then surely there is no difference between man nor woman, despite some quirks of their physiology. And when you got down to it, is the difference between male and female any more significant than between brother and brother?

Something to talk to Kit about, I thought idly as the duo of monks fell to a stop in front of us.

"Welcome to the Isale academy, Do'Seer Kit, Kehlem Temason," the Abbot said, arms wide in a welcoming gesture. He turned to Broch, arms falling to his waist. "And welcome back, Broch Farlison."

Broch winced at my side at the Abbot's much colder welcome. Kit cleared his throat.

"Thank you, Abbot-Primus, we've had a safe, if eventful journey."

The Abbot raised an eyebrow. "Well, I shall look forward to hearing your report. Kehlem, Broch, Do'Seer Arnett will show you to your room, and help you get settled in. Do'Seer Kit, if you'd like to follow me, I'd like to have a quiet word before you find your dormitory."

"Of course, Primus," Kit said, and with only a glance of farewell to Broch and I, he followed the Abbot back into the academy, leaving Broch and I standing with the silent form of Do'Seer Arnett.

"Don't worry about showing me to my rooms," Broch said, pulling the satchel he was carrying back onto his shoulder. "I remember the way." He turned to me smiling, "Well, this is farewell Kehlem, I imagine you'll be sleeping in one of the shared dormitories. I have private rooms in the upper east wing. I'll come find you later in the week once things have settled down."

Something about the way he said 'upper east wing' and 'rooms' plural, grated on me a little. Before Broch strode off to the entrance however, the monk cleared her throat.

"A moment, Broch. Those rooms have been surrendered and given to a Foclir. As you did not return by your requested date, the Abbot has seen fit to house you in the dormitories." The monk's tone was level, and professional. And yet, I could have sworn I saw a smirk from underneath her hood.

"What?!" Broch cried out. "But I've had those rooms since I first got here. They're mine!"

"Every room within the academy belongs to the Vin empire. Do not forget, Casere nobility means nothing this far north. You are given only what we allow." The monk turned on her heel, not waiting for us to follow.

The monk's tone surprised me a little. Sure, Broch was whining, but he was nobility, it's what they did.

Broch looked at me open mouthed, anger and shock written plainly on his face. I don't think Broch was used to people telling him 'no'.

I slapped Broch on the back, and we followed behind the monk, inside the awaiting doors to the academy.

Inside the great doors, I was greeted by an enormous entrance hall, which must have taken up the majority of the cliff it had been carved into. But instead of the cavernous, dark, dank cave I had been expecting, the hall was warm, filled with gentle diffuse light spilling from glowing lanterns that littered the walls. The floor was made from a stone so polished that it was almost reflective, and the walls and ceiling curved into one another, giving the appearance of an enormous barrel that had been hewn vertically, and laid on its side. There was a gentle background hum of voices and footsteps as students, monk's and presumably Foclir buzzed around the room, leaving through this door or that, descending or climbing up one of the many staircases that littered the room.

Broch tapped my chin. "You'll want to close that," he said. "You'll swallow a fly if you leave it open."

I slowly closed my mouth, and dragged my eyes back down to see the monk had peeled off to one of the small spiral staircases that were inset into the hall walls. We followed behind, and climbed the twenty or so stairs going around and around until they levelled out into a much smaller room. Made from the same stone as the hall below, this one was small enough that only two lanterns were needed to keep it warmly lit. The room was curiously minimal, with only a single ornate wooden door opposite the staircase. I could hear a steady 'clunk, clunk clunk' coming from behind it.

"Good luck with this, it takes everyone a while to get used to them," Broch whispered to me.

The monk strode over, and opened the door, and behind it was one of the strangest sights I'd ever seen. Small wooden platforms, only the width of the door frame, were rising slowly from beneath the ground, up and then past the door frame, disappearing to who knows where. Without a word of explanation, the monk stepped quickly onto a platform as it rose from the ground, and twisted so she was facing us. She rose with the platform, pulled by some mysterious force, and disappeared quickly from view.

"What the…" I whispered to myself.

"Don't forget to get off at the top!" Broch shouted gleefully, and he jumped onto another platform, also disappearing.

I walked over to the door frame, trying to figure out what it was. On a closer look, the platform I was apparently supposed to stand on was only a short step, barely large enough for my feet to fit, secured onto a row of wooden planks which had been affixed horizontally.

Was it some kind of waterwheel?

Step after step rose past me. Steeling myself, and not wanting to lose the others, I quickly stepped onto the next available platform and as it rose, banged my head on the door frame. There was enough room inside the contraption for me to spin around, and I managed to find a piece of rope dangling from the platform above me which I held gratefully. Inside the contraption was pitch black, and moving in the dark was starting to make me feel queasy. How long would this take? And what was its Broch said about the top?

Suddenly, light bloomed into the shaft as we rose into a tower which had regular, small, circular windows. I peered out, each window only providing me a brief frame. We appeared to be rising into one of the towers that I'd seen earlier, the courtyard falling quickly below us. So distracted was I by the vista, that I didn't notice the much larger window of light quickly appearing above me. Hands grabbed me, pulling me off the platform. I stumbled, falling onto solid floor.

"I did tell you to look out for the top," Broch chided, laughing as he pulled me to my feet.

I turned back, and saw I'd been pulled through another door frame, which the monk quickly closed. This new room was a lot different to what I'd seen so far. Gone were the soft, polished walls, replaced instead with heavy dark wooden floors, and roughhewn rock walls. The room was vaguely circular, with a spiral staircase in the centre of the floor. Around the walls were small circular windows, too high to see out of. Behind the staircase, and opposite the door to the lift contraption, there was a fireplace, complete with mismatched armchairs circled in, facing the hearth. To the left of the fireplace was an enormous, floor to ceiling window which looked out to the grounds below, providing a dizzying overview of the lake. There was the faint smell of candle wax in the air.

Giving me no time to look around, the monk was already climbing the staircase, which rattled unsettlingly as I followed behind. This next room, which judging by the shape of its roof was at the top of the tower, held five beds, all laid in a circle looking inwards to the staircase. Between each bed was a writing desk and chair.

"Broch, your clothing items have been in storage here since your expected day of return, please ensure they take up no more than your own storage." The monk pointed to a bed which had the most enormous pile of clothes I'd ever seen. Broch went running to the bed gleefully, pulling this piece or that from the pile and inspecting it.

"Kehlem, Themia sent word ahead of the hurry you left your home in. We've arranged to have some clothes ready for your arrival. Payment for tuition, room and board is thirty silver a month. You should make payment at the bursar's office by the end of this week." She gave me a sharp look. "Failure to make payment will result in expulsion from the dormitory, and punishment as seen fit from the Abbot. You're sharing this dormitory with one other Caserean." Her lip curled unpleasantly, like the taste of the word was bitter even to speak, "who will be joining you this evening after lessons I expect."

I walked around the room, finding a bed with neat bedding, and a pile of fresh, clean clothing stacked on top. Thirty pennies? A month? I honestly hadn't considered the academy might charge. I recalled suddenly the pouch Themia had passed me outside the Eastern Garrison, which I'd kept tucked, and frankly in all the excitement of the journey, forgotten about, on my belt.

"Broch, you have a disciplinary meeting at fifth bell. Kehlem, your Pattern Trial will begin at sixth bell." She nodded to us both, and disappeared down the stairs, the sound of a door opening and closing confirming she'd left.

I sat down on my bed, thankful to take the weight off after the morning's walk up from Isale town. I opened the coin pouch, and counted out exactly thirty pennies, and let out a sigh of relief. Of course she had known. That was the first month taken care of at least. I just needed to find a way to make enough money for the next month. Right now, however, I had another more pressing issue. "Broch?" I asked.

"Hmm?" He was busy holding tunics and waist coats up to the window, checking them for damage.

"What is a Pattern Trial?"

"Would you stop gawking?" Broch called over his shoulder to me, exasperated.

We were back in the main hall, and the fifth bell was about to ring. Broch had promised to show me where my Pattern Trial would be held on the way to his disciplinary. I'd been staring up to the barrel ceiling of the hall, where I'd noticed carvings similar to those I'd seen in the Eastern Garrison temple.

I looked back down, and caught up with Broch.

"Still feeling sick?" He asked.

"A little," I said, holding my stomach.

To get out of our tower, and descend to the lower levels, we had to get back in the platform lift. It carried on going a little higher up, and then began to level out as it reached the top. Broch had explained to me that it was like a belt that span on two wheels, one at the top of the tower, and one at the bottom. To descend, you had to travel up to the top of the upper wheel, walk across the zenith, and then stand on the platform in front of you, ready to descend. That's why the platforms were cut like a triangle, flat side stuck to the belt. It meant they were the same shape upside down. What Broch hadn't warned me about was that going down felt a lot worse than going up. Firstly, there were no windows on this side of the tower, so the journey down was pitch black, and seemed to make the ride feel faster. Secondly, the feeling of going down in the lift felt remarkably similar to how I'd imagined plummeting to your death would feel like and the whole way down I had an uneasy, pinching feeling just behind my navel. This time I kept an eye out for the door at the bottom and jumped out in time, but the whole sensation left me feeling ill, which Broch took great delight in.

I followed Broch up the grand stairs at the back of the hall, and through an archway I hadn't seen from the ground level. It led out to a balcony of sorts that wrapped around the edge of another enormous hall. This one I noticed had far more students in it. They were congregated on the lower levels, sat on desks and benches that had been neatly arranged in rows. Monks were also interspersed amongst the students, carrying out work of their own. The balcony we were on, perimetered the upper level, with wooden doors repeating occasionally along the wall.

"This is where you'll find most of your classes," Broch explained, still strolling quickly towards the other end of the walkway. I could see that on the opposite side of the room, the balcony swivelled into a small landing, with a set of wide stairs joining the lower and upper levels together.

"Handily, the Abbot's offices are just next door to where they hold the Pattern Trial. This is me," Broch said, coming to a halt just before the landing.

We stood in front of a heavy looking ornate door. "There should be a similar door, on the other side of the staircase. That's where your trial should be."

In the distance, a bell could be heard.

"Well, wish me luck," Broch said. He did not look confident.

"See you this evening," I said.

Broch grimaced at me, and then knocked on the Abbots door, stepped in and left me alone on the landing.

With nothing to do for another hour or so, I figured I'd try and explore a little and get a feel for my surroundings. Apparently, there was a mess hall nearby, which would provide free meals to students here. Having not eaten since the morning's pastries, that seemed like a good place to start.

I walked down the stairs to the lower levels, where the hum of conversation, and scratching sound of quill on paper grew louder. I walked past the students and monks cautiously at first, worried I'd be told I wasn't allowed here, that I was breaking a yet unknown rule to me. But not one of them looked my way, too busy deep in conversation, or heads buried in their books. Spurred on, I spotted a large corridor underneath the balcony I'd come in on, and made my way towards it.

A distant smell of food greeted me at the entrance of the corridor, so I decided to follow my nose. Unlike the study hall, this corridor was quiet, and dimly lit. There were patterns carved on the walls and ceilings that seemed familiar to me now, and with each step I took, the smell of food grew stronger. Around midway, two doors interrupted the smooth stone walls, one on one side and one on the other. I could hear a faint clattering, but couldn't decide which door it was coming behind, so taking a guess I opened the left-hand side door.

It wasn't a mess hall. It was far better. Immediately I was greeted by a familiar, comforting smell. It was a dry, musty smell that reminded me of comfortable nights at home in my study. Books. I was in some kind of library, except to call it that seemed like a gross understatement. We had a library back home in Barrowheld. This was gargantuan. Row after row of books, as far as the eye can see — admittedly not very far as the room was dimly lit by only a few glowing lanterns. But the shadows I could make out hinted of the enormity of the room and told me of unspoken secrets they held within. So busy was I staring around in wonder, that I almost jumped out of my skin when a hand touched my shoulder.

"Sorry!" I whispered, after I yelped. "You scared me." I laughed quietly to myself. I turned around, realising the hand belonging to a monk.

"You shouldn't be here," came a voice from under the hood.

Shit. This must be one of those rules I was supposed to know, but Broch conveniently forgot to tell me.

I kept my voice quiet, not wanting to make more of an arse of myself. "Sorry, Do'Seer. I've only just arrived, I wasn't sure where I was."

"This library is for Seer's only. You shouldn't be in this part of the Academy," the voice hissed, as he pushed me towards the door. "Especially not a Caserean." He pushed me through the library door, shutting it behind him.

Well I guess that explains why the corridor was so quiet. Not wanting to get caught by another monk, I quickly retraced my steps, and walked back into the study hall, noticing a few odd looks given to me from students. Not wanting to accidentally stumble into a monk only bathing room, I walked over to a table where only a couple students were sitting quietly working.

"Hi," I said. "Sorry to intrude. Do you know where I can find the mess hall?"

Not bothering to look up, one of the students lifted a free hand, and pointed to the other side of the study hall. There was another corridor, opposite the one I'd just left.

Of course.

The sound of the sixth bell echoed through the mess hall. I put my spoon back into my half-eaten bowl of egg and rice, and dropped it back at the counter. While filling, the rice grain was much chewier than what I was accustomed to at home, and had been spiced with a flavour that was unfamiliar to me, making it almost sweet. The mess hall was small, and far less grand then the study hall. Rows of benches filled the room, and a single counter serving hot food stood at the opposite end. It had been quiet when I'd first entered half an hour ago, but it had begun to fill up slowly as students came to enjoy an evening meal. Not wanting to be late for the trial, I left the hall and exited into the corridor that would take me back to the study hall.

Broch hadn't really explained what a Pattern Trial was, but from what I could gather, it was a way for the monks to understand if you had a natural propensity for a certain type of Aspecting. There were many areas of study; medica, alchemy, Destructia and Fabrica were the main ones I knew of from speaking to both Kit and Broch. The experience with healing Broch's foot had awakened something in me though. It had felt so natural and easy. Ever since I'd spoken to my father all those moons ago, about Job's amputation, I'd quietly fantasized about Aspecting to heal. Maybe Kit had already informed the monks, and they knew about me saving Broch's foot. I may not even have to do this trial. It could just be a formality and they'd just ask me to specialise in healing straight away.

I climbed the stairs out of the study hall, and back onto the balcony, where I took a left. In the corner, was an ornate wooden door, which matched the one I'd seen Broch use for his disciplinary meeting earlier. I took a deep breath, steadied myself, and with a knock on the door first, walked in.

16

Pattern Trial

It took a moment for my eyes to adjust to the dimly lit room. There was a smell of incense in the air, and that, coupled with the strange, echoey acoustics in the room reminded me immediately of the temple in the garrison. I walked hesitantly to the centre. It was hard to tell in the gloom, but there looked to be a podium at one end of the room.

I cleared my dry throat. "Hello? I'm here for the Pattern Trial?"

There was a sound of shuffling feet on stone, and a hooded monk appeared from behind a wall. I wasn't certain in the dark, but there must be a curtain separating this room from another. Maybe they connected to the Abbot's offices? The monk thumbed at a lantern and a soft orange light blossomed in the room. It was indeed a curtain the monk had appeared from. The room I stood in was very reminiscent of where I'd met the blind-Abbot in the Garrison. Small, square and laid completely in stone. The walls of which were carved with similar intricate patterns, which caught the steady light of the lantern, creating strange shadows. Facing me was a podium on a short-raised dais, which the monk placed a well-worn book on, and stepped back. As if he heard my earlier thoughts, the man I recognised as the Abbot-Primus strode through the curtain.

"I'm pleased you managed to find your way here, Kehlem. I hope you took the chance to eat first?" he asked, as he walked over to the plinth.

"I did, Primus," I said, recalling the honorific Kit had used earlier that day.

"And do you know what to expect from this trial?"

"Not really," I said, uneasy at showing my ignorance. "Broch mentioned it being to do with aptitude?"

"A correct, if not simplistic view of the trial," the Abbott conceded. "Of course, I would not normally be in attendance, but given the letter that Themia has provided, and the tale of your use of a full pattern of healing, I confess myself curious.

"There are many schools, within this academy, and indeed within the empire. There are those who are concerned with the elemental nature of things and harness the Aspect to create and understand artefacts of marvellous ingenuity. Others will use their strength and connection to the Aspect to heal, cure and remake those who have been left with the burden of physical aberrations. And of course, there are others who would use the Aspect to protect the Vin Irudur empire, against all those who would seek to undo what we have done. The Aspect teaches us that most people will have a propensity for a particular school, a particular language. I see from Themia's letter that you, for example, intuited a pattern of exothaumic dispersal, correct?"

Where was this going? "Well, I don't know the name of the pattern, but…"

"Of course, of course," he said, dismissing my concern. "Today, you will be shown different patterns. Only quarter patterns mind, nothing like the full pattern you performed on Broch. We shall observe, and from that, recommend to which school you should focus your efforts."

Taking his unspoken cue, the hooded monk opened the book on the plinth to a bookmarked page, and placed an item on the floor on the plinth.

"What about a tether?" I asked.

The hooded monk walked up to me, and held out a piece of leather cord, with a circle of metal wrapped in the middle. As I went to take it, his hands brushed mine aside, and instead tied the bracelet around my wrist, so the cold metal was held against my skin.

"We use these to train Nascents. They allow you to temporarily tap into one of the smaller sources here at Isale. You can Aspect with this on, and not

PATTERN TRIAL

worry about hurting yourself or others." He gestured to the dais, "Whenever you're ready, Kehlem."

Unsure what else I was meant to do, I walked up to the podium, and examined the pattern on the page. As the Abbot had said, this only filled a quarter of the two-page spread. This pattern seemed different somehow to the pattern I'd used to heal Broch's foot. This was all spikes, and irregular movements. I tried to picture how I could move through it naturally, but it seemed filled with pauses and staccato movements. I remember the monk had left something on the floor as well, so I knelt down to inspect it. It looked like a small lump of dark grey metal. I pressed a nail into it, which left a small mark. Lead?

Presumably this was the alchemy trial then. I turned back to the podium, and saw that both the monk and abbot were watching me. It was strange how I was stood at the pulpit, as if I were a Martyr priest giving my lessons to the monks. I shook my head, and tried to clear it. Trying to memorise only a quarter of a pattern seemed like a much easier task compared to the pattern I'd used on Broch. Once I thought I had it held firm in my mind, I closed my eyes, and lifted my left hand. Now I had touched the Aspect a few times, I knew what I was looking for. It was like running your finger across the closed pages of a book, and noticing by touch if a page was slightly askew. I felt a gentle ripple in the air in front of me, so I held my forefinger against it, pushing but not breaking the boundary between our world and the next. I recalled the starting shape of the pattern, and once again, felt an undertow from the Aspect, pulling my hand, directing it through the pattern I held in my mind. It danced my hand quickly, alternating direction this way and that, my wrist having to bend to take some of the strain from the rapid, halting movements. Quickly, I was running out of pattern, so on the final turn, I dragged the pattern down and touched my forefinger to the lump of lead, still on the floor. It glowed for a moment, lit within by a red light briefly, and then it faded to nothing. The metal against my wrist felt painfully cold on my skin for a moment, before it slowly was warmed again by the heat of my body.

"Please bring the metal over here, Kehlem," the Abbot called.

I lifted the metal, which felt warm to the touch and dropped it into the open hand of the monk. He prodded and rubbed the metal, and to my astonishment, the grey rubbed off a corner of the surface of the metal like a patina, revealing a golden skin beneath. The Abbot was staring out towards the dais still.

"A partial transmutation would you say?" he mumbled to the monk, who was still rolling the metal in his palm.

He considered the metal a moment longer, and murmured his agreement.

"Hmm," the Abbot mused to himself. "Not bad by any means."

The hooded monk pocketed the metal, and returned to the podium, flicking through the patterns until he found the page he was after. Smoothing the pages out, he disappeared behind the curtain, returning a moment later with a fat, brown rat, which he held by the scruff behind its neck.

"Up you go Kehlem," the Abbott said, nudging me.

I walked back up to the dais, a little confused as to why the monk was still standing next to me, rat in hand. I looked down at the pattern he'd opened for me. It seemed familiar, somewhat reminiscent of the pattern of healing I'd used on Broch, except this one was more straightforward, its intent more plain to see.

Oh Martyr.

I turned back to look at the monk, who had pulled a small, sharp knife from somewhere, and with a practiced ease, he sliced the rat across its belly. The rat squealed and thrashed in his hands. Before I even knew what I was doing, I'd touched the Aspect with my left hand, and whipped my way through the pattern, and touched the rat. In all, it had probably taken 20 heartbeats for the monk to slice the rat and for me to dart through the pattern. A familiar red light emerged across the rat's skin, and closing my eyes I could feel the trill of its terrified existence. I flexed the pattern, calming and soothing the rat, and then across the gulf of torn flesh, I let the pattern flow either side, and willed the flesh back together, stitching the wound closed with light. Again, the metal drew cold against my skin, although less painful than before, and the monk stepped down to the Abbot, who inspected the rat's belly.

PATTERN TRIAL

"Impressive. Quick as well," the Abbot said, running a finger along where the cut should be. "That looked to be a transference into the second phase as well. Interesting."

The Abbot took his hand away from the rat. No sooner had he withdrawn his hand, the monk gripped the rat by its tail, and swung the rat, smashing its head against a stone step. The sudden, casual violence took my breath away, and I stood rooted to the spot. The abbot didn't even blink.

Taking the remains of the rat with him, the monk once again disappeared behind the curtain, this time returning with what looked like to be a hay stuffed scarecrow, which he dragged until it stood about four meters opposite the dais. The monk and abbot then strode up to the dais, where the monk flipped a few more pages, and then retreated with the Abbott against the wall. I glanced down at the book, a sense of dread building and looked at the pattern. There was a strange tension in the air, like the Abbot was holding his breath. I knew this pattern. I'd never seen it before, but looking at it now, it felt like an old friend. I could easily see how it would be drawn, where the energy would go. I glanced back to the mannequin. It wasn't a scarecrow. It was a target.

I took a deep shaking breath. Already I could feel an ember of fury glow within the pit of my soul. Each breath I took fed it, causing it to grow brighter. Thoughts of nausea, dizziness crashed against my mind. A feeling of hopelessness as I realised I couldn't recall entire evenings, gentle words spoken between Eva and I vanished, taken by an insidious poison. I heard the sharp crack as the rat's skull shattered against the stone floor. The ember caught, and once again I was aflame. Not even bothering to consider the pattern, I braced myself, bending my knees slightly. With an open palm, my left hand found the Aspect and gripped the fabric between worlds. I pulled back with a fist, pulling the pattern down, letting it build inside of me. My right hand, three fingers open, danced a simple pattern in front of my chest, and as I pulled back my right hand, all the rage, the hurt and hatred poured into my arm. I threw my hand forward, towards the target and opened my palm.

A jet of blue flame erupted from my open palm, shooting towards the target. There was no point aiming, as the jet opened wide enough to engulf the width of the room. I struggled to keep my footing against the force erupting out of my hand.

Against my left wrist, the metal ring on the bracelet was like a needle of ice, as its temperature plunged. There was a metallic *ting* and the bracelet dropped from my arm onto the floor. As it fell, the blue light vanished.

It took a moment for my eyes to readjust, the room now being lit by the lanterns and the burning remains of the target, which from the waist up had been annihilated. Curiously, the stone walls looked untouched. I looked down to figure out how the bracelet had become untied, and saw that the metal ring had snapped cleanly in half.

"Incredible," came the hushed voice of the Abbot. He walked up to join me at the front of the dais. "I've never seen anything like it. I was wondering if Themia's account could possibly be correct." His voice was full of wonder.

I was horrified. Seeing the destruction, I'd wrought, being conscious to see the aftermath. How could anyone have survived that? How could my father possibly be still alive?

"I see no point carrying on the trial," the Abbot said. "Kehlem, you will focus your studies on patterns of destruction." He turned back to the monk. "Make the appropriate provisions, prepare a time-table for Kehlem. It's important that we…"

The Abbott carried on talking but I was barely listening. A familiar feeling of hopelessness as my life was once again being decided before me.

"You're back early," Broch said, as I stumbled out of the lift and into the common room of our dormitory. "Wasn't expecting you back until sun down."

Broch was lolling across one of the battered arm chairs, sat sideways, yet he still somehow exuded comfort. He reminded me of a cat. Golden sunlight streamed in through the arched window. I set myself down on the windowsill, considering the view down to the lake.

"We finished early," I said. "How did your disciplinary go?"

Broch waved a foot at me. "Oh, fine. They made some piss poor threats about me not getting my tether this year, having to repeat a year, blah blah," he said. "How come you finished early? Did they find you a specialisation? Wait let me guess, healing right? It's got to be."

I shook my head, still in shock. I didn't want this.

"Did you choke up? It happens to all of us, don't sweat about it." He pushed himself upright so he was facing me. "So, what did you get lumped with?"

"Destruction," I said, looking out through the window.

"Huh," Broch said, surprised. "I wouldn't have thought you'd be a match. You don't seem the type. There's only a handful of Casereans that get into the Destructia school each year as well."

Something about how he said it made me turn around. "How do you mean?"

"Well, the Vin are notoriously tight-arsed about teaching non-Vinnish people Destructia patterns. Think about it, would you want to teach the country-men you beat black and blue how to blow up a small battalion from one hundred yards?"

"Well, sure but that was years ago, they can't still be worried about an uprising."

"You're cute, Kehlem," Broch said, talking to me like I was a puppy. "Why do you think there's such tight restrictions on tethers? Why do you think only the Vinnish can teach Aspecting? If you ever want to get a tether, you're going to have to show the Vins that you pose them no threat." He eyed me up and down. "Not exactly an easy task if they cut your trial short and are sending you directly to learn Destructia." He paused, thinking a moment, and then shivered. "Mother of the Martyr, I'd hate to know what you can do with destruction if you can already use a full pattern of healing, and they decided you're better at killing people. Remind me not to piss you off."

Before I could say anything, the door to the lift opened, and out stepped a blond Caserean boy.

Quickly taking in the scene, he introduced himself. "You must be the new roommates I was warned about. I'm Thain."

"Charmed," Broch said, lazing back into his chair.

I rolled my eyes, and walked over to greet the newcomer. "I'm Kehlem, that's Broch," I held out my hand, which he shook, giving me a wide, earnest smile. Unlike Broch, Thain was dressed simply, in muted colours and he wore his shoulder length fair hair in a single tie behind his head. Despite his boyish complexion, complete with freckles and sharp cheekbones, he stood a few inches taller than myself.

"It'll be nice to have company," he said, brightly. He looked over my shoulder to Broch. "I've seen your face before. We were studying fabrication patterns together last year."

Broch grunted back. I wasn't sure if that was an agreement or not.

"I don't recognise you though, are you from another academy?" Thain asked, looking back at me.

"Actually, I'm a Nascent. I'm new to all of this." I gestured around me.

"Oh," Thain said, smile faltering a little. I could see a familiar question burning up inside of him, and then the effort he made to not ask it. I appreciated him for that.

"So, it would be you then who broke his iron tether during the Pattern Trial then? I heard some of the Foclir gossiping about it in the mess hall just."

I nodded, surprised other people had taken an interest. "I was just telling Broch, I've been assigned to destruction patterns." It was hard to keep the disappointment out of my voice.

Thain whistled. "Yeah no wonder. Those tether bracelets are tied to one of the minor waterwheels, so to overload it, you must have shifted a huge amount of energy in one go."

"Wait a moment." Broch sat up. "You didn't tell me you'd broken the tether bracelet they gave you." He almost sounded offended.

"I didn't think it was important," I said, shrugging my shoulders.

Broch rolled his eyes at me, the way a parent would at their child. He turned his attention to Thain. "Is this it? Is it just the three of us sharing the dormitory? There's enough room upstairs for another two of us, surely?"

"Just us three," Thain said. "They keep us Casereans housed apart from the Vins, and while there is a separate dormitory for the females, I don't think there are any female Casereans at the academy at the moment, not since Tibitha earned her tether last term."

Broch nodded to himself, listening to Thain.

Why did they need to house us and the Vins in different dormitories? I wondered.

"So Destructia then?" Thain asked, turning to me. "Well, as it happens, I was shifted over to Destructia school last term as well. At least you'll have a friendly face with you," Thain said.

It surprised me that it was actually a relief to hear that, and while it didn't stop the sinking feeling at knowing I wasn't going to be a healer, knowing at least one other person in the class wouldn't be a total stranger was a comfort.

"How come they shifted you out from fabrication?" Broch asked.

"The monks must have gotten sick of me accidentally blowing up whatever it was I was trying to make," Thain shrugged.

"That's why I didn't recognise you! The eyebrows!" Broch jumped to his feet, wiggling his own brows for effect. "I don't think there was a single class I saw you in, where you hadn't burned your eyebrows off."

Thain flushed a deep red, and sank into an armchair.

Taking pity, I sat across from Thain. "That's a bit rich coming from you," I said.

Thain looked between Broch and I looking for an explanation. I explained how Broch and I had first become acquainted, complete with a ridiculous imitation of Broch's accent. At first Broch sulked, silently listening, but as soon as I began singing the song Kit made, he surprised the hell out of me by jumping onto his chair, and with a rich baritone, gave perhaps the most ridiculous rendition of 'The One Foot Philander' there ever was. Thain and I cried with laughter, and joined in for the refrains. Thain even came up with a brand-new verse, and demonstrated he was a genius at rhyming innocuous words with atrociously filthy puns.

17

Kin and Kith

The three of us rose early the next morning, and ate breakfast in the mess hall. We'd stayed up late together, Thain and Broch filling me in on what some of their classes had been like and what to expect today. After breakfast Broch made his excuses and left, apparently part of his punishment from yesterday was to work in the library open to the students, cleaning and organising the books. Thain and I didn't have class together until the second morning bell, so he offered to give me a complete tour of the academy, which I gratefully accepted.

The study hall was essentially the main part of the academy, as far as students and Foclir were concerned. Most classes were held in one of the rooms that radiated out from the balcony above, and of course the mess hall and student library was attached to one of the corridors that stemmed from the lower student hall. The main hall, or entrance hall was the only way to enter the towers, via the system of stairs and lifts. The tower our dormitory was in was one of the oldest, and therefore most dilapidated, and so was reserved for the Caserean students. Some of the towers had rooms within their lower sections which took advantage of the tall ceilings, for experiments where violent spontaneous combustion was a real and present concern. East of the entrance hall were the dormitories for the monks, which was largely off limits to students, unless invited. There were also sets of stairs that descended below the main entrance hall, which Thain had never been down before, so couldn't tell me where they led, although supposedly it was mostly rooms for storage and overflow dormitories, for a time when Aspectors were more prevalent.

As one of the most inherently dangerous pattern series to learn, Destructia was never taught inside a classroom, and was instead only taught outside, whatever the weather. Less chance of blowing a hole through a load bearing pillar that way. Second bell rang, and so Thain and I made our way out of the entrance hall, and down towards the lake, where my first lesson would begin.

There was a small cohort of five or so students waiting for us by the flat lakeshore by the time we arrived. They were talking amongst themselves, but grew silent as Thain and I arrived. We awkwardly stood to the side of the group and waited for the Seer to arrive. I was about to ask Thain a question, when he nudged me with his elbow, and gestured to the front. A Seer monk was walking down the hillside towards us. He was dressed differently to the other monks I'd seen. Wearing the same brown robes as the others, his hood was down, but he didn't appear to be blind. The loose garments he was wearing had been bound tight against his wrists and ankles with long black rope, which only highlighted a strong physical form I had not expected from what I'd previously considered to be a bookish vocation. As he arrived at the front of the class, the whole group of students grew very quiet and still. He eyed the group silently for a moment, gaze falling on me and Thain at the back.

"You will have by now noticed we have a new student joining us." His voice was loud and clear, even out here in the open. "I have been assured by the Primus that despite being a Nascent, the new Caserean has already mastered up to the second form of the Destructia pattern two."

Muttering broke around the group, and Thain gave me an uneasy look.

The monk's voice rose above the muttering, drowning it out. "That either means, that our young Caserean here is a boy wonder, or anyone left in this cohort who cannot perform Destructia pattern two should consider taking up life as a wagon pusher."

The disdain in the Seer's voice made it clear which explanation he thought was more plausible.

"Thain!" the Seer barked.

At my shoulder, Thain jumped

"You will catch the newcomer up on pattern one."

"Yes Do'Seer," Thain called back.

"The rest of you. You will practice patterns one and two. First and second forms." The group stood still. "What are you waiting for? Get to it!"

The class lined up and collected our temporary tethers from the Seer, these ones made of bronze instead of iron. As I went to take mine, he held onto it for just a moment, holding my gaze before letting go. The Seer also handed Thain a parchment with a pattern, and he and I walked some distance away from the others, to give room for practice. The rest of the class had also spread out, and before long there were sputters of blue jets of light erupting out of palms, although I noticed with interest, not many of them seemed to spread beyond a meter in front of their respective Aspector.

"Well," Thain said, strapping his bracelet to his wrist. "If they didn't like you before, they're going to hate you now."

"How do you mean?" I asked, doing the same.

"Only one other person has managed to master a second form of pattern two. That's him over there, Frennic." He pointed to a Vinnish boy who was stretching, warming himself up. Curiously he stood apart from the main gaggle of his peers. "We've been studying the second form since the start of the year, so for a Nascent to walk in, fresh faced and show them up..." he paused, "You're going to have to watch your back."

Now he said it, I did notice a lot of the other students glancing our way, although we were too far apart for me to make out their expressions.

"So, what's this about pattern one?" I asked, changing the subject.

Thain passed me the parchment he'd been given, it held a single page of an unfamiliar pattern. "It's the first pattern you're supposed to learn in Destructia. It's essentially the opposite of pattern two. Instead of sending a projectile of energy, you take the energy out of something else. Here, let me show you."

I stepped back, giving Thain some room. He tied his blonde, almost white hair back out of his face, and closed his eyes. With a snap of his arm, he brought his left hand up and around in a circular motion, a faint red line trailing behind his movements. He danced his hand slowly, in a large sweeping motion, which mimicked the pattern on the page he'd given me. Closing his fist, he knelt and brought the pattern down to the shoreline, brushing the water with his fist. The pattern glowed just beneath the water's surface, and as it radiated out from his fist, a thin layer of ice formed as the water froze, spreading a few feet in radius before stopping. Thain opened his eyes, and walked back to me, grinning.

"Impressive," I said, genuinely. "I had no idea that was even possible. I thought you could only take energy from the Aspect."

"Not at all. The point of this pattern is that it allows you to withdraw energy from an object and release it into your tether using yourself as a conduit."

"What's the point of using it then? I mean, with the other pattern it's easy to see how it could work on the battlefield, but I can't see how this would be that useful."

"Well, it's not like Aspectors are really used on battlefields anymore. They're mostly used as manhunters, moving in small groups. The main purpose of this is to charge a tether."

"I didn't even know you could do that," I said, a little overwhelmed.

"Before I show you the pattern, do you think you could show me how you perform pattern two? I think I'm getting there, but it would be great to see it up close."

I nodded, a little apprehensive. I could hardly say no, if Thain was stuck having to catch me up on stuff he already knew. I took a deep breath, clearing my mind. I tried to remember how I felt yesterday, standing on the plinth, looking down at the straw target. That coal of rage was still burning, so I fanned its flames and closed my eyes. I didn't even need to see the pattern; the movements were so familiar it was like holding a loved one close. I grabbed at the Aspect, pulling and twisting with both hands as I directed the energies inwards and through me, where they mixed with all the loathing I felt, the loneliness, and the fear. I swung my right arm, and pointing out towards the lake, I shot it forward, opening my palm. As before a jet of blue light erupted from my hand, shooting six then twelve feet across the lake. The ice Thain had formed earlier was vaporized in a moment. The brass tether I was wearing grew painfully cold, and not wanting to break this one, I severed the connection I'd held to the Aspect with my left hand, letting the blue light die out. Steam rose across the lake's surface and ripples faded slowly into the distance.

There was an eerie silence, and looking around, I realised the rest of my class were staring at me, some in surprise, others in open distaste. The monk was watching me expressionless.

Thain ran up to me, and broke the silence. "That was incredible!" he rejoiced, breathless. "I had no idea the flames could grow that large. And that was just the second form?"

I nodded.

"Can I just ask you quickly, when you did this…" and Thain began asking me hundreds of small questions about form and placement. How did I hold my hips when I moved from this place to that? What was I feeling when I turned to this point? I spent the whole morning trying to explain to him what I understood instinctually. It was beyond difficult. It was impossible. How do you explain to someone how to smell? I may as well have tried to describe sound to a deaf person. By the time the monk called us back, I'd spent two hours running through the second pattern with Thain, and he had shown me nothing of the first. The class lined up, untying and handing back the bronze tethers we'd been given at the start of lessons. After each student handed the bracelet back, they burst into a run, not back to the academy, taking a right instead, around the lake. Confused, I handed the bracelet to the monk, and stood still, not sure what was going on.

"Well?" The monk demanded.

There was a pressure in my back and I stumbled forwards, as a Vin student who'd queued behind me shoved me in the small of my back, and shouted "Get running then!"

I could hear some sniggering behind me so broke out into a jog, following the path I'd seen the others take. A few moments later, the Vin student who'd shoved me ran straight past me, spitting on the floor as he went.

I wasn't exactly athletic. A lifetime of staying indoors and reading books would do that. I kept a slower pace than the rest of the group, who I could see were already halfway around the lake. Thain caught up to me, and slowed down to match my pace.

"Sorry about that," he said, barely out of breath. "I should have warned you. If you're working on Destructia patterns, they expect you to be physically fit as well."

There was a burning sensation in my throat, as I gulped down the cold mountain air struggling to catch my breath.

"Do you want a running partner?" Thain asked.

I waved my hand, gesturing for him to run ahead. There was no reason for him to be stuck at my pace.

"Meet you in the common room then!" he said, and he increased his pace with ease, speeding off into the distance.

It took me another thirty minutes to get around the first half of the lake, and my jogging speed had slowed to almost a walk. The rest of the class and the monk had long gone, my Vin Irudur peers shouting something undoubtedly obscene across the lake at me as they finished. My lungs were burning, my calves felt like stones and the balls of my feet were red raw. Still, I finished my lap, collapsing on the shoreline, hot and sweating, lying on my back panting for breath. I was close to vomiting. I swivelled over onto my front, and brought myself up to my knees. I knew that lying here would just make my muscles seize up, so hating myself the whole time, I slowly stretched out my thighs and my calves, and walked agonisingly slowly back up to the academy.

Thoroughly miserable and exhausted I arrived in the common room to see Thain relaxing in an armchair, flicking absentmindedly through a book.

"Martyr, you look dreadful," Thain said.

"Cheers," I said levelly, sweat still dripping from my brow.

He blushed a little. "Want me to show you where the baths are?"

I had intended on getting some food, but from the way students had avoided me on the way up to the academy, I assumed I stunk. "Yes please."

THE SOUL'S ASPECT

Thain kindly grabbed some of my spare clothes from the upstairs room, and took me down to the entrance hall and down a long, echoey corridor. As we walked, I noticed the corridor seemed to be getting lighter, and the sounds opened up. "Where does this lead? Is there another hall?" I asked, a little incredulous at the size of the academy.

"Patience, just wait a moment," Thain said, smiling.

A few moments later, I got to see for myself. It didn't open up into another hall, it didn't open up to another room at all. Instead the corridor led us back outside, into what I assume was a natural crevice in the cliff face, which had then been carved out, and turned into an open bath. Students, monks and Foclir intermingled, men and women alike, relaxing against the edges of the most enormous bath I'd ever seen, and judging by their red faces, and the steam evaporating off the surface, it was heated as well.

"I hope you're not shy," Thain said.

"How do you mean?" I asked, confused. And then I realised. No one was wearing any clothes. It was hard to tell because the water was murky, but when one of the older male monks stepped out of the bath, steam rising off his red and wrinkled body, I had no idea where to look. I flushed a deep red, and averted my eyes.

"Don't worry about it," Thain said, laughing. "It took me a little while to get used to it. The Vins don't have the same sensibilities as us. Just try not to think about it too much."

He walked over to the side, dropping my spare clothes on a bench. With a practiced casualty, he then stripped off his own clothes, and walked quickly into the water. Not seeing another option, I went over to the bench, and took a deep breath. Being around naked people wasn't exactly new to me, and sometimes it was unavoidable working as a physician. It was just the casual nature that shocked me, people having conversations with their friends as if they weren't naked like the day they were born. Taking Thain's advice, I tried not to overthink it, and quickly pulled my tunic over my head, took my shoes and trousers off, and walked quickly, if not carefully over to the steps of the pool. Thain was mercifully facing the other way.

"Not so bad right?" he asked, as I sank into the water opposite him.

The warm water surrounding me was exquisite. I hadn't properly bathed since I'd left the temple in Eastern Garrison, and it was like washing away a month of grime. I sank beneath the water, letting it cover my head. I was surprised to see how long my hair had gotten as it floated freely around me, like some kind of auburn halo. I grabbed a spare bar of soap that was dotted around the walls of the pool, and cleaned myself, massaging my aching muscles. Feeling fresh and clean, I sat back against the wall.

"Thanks for showing me this place," I said to Thain, who was busy washing his own hair.

"It's no bother. Especially after you spent all morning working with me on that pattern. I didn't even get a chance to run through the first pattern with you," he said, rinsing his hair.

"Can you show me back in the common room?"

"Can't. It's forbidden. Only Seer's are allowed to draw out the patterns."

"Oh, why's that?"

"It's just another one of their laws, don't ask me." His inflection made it obvious who 'they' were. "So, how does an almost adult Caserean man find himself a Nascent hundreds of miles from home?"

I almost sighed. I could feel the question coming for a while now, although now it was here, I found that I didn't really mind. So, while we bathed, I told Thain about Barrowheld, about my father and my medicine, and about Eva. He was a good audience, listening carefully, not interrupting or pushing for more detail. It was surprisingly cathartic, and by the time I'd finished, we were one of the few still left in the pool. After we dried off, and made our way to the mess hall, Thain told me a little of his own life. He had been raised in one of the northern cities, on the coast. Born to a bookkeeper, he'd lived a fairly comfortable life, but being in a larger city, close to the Vin border, had meant a higher prevalence of the Vin Irudur and their Aspectors. Apparently one morning they came to his parent's business, told them their child was an Aspector, handed them a silver penny and took him. He hadn't seen his parents since. Apparently, the break Broch was allowed is a privilege only given to the rich and favourites of the Vin administration. He told me all this under a bright veneer, but I could see he was still hurting, after all these years of being ripped away from his parents, from his life. I'd left my life somewhat willingly, but he had been stolen from his. Before we returned to the common room after we ate, he pulled me aside.

"I know what it's like to be pulled from people you love. To be taken from a life you thought was set in stone. I promise Kehlem, I'll help you get your tether. If it's within our reach for you to get it this year, I swear by the Martyr's ashes we'll do it."

His gaze was fierce, and steely. For once, there was no smile on his lips.

I studied him a moment, looking into his green eyes. They did not waver from my gaze.

"We're in this together," I said, grasping his hand. "We'll get our tethers together, and leave this academy together."

18

Aberration

The next day, on Thain's suggestion, we woke up early and went down to the lake side for a morning run together, before the majority of the academy woke up.

"It's how I got through my first month in these classes," he had explained to me.

So, despite my aching muscles, I agreed, and found myself jogging slowly around the lake side. There was a fine mist in the air as low clouds descended into the valley, and this time Thain jogged next to me, keeping me company. The aches and pains from yesterday's run made today's even worse, and there was a burning at the back of my throat, one which the cold air exacerbated as I struggled to keep my breath. Despite the pain, and the nausea that was coursing through me, when I finally finished, I was oddly happy. Thain had taken the time to rise early with me and help me exercise. He'd ran with me at my own, much slower pace, and all because he'd gone through the same struggles himself. Besides Eva, I'd never had a friend like that. It was a novelty, and one that would take some getting used to. We warmed down together after the run, and made our way to the empty baths to clean before meeting Broch for breakfast in the mess hall.

Ravenous, I grabbed as many eggs and bread that I could fit on my plate and joined the other two at a bench.

"How did your run go?" Broch asked, pouring himself a mug of warm coffee.

I grunted in response. I was drained, and all I wanted to do was crawl back into bed. Worst of all we had class again in another hour, and we'd be expected to run another lap of the lake.

"He'll get the hang of it," Thain said, annoyingly unaffected by the morning exercise. "How was the library work yesterday?"

"Dull as all hell. They just had me stacking books all morning. For the money, I'd rather be running laps outside with you."

"You can gladly take my place," I said, through a mouthful of egg. The thought of idly flicking through books sounded like a dream right now.

Broch casually wiped a piece of egg that I'd spat at him off his collar. "I heard that our Nascent here is growing quite the reputation," he said, changing the topic. "Rumour has it he sent a jet of flame large enough to cross the lake on his first day."

"It wasn't that large," I protested. "Besides, how did you even hear about that?"

"Oh, come on Kehlem. Look around, there aren't that many people here. What are we to do but gossip? Besides," he said, looking at me with distaste as I shovelled more food into my mouth, "a grown Nascent, who not only breaks an iron tether during his trial, but also specialises into Destructia despite being a filthy Caserean? You're a tongue wagger's dream."

"It's true Kehlem," Thain said as I blushed. "It's one of the reasons I didn't run through the pattern I was supposed to teach you yesterday. I figured it would be better for any onlookers to see what you already can do, rather than you struggling to learn a new pattern."

"Good thinking that," Broch said, sipping his coffee.

I chewed my eggs, thoughtful as I mentally readjusted my image of Thain. When I'd first met him, I'd assumed him to be a sweet, eager to please young man, but this shrewdness, along with what he told me yesterday, made me think I had judged him too swiftly. The truth was he had done me a great favour. No doubt many here at the academy probably judged me unworthy to be here, or didn't believe that I was capable of learning Destructia. He'd saved me a lot of trouble by guiding me so deftly yesterday.

"You heard anything from Kit?" I asked Broch, not wanting to leave the conversation focused on myself.

"Nope, he's probably stuck shadowing some dull Alchemy class or something. I'll keep my eyes out for him. Speaking of class, I better get moving." Broch put his mug down, and stood to his feet. "I'll see you ladies later."

"He's not at all like I thought he would be," Thain said, watching Broch disappear.

"How do you mean?"

"I was in the same class as him last year, in fabrication. He always seemed... aloof. Never really spoke to anyone. I don't know, he's a lot friendlier than I thought he would be."

"He was probably just concentrating on his studies. He's been here how long now? I know he's been trying to get his tether for years now," I said, dropping my cutlery onto my empty plate.

Thain gave me a funny look. "Is that what he told you?"

"About the tether?" I furrowed my brow, confused. "Yeah, he said something about how he'd been trying to get his tether for a few years. Why?"

"You're not the only one people gossip about. It's well known Broch could have gotten his tether years ago, he's better in fabrication than most second degree Foclir. He just always seems to find excuses to fail his test."

Thain wasn't the only person I'd apparently misjudged. Why wouldn't Broch want to get his tether so he could go home?

Thain and I were already stood waiting by the lakeside by the time the rest of the class appeared, walking together as a small group. While most of them seemed to avoid looking over to us, the one Thain had pointed out as Fennric stared at me with a slight sneer on his lip. Thankfully the Seer monk wasn't far behind the rest of my classmates.

"Same as yesterday, fall in!" He boomed, and the class formed a line in front of him, collecting the bronze tethers. As Thain and I collected ours, he passed the same parchment over to Thain. "I expect to see some progress today. If I wanted the newcomer to teach you what you should already know, I would have asked."

"Yes, Do'Seer," Thain said, looking suitably abashed.

The monk said nothing, and simply walked off to inspect some other students practicing their patterns.

"Come on," Thain said to me. "Let's get started."

We found a spot by the lakeshore that would hopefully be secluded enough to not draw attention from the academy. Thain passed me the parchment so I could take a look at this new pattern. It was different to all the others I'd seen. This pattern was wide and sweeping, all slow movements, and none of the tight twists and turns I'd been used to.

"Got it?" Thain asked.

I nodded, trying to keep the picture of the pattern in my mind's eye. I stood next to the shoreline, and closed my eyes. I brought my left hand up to eye level, and let it drift until I caught the now familiar feel of the Aspect. With the pattern held firmly in my mind, I traced a crack through the Aspect, making large gentle swoops with my hand, and gently bringing my closed fist to the water's surface. Towards the end of the pattern, I felt the tug of the Aspect wanting to direct my hand in a different motion, counter to the pattern Thain had shown me. I resisted it, and finished the pattern per the drawing. A flood of warmth swept through my left hand, and opening my eyes, I saw a thin layer of ice spiderweb out from my hand, across the surface of the water. The hold I had on the Aspect was getting harder to maintain, as the energy that coursed through my hand made the connection feel almost slippery, and suddenly, it was gone. The ice stopped its formation, and I stood back up. I'd managed to cover about half the distance Thain had when he'd demonstrated the pattern to me yesterday.

"You are a fast learner, aren't you?" Thain said, holding a hand over his eyes as he looked over the lake. "It took me a couple days to be able to hold on for that long."

I shook my hand, trying to get rid of an ache that had developed after losing control of the Aspect. The tether at my wrist had warmed slightly, having absorbed some of the excess energy.

"It feels different to the other pattern's I've used. It's a lot harder to keep control of the Aspect."

Thain nodded, agreeing. "That's the hardest thing with this pattern. You have to actively work against your instincts, otherwise you'll lose control. Try again."

Better prepared, I ran through the pattern, and again it felt like the pattern was running incongruent to where the invisible undertow wanted to take me. It was even harder this time to keep that grip on the intangible, and I'd barely started before the connection flew out of my hand. The tether was growing uncomfortably warm against my skin.

"Try not to force it," Thain said.

Not wanting to get burned by the Tether, I loosened the strap, so the metal no longer touched my skin. Once more I ran through the pattern. I held a looser grip on the Aspect, but this time when I felt the drawn pattern and the will of the Aspect diverge, I let the Aspect direct me. I finished the pattern and found I could hold it for longer. Ice flew across the lake, doubling the distance of my first attempt. I also noticed that the warming sensation I'd felt across my hand was now spreading up my arm, and into my core. As it spread, the tension in my muscles from the morning run eased, and the weight against my eyes also seemed to let off. I cut off the pattern and stood up.

"I officially hate you," Thain said, admiring how far the ice had travelled. His eyes flickered down to my wrist, noticing the tether bracelet hanging loose. "Kehlem!" he whispered sharply, alarmed. "Tie that tight before anyone spots you."

I pulled the strings on the tether so once more the metal was held against my skin. "What's the big deal?" I asked, shifting the metal around absent-mindedly.

"The big deal," Thain said, voice still barely above a whisper, "is that the metal needs to be touching your skin to work. You're lucky it must have been touching you when you just Aspected, otherwise Martyr only knows what would have happened."

Had it been touching my skin? I didn't notice it getting hot this time. Was that why I felt restored? Was the energy flowing into me instead of the energy flowing into the tether?

"What if you don't need a tether for this pattern?" I asked, my mind putting the pieces together.

"What do you mean?" Thain asked, eyebrows furrowed. "How would you charge the tether if you weren't wearing it?"

"What if the energy flowed into the Aspector instead?" I kept my voice quiet. I looked out to the lake so it wasn't obvious to any prying eyes that Thain and I were talking.

Thain looked at me sharply. "How do you mean?"

I explained to him what I just felt. "I was exhausted earlier. My calves have been killing all morning. But now, I feel great. Like I've just woken up. Is the Seer looking this way?"

Thain shook his head.

I explained what I'd done, changing from the pattern he'd shown me, how I kept a looser connection to the Aspect, and suggested Thain try it for himself. He stepped up to the lakeshore, quickly performing the altered pattern, ice forming, reaching out to meet mine and beyond. He stood back up and walked over to me.

"And?" I asked, impatient to see if it had worked.

"Martyr's Ashes," he swore, a wide grin broke over his face. "I had no idea that was even possible!"

"I'm going to try it again," I said, excited to try and pull more energy, but Thain gripped my arm.

"Don't," he whispered. "The monks keep an eye on these tethers, what they're tied to. They'll figure out that the energy we're pulling isn't going back into the tethers."

Shit. Why was everything so locked down in this place?

"Fine," I said, a little disappointed. "I guess we should practice the second pattern anyway."

Comfortable that I now knew pattern one, as instructed by our Seer Monk, Thain and I worked on his Pattern two, and by the end of the lesson, he was able to shoot small, hot jets of blue flame, to the chagrin of some of the Vinnish students who were still struggling with the pattern. We handed our tethers back, and broke into a comfortable jog around the lake, and with my energy restored, I found I didn't need to slow down as much today, and surprisingly didn't even need to collapse after we finished. Frennic still overtook me though, the smug bastard.

"Kehlem! A word," the Seer monk called. I glanced over at Thain nervous, and walked slowly over to the monk. Had he noticed what we had done?

"The Abbot Primus has asked to see you, go straight to his office."

My stomach dropped with dread. Could they have checked our tethers and realised we'd figured out how to use pattern one differently? I tried to catch Thain's gaze, but he was busy warming down. Not sure what else to do, and not wanting to keep the Abbot waiting, I made my way back up to the academy.

I knocked on the ornate door, waiting to be called in. I was back on the balcony, above the study hall. I'd walked the whole way up to the academy fretting, worried that someone had spotted what Thain and I were up to. It was stupid, to experiment like that after Broch had just warned me that people were watching what I was doing. What would the Abbot do?

"Enter," called a voice I recognised, and walked into the Abbot's office, bracing myself. Only the atmosphere was all wrong. He sat at his desk, relaxed and waved me smiling to a chair opposite him. A hooded monk stood silently at his side. Some of the tension bled out of me a little.

"Thank you for coming so quickly, Kehlem," the Abbot said, voice warm and lilting. "Now that you've had a chance to settle in a little, there are some things I wished to discuss."

"Oh," I said, uneasy, "What kind of things?"

"One thing we Seers know and understand about the Aspect is its rigidity. In fact, Seers and Aspectors alike rely on that very fact. The very language, the patterns you use to commune with it, have remained unchanged for millennia. There is much we don't know about the Aspect, but Seers believe, in fact it is a core principle, that if we can glimpse the start of a pattern, we can perhaps predict where it may end.

"We, and by that, I mean everything, all of creation are slaves to this fact. Patterns emerge in nature, in disparate species, across flora and fauna. These patterns are driven by the indelible tracings which the Aspect influences on this world. Can you perhaps see where I am going with this, Kehlem?"

A knot in my stomach told me so, but not wanting to tie the rope myself, I kept quiet.

"This pattern, this sacred geometry, we see it even in our own Aspectors. Without fail the calling to the Aspect is felt by all those on the day they begin their transition between childhood and adolescence. Many, many years of study, and research has proven this immutable fact, and yet here you are, an adolescent on the verge of being a man, a Nascent. You are, through no fault of your own, an aberration." The way he pronounced that word made it sound like gristle, stuck in his teeth. He sat back in his chair.

I tried to keep my face still, as inside my emotions whiplashed from fear of being found to be experimenting with the Aspect, to hurt at being referred to as an aberration.

"To make matters worse," the Abbott continued, "you continue to demonstrate burrs within the pattern. You instinctively use a second form of a Destructia pattern with no tether, and no training, to an extent large enough to level a house. And then through the incompetence of a Seer monk, you learn a full form pattern of healing, again tetherless."

The monk stood next to him shifted slightly from foot to foot.

"Never in my thirty years as Abbott has anyone broken an iron tether during their Trial of Patterns. You are a burr in an otherwise perfect pattern."

The Abbott paused, taking a breath. Not sure what to say, but feeling more than a little uncomfortable, I remained quiet.

"What do you understand about the Aspect, Kehlem?"

"Well," I said, voice dry. *'Not much'* is what I wanted to say. I coughed, clearing my throat. I thought back to what Themia and Kit had told me. "It's a world that overlays ours. Filled with the energies that fill our world. We're all made from it, and when we die that's where we return." I still wasn't convinced on that last part.

The Abbott raised an eyebrow. "Unusual for a Caserean to disavow his faith so quickly."

I shrugged my shoulders, forgetting the futility in doing so. "Father and I never listened particularly closely to our Priest."

"There can sometimes be a misunderstanding, an oversimplification of the Vin Irudur belief, Kehlem, that the Aspect is this cold void of nothing. We know this to be furthest from the truth. The Aspect itself is alive. How can it not be if the very spirit that lives in you was once a part of itself? If one was to believe this, and believe that all spirit was once part of the Aspect, then how could it be that the Aspect created you faulty, as a ruin of its own machination?"

Realising it wasn't rhetorical, I hedged a bet. "It can't?"

"My thoughts exactly. So, if we assume you are not an aberration, then you're merely a piece of a larger pattern, one we do not yet understand. By that token, I have decided to take a perhaps unusual decision, and have devised an experiment. I want you to study with Do'Seer Kit, here," he gestured to the monk stood next to him. I knew I'd recognised that awkward shuffle. "You will learn some basics of seeing. If we have any hope of understanding the role you play in the pattern, I think we must perhaps move away from tradition a little. Do'Seer Kit will explain more to you, but I will expect updates on your progress. I'll be watching with great interest."

On my way back to the dormitory I stopped a passing Foclir for directions to the bursar's office. I'd been carrying around my pennies Themia had given me, their weight an odd comfort. While they gave me a month's reprieve, they wouldn't change the fact I needed a way to make money. And quickly.

19

To See

"Do you miss her?" Thain's whispered voice travelled across the darkness of our room, just audible over the sounds of Broch's laboured snoring. I'd been laying flat on my back, unable to sleep, thinking about the Abbott's words.

"Who?" I whispered back.

"That girl you were telling me about. Eva."

Unbidden, her face appeared before me. Amber eyes set within soft skin, long flowing black hair. The half-smile she would give me when she mocked me softly. I let out a deep sigh.

"Of course." I'd been trying not to think of her, but it was impossible. It was like trying to not think of an open wound. You can pretend you don't feel the pain, the way cold air agitates the nerves, or how each movement opens the wound afresh, but you're just lying to yourself and the dull, constant ache is ever present waiting for you.

"What about you?" I asked. "Is there someone at home waiting for you?"

I could hear him laugh softly. "No," was all he whispered back.

The silence of the room lay thick, punctured only by the occasional snore from Broch.

"Kehlem?" another whisper.

"Yes?"

"That pattern, the one we changed. Do you think the others know about it?"

I paused, considering. "Probably." It seemed unlikely that monks who had devoted their lives to understanding the Aspect weren't aware that that particular pattern could be used in that way. Maybe Thain had the same thought, because he remained quiet. I closed my eyes, the words of the Abbott ringing in my ears.

A splash of cold water fell onto my forehead, waking me from my slumber. I tried to sit up, but my hands and feet had been restrained against something. The cold I felt against my cheek, and the metallic tang in the air told me whatever I was tied to was probably some kind of metal. There was little light wherever I was, but there was a darker shadow in the room, which moved towards me. I couldn't move, or even cry out in fear. I felt a hand on the back of my head, gripping and twisting the locks of my hair. It pulled my scalp tight, and when it had a firm grip, it pushed my face into the metal I was held against. Pressure and pain melded into one, and I grunted in agony. The unrelenting force continued, silent and uncaring. Tears of pain fled down my cheek, pooling and dripping into my open mouth. They mixed with the blood that was now pouring from my nose, as it was pushed against the unmoving metal. The pressure built, the hand pushing harder still. I let out a strangled cry, as my nose popped. I gasped in blood and sweat, choking as it aspirated into my lungs.

"Kehlem!"

I thrashed, arms and feet caught and still bound by something. I twisted, now free of the grip on my hair.

"Kehlem, wake up!"

I needed to get away, break free of whatever was gripping me. Fire struck across my face, and I inhaled in shock, opening my eyes.

Broch and Thain stood over me, Broch's open hand raised as if to strike me. Daylight streamed in through one of the windows of our dormitory.

"Sorry for slapping you, but you wouldn't wake up. You ok?" Broch asked.

I rubbed my cheek, sitting up, as I tried to untangle myself from the sheets. They were drenched in sweat.

"Just a nightmare, sorry," I said, my mind still a little muddled. I rubbed my nose, straight and unbroken.

"Just a nightmare he says!" Broch said. "You're lucky it's just the three of us up here, you could have woken an entire tower with that screaming."

"You sure you're ok?" Thain asked, concern etched in his eyes.

"I'm sure, I just need to get some fresh air. Thanks for waking me up."

The two of them shuffled back to their beds while I got up, stripped my bedsheets, and changed out of my night clothes. It was still early, but I knew I wouldn't be getting any more sleep.

With the mess hall closed for another few hours, I decided to take another jog around the lake, letting the exercise clear my mind. Each time my mind floated back to the nightmare, I ran quicker. I ended up doing three laps of the lake before my body forced me to stop. My legs were on fire from the exertion and my body was covered in sweat. I bent double, hands on my knees, gulping in air as I tried to recover my breath. Exhausted and limping, I walked to the far end of the lake, where there was the most cover from potential onlookers in the academy and closed my eyes. Lifting my left hand, I found a disruption in the air where the boundary between us and the Aspect was weak, and traced long sweeping patterns through it, arcing them down towards the lake surface, where ice began to spiderweb out from the shoreline. As before I kept a loose connection to the Aspect, and with no tether to soak up the excess, warmth ran through my body, replacing the energy spent from my earlier exercise. The heat the lake had soaked up and stored in its waters was now replenishing my tired muscles. The rise and fall of my chest slowed as breath became easier to hold. Not wanting to create too much ice, I severed the connection. Satisfied, and with a clear head, I cleaned in the deserted baths before fetching three portions of food from the mess hall, to take back to my friends by way of thanks.

The entrance hall was filled with clusters of monks and students, moving this way or that to their afternoon classes, feet slapping against the smooth stone floor, sending hundreds of echoes bouncing off the barrelled ceiling. I was on my way to the eastern wing, for my first session with Kit. Broch and Thain had been as surprised as I was when I'd told them of my conversation with the Primus. The boundary between Aspectors and Seer's had always been finely drawn, yet another piece of this grand pattern the Primus was talking about that I appeared to be interrupting. I saw a few questioning glances as I walked into the corridor towards the monk's enclave, but paid them no mind. The further in I walked, the more I was reminded of the temple back in the Eastern Garrison. The smell of incense filled the air, and there was a heavier silence that seemed to mute the echoes from the entrance hall quicker than distance should have allowed. The further down the corridor I went, the dimmer the lights got, until an artificial twilight surrounded me, punctuated by the steady glow of soft lanterns. I drew to a halt as a familiar hooded figure strode to meet me.

"It's good to see you again, Kehlem," Kit said, trying to keep his voice level.

"You too, Do'Seer," I said, keeping the proper honorific.

A half smile touched his lips at that.

"Follow me," he said, walking deeper down the corridor. A wave of dejavu hit me, and for a moment, I was back in the Eastern Garrison, lost and confused at having just left Themia. I shook my head, trying to physically clear it, and trailed behind Kit as he led me into a small room.

This room was decorated like an extension of the corridor, simple stone walls surrounded us, and smooth flagstone beneath us. Two thin cushions were set on the floor, and Kit gestured for us to sit opposite each other on them. As we lowered ourselves onto the floor, Kit lowered his hood, and smiled at me.

"So," he said, "the Primus has already explained why he wants you to learn some of the basics of Seeing. The plan is you'll meet me here twice a week for sessions, and hopefully I'll be able to instruct you."

"Do we know why the Primus has asked you to teach me?" I asked. "No offense," I quickly proffered, after realising how that must sound.

"None taken. The Primus was surprised by the tale of you healing Broch's foot with a full form pattern of healing. I think his hope is that by having the same teacher, we may be able to recreate some of that success."

"Fair enough. So where do we start?"

"Well, the first step, you will need to learn how to meditate which will not be as easy as it sounds. Once we've got that sorted, we can move on to the next step."

"Oh, that's fine. My father taught me how to clear my mind when I was younger," I said, dismissively.

"This isn't the same thing. If you assume it is, it's just going to make these sessions harder."

I listened dutifully to Kit's instructions, which seemed mostly around correcting my breathing, something I didn't even know you could do wrong. There were a hundred thing's Kit corrected, or pulled me up on throughout the session. I started to get frustrated. How could anyone meditate when they're only allowed to sit and breathe in a single, specific way. As we sat in silence, my body seemed to rebel against me. Constant itches rummaged across my skin, compelling me to react. Each time I moved, I could feel Kit's frustration at my lack of self-control. Even when I was able to sit still for ten minutes at a time, I was so distracted by thoughts of Eva, patterns or even the thought of food, that I barely managed any actual meditation. Finally, Kit called an end to the session, and I jumped to my feet, eager to spend some of the nervous energy that had been building. I helped Kit put the cushions back against the wall and I noticed Kit's demeanour shifted a little too. His mannerisms became softer, and he seemed less tense. I had to remember this was hard on him as well. I shouldn't let my frustrations out on him.

"There's a book the Primus has asked for you to read," Kit said as we strode to the exit together. "You should be able to get it from the library. It's called the Ars Exemplar."

"What's it about?" I asked, falling in step with Kit.

He smiled at me warmly. "Everything. You could say it's a history of the Aspect. It's one of the core tomes of the Seer monks."

We drew to a halt at the edge of the corridor, and Kit left me to go get some food with a promise to find me later in the evening. Of course, I wouldn't be able to get the book from the Seer library, so I'd have to use the student's instead. Thain had spoken to me about it briefly, explaining it as this huge ponderous room with an impenetrable sorting system and hundreds of hidden rules of etiquette. Thankfully for me, I had a friend who happened to be working most days in the student's library as punishment.

"Kehlem!" Broch's loud drawl reverberated across the silent, dusty room. I'd just stepped into the library, barely taking in my surroundings before Broch evidently had spotted me first. A chorus of tutt's and huffs called out in response in the twilight like a bizarre dusk chorus. The student's library appeared to have a similar layout to the Seer's, with a single reception desk at the opposite end of the room behind which a wealth of shelves stacked with ponderous tomes spread behind. Armchairs, desks and tables were scattered between entrance and reception, where students sat by themselves in deep study. By each chair a lamp was fitted, each bearing a clever shade, directing a soft light only onto the pages of the book held in the student's hand. With the rest of the room in shade, the room appeared like some strange forest glen lit by fireflies, moving slowly as a student adjusted the direction of their lamp.

A figure, which I assumed to be Broch's came striding from behind the reception desk and over to greet me.

"What are you doing here?" Broch asked, voice still cringingly loud.

"I'm looking for a book," I whispered back, distracted. It wasn't like Broch to be this enthused or energetic about anything, let alone the sight of me.

"Of course, of course," Broch said. "Oh! I forgot, how was the Seer's class?"

The pointed looks and coughs were becoming too much for me, and I was about to suggest Broch lower his voice, when I noticed another figure from the reception desk striding over to us. As the figure got closer, it resolved to reveal a woman, probably a few years older than Broch and I.

"A word," she hissed, grabbing Broch's elbow and pulling him to the door. Her lilting accent confirmed her to be a Vin.

I followed the two of them out of the library and into the now startlingly bright corridor, blinking spots out from my eyes.

"Look, if I have to suffer you working with me, the least you can bloody well do is keep your voice down. Some of us work here by choice. Anyone would think the Primus was punishing me by sending you here," the woman admonished.

Something about her demeanour told me this wasn't the first time she'd had to have this conversation with Broch.

She turned, noticing me for the first time. "Who's your friend?" She asked.

"Oh, how rude of me," Broch said, visibly relieved to change the subject. "Adléta, this is my good friend Kehlem." He gestured expansively to me with his hand, as if introducing the two of us at a ball. "And Kehlem, this darling is Adléta, a most formidable librarian and physician in training."

"What have I told you about calling me darling?" Adléta demanded, turning once more on Broch.

Broch looked completely lost. "Erm…don't…?" he ventured.

"I have not been anyone's 'darling' since I was five years old. Unless you plan on introducing all your male friends as darling, I see no reason why I must suffer it."

Broch stammered a little bit, clearly flustered.

Adléta sighed. "Just don't do it again." She turned to look at me, and held out a hand. "Pleasure to meet you Kehlem"

I shook it. "Pleasure is all mine. I think that's the first time I've seen my lordling friend flustered."

"Oh please," Broch said, rolling his eyes at the two of us. "What was this book you were after?" he asked, changing the subject.

"It's called the Ars Exemplar," I said.

Adléta raised her eyebrows. "And why exactly would you be looking for that particular book?"

I flushed a little, embarrassed at stepping on another hidden etiquette. "I'm having lessons with the Seers. One of the monks asked me to read it. For my studies."

"The Seers are teaching you one on one? And asked you to read that book?" Adléta seemed almost offended.

"Don't be so prickly, it's true," Broch said, interrupting. "The Primus has asked Kehlem to be trained in Seeing. I'm sure if you wanted, you could speak directly with the Abbott to check?"

It was Adléta's turn to flush. "You're right," she said, and turned to me. "I'm sorry Kehlem. It's not my business to poke into yours. I was just surprised." She did seem genuinely apologetic.

"It's fine, don't worry about it," I said, relieved to not have offended her.

"It's just the Ars Exemplar, it's a monk study book. Only monks ever take it out, and usually they would use their own library. We have a copy here of course, but I don't think a single student has ever taken it out," Adléta said, leading us back into the library and lowering her voice.

"Is it really that unusual for an Aspector to study Seeing?" I asked. The Primus had said as much, but I'd thought him to be exaggerating.

"It's unheard of," Adléta whispered, "and if I were you, I would keep it to yourself. Some *people* may not take too kindly if they found out." She gave me a pointed look, and then eased it with a warmer, half smile. "I personally don't give a damn, but some Vins have a stick up their arse about this kind of thing."

I snorted, taken completely by surprise and earned myself some of my own tutt's.

"Wait here," Adléta said smiling, and disappeared behind the desk.

"While she's gone, I'm going to sneak off," Broch whispered to me. "Fancy going for a drink tonight?"

"Absolutely." It would be good to get some fresh air and get out of the academy for a little while.

"See if you can find our monk friend as well, and we'll drag him with us. I seem to recall owing you both a drink."

We both heard footsteps from behind the desk growing closer, and Broch darted off, leaving me alone, leaning against the wooden desk.

"Here it is," Adléta said, dropping a thick leather-bound book on the desk between us with a thump. A cloud of dust erupted from the sides as it fell, swirling in the amber lights. Adléta looked up, and noticed the Broch shaped nothingness next to me. She let out a heavy sigh. "He's disappeared, hasn't he?"

I nodded, but figured it was a rhetorical question. "Give him time," I suggested. "He's a good person when you get to know him. You just have to rub through that privileged exterior."

Adléta didn't seem convinced. She pushed her long brown hair out of her eyes, and tied it behind her head. "You can't take that book out of the library, but when you're done with it, I'll put it aside for you, so no one else can take it out. Come find me when you're done. It's nice to meet you Kehlem."

Before I could give her my thanks, she'd disappeared back behind the shelves, pulling a cart of books behind her.

I retreated to a spare seat. Turning on the lamp beside me, I sank deep into the cushioned comfort of the chair and began to leaf through the pages of the book. It was heavy set with tiny scrawls of writing. Broken up into sections, the introduction seemed mostly to repeat what Kit, Themia and the Abbot had already said about the Aspect, just in a more formal style. Every so often a full page would be set aside for an intricate drawing; a vista of a farm with workhands gathering a harvest of some unknown crop, an intricate map of a city and even a crude anatomy of an adult male. In each of these drawings there was a common theme; amongst the shading and the linework was a single, thin, gold-leaf thread which swirled down city streets and across alleys, branching across arterial systems and through fields of grain. I sat and stared at these drawings for what felt like hours, and for the first time I began to feel the true weight of the Aspect, and grasping the edge of the belief that the Seer's held.

"How are you getting on?"

The voice shook me awake. I'd been staring at one of the drawings, my eye's absentmindedly following the golden pattern amongst the ink. How long had I been here? Looking around, the library was mostly deserted. Stood across from me was Kit, his heavy robe still swaying slightly.

I thumbed through the pages I'd read up to. Barely twenty pages in.

"Not bad?" I ventured.

Kit laughed. "I figured I'd check if you were still here. I didn't want you to try and struggle your way through it all in one night. It's a ponderous tome."

"What time is it?"

"Just after sixth bell."

Sixth bell? I'd been here hours. How had time slipped past so quickly?

"I'm glad you caught me, I probably would have slept here otherwise. Actually," I said, remembering Broch's suggestion, "you'll be glad you found me as well. Our lordling friend has offered to take us for drinks tonight, if you're up for it? As long as that's allowed?" I had no idea how keen the Abbot would be on the Seer monks mingling with the students.

Kit waived his hand eagerly. "It's fine, there's no rules against it. Drinking isn't forbidden."

"Great," I said, easing myself to my feet. "Let's go find Broch, let me just return this book."

I walked over to the reception desk and rang the bell, unsure where Adléta was. The sound of footsteps came from the hidden shadows of the library shelves, followed shortly after by Adléta herself. How far back did those shelves go?

"Hi, I just wanted to drop this off." I set the book on the table with a light *thump*. "Wasn't sure where I should leave it."

"Oh, thank you," Adléta said. "I'll put this aside with a note, so you don't have any issues from other librarians next time you pick it up."

A sudden thought crossed my mind. "I don't suppose the library is looking for any more workers, are they?"

Adléta gave me a sympathetic smile, "Fees, right?"

I nodded.

"I'm afraid your friend took the last open spot, although if it's any consolation, the Seers have ensured he doesn't get paid for his time."

"Black damn it," I swore. Unlike Broch I would have loved to have worked in the library.

"You should see if anyone is looking for help in the town," she suggested with a shrug. "They're well used to students looking for work. Some even will pay directly to the bursar."

"Thanks for the tip," I said, "I appreciate it."

"Any time," she smiled.

We found Broch studying a book in the dormitory, lazing across one of the beaten-up armchairs, with Thain making some notes at a desk he'd had from upstairs and pushed next to the arch window. As Kit and I entered the room, Broch looked up from his book.

"If it isn't my favourite Do'Seer!" He called, sitting himself upright.

Kit winced. "Just Kit will do when we're out of earshot of the other monks."

Broch shrugged his shoulders. "Fine by me. You both ready for drinks?"

"Absolutely," I said. I was drained from both the session with Kit and then reading that book in the library. My head felt stuffy and full, and all I wanted to do was think of other, lighter things.

"You coming as well Thain?" I asked. I hated the thought of him feeling left out, and the look he gave me when I asked him made my heart sing, the joy that blossomed on his face. He lept off his chair, and came bounding over.

"As long as I'm not intruding!" he said.

"Of course not. Thain, Kit, Kit, Thain," I said by way of introduction to my two friends. Kit nodded his head.

"I've heard a lot about you," Thain said, falling in line with the rest of us as we made our way to the lift contraption.

"I'm sure whatever Broch told you was greatly exaggerated," Kit said laughing as he stepped into the lift and out of view.

There were of course no taverns on site in the academy, but thankfully the wonderful town of Isale was well familiar with living next to a student population, and so the four of us took the winding path down the mountainside to the town below. On the way Thain taught Kit the new verses he'd made for 'The One-footed Philanderer', and the rest of us joined in on the chorus, no doubt terrifying any wildlife that hid in the woods that surrounded our path down to the tavern.

We found a place based on Broch's recommendation, just off the centre square. It was warm and quiet inside, lit by candles which had been stuck onto each table by globs of wax. It reminded me so much of the Rosen Pyre. The smell of spilt ale and the gentle hum of the tavern patrons talking brought about an ache within my heart that made me think of home.

We found a table and chairs by the hearth and Broch raised his hand to get the barkeeps attention.

"So, how's your first week been?" Kit asked me.

"Stressful," I said. "I've probably ran more in this one week than I have in my entire life."

"Hello?" Broch called loudly, waving his arms at the tall, be-aproned man in the corner.

"At least you're not collapsing on the floor after each run anymore," Thain offered.

"Finally," Broch said as the innkeep made his glacial progress over to us. "I thought you said you were from a tiny village? I'd always pictured you chopping wood and lighting fires. I'd have thought running a few laps around a lake was nothing new for you."

"I wasn't an outdoorsy kid. The first time I tried to lay my own fire, Eva had to re do it all, and teach me how to do it properly."

"What can I get you?" The barkeep asked, his voice like deep rich mahogany, which suited his tree-like frame. A bald, cherry-oak head sat betwixt two of the biggest ears I had ever seen.

"Four ales my good sir. Nothing fancy, whatever's on tap. You can just place it on my tab."

The innkeep leaned down to squint at Broch. "Oh," he grunted, "It's you. Thought you were dead. Fine. Four ales."

"And sometime this month would be good."

The innkeep froze mid step. I was suddenly very aware that his hands looked to be twice as large as Broch's slender face.

I cringed, holding my breath. Thain and Kit eyed each other, their eyebrows raised.

Eventually, the innkeeper huffed. "We're short staffed," he said, and turned away, retreating back to the bar.

"Bloody hell," Thain complained.

"What?" Broch asked, turning to look at us. For his part, he did seem genuinely confused.

"I better go apologise," I said, getting to my feet, "Before he gobs in all our drinks."

I made my way quickly over to the bar where the innkeeper was pouring our ale. "Sorry about that," I called. "My friend, he's a bit..." I stopped, not sure what I was about to say.

"Noble?" the man grunted.

I laughed, "Aye. Noble." I held out my hand, "I'm Kehlem."

For a moment, the man stared at me, but then he reached out with his shovel-like hands and gripped my own, enveloping mine entirely. "Brin," he said, simply.

"Brin, nice to meet you." I gave him my most charming smile. "I hear you're short staffed."

Five minutes later I returned to our table carrying our four tankards of ale.

"What was all that about?" Thain asked.

"Did our tree of an innkeeper take a liking to your pretty face?" Broch asked.

"Actually," I said, setting the tankards down on the table, "you're looking at Brin's tavern's latest barmaid. Or barsevernt?" I looked at Thain, "What's the male version?"

"I think it's just 'barmaid'," Thain smiled, taking a sip from his ale.

"Regardless!" I ploughed on as my friends laughed, "For working here most evenings, our friend Brin there will pay thirty silvers direct to the bursar each month."

My friends cheered, but I held up a finger. "However, as I have already paid a month in advance, and Brin would like his fresh barmaid to start tomorrow, I struck him a deal." I strode back to the bar, and returned quickly, thumping a quart barrel of ale onto the table top. It had been tapped of course, and was already half empty. But there was enough ale left in there to stand us all five or six rounds each.

Broch stood up, and placed his hand on his heart. "Kehlem, I think I may just love you."

"To Kehlem and his pretty face!"

"To Kehlem and his ale!"

"Kehlem the barmaid!"

I bowed to my friends, my cheeks burning from grinning, and took a long sip from my tankard while Thain and Broch eyed up the barrel.

"I hear you all but set the Pattern Trial room ablaze on your first day," Kit said, turning his head to look at me.

"His second pattern of Destructia is insane. I've never seen anything like it!" Thain interjected, spilling some of his ale as he gestured eagerly with his arms.

"Is that so?" Kit asked, wiping the ale off the table with the edge of his robe.

"He's exaggerating," I said, patting Thain on the arm.

"I am not! I thought Frennic was going to shit himself when he saw your pattern that first day."

I rolled my eyes, but all the talk of the Destructia patterns gave me an idea. "Say, Kit. have you ever heard of patterns being changed slightly so that it changes what it was originally intended to do?" I asked, trying to keep my tone casual. Thain's eyes watched us intently as he understood the real question I was asking.

"Why?" Kit asked quickly. "What did you do?"

"No, nothing," I said. I hastily tried to think of another way of asking the same questions. "I was just curious. I'm having to learn the Destructia pattern one, you know the one that can charge a tether"

"The endothaumergic pattern?" Kit asked.

"Sure, that one." I had no idea what its actual name was, but hoped we were talking about the same pattern.

"What about it?"

"Well at the moment, whenever I use the pattern, I can sense the energy just passing straight through me and into the tether. But I can almost feel like there's another pattern, one that the Aspect is trying to show me, linked to the first."

Thain and Broch were sitting quietly watching Kit now as well, obviously equally interested.

"Well, it's not really something that will be taught to you until you've gotten your permanent tethers…"

He trailed off, although something in his tone told me he would continue, if we offered him reassurance.

"We won't tell anyone else. It's just out of curiosity," I said. I looked over at the other two. "Right?"

"Oh, of course."

"Not a word from me."

Kit looked around the table. "Fine, but keep this quiet. I don't really fully understand it, as I'm still learning to teach Aspecting myself. The thing you've got to remember is that the patterns you're learning, they're like a language, words that are used to show your intent to the Aspect. But they aren't the only patterns."

I had to stop myself from leaning forward, trying to keep a casual composure to not spook Kit. He carried on regardless, his cheeks rosy from the fire and ale.

"The patterns taught by the monks have been collected and studied for centuries. But it is known, amongst the Seers at least, that there are many more patterns, variations on the ones taught here as well as more *esoteric* patterns, ones whose intent we could never hope to decipher."

"So why did the Academy settle on the ones they currently teach?" Thain interjected, drunken eagerness plain in his voice.

If it weren't for his earnest grin I could have thumped him for stopping Kit midflow.

Thain's eagerness obviously reminded Kit where he was and who he was speaking to. He leaned back in his chair, elbows lifting off the wooden table.

"We stick to The Book of Patterns. It's been agreed and unmodified for centuries," Kit said. He looked at me. "To experiment and to change patterns from those that have been prescribed. That is forbidden. I trust you understand."

The atmosphere between our group grew noticeably chillier, as Broch looked anywhere but Kit and I, and Thain gave me a worried look.

"Of course," I said, keeping my voice level. "It was purely academic," I lied. Nevertheless, Kit seemed satisfied.

"Huh," Broch said, breaking the tension. "Well, you don't have to worry about me. I can barely manage with the patterns I've got."

"Oh, come on, that's not true," Thain protested. "Everyone knows how great you are! You could get your tether anytime you like."

To my surprise Broch flushed a little at the compliment, and the two of them bickered back and forth, meanwhile I sat back and digested what Kit had said. What did he mean, 'esoteric patterns'? What was it that the empire didn't want us learning?

That evening, by unspoken agreement, we made it our mission to reach the very bottom of the ale barrel. There was a moment, where we were all sitting around the table which had been filled with our empty mugs and glasses. Thain and Broch were in some deep conversation giggling like a couple of children, and Kit was, despite his inebriation, trying to explain to me something very earnestly about the nature of Seeing. I remember looking around fondly at the small friendship group I had found myself in and feeling a sense of peace. Here I was, hundreds of miles away from my hometown surrounded by some of the closest friends I had ever had. It felt good. Of course, the dull wound that was my longing for Eva was ever present, and curiously, the drunker I got, the more keenly I felt it.

I assume Thain sensed something of what I was feeling as he suddenly chippered up, nudged Broch who was currently snoozing in the crook of his arm and, regaled us with the time his pet cat back home bought a live rat into his parent's shop, much to the horror of the gentlefolk and merchants who frequented his family's business. Apparently, the wife of one of the merchants fainted at such a wretched sight. Despite the increasing inebriation of our group, Kit somehow managed to pull a song off the cuff to commemorate Thain's now dead pet, in which he — to laborious and impressive detail — told the brave tale of Scarpi the housecat, and his fight with the be-tailed Sir Dreadtooth. In a deep baritone, he could have given many a minstrel a pause of, if not thought, then at least mild concern. When he finished we howled and hammered the table with delight. Broch bought Kit a tankard of his favourite ale, and Thain even had a few tears in his eyes and a sad, drunk smile on his lips.

The night drew on and eventually, worried we would stumble down a crevasse if we were to make the walk back to the academy in our inebriated state, Brin insisted we sleep upstairs in one of his guestrooms to sleep the night off.

20

Break

The weeks during that first month I was at the academy all followed a similar routine. The first few days of the week were taken up with practicing the two Destructia patterns, progressing from sending swathes of blue fire across the lake, to trying to aim and focus the blast of energy at smaller and smaller targets, that would end up further and further away. It became a not-so friendly competition, with me trailing just behind Frennic in second place. I was no longer exhausted after each run after class and could even keep up with the bulk of the runners, although I was heavily subsidised through my nefarious use of the first Destructia pattern to help relieve some of the strain on my body. The seemingly rapid improvement in my fitness just alienated me from the rest of the class further, to the point that no one other than Thain and the Seer monk even looked in my direction during those classes.

Later in the day we would be sent to the library, instructed to study the history of the patterns we were learning with Thain and I specifically directed to learn about the history of the Vin empire. Thankfully Thain and I often had Broch to help guide us around the library and the three of us would often retreat to the study hall together, Thain and I making notes on the various calculations for direct or indirect energies required and Broch would work on his fabrication research. Then as daylight began to fade, I would bid my farewells to my friends and head down into Isale town, to

Brin's tavern. The work was hard, but Brin kept me busy enough either serving patrons or cleaning, which made the shifts go quickly. I began to realise that past his hard exterior was a gentle soul. There were many times when the evening drew to a close and business was slow where Brin would bring me a bowl of curry from the hearth pot, and a mug of ale. He'd sit opposite me, his hands cradling a wine glass, usually in silence, passing only a few comments here and there. Eventually Broch and Thain began coming down to the tavern to visit while I was working, sometimes even bringing Kit as well. They often used it as a second study space, bringing their paper and books to read. Brin would give them a hard look, and would grumble to me about 'that gaggle of rakes, rogues and reprobates', but I often caught him cleaning down their usual table if he saw them sauntering through the square, pulling extra stools to the table for the group. When the nights were quiet, I would call him over to sit with us, and while he did so begrudgingly, he would inevitably pull out a deck of cards, dealing them to us all far more deftly than you would expect for a man with hands built like bricks.

Needless to say, Brin quickly became a de facto member of our friendship group, to the point that even on my days off, we'd end up at Brin's tavern, drinking, studying and sneaking in a game of cards whenever there was a lull in business.

The second half of my week was taken up with my Seer meditations with Kit, where progress was glacial. Whether from ineffectual tutelage from his side, or more likely blind pig-headedness from mine, I was finding it almost impossible to get my mind in the place it needed to be to meditate. By the end of the month I could just about manage twenty or so minutes of quiet meditation on a good day, and zero on a bad. The bad days outnumbered the good by a hefty margin.

Blue flames roared out of my open palm, racing away from me to a straw figure that had been dropped some 80 yards away. It was the furthest target I'd tried to hit, and I already knew it was too far away. The bronze tether I wore against my wrist grew uncomfortably cold, and I cut the connection, letting the flames curl around themselves as they vanished into the air.

"Not bad," Thain said in my ear. "Better than I could have done anyway."

"Hmm." I looked over to Frennic who was standing next to me. He'd just fired his own shot which had managed to singe the edges of the target.

What was I doing wrong? What was Frennic doing right?

With the Aspecting part of the lesson drawing to a close, we all lined back up in front of the Seer monk, ready to run around the lake. But before he took the tether off the first student, he cleared his throat.

"Now that you have all finally learnt the second pattern, we shall be moving on from the lake runs."

"Oh, thank Martyr," I heard Thain whisper behind me.

"Learning to fight with Aspecting is only half of your tutelage. You must also learn to fight without it. We will begin today with simple sparring, hand to hand and grapples, and slowly learn the basics of short sword and dagger. You will each be given a sparring partner. The safety of your partner is your primary concern. No direct blows to the face, no reckless throws to the ground. Am I understood?"

A round of slightly bewildered 'Yes, Do'Seer's echoed from the lakeside.

"Good. These are the techniques I would like you to practice. Kehlem, to the front."

I jumped at the mention of my name, startled and walked cautiously to the front of the line.

"Right, now stand here." He pulled my tunic so I stood opposite him. "Yes good. Now, mirror my stance," he said.

I shifted my feet to match the same stance he was standing in, one foot pointed towards me, the other pointed to the side, and lowered myself a little so my knees were bent.

The monk bought his hands up, close and guarding his face. "Mid body jabs," he said, and he threw his fists one after the other in straight lines towards my trunk.

I flinched, not able to help my reaction, but he'd already pulled his punches short. Laughter rippled through the audience. Cursing myself, I set myself back down into the stance, and tried to keep still.

The monk reset himself opposite me. Raising his hands again he barked, "Double leg takedowns." He dived towards me, quicker than I would have thought possible for a man of his size. Again, I reacted instinctively, bringing my hands up to block whatever he was planning to do. He ducked underneath my guards, grabbed both my thighs and with the momentum he'd built from charging me, tipped me ever so slightly. It was more than enough. Before I knew it, I was falling and had hit the ground with a heavy thud. I wheezed as the air was knocked out of my lungs. Another smattering of laughter. I struggled back to my feet, wheezing. The monk had turned away from me, and was looking back at the class.

"I want you to practice those two for now, punches and throws. Punches to the trunk only. Take it in turns attacking and defending. You're paired as per the current standings for the second pattern targeting."

Oh shit. That meant I was sparring against Frennic. He turned to me, realising the same thing, and gave me a wide smile telling me this was just the opportunity he'd been waiting for. The class quickly disintegrated into pairs and the Seer monk circled around the group to watch and offer suggestions on the sparring. Unfortunately, it seemed the route he was taking would leave Frennic and I alone for a while.

We both fell into the same stance the Seer had demonstrated and watched each other. I was about to ask if he minded if I attacked first, but before the words could leave my mouth he had already launched at me. With a sinking feeling, I noted his foot work looked very practiced.

Ah fuck.

Frennic was uncomfortably close to me within two strides, and shot an extraordinarily fast right-hand jab which connected heavily with my upper stomach. The wind rushed out of me once more. I gasped for breath. As he brought his right fist back, his left curled around and hooked me straight into the side of my ribs. Shocked by the speed and precision of his violence, I staggered backwards, stunned and barely able to keep my guard up. Frennic took the chance, charged forward and grabbed one of my legs and lifted me quickly. Before I knew it, I was on my back looking up to the blue sky. I took a second to catch my breath and eased myself back to my feet, my ribs aching. Either he was excellent, or I was shit. Probably the answer lay somewhere in the middle of that scale. The monk was still circling around, so not wanting to give Frennic another chance to lay into me again, I dived forward and threw a clumsy jab aimed at his stomach which he easily blocked by sweeping one of his hands down from his guard. Determined to land a punch, I threw a wide right hook, which connected with the meat of his left arm. Wanting to press the advantage I stepped forwards and aimed a straight left jab towards his chest which he somehow dodged by twisting his upper torso, causing me to lose balance. He grabbed my overextended wrist and yanked me forwards. As I fell to the floor he casually twisted his knee so that as I fell, my nose collided directly with the hardest part of his kneecap. I heard a sickening pop, and felt a wetness spill down my face. I fell onto the grass face first tasting iron. My face was on fire. I pushed myself to my knees and tried to pinch off the blood flow from my nose. Through my watering eyes I saw the Seer monk approaching.

"What happened?" he demanded.

"The fool threw a punch he couldn't land. He slipped and headbutted my knee. Honestly Do'Seer, he'd be a better jester than Aspector," Frennic laughed.

The bastard wasn't even out of breath.

The monk eyed Frennic a moment, before looking down at me. "Go back to the academy. Get yourself cleaned up," he said, dismissing me. "What are the rest of you looking at? Get back to work!"

I struggled to my feet, and with my head down I walked slowly back up to the academy, avoiding the gaze of the onlookers.

I made my way to the Medica wing, ignoring the pointed stares from students, Foclir and monks alike as I pinched my nose. The blood had thankfully stopped pouring, and was beginning to dry on my face, leaving a horrible sticky residue across my lips and chin. Now that the adrenaline was fading, the throbbing pain in my nose slowly escalated. I knocked on the door to the main Medica reception, and let myself in. It was a large quiet room with some beds and benches laid out in equal spaces. A monk came over and without a word grabbed my chin, inspecting my nose, twisting my face this way and that.

"Take a seat on the bench. I'll be back in a moment," he said, abruptly dropping my chin and walking towards one of the doors that littered the reception.

I eased myself down onto the bench, my ribs also beginning to graduate to a sharp pain. I prodded them carefully, but they didn't feel broken, thank the Martyr. Broken ribs were a pain to heal.

The monk returned with a young Vinnish student, he'd just pulled out of class. A dark young girl, probably three years my junior. She copied the monk's inspection, and rolled my face left and right inspecting my broken nose.

"Are you ready?" The monk asked.

"Mhm-hm" I said, trying to concentrate anywhere else but the pain radiating in my nose.

"Not you," the monk said testily.

"I am," the girl said, closing her eyes and raising her left hand. Curious to see what pattern she would use, I watched as she danced her hand hesitantly through a pattern I didn't recognise. Unfamiliar as it was, the more I watched, the more frustrated I got. It was like I knew where the pattern wanted to take her, but she was resisting, flexing a finger too early, or sweeping her hand slowly when it should be fast. As clear as any of the other patterns I had learnt, I knew what this pattern wanted to be.

She drew the pattern to a close and touched her Aspected hand to my broken nose. A warmth spread through my skin, and deep into the meat of my face, stretching and uncoiling through tissue and sinew. There was a sharp tug as my nose reset. I grunted in pain and my eyes watered from the sharpness of it. She withdrew her hands, and it was over.

"Not bad," the Monk said to his student. "Ideally there should be no pain in the patient with a second form of Pattern three, but that's something to work on next time."

"Yes, Do'Seer," the girl said meekly.

"What are you still doing?" The monk asked, looking at me. "You can leave."

A little shaken by the whole experience, I left the Medica and made my way back to the dormitory. That was the oddest interaction with a physician

I'd ever experienced. I'd had it drilled into me since I was a child that actual healing makes up only half of a physician's work. The other half is how they approach their patients, informing them of what they're doing, calming them and providing a gentle touch. It disturbed me to know that the Academy was training Aspected physicians to be so detached from their patients.

Was that how they treat everyone? Or was the student and monk purposefully dismissive because I was Caserean?

Lost in thought, I stepped on to the elevator that would take me to the dormitory. I also couldn't get the pattern I'd seen out of my head. It had wormed its way into my mind as I'd watched. More important, I could see all the clunky mistakes the young Vin student had made. It wasn't the first time since I'd arrived at the academy that I wished I could have been learning Medica rather than Destructia.

"Martyr's charred body, what happened to you?" Broch demanded.

I had just walked into the dormitory. Broch and Kit sat opposite each other, both of them with looks of horror on their face.

"Huh?" I asked, confused. I lifted my fingers to my nose, worried the Medica student had set my nose wrong. No, it felt straight. I let my fingers drop, but then realised she hadn't bothered cleaning the blood off my face. I'd been walking around with a huge bloody stripe drying down my lips and chin.

"Oh," I said, walking over to a small water butt where we kept some drinking water. "Frennic decided to give me a lesson in arsery." I swirled a rag in the water, and then lifted it, washing my face, wringing the bloody water from the rag over an empty mug. I kept cleaning until the water ran clear. I joined my friends in the centre and explained to them what happened. Kit seemed appalled, but Broch remained uncharacteristically silent.

"You must speak to your trainer Kehlem, explain what happened. You shouldn't be partnered up with Frennic again." Kit said.

"It won't make a difference," Broch interrupted.

"What do you mean?" Kit asked.

"The monk isn't an idiot. Especially that one. He knew exactly what happened."

"That doesn't make any sense, why would he not have punished Frennic if he knew he broke Kehlem's nose on purpose?"

"Kit, you're a good friend, but you're blessedly naive sometimes. Look at us, look at where we are. Caserean Aspector's aren't exactly a celebrated population here at the academy. The monks turn a blind eye to this kind of stuff. Some of them actively encourage it."

"That doesn't make any sense," Kit blustered. "The Primus wouldn't allow it."

"The Primus is just as big of a part of it as everyone else!" Broch said, raising his voice. He seemed genuinely angry. "Do you not think it strange," he said, "that Kehlem learnt a full form pattern of healing in less than half an hour, without a fully trained teacher, and yet the academy saw fit to only teach him Destructia?"

"The Primus has his reasons!" Kit shouted back, angry as well.

"And while we're at it, explain to me why Vin Irudur students can learn more than one school at once, while us lowly Casereans are stuck with a single school?"

Vinnish students can learn multiple schools? That was news to me. Kit looked between me and Broch, looking perhaps for some support. I had no heart to offer it to him.

"That was part of the accords!" Kit said, rising to his feet. "I shan't sit here and listen to you spout this nonsense." He stormed to the lift, slamming the door behind him, the sound of which echoed briefly around the stone walls of the lounge. Broch rolled his eyes at me and lay back down across his arm chair.

"Is it true? Vinnish students can learn multiple schools?" I asked

Broch nodded.

A familiar seed of rage sprouted in my gut. My time at the academy so far had not been at all how Themia had led me to believe. I realised now she had described it through the lens of a privilege I, and my fellow countrymen, were not privy to. I wasn't going to get the shit kicked out of me each week for the trainer monk to look on with a blind eye. I thought back to the awkward pattern the young Vinnish Medica had used, my mind's eye seeing the connections that she should have made.

"Let's wait for Thain to get back from lessons," I said, absentmindedly to Broch. "There's something I want to discuss with you both."

21

The Scribe

"So, you're telling me, you've both been able to modify a pattern?" Broch asked.

I looked over at Thain, and we nodded in unison. A summer storm lashed rain against the window in our dormitory, and there was a gentle tattoo of rain heard on the wooden roof above us. Thain had lit the fire to dry off some of his clothes after getting caught in the storm.

"I've been thinking about it, and the modification we made to the pattern, I think with a slight change, we could figure out how to direct the energy elsewhere," I said, looking intently at Broch.

"Well, what good would that do?" Broch asked.

"You study Fabrica patterns, right? You know how to engrave patterns, and imbue metal, right?"

"Of course, but what's that got to do with —"

"And I bet if pushed, you could make your own iron or bronze temporary tether."

"In principle of course, but they wouldn't do any good without an actual physical tether to tie it to," Broch protested, not understanding what I was getting at.

"You want to make one, don't you?" Thain asked, looking at me.

I smiled at him. "Exactly. There's nothing stopping us making our own tether. We could each have our own temporary tether. We could even teach each other the patterns we've learned from the different schools. Why should Vin Irudur get to decide what we can and can't learn?"

Broch looked stunned. Thain looked eager.

"What if we get caught?" Broch demanded. "Do you know what they'll do to us?"

"Do you?" I shot back at him. "Look, I don't know about you, but I'm sick of my life being in the hands of other people. Why should people who don't even Aspect, dictate to us what we can and can't learn?"

Broch did not look convinced. "It's not that simple, Kehlem. You need energy to make the tether in the first place. We'd need a tether to make a tether."

It was now or never. I quickly stood up, and walked over to the fire place. I took a sharp knife I'd grabbed from the mess hall for this very purpose, and slashed myself across the back of my hand. Both my friends recoiled in horror.

"What the fuck Kehlem?" Broch cried.

I ignored them, and closed my eyes, ignoring the stinging on my hand. I lifted my left hand, and let it dart quickly through the first Destructia pattern, keeping a loose hold on the fabric of the Aspect. As I finished the pattern, I thrust my hand into the fireplace, straight into the middle of the flames. I heard a sharp intake of breath as my friends reacted to my madness. But there was no burning, no pain. There was a warmth, but it was gentle, and it coursed through my hand, and into my body. Some tried, and failed to spill into the Aspect, instead reverberating uncomfortably on the ineffable boundary, threatening to shake my grip, but I held tight. Most of the energy poured into me. As the fire waned, an uncomfortable warmth spread through my whole body. My heart was beginning to beat faster and faster, and sweat was soaking into my clothes. I smelled smoke as the fire fully extinguished. I immediately dove into another pattern, the healing pattern shown to me during the Pattern Trial. I touched my left hand to my cut on the right. It slowly stitched itself closed. Continuing into the next pattern, I used the first form only of the second Destructia pattern, and sent a jet of flame back into the fireplace, working hard to limit the amount of heat and fire I was producing so as not to set the dormitory alight. I cut the stream quickly, not wanting to spend any of my own energy. I opened my eyes. I felt good. My heart was again beating at a normal pace, and the sweating had ceased. Thain and Broch on the other hand, could not have looked more ill. Both were pale, looking at me with a mixture of horror and awe.

"What did you just do?" Thain asked.

"How are you not dead?" Broch managed to stammer out.

"I just cut out the middle man," I explained. "I figure that all a tether is, either the temporary bracelets, or a full tattoo, is just a way of bridging back to an energy source over distance. I'm correct aren't I Broch?"

"Well, yes, the main purpose of the pattern you can find on any tether is to allow energy to skim along the boundary of the Aspect..." he trailed off. "I still don't understand how you aren't dead. You shouldn't have been able to use that much energy without the Aspect killing you."

"The Aspect had nothing to take back," I said, simply. "I didn't use any energy from the Aspect. I took the energy from the fire, and stored it within me, using that modified first pattern. I just tapped into that excess energy for the pattern of healing and then the Destructia pattern. As long as you don't hold on to the energy for too long, and don't pull too much, you should be fine."

I flopped down onto the arm chair opposite them both, grinning from ear to ear.

"Don't you get what this means?" I asked. "If we can do that with what Thain and I already know, then we can use that to make our own tethers. I can teach you all that I know about healing patterns, Broch you can teach us Fabrica, and Thain can teach you Destructia."

There was a stunned silence for a moment.

"What are we even going to tether to?" A simple, but obvious question.

"I've thought about that. We can use the water butt," I pointed to the barrel, "as our shared tether. If we each take turns charging it when we can, then we can draw from it when we need. If we keep it up here, how will anyone know?"

"But what about the pattern, the one for the tether? Do you know it off the top of your head?" Thain asked Broch.

"It's...complicated," Broch explained. "There's different types. All of the tethers made at the academy use the same pattern, one that can be mass produced by students and Foclir. That's the pattern I know."

"Well what's the issue with that pattern?" I asked.

"They only teach us the one half, the ones that go on the actual bracelets. There's a pairing step they only teach the Foclir which binds the tether to their sources. If I just used the one I know, it wouldn't work. I know there is another pattern, one that doesn't get used anymore because it's woefully inefficient. But I don't know it, it's restricted to only the Foclir." Broch said.

"Fuck," Thain dropped heavily into his seat. "It was a good idea Kehlem."

There must be some way to get our hands on a copy of the pattern. I couldn't ask Kit, he was already skittish about telling us modifying patterns.

"Leave it with me," I said, with more confidence than I felt.

Broch and Thain looked at each other for a moment, scepticism written loudly across both their faces.

Frennic's knee connected with my inner thigh, and my leg grew numb almost immediately. I skittered back clumsily so I was out of his reach, hoping the pins and needles would dissipate from my leg quickly. It had been a week since Frennic had broken my nose, and these sparring matches had become a regular feature of our Destructia lessons. Sweat was plastering my hair against my face as the summer sun bore down on us. Frennic slowly circled around me, and I mimicked his movements, following him. In the past week of fighting, I hadn't won a single bout.

He rushed into me, side on, making his frame too slim to aim a punch at. I sent a few clumsy jabs at him anyway, trying to keep him at a distance, none of them connecting. He ducked under my exhausted guard, and grabbed my numbed leg. As he charged, he lifted it sharply, and I lost my footing, falling heavily to the floor. Frennic didn't let go as he fell, and made sure to keep my leg at an awkward angle, stretching bone and ligament almost to breaking point as he fell bodily on top of me. This had been Frennic's little game as of late. How many little tortures could he get away with, what could he sneak under the Seer's eyes. The answer was quite a lot, especially when the Seer monk in question always seems to be looking away when it happened.

"Enough!" The monk cried, and the class slowed their sparring to a halt. Frennic gave me a smile I had come to loathe. That one smile spoke more words to me than he had since I'd arrived. It told me he enjoyed this. He took pleasure in hurting me. He would keep doing it for as long as he could. And there's nothing I could do about it.

I stood up, pushing myself back to my feet, and limped over to where Thain was standing, his blond hair also slick with sweat, making it look almost transparent in the sun.

"How did your match go?" He asked, slightly out of breath.

"Well he only floored me twice this time, so perhaps I'm improving," I said, only half joking.

Thain ducked underneath my arm, supporting my weight on his shoulder so I didn't have to limp all the way back to the academy. As we made our way, I noticed that all the Vin students were walking together, except Frennic who seemed to be trailing the tightly pressed group always a few steps behind. What's that about?

"How was your bout?" I asked, tearing my eyes away from Frennic.

"That Thena is a real git," he muttered. "You know, she's a ridiculously good fighter. She's half my size but manages to beat me black and blue each time."

"Have you considered you might just be too slow?" I asked, laughing.

Thain ducked, causing me to lean heavily on my hurt leg.

"Ow, ow ow!" I said, struggling to lean my weight back onto Thain, "I get it, I'm sorry!"

"It's ok Kehlem, I'd be bitter to my friends as well if I'd lost every single fight I'd had this week," Thain said dryly.

"You know, I think you're spending too much time with Broch. I liked you a lot more when you were less sarcastic." I joked.

I'm not sure Thain realised it at the time, but he flushed ever so slightly at my comment. We walked into the entrance hall.

"You can leave me here," I said to Thain, taking my arm off of him. "I've got a meditation session with Kit. Meet you for dinner later."

"Have fun!"

I rolled my eyes at him and hobbled off into the east wing.

"You stink," Kit said, wrinkling his nose as I sat down opposite him.

"Sparring," I said by way of explanation. My thigh hurt, my groin was sore from where Frennic stretched my ligament, and to top it all off, I hadn't eaten since breakfast. I was exhausted. My sessions with Kit had continued despite the rift that had grown between him and Broch, leaving me stuck in the middle. I avoided talking about it with either of them, especially as I agreed with Broch.

"Well, you know the drill," Kit said.

I certainly did. I still hadn't made any significant process with the Seer sessions. I was able to meditate for longer now certainly, but the next step had so far eluded me.

I closed my eyes, and focused on my breath, trying to keep my back posture both straight and relaxed. By now falling into that meditative stance was becoming familiar. I listened to the sounds of my breathing, feeling the weight of the air around me against my skin. I focused on my heart's rhythm, letting it lull me into a state of relaxation.

As always, I heard Kit's voice from a distance. "Listen for the pattern," he guided. "Listen, and watch for it with your eyes."

Watch for it with your eyes. What nonsense was that. My eyes were closed, at whose instruction? How can I watch anything if my eyes are closed?

I tensed my jaw, realising I'd let myself get distracted and fall out of the meditation. This always happened. Whatever it was Kit wanted me to hear or see next was completely lost to me. May as well ask a tree to swim.

I flexed my hands to try and ease an ache that was developing in my wrists from the morning's fight. As I brought my left hand to a close, I noticed one of the familiar snags in the nothingness. It was a thinness between us and the Aspect. I let my hand linger on it for a while. My arms were resting on my crossed legs, so I hoped Kit wouldn't notice. Seeing and Aspecting were always supposed to be separate. Touching this boundary however, comforted me a little, and I could feel myself slipping back into thoughtlessness once more. For some reason, despite being sat in a cold, stony room with no windows to the outside, I felt the warmth of sunlight brush against my face. I was reminded of being sat on top of a wagon, thinking of Eva.

Eva.

Like a familiar song, the sound of her voice filled my head, as if we were just a step away from one another.

"...taxes are extortionate. Do you think it's targeted?"

The sound of her voice shocked me, and my body jolted suddenly. Was she talking to me? Before I could respond, her voice echoed through my mind once more.

"They can't do that! Veriah, this has been your business for the past twenty years, they can't force you out of it because you're not Vinnish!"

Veriah? That was her uncle's name. What was going on? Her voice drifted through my mind again, softer and quieter this time.

"There's a meeting tonight that Cera told me about. We should go, if only to figure out what's going on, see if there's anything we can do to help."

Her voice trailed off into soft echoes that whispered gently through my mind. I knew whatever had happened was over, but I savoured the moment a while longer before taking my hand away from the Aspect and opening my eyes.

Back in the meditation room, I noticed Kit was staring at me, a strange look on his face.

How long had he been watching me?

"What were you doing? Just now?" His voice was sharp, almost angry.

"Nothing," I stammered, defensive.

"Don't lie to me Kehlem!" Kit's voice rose to a shout, and he jumped to his feet. "I know you were Aspecting just now!"

"I didn't mean to!" I said defensive, jumping to my own feet. "Why are you getting so worked up? What's the big deal?"

"You need to leave Kehlem," Kit said, taking a steadying breath. "I don't have time to explain it to you, just go. I'll send for you if you need more lessons."

He was barely looking at me. What did I do wrong? I quickly walked slowly to the door, still confused. I turned back to say something, but Kit was already busy tidying away the pillows.

What did he mean, *'if'* I need more lessons'?

I walked through the empty corridors of the academy in a state of confusion. Why had Kit reacted so badly earlier? I'd never seen him lose his temper like that before. And more importantly, was that really Eva's voice that I'd heard? How was that even possible? If it was truly her voice, then something was going wrong in Mercy. I hoped she was safe.

It took me a minute to realise I'd stopped walking. I'd been so lost in my head that my body had taken over and had walked me to the library. A sudden thought crossed my mind. It's possible there might be some answers in the Ars Exemplar. I'd been reading the book on and off for the past month, and the writing remained as impenetrable as always, the authors speaking in formal riddles. But what kept drawing me back was the illustrations. They had a calming impact on me, one I could not explain. I'd find my eyes following the intricate patterns hidden just beneath the surface of the drawings, longing to understand their intent, and marvelling at the skill and prowess of the illustrator.

I stepped into the library, and was relieved to see Adléta was working today. True to her word, she'd put the book aside for me, with an explanatory note, but that didn't stop less amenable librarians giving me a hard time when I asked for it.

I stepped up to the counter while she had her back turned, and rapped my knuckles against the desk to get her attention.

"Kehlem," she said, as she turned to face me. She looked resigned, as if she'd been expecting me.

"Something the matter?" I asked, genuinely concerned. While Adléta had always been quiet, and we had spoken little, I still considered her a friend.

"We should talk. Have you got a moment?" She asked. She lifted up the counter to let me past the desk.

I stepped through, curious to see what lay behind the desk. "I was just here to pick up the Ars Exemplar."

"That's what we need to talk about. Come on, let's talk somewhere quiet."

I looked around. The library was deserted apart from one or two students buried in their work. Where could be quieter than the library? Still, I followed her past the tall shelves, into the twilight gloom of the stacks. The smell of leather, dust and dry paper became stronger, and with a heavier darkness around us, the ceiling seemed to vanish off into the unknown leaving the two of us to trek through the cathedral storage of the library. Adléta was following some invisible path, twisting left at the geographies, down a tight alleyway of recent histories and out into a clearing of travelogues. Here the shelves of books opened up, creating an artificial open roofed room within itself, complete with a table, chairs and lantern.

"What is this place?" I asked, stunned at how far back the library seemed to go.

"The student librarians have made spaces like this all through the stores. The academy's libraries are all interconnected if you go deep enough. Occasionally we need to fetch books from deep into the stores. So, these little respites were created as travel stops. They help you map out the place."

The libraries were interconnected? I struggled to picture how large that would make the library in total. The student and monk library were on opposite wings of the academy, with the study hall in between, which meant the stores must go underground, beneath the hall. And it was all filled with books. An idea brushed against the edge of my subconsciousness.

"Come on," Adléta said, sitting down at the table and thumbing the lantern on. "Take a seat."

I sat down opposite her. "What's going on?"

"I got a message, a few moments before you came in, instructing me to restrict your access to the Ars Exemplar, and taking our only copy back to the Seer library."

"Oh, for fuck sake," I gasped, exasperated. What was Kit playing at?

"What happened, Kehlem?" Adléta asked. She was looking at me sincerely.

I considered for a moment. She wouldn't have taken me down here for no reason. Could she be able to help? I decided to trust her, and told her what happened, about hearing Eva and Kit's reaction. She stayed quiet the whole time and listened patiently.

"...and I came to the library hoping to figure out why he acted so strange, but I guess I can't even look at the book anymore to figure that out." I finished, a little petulant.

"It's true I can't be seen handing the book over to you," Adléta said, each word said very carefully. "But maybe I can help fill in some gaps for you."

"I'm listening," I said.

Adléta leaned back in her chair, almost disappearing out of the small aura of light the lantern was emitting.

"The Seer's like to pretend that all Vin Irudur are united under a single banner of belief. I'm sure you've heard by now how the Aspect is the store of all energy within the world, and how everything returns there once they die."

I nodded in agreement.

"And I'm sure the Seers have gone to great lengths to tell you that the Aspect isn't sentient, that it's just a pattern, a natural force. Well, that is only one side of the coin. There are some Vin Irudur, a denomination of the Seers, that believe that the Aspect is much more than that. They believe that the Aspect is not just a source of consciousness, it *is* consciousness."

Adléta was watching me carefully for my reaction.

"You've lost me," I said, honestly.

"Those of this particular denomination believe that the Aspect created the spirit. That it created the spiritual world, which the Aspect itself resides in. They believe it to be a God. The God."

I looked at Adléta, realisation bubbling to the surface. "You believe this don't you?" I asked.

She nodded her head slightly. "The Seer's believe it to be heretical, and wish to root out any dissent. It's one of the reasons I took you so deep into the stores."

"Your secret is safe with me," I smiled. I was touched that Adléta would share such a personal, and dangerous secret with me. "But what has this got to do with what happened with me?"

"Do you believe in the Martyr?" Adléta asked.

I blinked, surprised by the non sequitur. "Not really," I said, honestly.

She rolled her eyes. "Figures, "she said. "Well, you should. Those of us that follow this belief in the Aspect, we believe in the Martyr. Except as we understand it, the Martyr was the first Aspector. The first prophet of the Aspect." Adléta cleared her throat, as if preparing herself for a sermon.

"Long before the world was created, the Aspect was born of itself. A realm of spirit, in single commune with itself, and all was in harmony. The Aspect wished to create, to share its existence with others, and so it began a pattern. A new, and strange pattern, one both beautiful and terrible. With the first design, it created the world, a lifeless rock filled with a stillness that repulsed the Aspect. With the second design, it filled the world with energy. Lava flowed beneath the rock, water flowed from the skies, and wind flowed through the air. With the third design, it created husks. Soulless plants stood fixed in the ground, where animal's bodies lay, lifeless and unmoving. Humans lay as if in permanent sleep. With the fourth and final design, the Aspect breathed itself into these husks. Humans woke from their sleep, birds flew across the sky. Insects crawled across the ground, and cows grazed on the fields. For many centuries, the world lived in peace with itself, all knowing they were connected, just as the Aspect was once whole before creation. The Aspect was well pleased, and continued the pattern it had begun at the birth of the world, to ensure the plants would still grow, the animals would still birth and the energy of the world would continue its cycle, nourishing all. But as time grew, the more people forgot about the Aspect. Humans began to create material things from what the Aspect had given them, and saw themselves as their own Gods. And before long, they forgot the Aspect entirely. Eschewing the nature of their being, they focused on their differences, and they formed tribes. Tribe warred against tribe, and the world fell into the conquerors and the conquered. Tribes became villages, villages became cities, and cities became countries. Lines were drawn in the sand, and the differences between the Aspect's people became set in stone. War was becoming commonplace, and hatred between the peoples was the single common language spoken. Seeing that its creation was in turmoil, the Aspect reacted. It added a new design to its pattern, and the first prophet was born. Like any human, she was born with a soul, given by the Aspect, except the Aspect gave this human the strength to see into the spiritual world. To glimpse at the patterns that permeate all of creation, in the hope that the prophet would remind the peoples of the land of the long-forgotten truth of the Aspect.

"But it was too late. Humans were too buried in their hatred to see the truth for what it was. There were a few that believed the woman, and listened to her teachings, but not enough to turn the tide. Enraged by their arrogance, the Aspect communed with the woman, and taught her patterns of power, patterns of nature. Allowed her to touch the spiritual, not just see it. And so, the first Aspector was created. This Aspector demonstrated feats of wonder and terror, and all who saw her wept to know the truth once more. But greed and hatred are a powerful force. And there were those who, despite the truth written so plainly for them to see, conspired against her. With treachery they stole the Aspector, bound, poisoned and blinded her, and demanded she renounce her claims. They tried to steal away her power so that they might have it for themselves. Deny the Aspect, they demanded, or be burned. Four times she rejected their demands. On the fifth they lit the pyre. The woman did not scream, did not plead, did not cry out. Despite being beaten, blinded and bound, she knew she was returning once more to the Aspect. Thus, the first Aspector was martyred. The soul of the Martyr dispersed into the Aspect, and from then on occasionally a new child would be born, with a piece of what once was the Martyr instilled within their soul. The children would be born as Aspectors, or Seers. Sometimes both. Thus, it was, and thus it will be, until the pattern ends and begins anew."

Adléta finished, and leaned forward in her chair.

It was fascinating to hear someone speak about the Martyr in such a way. There were aspects of her tale, the quadrille refusal to deny and the burning of the Martyr which were the same as how the priest had explained things back in Barrowheld, but in our version the Martyr wasn't an Aspector. She was God born anew in flesh, a deliverer of hope and peace.

I wasn't sure I understood the ramifications of Adléta's belief in an

Aspected Martyr, but it was incredible to me that hundreds of miles from my own country, from the nearest church of the Martyr, here someone was telling me a tale of my own religion, one I had never heard before.

"I can see why the Seer's aren't keen on this tale," I said, considering Adléta's emphasis on all people being equal. "I still don't follow why Kit would be upset about what happened earlier though."

"The Seer monks have never believed in the Martyr, and do not believe it is possible to be both a Seer and an Aspector. I don't know why the Abbot decided to test that theory with you. But if what you say happened is true, and I do believe you, then you've demonstrated it is possible. When you heard Eva's voice, you heard her because of a connection you share, and you found it while meditating in the Aspect. Distance means nothing in the Aspect. I'm not a Seer, so I cannot truly explain why you heard what you did. But the fact you've shown it's possible..." Adléta paused, lost for words. She looked truly concerned. "It can't bode well for you."

I tried to let it all sink in. Seeing, the Martyr, the Abbot. Eva. It was too much.

"Why tell me this? Why put yourself at risk?" I asked.

"Not all of us have faith in the Seers. You've barely scratched the surface of the history of your own country, you have no idea the blood-soaked history of our people. Besides, in showing the Seers were wrong, you have vindicated what we have been saying for centuries. Of course, I want to help you. That's the other reason I took you down here. I may not be able to give you access to the Ars Exemplar in the library any more, but I can show you how to find it yourself."

That made me sit up straight. "You'll show me how to navigate this place?"

"All you need to do is be able to sneak into the stores of the Seer library. They have loads of copies of the Ars Exemplar. Maybe you'll find more answers there."

I broke out into a broad grin, excited. The Ars Exemplar wasn't the only thing I'd find in the Seer Library. Maybe I would be able to get my hands on a Book of Patterns as well.

"Lead the way," I said.

It was hard to tell how long we spent in the warrens of the library. Adléta showed me the winding paths and roads of the stores, how to spot landmarks to gain my bearings, and importantly, where each of the rests were. These were important because not only were they often stocked with food, water and light, but they would be the main places where other librarians congregated. As I wasn't supposed to be down here, I'd need to avoid them at all costs. To pass the time Adléta told me about her studies in Medica, how she was close to getting her tether, and I tried not to let any jealousy inch into my voice. She planned on returning back to her town, which was many hundreds of miles from Isale, on the eastern coast of Vin Irudur and take up residence as the area's physician. She explained that she would likely serve as physician to the surrounding villages as well, and as an Aspected physician, other non-Aspected healers would report into her. She eventually moved onto asking about my studies, but when I explained the issues I was having with Frennic she interrupted me.

"Frennic broke your nose? Surely it was an accident?"

"Trust me. He's excellent at making things look like an accident but he broke it on purpose. Why do you ask? Do you know him or something?"

"We were good friends during the initial intake," Adléta said. "He seemed like a sweetheart."

Broch had explained that for the first five or so years at the academy, Nascent Aspecters were given basic schooling before they were taught Aspecting, known as intake. It ensured that all Aspectors, regardless of stature, could read, write and had command of basic arithmetic.

"Well something must have changed, because he's a royal shit now. He seems perfectly lovely to his own countrymen though," I said, bitterly.

"Oh. Of course," Adléta sighed. "Frennic lost his grandfather and uncle in the war. His father avoided the draft, and from the bits Frennic told me, was branded a coward by his mother, Frennic's Grandmother."

"Oh, I see," I said, dryly. "He's trying to prove his bravado by breaking each bone in my body. Makes perfect sense."

"These things rarely do Kehlem," Adléta said seriously. "It's a lot easier to hate than forgive. Especially if the one you're forgiving did nothing wrong."

We walked mostly in silence after that, while I stewed on the titbits Adléta had fed me about Frennic. Understanding his motivation for hating me did not make me pity him, they only served to make me more annoyed at how weak a man must be to be driven by his family's prejudice.

Not long later, Adléta showed me the pile of fallen books which demarcated the start of the seer library, and we turned back. She made me call out the names of the landmarks as we passed them, and encouraged me to choose the direction to get back to the student library. It wasn't an easy task reversing the order in my head, but thankfully the majority of the path was obvious, being well trod over countless years by hundreds of librarians.

Much quicker than I was expecting we arrived back at the student library, and I was back on the other side of the reception desk. The room was totally deserted.

"Thank you Adléta, for trusting me, and showing me all of this." I gestured widely to the whole place.

She smiled at me. "Any time, Kehlem. Just promise you'll be careful. Watch your back. I don't know how the Abbot will react to what I'm sure Kit has already reported to him."

I nodded, and left for the dormitory, leaving Adléta to finish her shift alone.

Later that evening while I was working in the tavern, I heard the familiar deep voice and subsequent bright laugh that told me Broch and Thain had both walked through the door.

I walked over to the bar. "Do you mind if I have a moment?" I asked Brin, who was pouring a tankard. "I need to speak to those two quickly."

Brin looked between me and Thain and Broch who were pulling up their usual seats. "Fine," he said. "But remind Thain that he owes me five silvers from last night's game."

I smiled, "Thanks Brin."

I strode over to my friends' tablet, and sat down heavily next to them.

"How did it go?" I asked Broch

He nodded. "It's in the dormitory."

A palpable weight fell off my shoulder. It would be no good finding the pattern we needed if Broch wasn't able to sneak the metal out of fabrication class.

"I've been thinking," Thain said, "It might be a good idea for us to practice sparring between the three of us."

"And ruin my pretty face?" Broch asked. "You two may go at it, but you can count me out."

"Kehlem?" Thain looked at me.

"It's a good idea," I agreed. Martyr knows I wasn't getting any better fighting Frennic again and again.

Thain smiled at me, and gave Broch what almost seemed like an 'I told you so' look. I didn't bother asking them what it meant. I had no doubt they had been talking about me on their way down, concerned that I was getting the shit kicked out of me each day by Frennic. They'd probably already talked about spar training before they got here. If I'm being honest it felt nice to have friends that were concerned enough to conspire together to help.

I got back up and finished the rest of my shift, while my two friends relaxed and drank in the corner, giggling amongst themselves about Martyr only knows what. Still, with the bronze ready, I could finally begin plotting the next steps of my plan.

22

A Burning Soul

While I was limited to when I could explore the stores to when Adléta was working in the library, Kit hadn't called me back for another lesson since the incident, so I found myself with a sudden excess of free time. I started going to the library in my spare afternoons and evenings, even on days Adléta and Broch weren't working. I couldn't get a hold of the Seer restricted texts on these visits, but there was still plenty for me to read. I was particularly interested in their books on anatomy and other Medica texts. Most of the books I had read back home in Barrowheld were fairly dated, so I often found myself pouring over the newer anatomy books, lost in the intricate details held within. On days that Adléta was working, I would wait for the library to empty and then sneak behind the counter. The first few solo trips into the stores were thrilling, both from the sense of adventure, and the worry of getting lost. There was just enough light within the stores that I could explore without a lantern, if I let my eyes grow accustomed to the dark first. It was the only way I could guarantee not being seen by other librarians, whose occasional presence was announced by distant glows of light, travelling like slow carvels on a smooth sea. In that first week of exploring, I was tentative, still getting used to the layout of the stores. Each trip I would push further and further towards the Seer sections, while still hovering on the border.

All of this was unbeknownst to Thain and Broch. Adléta had sworn me to secrecy about the stores, even from Broch, who of course knew of the stores, but had never bothered to venture far enough in to realise their true nature. I also refused to get my friends' hopes up until I had what I was seeking.

During the second week of my exploration into the stores, I grew more confident in my ability to navigate through the ponderous tomes, and became braver through the distinct absence of librarians. Initially I had jumped at any sign that another librarian was also in the vast city of books. I would scuttle away, deep into the city of books until they had passed. But such meetings were rare, and few librarians delved deep into the stacks of books like me, and so my progress of charting the city became quicker. I began delving into the Seer section, navigating the new and unfamiliar territory. Whereas in the student section, the grouping of books by genre made sense to me, here the grouping where entirely unfamiliar, and un-signposted. Finding a Book of Patterns would not be as simple as I had hoped.

Stepping between the towering shelves of books, I placed each unshod foot carefully, each footstep quieter than a whisper. I had explored much of the deeper Seer section with no luck. Today I was pushing closer to the Seer library than I had ever done, close enough that the light from the main seating area was casting shadows towards me. A movement caught my eye, and I halted, eyes wide as I tried to take in as much light as possible. It was a tall shadow cast against the smooth stone floor, slowly drifting from left to right.

Was it a monk librarian at the reception desk? Or even a Seer moving to their armchair in the main antechamber? It was too hard to judge distance, and I needed to avoid looking towards the brighter light coming from the main library. I needed to maintain my night-vision.

I slunk behind a bookcase which was parallel to where I assumed the desk was, hoping to hide my figure from any prying eyes. I moved quietly, stepping achingly slowly to avoid making any sound. I'd left my shoes hidden in one of the deeper alcoves.

I continued a slow winding path, tracing the dustier volumes of books which would take me closer and closer to the reception desk of the Seer library. I needed to avoid the main thoroughfare.

The sound of a cough made me freeze. It was heart-stoppingly loud, and it took all my willpower not to dart away.

I must be no more than a few meters away from the main antechamber. And still I had not found a Book of Patterns yet. I knew it wouldn't be easy of course. They were probably the most requested book in this library. They would be near the front, somewhere easy to find.

I rounded the corner of a bookshelf, and had to pull myself backwards. This was it. End of the cover. Past this bookshelf, I would be directly behind the reception desk, and illuminated for anyone looking past the desk to see. My heart was hammering in my chest. I took a long deep breath, and waited for my body to calm. But it refused. My hands were sweating, and the perspiration was starting to make the soles of my feet slick also. The longer I waited here, the more likely it would be that I'd get caught. I creeped closer to the edge of the shelf, and peered around, taking stock of my surroundings.

And as simple as that, there it was. The end of my quest. A whole bookcase, filled floor to ceiling with Books of Patterns. It even had a sign hanging from the edge facing me identifying it as such. Even better, there was a bookcase in front of it, obscuring it from view from the main chamber. The only issue was that the only path I could see to get to the shelves took me right past the desk, in full view of potential onlookers.

Deciding that a darting figure would draw more attention, I waited until it seemed all shadows were still, and I walked carefully and purposefully towards the bookshelf. Each step trod in the light could be counted with four of my heartbeats. There was a pressure in the back of my legs, urging me to run. I resisted. I was waiting to hear a voice call out, demanding I stop. But none came. And before I knew it, I was once more in the cover of the bookshelf. I could have laughed with joy. But there was no time.

I passed my finger across the spines of the books, and found the volume I was looking for, *Fabrica III*. I wouldn't be able to take the book with me; its absence would arouse too much suspicion. I quickly sat down on the floor, and flicked through the book, various patterns flickering past my eyes, until I spotted the one design I had been searching for. I slowly let both sides of the book down onto the smooth floor and lay the pattern out to face upwards. Like all patterns in the book, it filled the two pages, and there, written in a tight cursive font in the upper right corner: *Fabrica Pattern XII; Individual Tether.*

This was it. This was the pattern we needed. I pulled out a folded blank parchment from one pocket in my tunic, and a piece of sharpened charcoal from another. I lay my blank piece of parchment next to the book, and working quickly, I copied the pattern. Drawing the pattern physically felt wrong. There was no connection to the Aspect, nothing familiar, nothing guiding my hand like there usually was when Aspecting. Twice I made a mistake, sending a spiral too tight, and a fractured line too straight. I rubbed these marks with my finger, smudging them out and redrawing them. Around thirty minutes later, I was done. My hand ached from the speed I had drawn, but there was no time. I folded my parchment, stuffing it back in my pocket, and lifted the book back to its slot in the bookshelf. I waited for stillness from the library once more, before stepping quickly across the illuminated gap, and back into the warm and comforting shadows of the deeper book-city.

"Oh, look who it is!" Broch called out to me, as I stepped through the door into the warm dormitory. Night had fallen and my two friends had twisted their chairs to face the fire, so all I could see was Broch's head peeking out from the tattered wing of his armchair.

"I was beginning to forget what your face looked like," Broch said, turning back around as I sat to the left of the fire on an empty chair.

It was true, I had been neglecting my friends while I'd been exploring the library, an absence felt undoubtedly stronger by them due to its mysterious nature. But I hoped the folded parchment in my pocket would make up for it.

"Well," I said, stretching out, "you'll be pleased to hear that you'll be seeing my face each and every night from now on. We need to get practicing." And I casually tossed the parchment onto the table between us.

"What's this?" Thain asked, reaching for the paper.

"Martyr take me," Broch swore, as he peered over Thain's shoulder to look at the drawing.

"Is this it?" Thain asked, looking between Broch and I.

I kept my smug silence.

"How in the seared flesh of the Martyr did you get your hands on this?" Broch demanded, looking stunned.

"That's not important," I said, trying to change the subject. I wasn't about to break Adléta's trust. "What is important is whether you're both in?"

My two friends looked at each other and grinned, a hungry look in their eyes.

"Here," Broch said, tossing Thain and I a blank circle of bronze. I caught it, lifting it up to the late afternoon light, marvelling out how smooth the metal was. We were back in the dormitory, later than planned, but ready to finally get started.

"Who's going first?" I asked.

"I'd better go first so you both can see how it's done for real," Broch said, picking up an inscribing stylus.

For the past week we had been practicing the stolen fabrication pattern, which we had drawn in material, like iron or wood. The pattern we had been practicing was one that would tie the energy produced by one object, to another. The plan was simple, we would have a single piece of flat bronze inscribed with the first half of the pattern stored in the bottom of our water butt. Then, we would each inscribe the second half of the pattern on our three bronze rings. A fully sealed unit would be better, but with the amount of water we could store in the barrel, it should make for an efficient tether, as long as we all charged it when we could.

The tricky part of tonight's plan would be the binding of the tethers. It's not enough to simply inscribe a pattern into an object, anybody could do that. Once finished, the two objects need to be connected via the Aspect, which would need energy.

"Gather around, students mine," Broch intoned, as he leaned over his own disk, Thain and I stood behind him, peering over his shoulder. We'd practiced these patterns during the week, but only on scraps of wrought iron we could find around our dormitory. The bronze was a harder material than iron, so the practice could only help us so much.

Broch's inscription was beautiful and it was easy to see this was an area he excelled in. It was incongruent with his personality, which was sometimes excessively foppish, but he was a tremendous Aspector, when he felt like it.

"There," he said, wiping some of the scrap shavings off the surface. "Done."

He passed the bronze ring up so we could have a look. The pattern covered almost the entire surface of the ring, curling around itself and finishing next to the beginning. Studying the tether up close, it was easy to see the beauty held within these patterns.

"Let me get mine over and done with," Thain said, and swapped places with Broch. "And don't hover over my shoulder," he snapped, uncharacteristically sharp for him.

I could understand his nervousness. The only reason we were able to get a hold of the rings was thanks to a Foclir class using the blanks to create more temporary tethers. Apparently, they'd been left on the side in the workshop Broch used. Taking three was already a gamble, we had no idea if they kept stock of numbers for the blanks. We hoped not.

For this particular tether pattern, each tether needed to be inscribed by the tether's owner, even though the pattern was the same. Broch had tried to explain the reason why, but had lost me when he started using words like 'harmonic resonance'. Clearly there was still much I didn't understand about Aspecting.

Not wanting to stress Thain out, I stepped away, and paced around the edge of the circular common room. Each step I took, I struggled to not let my mind get distracted from the earlier events of the month, which had led to this moment. Thinking about Eva, about seeing her, could wait until after tonight. It was going to take all my concentration just to get the pattern right, let alone having to pair the two disparate pieces into a single tether later on.

"I'm done," Thain said hoarsely. I stopped in my tracks, too nervous to see if he'd ruined the piece or not. Broch took the piece out of Thain's hand

and inspected it, turning this way and that in the candle light.

I saw Broch look at Thain, and declare; "Beautiful."

Thain's face lit up like a sunrise and Broch pulled him into a tight embrace. Like a lightning bolt, a thought struck me and suddenly a few things clicked into place.

"Your turn Kehlem," Thain called.

That particular revelation would have to wait until later. I walked over to the table, and sat down, laying my bronze ring down. I took the stylus from Thain, and held it like a quill in my left hand.

Thain and Broch stepped back to give me some space, and I looked down at the ring, concentrating. Like I would with any other type of Aspecting, I let the picture of the pattern fill my mind, but instead of letting my hand drift and find a weakness in the boundary between us and the Aspect, I put my stylus onto the bronze ring. With the motion Broch had taught me, I loosely pulled the stylus across the surface, letting it glide across, scoring the metal. With my right hand I slowly twisted the metal ring, so that I could manage the intricate swirling geometry of the pattern. The process reminded me a little of meditation. My mind was so focused on holding the pattern at the forefront that it left little room for anything else. Before I knew it, I'd finished the first pass and the metal had faint lines scored across it. Next, I needed to go back over the lines, pressing harder to make grooves out of the metal. This was less meditative. Twice I made mistakes, pushing too hard on the stylus, causing it to skit off the surface. The first time I was lucky, and it didn't leave a mark. The second however, a faint line was scored across the inner edge of the ring. The final stretch was the worst. Not used to holding a quill for so long, and certainly not with the same amount of force, my hand was growing numb, and my engraving was becoming more and more clumsy. I finished the pattern, and dropped the metal in scorn.

"I've finished," I called to the others. "I think I may have ruined it."

Broch rushed over and inspected the ring. "Well, you may not be a natural," he said, placing the metal back on the table, "but this should work fine. The pattern is clear, and while there are some slight scuff marks, they seem inconsequential."

I let out a deep sigh of relief. If I'd ruined my tether, the others could have still gone ahead with their own, I would have just been left tetherless. And since we'd set this plan in motion, I had a burning desire to learn, and practice. More than anything I wanted to delve deeper into the possibilities of Medica Aspecting.

"Well while you too were busy, I finished the other half with my naffer stylus," Broch said, passing me a flat piece of bronze which had been beautifully engraved with a dramatic shifting pattern.

"Do you really think this will work?" Thain asked, as I strode over to the fire.

I wasn't sure. I knew from speaking to Broch that the energy required to bind two pieces into a tether was around the same amount as a second form of Destructia pattern two. The one that broke my iron tether back in the Pattern Trial. Easily enough energy to kill me tetherless. Nevertheless, I had a plan. I figured that if I used our modified Destructia pattern to let energy flow inside of me, and at the same time call the pattern to bind the tether, then hopefully I could let the energy flow straight through me. The alternative is that my body absorbs some of the energy. Which would kill me. That wasn't exactly a comfortable margin of error.

Calling twin patterns wasn't an unknown thing to do, it was actually one of the tests that decided if a Foclir is designated third degree or second, but it is damned hard. It essentially involves capturing the Aspect in both hands, and drawing two different patterns at the same time. Most people can't pat their head and rub their stomach at the same time. Imagine now that the consequence of failing is spontaneous combustion from absorbing too much energy. I'd practiced the patterns during the week, but only yesterday was I able to draw them both at the same time without messing one of them up. In none of my practices had I tried to Aspect as well.

I took a deep breath. I was only going to talk myself out of it if I hesitated. I took the three engraved bronze rings and the bronze plate in my right hand and stood next to the fire. Broch and Thain stood watching me.

"Good luck," Broch said, serious for once. Thain just nodded at me, too nervous to say anything.

I smiled at both my friends and closed my eyes. Lifting both hands, I let my forefingers search for the weakness in the boundary to the Aspect. My left found one almost instantly. My right, not used to the sensation took a little longer, but eventually found one.

Exhale.

There could be no hesitation. My left hand drew large sweeping motions, a pattern that was more than familiar to me. At the same time my right moved in a staccato, sharp twisting motion. In both of my hands I felt the tug of the Aspect as its currents caught a hold of my intent, and wanted to guide my hands the rest of the way. I smiled to myself. It was almost effortless. It was like my hands had a will of their own, drawn on warm winds, pushed through a route familiar to both of them.

Inhale.

Both patterns were drawing to their ends. I bent my knees, eyes still shut, and plunged my left hand into the fire. Once again there was no burning, only a gentle heat. In my right, a strange vibration was coming from the bronze objects I held in my now open palm.

Was it working?

There was no heat spreading inside of me, no excessive heart rate, no rapid breathing. Instead, there was a piece of string, connecting one hand to the other, traveling through the centre of my being. As the tethers in my right hand drew energy, they pulled on this string continuously from the left. It began slow and gentle but rapidly increased in speed. It was like no feeling I'd ever experienced before, like light itself was boring a hole through my spirit. Surely there must be brilliant smoke pouring from my skin as my very essence burned. And yet it didn't hurt. Not in so many words anyway. It transcended pain, pushed through right into pleasure and out into absolute dread. I was being torn asunder.

Will I die? Again?

Through gritted teeth, I dropped my left hand lower into the fire, and grabbed one of the burning coals, squeezing it in my palm. The string in my core slowed, and I felt present once again within the dormitory. Smells and sounds returning to me. The string was slowing now to a halt, and the vibration of tethers slowed with it, until they lay still in my palm. I cut my connection to the Aspect in both hands and collapsed backwards onto the floor, drained. The tethers fell from my hand with a metallic clatter as they hit the hardwood floor.

I sank down to my knees exhausted. Thain rushed over to me, and Broch picked up the fallen metal.

"Are you okay?" Thain asked, his eyes searching my face nervously.

I could only grunt through gritted teeth, the sensation in my chest slowly dripping away to nothingness.

"Did it work?" I asked, changing the subject.

Thain's eyes danced with excitement.

"Come see."

Thain grabbed my wrist and pulled me over to the water butt, where Broch just emerged, sleeves rolled up to his elbows.

"That was," he said, shaking his hand dry of water, "the most ridiculous thing I've ever seen in my life."

Thain whacked him on the shoulder reproachfully.

"It was beautiful Kehlem. I've never seen anything like it. You made it look effortless."

"That's what I said!" Broch protested.

Thain rolled his eyes.

Effortless? It certainly didn't feel effortless. I placed a hand over my chest where I'd imagined my soul had been smouldering. Whatever it was, had passed, but the memory remained.

"Here," Broch said, passing each of us back our own bronze rings and some short leather cords. "Use these to tie them, I'd recommend somewhere not easily seen." He passed around some leather cord.

I opted to tie my tether to my upper right thigh, figuring it'd only be visible when I stripped at the baths, in which case I'd just take it off.

"How shall we test them?" Broch asked, tying his tether around his upper arm.

"I've got an idea," Thain said, walking back to the now smouldering fire.

With a practiced ease, he danced through the Destructia pattern, and picked up a smouldering charcoal in his hands. The amber glow faded, dimming as he cupped his hands around it, and at the same time there was a warmth against my thigh, where the tether was tied.

"Feel that?" Thain asked.

Both Broch and myself nodded.

It worked.

We danced around like fools. Each of us now had our own secret tether, a tool that would allow us to practice Aspecting, allow us to teach each other, accords be damned. We agreed a rota. The tether in the water butt would need to be charged periodically, and it would need to be done subtly. Thain and I could siphon energy from the lake after it had warmed in the summer sun, excusing it as practice. Broch would try and siphon energy from some of the furnaces in the Fabrica workshops, once we'd taught him how to use the pattern. And we each agreed that we would only use the tethers for practice and teaching each other. We had no idea what the consequences would be for being caught with them, but it didn't take a great deal of imagination to guess.

The rest of that night wasn't for planning however. Thain disappeared upstairs into the dormitory, reappearing down the spiral staircase a moment later with an unopened bottle of Vinnish wine, overstock from one of our previous nights in Isale. Broch and I cheered his return, and we spent the evening celebrating our successes, passing the bottle between us.

As the stars began to shine their brightest, and our excited prattling slowed to a thin silence, I noticed Broch had begun humming a haunting melody, audible just barely beneath his breath.

"What is that?" I asked, lolling my head to the side of my armrest.

"Hmm?" Broch asked, distracted, his eyes staring thoughtlessly over to the window where Thain was sat. "Oh, nothing. Just a song my mother used to sing me to sleep."

There was a subtle quality to his voice that night, that caught my attention, like all the snark and sarcasm which cocooned him had been shed away, and for once the real Broch was laid bare.

I perhaps wasn't the only one to notice, as Thain called over to him. "I'd like to hear it."

"Pish," Broch said, half-heartedly, and reclined deeper into his chair.

"Come on Broch, let's hear it," I said, joining Thain's encouragement. Broch rarely spoke of home, and I was intrigued to push beyond this veil he held over himself.

Whether it was the drink in his blood, or a longing for something familiar, I do not know, but he relented to our words.

"Fine, fine. It's a maudlin song, but it reminds me of sweet words from my mother." He looked me in the eye, "Mock me for my voice and I promise to thrash you."

I smiled at him and held my hands up.

Broch sat up in his chair, and twisted so he was once more looking over to the window near Thain. He cleared his throat, and with a warm tenor broke out into a gentle song.

"Weep 'neath the willow my love,
Wet by the swell of the flow,
Restless the leaves, surrender to sleep,
Weep 'neath the willow my love.
Wax in the strength of the oak,
Sway from the strength of the blow,
Root in the ground, coiled and bound,
Wax in the strength of the oak.
Wain in the shade of the yew,
The warm earth a blanket below,
Rest and sleep, the Martyr you'll meet,
Wain in the shade of the yew.
Weep 'neath the willow my love,
Wax in the strength of the oak,
Wain in the shade of the yew,
I'll weep 'neath the willow for you"

He held the last note just barely above speaking volume, his voice cracking a little as he finished. I took a deep breath, surprised to find I'd been holding it while he sang. I wiped away the few tears that had wet my eyes. I'd never heard that song before, just a simple folk verse to sing to a babe, but to hear my friend sing it, with a vulnerability that was most unlike him, it became the most beautiful melody I'd ever heard. I told Broch so, but he just smiled at me sadly, still watching the window, where Thain was now silently weeping.

23

To Rend a Heart

Summer deepened over the mountain glen, and golden light spilled across mountain sides and slipped across valleys. The winds dropped to a mere hint and the long grass in the grounds of the academy lay still. Students were spending more time outside, studying under shade from trees during the day, then laughing and drinking late into the evening. Twilight dropped quickly in the valley, as it was surrounded on all sides by sloping hillside which occluded the sun before it could approach the horizon, leaving a purple hue to all within on clear nights.

Most afternoons, before I left for the tavern, Broch, Thain and I were in our dormitory, teaching each other patterns and practicing with our new tethers. The rota we had assigned was working well, and we had been able to keep our tether counterpart well charged with energy siphoned from the lake and furnaces. Broch had taught Thain and I some more intricacies in fabrication patterns, some of which Thain was already familiar with having studied with Broch a few terms ago before moving to Destructia. Unlike Medica or Destructia patterns, the Aspecting Broch was teaching us came slowly to me. I was used to Aspecting feeling like second nature, as simple as breathing, but the effort required for Fabrica was quite unlike traditional Aspecting. It required a skill and deftness that I apparently did not possess. Broch didn't blame me for my slow pace, telling me that it was to be expected. Usually students would learn some Alchemy first and get an understanding of the materials at hand. Broch explained it to me as though every object had a soul. But rather than the Caserean sense, where souls were where consciousness derives, in the teaching of Aspecting, a soul was the piece of us that once resided in the Aspect, and it was found in everything. This piece of Aspect, this soul, would call out to those sensitive to it. It could be felt and understood by those listening for it and to the trained Aspector, it would sing volumes about the very nature of the thing the soul resides in. This technique was taught to all fledgling Alchemist, and therefore all those studying Fabrica knew it as well. Without it, I was struggling blind. That isn't to say I was totally useless and I did pick up some stuff here and there, but we mostly relied on things Broch could teach us from memory. In return I taught Thain and Broch as much as I could about Medica, including useful information from the natural side of a physician's work. Both of them took to it instantly, although they could only get as far as the second form of the pattern of healing, neither of them managing the third or the full, fourth form. While I spent more time practicing my engravings and fabrications, Thain spent time teaching Broch the first two patterns of Destructia. The first, which we had come to refer amongst ourselves as the 'siphon' pattern, Broch struggled with, to the point Thain had to coach him through the pattern multiple times, sometimes grabbing his hands for him and taking him through the pattern himself. Eventually he did get the hang of it, and was able to contribute to the charging of the tether. The second Destructia pattern while we could teach it to Broch, he was unable to practice. Not in such a small room at least. The risk was too high. We taught him the pattern regardless, with a promise that when we could, we would practice it for real with him.

Since Kit hadn't requested I join him again for Seer training since the last incident, Thain and I had been using that time to practice sparring together. Neither of us were excellent fighters, but having the opportunity to spar with someone you could trust not to either kick you in the groin at every opportunity or to sadistically hurt you whenever the instructor's gaze wasn't upon you, did wonders for our form. My fights with Frennic, while I still wasn't winning any, had stopped becoming so hideously one sided.

"You heard the rumours?" Thain asked, pulling off his tunic so he was naked to the waist. He grabbed a cord and tied his hair back behind his head.

"What's that then?" I asked, throwing my own shirt to the grass.

It'd been a month since we'd made the tethers in our dormitory, which coincided with the start of mine and Thain's sparring matches. Thain dropped into his crouched stance, and I mimicked him.

"There's a Foclir coming. A Destructia Foclir. First degree. I heard one of the Vinnish kids mention it in the study hall."

He aimed a low sweeping kick to try and hook my front leg. I darted back, out of range.

"Why's that?" I asked. I lunged forward, trying to take him by surprise. I threw two quick jabs, aimed at his trunk. The first he blocked with his wrist, pushing my arm wide, the second connected. I pulled my punch in time so that it wouldn't leave him winded.

"Good shot," he said. "Apparently to teach us."

He sounded uncertain. I pressed my advantage and sent a quick kick to the side of his leg, which he brought up so I only connected with the hardest part of his shin.

"Isn't that what the Do'Seer is for?"

"I guess they must be here to teach us stuff other than Aspecting," Thain said, sending a wide hook punch to my right which I stepped away from easily. Having practiced fighting so often, it was becoming easier to think clearly and quickly, and not just panic during these bouts.

"What even is it Destructia Foclir do?" I asked, slowly circling Thain. "You know, other than serving in the Army. It's not like the Vins are invading anywhere at the moment."

"Most become Hunters, I think." Thain moved quickly, trying to grab a hold of my leg to toss me to the floor. I managed to slip out of his grip, but not before he landed a couple of jabs into my stomach.

Hunters. The word rang through my head as we sparred. Hunters were probably the only Aspector that everyone had heard of back home. They were the enforces of the Vin empire. There were stories aplenty in the

Rosen Pyre of entrenched bandit camps that had been destroyed by only two or three Hunters. Hunters were also responsible for the tracking, and capture of rogue Aspectors, those who broke the accords. To think that this was what lay ahead of me, a weapon of the empire, made me feel sick.

One of Thain's blows went wide, leaving him open, so taking my chance, I rushed him, kicking as if towards his leg, which he moved to block reflexively. I changed my momentum midway, and instead I leaned back, kicking him in the stomach. Quickly back on both feet, I grabbed his leg whilst he was off balance, and threw him to the ground.

"That one goes to you I believe," Thain said from the floor.

I reached down and grabbed his hand, pulling him back to his feet. I grabbed my tunic, and pulled it back over my head.

"You heading to the baths?" I asked, knowing what the answer would be.

"Not today," he said, "I'm meeting —"

"Broch for more pattern practice," I said, finishing his sentence, eyebrow raised.

He couldn't help flushing. "What do you mean?" he asked, almost stammering out his question.

"Oh, come on, Thain. Do you think I'm that dumb? You don't have to pretend with me, I don't care," I said, exasperated.

"Kehlem," he protested, "I honestly don't know what you're talking about."

"So, you and Broch haven't been sneaking out together after you think I'm asleep? You've been making cow eyes at each other for months now. I'm happy for you!" I said, genuinely.

Caught, Thain's face fell, and he stopped. "How long have you known?"

"I twigged the night we made the tethers, but honestly I probably should have guessed weeks before that. Why didn't you both just tell me?"

"We didn't want to make you feel uncomfortable, it's always a bit weird if you find yourself the third to a couple…" Thain trailed off, looking down at his feet and blushing.

"Don't be ridiculous Thain, I couldn't be happier for you both!" I said, fully earnest. I'd grown to love Thain like a brother, and while Broch knew how to wind me up, I knew he was a good, caring soul. Other than Eva, they were my closest friends.

"Honestly we weren't sure how you'd react," Thain said, cautiously.

"Pish," I said, mimicking Broch. "Like I give a damn. If you two are happy, then I'm happy. I'm not some jealous lover who's going to start wailing because the two of you want to spend some alone time together."

Thain grinned at me, looking distinctly relieved.

"I still don't understand why you didn't just tell me," I said.

"Honestly, I wanted to, Broch is just a little more cautious about these things..." Thain said, trailing off.

I waited for him to finish, as he so clearly wanted to.

"Oh Martyr," Thain said, rubbing his face. "Promise me you won't tell Broch I told you this?"

"Tell me what?" I asked. "Alright, I promise!" I said, taking note of Thain's serious expression.

"The reason Broch hasn't gotten his tether, the real one, not the one we made. The reason why he somehow always seems to miraculously cock up and piss off the monks so they delay his testing, he does it all on purpose."

"What? Why would he do that?" I asked.

"He told you his father wants to use him as a leverage for the Vin court, yes?"

I nodded, remembering him saying something to that effect on our journey to Isale all those months ago.

"Well Broch and his father don't exactly get along. From what he's told me, his father was none too kind to him as a child, at least not up until he found out his son was an Aspector. Of course, ever since, his father tries to pretend nothing ever happened, acting like Broch is suddenly this golden child. It really messed Broch up. He tries to hold people at arm's length sometimes. I think when he does finally let people in, he worries they'll abandon him at a moment's notice. He just wants to keep the status quo."

Thain said all of this with such a tenderness in his voice, it made my heart weep at the blossoming love between my two friends. I also felt shame at not having realised some of this myself, having not taken the time to speak with Broch about it. Some of what Thain was telling me rang true for me.

"I had no idea," I said, seriously. "You both didn't need to hide your relationship from me though," I said. "I love you both, and I'm thrilled for you."

Thain's expression softened. "If it were up to me, I wouldn't have lied to you Kehlem, but Broch is understandably nervous about these things." Thain stopped walking and turned to look at me. "Could you do me a favour?"

I nodded, "Of course Thain, what do you need?"

"Can you talk to Broch? Tell him gently, that you know about us. I think if he knows that you figured things out a while back, and nothing's changed, it will put his mind at rest. He's been losing sleep over it."

Losing sleep? Martyr, he must care an awful lot about both myself and Thain to be so concerned.

I nodded. "I'll go speak to him this evening. He's working in the library I think."

During the walk back to the academy, and then over lunch in the mess hall, Thain filled me in. Thain and Broch had kissed after one of our drunken evenings in Isale town, and things had progressed from there. They'd been seeing each other for over a month, and from the way Thain smiled whenever Broch's name kissed his lips, I could see they were besotted with each other. My heart ached for them both.

It didn't take much prompting from Thain for me to start talking about Eva that evening as well. As much as I was thrilled at both of my friends' happiness, it just reminded me of what was absent from myself. That afternoon, in the dormitory as Thain and I sat opposite each other on arm chairs, I let myself unravel. I spoke for hours on end. I told Thain everything. Once I started, I found I couldn't stop. It was like picking at a thread in a woven rug, and before long the structure I had held so rigid was reduced to loose yarn in my hands, and I couldn't make sense of the start or end. I told him about her long raven hair. I told him of her wicked intelligence, her fierce determination to make something for herself, away from Barrowheld. At some point, I must have started crying, because I paused, taking a breath to find Thain comforting me, his arm around my shoulder. I let myself cry, and together we watched the afternoon light fade until the glimmer of stars shone from their twilight blanket.

As promised I left Thain that evening to go speak with Broch, to try and put his mind at ease. The early evening stroll through the academy was quiet, with few students and Foclir around, leaving me alone with my thoughts. I was drained from speaking to Thain about Eva, and now walking towards the library, a nervous energy rose within me, anxious at the thought of my conversation with Broch. His relationship with Thain was clearly important to him. I'd need to navigate the conversation deftly to put his mind at ease.

Too soon I was standing at the student library door, but was surprised to hear laughing coming from the other side. I stepped through and though the main seating area was empty of students, Broch and Adléta stood at the reception desk, laughing, and both with a drink in hand.

"What are you two laughing at?" I asked. I was pleased to see the two of them getting along finally, but also shocked to see Adléta drinking, in the library no less. She usually took her job so seriously.

Both of them jumped, startled when they heard my voice, but relaxed when they recognised me.

"Kehlem! I'm glad you're here! We're celebrating!" Broch called over to me.

I joined them, standing opposite the two of them at the desk. Broch pulled another glass from behind the desk and poured some amber fluid from his own glass into it.

"Here," he said, pushing it over to me.

"And what is this in aid of?" I asked, bringing the drink to my lips. Was that whiskey?

"Adléta is getting her tether. Her *permanent* tether," Broch said.

I looked over to Adléta, who was grinning ear to ear.

"Congratulations!" I reached over to pull her into an awkward one-armed embrace. "I'm so happy for you! When do you leave?"

"Three days from now. I've had my assignment confirmed, back in my hometown. If you are ever in the area, you're all more than welcome to visit."

"We'll hold you to that," Broch said cheerily.

The eastern coast of Vin Irudur was well known for its span of coastal cities and long, hot beaches. Casere by contrast bordered Nalbin on its own eastern border, and so had access only to the much colder western waters of the truanic sea.

"What brings you to the library this time of night?" Adléta asked. The subtext was clear. *Do you need to get to the stores?*

"Well actually, I needed to speak to Broch about something, in private if that's ok Adléta," I said, watching her expression carefully. "Do you know anywhere we might talk?"

Can I show him the stores?

She looked at me, and then to Broch who was now looking thoroughly bewildered. "Oh, what do I care, I'll be leaving soon anyway. Go ahead."

"You mean to tell me this has been here all along, and you never told me?" Broch demanded.

I was leading him deeper into stores, to the first alcove stop that Adléta had first shown me. Adléta had kindly stayed behind to give the two of us some privacy.

"Well to be fair, there was nothing stopping you from finding it yourself. How long have you been working at the library?"

"I just thought there were more dusty books back here. Blimey, how deep does this thing go."

"All the way to the Seer library. It's a single room."

I waited for Broch to put two and two together.

"That's how you did it. I was wondering how the hell you got a hold of the tether pattern. Fuck me Kehlem. The balls on you."

I smiled as the pieces fit together in Broch's mind. "Here we are," I said, leading Broch into the alcove, and turning on the light. I sat down at one of the chairs and indicated Broch to do the same.

"What are we doing here Kehlem?" He smiled at me. "Look if you're trying to seduce me, as lovely as you are, you're not my type," he joked.

"Funny you should say that, you're not far off why I wanted to talk to you. Look, there's no gentle way to say this. I know about you and Thain."

Broch's eyes went wide, and he started to interrupt me. I held my hand up and pushed on.

"I realised a while back, and I just wanted to say, if you're happy then I'm happy. You two are my best friends. You two being together won't change that. I love you both." My voice caught as I finished what I was saying, and I brushed away a wetness from my eye. I decided not to tell him I'd already spoken to Thain.

Broch was very still, and was staring at me with wild eyes. He looked very pale.

I reached across the desk to comfort him, and grabbed his hand. It was ice cold, and trembling.

"Look. I don't know what's happened in your past. And frankly I don't care. You don't need to tell me anything. Blood ties and family doesn't mean shit. Being related to someone by coincidence of blood doesn't mean anything. As far as I'm concerned you and Thain are my family."

I meant every word. It had been a long time since I had thought about my father. While I could never excuse his actions, I could no longer feel the same burning anger anymore, and instead there was only a numbness. It seemed to me that choosing your family was a stronger bond than blood would ever be.

My words apparently resonated with Broch, as he seemed to relax a little, sinking down into his chair. He pulled his hand out of my grip and rested his head in it, closing his eyes.

"I've always felt alone. Always." His voice was quiet, and level. The dry smirk that seemed ever present in his mannerisms had all but evaporated. "Even at Isale. I'd been housed alone, and kept to myself. And then I met you and then Thain. You were both so open, and kind. And Thain has this ability, this wonderful, dreadful power where you find yourself opening up to him. Telling him things you swore you'd never tell anyone. All the bits about yourself that you hate, and the bastard listens. He listens and he cares. I don't think I have ever met a single soul who is as genuine and beautiful as Thain."

I knew exactly what he meant.

"I'm glad you have each other. You're well matched."

Broch smiled at me through his wet eyes. "I'm sorry we didn't tell you Kehlem. It's my fault, don't blame Thain. I just didn't want anything to change."

I waived him away. "It's fine. I understand. I just want you both to be happy. Don't hide yourselves for my sake."

Broch nodded his head.

And that was it. I could sense that unlike Thain, Broch didn't want to talk anymore about it, and I was perfectly happy not to. Let him keep that to himself to cherish and store. I embraced him like a brother, and we returned to the library to celebrate Adléta's tethering as a fully-fledged Aspected physician.

Ice formed across the lake before me, the heat from the morning sun battling quickly to melt it before it could spread a few inches away from me. I rubbed my eyes, trying to wake myself up from my dreary stupor. We were doing pattern drills this morning, and I had slept little from the night before. My head was sore from the drinking and the sun seemed a little too bright for my dry eyes. Thain caught my eye giving me a sympathetic shrug of his shoulders. I nodded back, and restarted the siphon pattern, as always letting some of the energy flow into the hidden tether at my thigh, and also letting some flow directly into myself, trying to wake myself up. It wasn't having much effect, I simply couldn't direct enough energy to make a dent. I closed my connection to the Aspect, and shook my head. I could still see the siphon pattern etched in red every time I shut my eyes.

"Gather around!" the burly Seer monk shouted.

Ugh. Sparring already? Frennic was going to take full advantage of the fact I'm exhausted today.

"Before you break off for sparring, I wanted to let you know, we will be joined next week by Wolv, a first degree Destructia Foclir. She will be instructing you for the remainder of the season."

There was some excited chattering, and one of the Vinnish students, a quiet dark boy called Rulf called out. "But what about Pattern learning? I thought only Monks could teach that?"

Thain and I shot each other a look.

"Wolv will not be teaching you patterns. The two patterns that you have learned so far are all that you will need this year. Pass Wolv's class and then you will move on to the next year session. Don't pass Wolv's class and you will repeat this year. Now, begin your sparring."

The class broke off into pairs, Frennic strode over to me, and immediately crouched into a fighting stance.

"You hear that, gentle Kehlem?" he asked, imitating a concerned parent. "Sounds like we won't have to suffer you in the same class soon."

He darted towards me with a quick jab, which I avoided barely. I was still trying to clear my mind from the siphon pattern.

"Don't be so harsh on yourself, Frennic," I said, trying to distract him and buy myself time to clear my vision. "I'm sure if you work a bit harder you'll be able to pass Wolv's class just like me."

It had the opposite effect. He lunged at me, this time catching me in the side of the rib with a fist.

"As if the Vin Irudur, would ever allow a Caserean Destructia Foclir." He spat the name of my country like it was a curse.

I aimed a sharp kick at his midriff, which he blocked easily. The siphon pattern still hadn't faded, and worse each time I blinked it seemed to burn itself deeper into my brain. I stifled a yawn, still absolutely drained from the night before. If I couldn't concentrate enough to Aspect properly earlier, there was no way I would be able to think clearly to block Frennic's attacks properly.

Struggling to contain my yawn, I squinted, and seeing an opportunity, Frennic landed a brutal blow to the side of my temple, dazing me further. Pain blossomed in my neck as it tried to control the force to my head. My thoughts were now totally scattered. All I could hope for was a quick win from Frennic.

A familiar tugging sensation caused my left hand to twitch, involuntarily, I realised that in my exhaustion, my hand was circling through the siphon pattern. I had used it so often, and had been Aspecting so frequently, it had become almost instinctual. Still. It wouldn't stop me from getting the shit kicked out of me. Trying to blink the sluggishness out of my eyes, I clumsily blocked a kick Frennic had aimed at my ribs with my right hand, and tried to shove him away with my left. A sudden wave of energy rushed into me as my hand connected with Frennic's chest, rejuvenating me. There was a faint red light that blossomed beneath my hand, which faded as Frennic staggered away, falling heavily to the ground.

"What was that?" he hissed, as he struggled to get to his feet.

What had just happened? Did I just siphon energy from Frennic? Was that even possible? The class was drawing to a close, and students were starting to gather their things and returning back to the academy, so following a lead that Frennic had been performing for the past month, I left him on the ground, and chased after Thain, walking together back to the academy. As I caught up with Thain, I spotted a couple of classmates giving me a thumbs up as they glanced back to Frennic, laughing as they watched him limping behind them.

24

Waterfel

After my fight with Frennic, Thain and I met up with Broch in the study hall, the two of them sharing a kiss as they greeted each other. I smiled to myself, happy they no longer felt the need to hide their relationship in front of me. We were approaching the time of year where examinations for permanent tethers were taking place, so students were trying to cram in as much work as possible. For those studying schools of Aspecting less physical than Destructia, that involved extensive research in the library and note taking. That isn't to say Thain and I never had any written work to do. On the contrary we would often be set tasks to calculate the required amount of energy produced by a tether to perform the patterns we'd been demonstrating that morning. The unintended effect being that Thain and I became excellent at anticipating when and how we should charge our very own illicit tether in our dormitory.

"What are you two grinning about?" Broch asked as we sat opposite him. He was surrounded by books.

"Kehlem just took out Frennic, finally," Thain explained.

Broch's eye peaked over the pile of books. "Please tell me you stuck the knee in. Just a little."

"I'm afraid not," I said. I'd kept my word and had said nothing to Broch about mine and Thain's conversation, but it was hard not to look at him in a more sympathetic light.

"Kehlem's too much of a gentleman," Thain said. "Besides, that's not the most interesting part. Tell him Kehlem," he urged me excitedly.

I explained what had happened with the pattern and how it felt like I'd siphoned energy out of Frennic. Broch listened with rapt attention, his eyes wide.

"There's just too much we don't know about Aspecting," Thain said, after I finished. "They must know this stuff is possible, so why don't they teach it to us?"

"I could probably guess," Broch said, dryly.

We all could. How much would you be comfortable teaching your old, beaten enemy?

"Do you think there's information about this somewhere in the academy?" Thain asked. "Is there anything in the library?"

"Not that I've seen. If it's anywhere, it'll be deep in the stores towards the Monk's library."

Broch and I had since filled Thain in about the stores, and I explained to them both exactly how I found the tether pattern.

"It's a shame Kit had a pissing fit the last time we spoke," Broch said. "We probably could have convinced him to help us out. How is Kit anyway?"

I shrugged my shoulders. "I wouldn't know, we haven't spoken in months."

Thain looked at me curious. "What about the Seer lessons you were taking?"

Did I not tell them? I thought I had. I filled them in on what happened, the meditation, hearing Eva and how Kit rushed out of the room, giving me no explanation. I didn't tell them about what Adléta had told me. I wanted to, but I couldn't think of a way without having to explain her secret. I wouldn't jeopardize that.

"Martyr, Kehlem, why didn't you tell us that happened?" Thain asked, exasperated.

"What's the problem?" I asked, "I'm telling you now."

"The problem, you dolt," Broch said, "Is that you've had a target on your back since the moment you stepped through the door. You said yourself that the Abbot thought you were 'outside of the pattern' or whatever. Clearly whatever it is you did wasn't supposed to have happened, otherwise Kit wouldn't have wet himself and ran away."

"But it's been over a month," I explained. "I'm sure if the Abbott was going to do something about it, he would have by now."

Thain and Broch shared a look, which said all that was needed. They weren't convinced.

"Have you tried again?" Thain asked. "You know, to hear Eva? It might," he paused, lowering his voice, "you know, it might help how you've been feeling."

Broch gave Thain a questioning look as I flushed.

"I haven't," I said. "Not that I haven't thought about it, it's just I've been too busy lately. Not in the right frame of mind," I lied.

"Don't bullshit us," Broch said, surprising me. "Anyone who's ever heard you speak of her could tell you're mad for her, so don't lie to us, trying to say you've been too busy."

Next to me Thain kept his gaze firmly on the floor, as the irony of the situation caught us both. I let out a long breath.

"You're right Broch, I'm sorry," I sighed. "I haven't tried again, because..." I paused as I tried to sort through the muddle of what I had been feeling. "I'm afraid of what I'll see. I'm afraid she'll have moved on."

"I've been thinking about that," Thain said, "and I've come to the conclusion that you're an idiot."

I burst out laughing, taken aback by his sincerity.

"I concur," Broch agreed, nodding sagely, and then looked to Thain. "But... why exactly do we think Kehlem is an idiot, sweet?"

"Because," Thain stressed, "from everything our sweet idiot has told us about this Eva, she's the one that led everything. She came back to the town, even though her apprenticeship started in only a few months, when it would make more sense to have just stayed in Mercy. She followed our dolt along on every excursion she could, and more importantly, was the one to kiss him first." He punctuated each sentence by raising a finger. "I suspect that Eva is more tightly bound to you than you realised."

I flushed at Thain's words. Of course, when you listed it like that it made it seem so straight forward. "It's not that simple," I protested "She did those things because we're friends, it's not like she loves me!"

Broch glanced over to Thain. "You're right, our sweet boy is an idiot"

True to the monk's word, a week after my fight with Frennic, a new Vinnish person was waiting for the class to arrive by the lakeside. What's more she was armed with a short sword at her side. I stared at the weapon as I came to a halt with the rest of the class. She was the first armed person I had seen at the academy. As the last of the class joined us, she cleared her throat.

"Greetings class. You should have been expecting my arrival. My name is Wolv, first degree Foclir and Hunter for the Vin Irudur empire."

"Each year I return to the academy to teach the new cohort the more practical attributes of a Hunter for the Empire. Woodcraft, weapon craft, navigation and tracking." She reeled her list off quickly and sharply. Wolv wasn't particularly tall, probably a head shorter than myself, and was slenderly built. There was an unspoken question in the air, and Wolv must have heard it as well.

"I am told by your Do'Seer that you have all been practicing sparring. I will see a demonstration. You," she pointed at Frennic. "Come to the front, and try to take me down."

Frennic did as commanded, albeit with a slight swagger. He stood a head and a half taller than Wolv, and with significantly broader shoulders he probably weighed twice her weight in muscle alone. I watched curiously as the two of them stood opposite each other. Frennic to his credit didn't immediately try and rush her, and instead sent some quick, almost exploratory jabs to test her guard. She swatted them away easily. Wolv's guard seemed fairly open, and high. Frennic must have noticed this as well, and rushed forward for a double leg takedown. He charged forward, quickly and dove down aiming for Wolv's midriff, hands out ready to hook around her legs, except her legs were no longer occupying that space. In the blink of an eye, as soon as Frennic had charged, she had stepped gracefully to the side and grabbing the back of Frennic's tunic, carried his weight and threw him face first into the ground.

Thain let out a bark of laughter in surprise. I smiled to myself, pleased to see Frennic getting his own arse handed to him for once.

Frennic seemed shocked as well, and quickly pushed himself to his feet. Red faced, and perhaps not particularly pleased to have been beaten so easily, he darted again at Wolv, except this time sending much harder jabs aimed at her face. Wolv blocked the first easily, and then twisting her frame slightly, she caught — actually caught — Frennic's wrist as she sent a jab errant, and then using his own momentum, twisted his wrist behind his back, pulling it at a painful angle, and then twisting it again. With her heel behind Frennic's leg she threw him once more to the ground. All in all, the bout lasted less than five minutes. Frennic had enough sense to stay down the second time.

"Not particularly impressive," Wolv said, her back to Frennic, now facing us. "Two weeks from now the class will be taken into the forest fifteen miles north of the academy. You will be expected to survive for three nights, and you will be given only a knife and an iron tether. After the third night you will return to the Academy. The first three students returning to the academy will be eligible for the next stage of testing. The rest of you will either resit the year or will have to find a new school."

Thain and I looked at each other. Three places? There were seven students in the class. We needed to be in that group of three that passed. If I had any hope of getting my permanent tether and freedom, I needed to pass this test.

The rest of the mornings lesson were reserved for Wolv teaching us some basic shelters that can be made in various settings, as well as some easy traps that can be laid to catch small animals. We were also set the task of reading up on navigation in preparation for tomorrow's lessons.

Later that evening after Thain and Broch made their excuses to leave the dormitory together, I found myself alone once more, with the evening stretching ahead of me. Like a piece of gristle stuck between my teeth, I hadn't been able to let go of the conversation the three of us had about Eva. Could my friends possibly be correct?

It felt like my whole body was itching as I was filled with a nervous energy.

No matter which way I sat, I couldn't find a comfortable spot to sit and read the book on navigation Thain and I had loaned from the library. I'd sit and read a paragraph, only to realise halfway through my mind had wandered off while my eyes continued their march to the bottom of the page, none of the information sinking in. The longer I tried, the hotter and sweatier I was getting, not helped by the fact this Martyr forsaken room seemed to trap heat better than our handmade tether. I threw my book across the room in frustration. None of it was sinking in. Grabbing my boots, I stomped out of the room and descended to the lower floors of the academy.

Since my arrival, I hadn't really explored the academy much, only following Thain and Broch around, so while my friends were otherwise indisposed and with a night off from Brin's, I decided to wander around, and see what forbidden areas I could discover.

This time of the evening the academy seemed hesitant, like all the walls were waiting for the breath of the morning to arrive. The lanterns were thumbed down by some universal machination, letting the shadows grow deeper. The atmosphere was reflected in the rushed footsteps of students and monks trying to get to their destination as quickly as possible, footsteps echoing deeper and louder than normal. Hushed voices added to the texture of the atmosphere, which the unusually shaped walls reverberated back to you, giving you the impression, you were never far away from prying eyes, despite how deserted the academy was this time of night. For me, it reminded me of being in the woods on a moonless night, with no fire to light your way. You look up through the canopy, and a thick blackness sits heavily atop the branches, and seems to encroach down upon you the longer you gaze in trepidation. At night sound seems to travel further, and even the gentlest of winds will send branches and leaves rustling, whispering, promising hidden malevolencies to any who dare trespass. The feeling in the back of your neck, or behind your legs, when you know someone is watching you, pacing behind you, that's how it felt to be walking in the academy at night.

Despite this, I stood firm and tall, unwilling to be bent to the whim of an inanimate object. I would not cower. I strode calmly, and slowly across the entrance hall, with neither aim nor intent. I walked through doors I'd never crossed before, up staircases I hadn't seen and followed wherever my feet led me. I walked for some time and eventually found myself in a slowly sloping corridor which spiralled in on itself upwards and inwards. The further I walked, the tighter the spiral became until the infrequent lanterns were no longer enough to make a dent on the creeping shadows. I would have stopped, turned back there and then, if it had not been for a noise. It wasn't a sudden noise, rather it was the realisation I had been following this noise for some time, but it had only just become loud enough for me to have enough resolution to notice it above the sound of my own breathing. A rushing, rapid sound. My curiosity tempering my unease, I continued the upward walk, reaching a hand out to the inner wall of the spiral to guide me. Even in the dark I could feel once again the strange yet familiar patterns that had been carved into the stone walls. For some reason their presence comforted me. I climbed up the spiralling slope and with each step the sound I was following grew louder, and the air around me seemed to become noticeably more humid, making the sweat stick to my skin. Just as I was regretting my decision to carry on, the spiral levelled out, straightening on to a short landing, lit with only two lanterns sat bracketing a short, simple wooden door. From the sound and smell, it seemed like it opened to the outside. With a mental shrug, I walked to the door and pulled it open.

Immediately I was greeted by the thunderous sound of falling water hitting stone, wood and metal. Loud enough to demand shouting, it almost made me slam the door shut again, were it not for the sight. Before me was a narrow stone pathway, slick from the aerosolised water, reflecting shimmered lights from lanterns that hung from poles above the walkway. Intrigued to figure out where I was, and with some suspicions of my own, I took some careful steps out onto the walkway, each step slow and with purpose so as not to slip. A few steps onto the walkway and the source of the noise became clear. At my back was the raw cliff face, but the direction I was facing was a sheer drop. Below me were some of the great waterwheels that powered the more important tethers, designated for use to those of First degree and nobility to the Vin Irudur. The stone walkway ended before it hit the waterfall, but if you were so inclined, you could probably walk to the end, reach a hand out and take a cup full of water from the falling torrent. Or the torrent would take you with it. I opted to stay where I was. From this height the dim lights of Isale town could be seen, arranged in discordant rows with a large square patch of darkness where I pictured the town square would be. I was lower than the dormitory tower, but that had only a single window large enough to peer out, so I took my time to appreciate the view. My legs were tired from the climb, so despite the wet floor, I sat down, enjoying the cool mist as it breezed against my body.

I'm not sure how long I was sat there, looking out into the night, but at some point, my musings were interrupted by the sound of feet hitting the stone walkway.

"Fancy seeing you here," Kit called to me, sitting down next to me.

"I could say the same to you," I said, raising my voice above the sound of the torrential water. It had been over a month since we had last spoken. From the shimmering light of the lanterns, I could see dark patches under his eyes.

"I come here most nights," he said. "It's a good place to clear your head I've found." He let out a heavy sigh. "I'm sorry we've not spoken in a while Kehlem. I'm sure you have your questions, I'm just not sure I can even begin to answer them."

His shoulders drooped, and his voice was slow and heavy. I decided to change the subject.

"How have things been for you? How is your learning going?" I asked.

Kit scoffed. "Not really what I expected."

I nodded in agreement, and for a while the two of us sat in silence letting the wind carry the fine spray of water around us.

"You should come out for a drink with us again some time," I said, breaking the quiet.

"I appreciate the offer Kehlem, but it's probably not appropriate." He looked around, and pulled his hood back up, getting to his feet. "I should be getting back. Be well Kehlem."

"Kit?" I called out to him as he turned to the door.

I saw his figure pause, turning slightly.

"Are you ok?" I asked earnestly.

Remaining silent, he turned back and left through the door, descending into the academy.

25

Forest

The wagon rocked as it trundled across the uneven path, the seven of us in the back swaying like stalks of grass planted on the rough wooden benches. Wolv was sat up front of the horseless carriage, taking us deep into the glen and into the cover of the woods. Today was the start of the woodland trial she had spoken about.

"I don't feel so good," Thain gasped next to me, pallor noticeably tinged with green.

I rubbed his back sympathetically and he shook me off, keeping his lips tightly pursed. I smiled to myself and watched the scenery of the forest go by. Thin, sporadic saplings gave way for thick, luscious pines, whose arms spread far and wide providing significant cover from elements outside and within. Despite the morning sun, the light grew paler as it struggled to penetrate through the thick plumage of the canopy. The floor beneath us became brown and soft, not from mud, but from the fallen pine needles, and the aromatic smell of pine sap filled the air. As with all forests, this had a silence to it, one that had been simmering for centuries. The sound of the wagon's wheels trundling on their spokes barely made a dent in the pitch-silence of the woods.

With the silence, came a rising anxiety in me. Wolv had explained what was at stake. We had to survive three nights in the woods, and be in the first three to return to the academy. We'd spent the past two weeks preparing,

THE SOUL'S ASPECT

learning how to find fresh water, to lay traps and to build shelter. Summer was drawing to a close, and autumn would be falling first in these higher altitude woods. We would only be given a knife and an iron tether. Water and shelter would be more important than food. If needed we could go without eating for three days. We would also be completely alone. It was forbidden to team up in the woods, and even if you wanted to, it would be counter intuitive. No one wanted to repeat this year, or drop out of this class. For me, this was my best hope of getting my freedom. If I failed, it would be another year, probably two before I could earn my tether and leave this place a free man.

As the cart continued its journey deeper into the woods, I could feel my stomach start to rumble from hunger. Last night Thain, Broch and I had descended on Isale town, with honourable intentions of a quiet drink and meal at Brin's before the trial. When we had arrived at the tavern however, we found atop our usual table another quart barrel of ale, with Brin smiling at us sheepishly behind the bar. I had warned Brin a week prior that I would be away for a few nights for the test, and it seemed he wanted to send Thain and I off properly, with enough Ale to drown a man. Being the sensible students, we were, we resisted for all of three heartbeats. The three of us, and with some incessant cajoling, Brin also, drank late into the evening, grinning and laughing like fools. I had woken up the next morning with an unpleasant, but not unmanageable headache whereas Thain, under the irresponsible tutelage of Brin had also imbibed some fine Vin wines, and judging by his viridescent demeanour, was paying a heavy price for mixing his drinks. I couldn't help but feel a little concerned for him. Thain was a gentle soul, and was raised in a city. This would not be an easy task for him.

I wonder if they'll leave us in a single spot? Maybe I could tail him for the first few days, make sure he's ok?

Around mid-afternoon Wolv pulled the cart to a stop. We were still on a narrow path, with no obvious sign as to why she stopped. She jumped off the cart and walked to the back where we were all sat, silent.

"Janus," she called. The Vinnish girl sat opposite me jumped. "You're off here."

The girl looked around, wide eyed. I'm sure we were thinking the same thing. Wolv would be dropping us off one by one. There goes my plan for trailing Thain then.

Janus stepped off the cart, looking very pale. Wolv handed her a short-sheathed knife and an iron tether from a sack she'd slung on her back. "See you in three days," Wolv said. And without a second glance, she strode back to the front of the wagon and pushed onwards, the figure of the girl stood still in the path in shock as we left her, continuing to climb up with winding forest path. This continued for the next hour, with Wolv stopping the cart and dropping another student off one by one, until Thain and I were the last in the cart.

Of course, I thought to myself. Of course, she'd leave the Caserean boys till last. We'd end up with the furthest to travel back to the academy. A glance at Thain told me he'd figured the same thing. And it may have been my imagination, but the next interval where she called the cart to a stop seemed to take a lot longer than the other ones prior.

"Thain," She shouted, not bothering to get off the cart this time. She reached back and threw him a knife and tether, which he caught clumsily.

"Three days," was all she said.

Thain looked at me, the green gone from his skin, replaced now with a pale white that matched his hair.

"Good luck," I said. "See you back at the academy." I smiled at him, trying to encourage him. Inside, I was filled with dread for him.

He nodded at me, and hopped off the cart, leaving me alone. I was relieved to see Thain immediately walking off the path, and walking confidently into the undergrowth as we continued our pace deeper into the woods.

Despite it being just the two of us, Wolv continued on in silence, following the quiet twisting path higher and deeper into the mountain woods. The anxious feeling in the pit of my hollow stomach began to rise and I began nodding my knee up and down, restless. Each time the wagon slowed for a bump or turn, I wondered if this would be my spot, but the cart carried on, endless, much further into the woods than any of the others had been dropped.

The silence of the forest grew thicker, and the light from the sun was coming from a decidedly lower angle, when finally, the cart drew to a stop.

"Out," Wolv commanded me.

Hungry, and eager to get started I jumped out of the cart.

"Be back in three days," She said, tossing my tether and knife to the ground next to me. By the time I picked them up, she had left, the racketing sound of the wooden wheels already fading into the cushioned quiet of the woods.

I sighed, and setting myself downhill, began to trudge slowly back the way we had come, south and into the depths of the forest. By how long it had taken Wolv to drop me off here, the worst-case scenario would mean I would have to walk for the three full days just to make it back to the academy. Those Vinnish students that had been dropped off first would likely just need to walk a day's march and then find a nice cosy spot to camp for the next few days. It was hard not to be bitter. The one hope was that Thain and I had been dropped off last, so it's possible that we may bump into each other.

I was hungry, but if I had any chance of getting back to the academy to win my spot, I'd need to use the last of whatever light there was to make progress south, and find somewhere comfortable to sleep. I also had a plan. Strapped to my thigh was my illicit bronze tether. If needed, I could try and draw energy from our physical tether back in the dormitory to replenish myself. That would mean I wouldn't need to waste time looking for food, although I'd still have to find water. I also couldn't rely on it. Whilst Broch had promised to keep the tether charged whilst we were away, if Thain was using at the same time, we'd quickly run it dry. The iron tethers that Wolv had given us were tied to one of the weaker energy sources in the academy, and would probably only be good for a single pattern.

Progress south was slow. To try and save myself time I was taking as straight a path as possible, which often meant climbing over fallen trees, or trying to navigate through tightly packed spruces. Not helping matters was the fact my attire was absolutely not made for this type of terrain. After less than an hour walking, I could already feel blisters forming on my feet, and as the sun dropped lower in the sky, a chill sent goose pimples across my skin.

The more urgent matter of course was finding a source of water. I could perhaps go a couple days without drinking, but it would be a miserable experience, and I'd need all the energy I had to be able to make the three-day march back to the academy.

After around two hours of walking, I paused for a moment, wanting to catch my breath, and take stock of where I was. The journey so far had been steep downhill, and my knees and thighs were aching from the effort of keeping me upright. I sat down on a fallen tree trunk, and rested, sweat dripping off my forehead and onto the forest floor. As my breathing slowed and quietened, I heard the faint but unmistakable sound of running water. Not caring if it took me off route, I followed the sound, regretting giving my legs a chance to realise how tired they were. Sure enough, the sound got louder until I found a small creek bubbling with fresh mountain water, no doubt leading down to the lake in the grounds of the academy. The creek was narrow and flat, the water having eroded away the topsoil leaving bare slippery rock beneath. We hadn't been given any water skins, so I dipped my hands straight in, scooping the frigid water to my lips. There are few things more refreshing than quenching a thirst with ice cold water. Drinking enough to sate my thirst, but stopping short of giving myself a stitch, I splashed some of the cool water over my face, and as the fragile dusk began to settle across the woods, I followed the edge of the water down, and towards the south.

Following the banks of the creek made my journey substantially easier, a lot of the ground was already flat, cleared probably from springtime floods when the creek would widen into a river of snowmelt, but this easier time came with a cost. The water's progress through the woods was meandering and at this time of the year, the water flow was small. Often the creek would disappear completely beneath the undergrowth, and I'd find myself once again tackling roots and uneven ground.

Evening fell quickly in the woods and the little light I was using to navigate was soon extinguished. I considered trying to press ahead, inching closer to my destination by feel alone, but after I almost twisted my ankle on a stray root, I decided to call it quits for the night, and find a good place to sleep,

THE SOUL'S ASPECT

rather than risk having to limp back to the academy.

With only the short knife, building a big, comfortable shelter was out of the question. Not to mention, I'd hadn't eaten all day and the pains in my stomach were beginning to become a distraction. I found an area nearby that was relatively flat where the fallen pine needles had softened, forming an almost spongy bed to lay upon. Wrapping my cloak tightly around my shoulders and laying down on the ground, I tried to will myself to sleep.

I woke suddenly, heart racing. The forest was still dark, and above me I could see distant stars blinking above the canopy. I groaned quietly. I'd hoped to sleep through until at least sunrise. It was too dark and too cold to get started walking again. I'd probably only slept for a few hours, if not less. Annoyed, I sat upright, leaning against a tree. I'd been woken up by stomach pains, unused to going a full day without eating. My hope of lasting three days without food was dwindling. Still. There was something I could do about that.

If I'm not getting any sleep tonight, I may as well be comfortable while I wait for the dawn.

Squinting in the gloom, I gathered some of the broken branches around me, trying to resist the urge to itch as each movement sent dead pine needles from my cloak down my back. I piled the twigs up in front of me, and concentrating, I used only the first quarter of the second Destructia pattern, linking myself to the iron tether we'd been given at the start of the trek. A pitiful blue flame sputtered from my palm, aimed down towards the pile of twigs. My eyes ached at the sudden light, but when it disappeared, it was replaced with the welcome sight of an amber flame, as my makeshift camp fire took light. We had figured out in our nefarious practises that you can shorten the forms of the patterns, particularly the second Destructia pattern, to produce smaller and smaller flames. Particularly handy when trying to conserve how much of a finite tether you use up. I held my hands up to the flames, warming them as the fire produced enough light to take stock of my surrounding. I'd slept beneath a great pine tree, its needled branches swaying gently overhead. In fact, the branches I was burning gave off the unmistakable sweet smell of pine sap. I concentrated again, this time linking myself to the bronze tether on my thigh. I quickly ran through the siphon pattern, hands clumsier than normal in the cold, and felt the soothing effect as energy from our tether in the dormitory filled me, and warmed me from the inside out. Not wanting to take too much, in case Thain needed some, I cut the connection. While it helped ease some of the aches from the walk and I was a lot more awake, it did nothing to stop the hunger pangs from my stomach. I couldn't sit here all night, pitying myself for my hunger, I needed a distraction.

Like smoke, seeping beneath a door blocking a burning room, an insidious thought crept into my mind, whispering a suggestion to me. It had been there, waiting for me to give in, for when my resolve was weakest, and now, while I was desperately wanting a distraction it pounced, knowing I had not the willpower to resist.

Before I could talk myself out of it, I sat up right, and slowed my breathing, concentrating on only the sounds I could hear. The crackle of the fire. The '*hiss*' as sap from a branch was boiled out of a twig. The sound of branches and leaves rubbing against one another in the canopy above. I laid my left-hand palm upwards on my lap and like a loving friend, the Aspect was there waiting for me. I held the boundary in my hand. and thought of Eva.

I was looking down on her sleeping form, curled tightly on a bed, covered with a blanket. The window next to her was shut, but the curtains were open, letting in light from the large harvest moon, sending orange moonbeams scattered across the bedroom. The room was sparse, but comfortable, I assumed it was her uncle's house judging by the decor. It was dark in the room, and I could barely make out her features, but I knew instinctively it was her. It was like when you close your eyes, and are told to point to your own nose, your body does so instinctively. It was the same with my soul and hers.

Not wanting to trespass on her privacy any longer, I left, clearing my mind. Before I let go of the Aspect however, another name, one that I'd tried to keep weighted down in my mind floated to the surface.

Tema.

My mind's eye went dark, and I was surrounded by pitch black on all sides. Where was I? Was this Barrowheld? Why is it so dark?

'Pa?' I called out by instinct, my voice having a strange, rich quality to it.

The blackness changed around me, morphing into something else. Back when I was working with Themia, she showed me some of the nastier solvents and how they worked. Some of them had a strange property where the surface of the liquid seemed to float atop the liquid itself, refracting light into strange and wondrous colours. That was what these new colours felt like. All around me the blackness was fading, replaced by a sluggish, yet frictionless prismatic transition of colours. I couldn't bear to look at it, and tried to close my mind's eye to it, to return to blackness, return to the forest. There was a loud, deep noise that reverberated, rattling my very soul, and I felt like every nerve, every part of me was aflame. I wasn't welcome here, wherever here was.

With an immense struggle, I found my hand, back in the forest and shifted it closing the connection to the Aspect. My chest was heaving, and cold sweat was dripping down my neck. I looked around and was relieved to see trees and sky and ground around me. I was back in the forest. The fire at my feet had burned out, and the sky above had a blue-ish tint as sunrise was beginning.

I took a long, calming breath, and tried to forget how the deep, awful noise I heard in wherever I just was, sounded so alien and yet so familiar.

26

Trail

The morning mist boiled around my feet, swirling in gentle patterns as I disturbed its sluggish progress across the forest floor. Using the faint early morning light, I journeyed back to the stream which was just a faint trickle surrounded by thick, green foliage. I continued to follow it south, forever downhill, where the stream opened a little, wide enough for me to drink from if I cupped my hand. As I washed my face, and quenched my thirst, I thought back to the images I'd seen from the night before. Why hadn't I been able to see my father the same way I'd seen Eva? What was the difference? And what the blackened hell was that place?

I rubbed my eyes, trying to ease the slight pressure that had been building up behind them, probably caused by a lack of sleep. Maybe that was it, maybe I'd just imagined it. The mind can do horrible things to itself when it thinks it's still dreaming. As a child I would have hideous nightmares, where I would wake screaming, paralysed in my own bed. Each time father would come running into my room, comforting me back to sleep. He told me that my mind thought it was still asleep, still dreaming, so it wouldn't permit my body to move, even though it continued to show me horrors from my dreams before my eyes. Maybe whatever I saw last night was just that, another waking nightmare.

I knew it was a lie I told myself, but it was a comforting, easy lie. One of the many hundreds we tell ourselves each day. What was one more stick to a pile of dry kindling?

With my thirst satiated I continued south, leaving the stream for a more direct route hoping to cover as much ground today as possible, so I'd have an easier final day. The hunger pangs in my stomach had blessedly abated, and all that was left was a curious hollow feeling. Using the tether last night had helped replenish my energy, but it couldn't sustain myself for the rest of the trial.

By mid-morning I had made good progress, the trees had become further spaced out, and the slope had become gentler, easing the pressure on my thighs and calves. I'd stumbled across a fallen log which had been overtaken by a fungus, one which I was fairly sure from recent lessons was edible. It grew from the fallen trunk wide and wrinkled, its gelatinous form making it look almost ear like. An uninspiring beige colour, it seemed harmless and with my empty stomach egging me on, I cut a handful of the lobes of fungus off the tree, and took a small bite. Surprisingly, it had very little taste, other than a faint nutty aroma, however its texture was awful. It squelched and splutted with each chew, squeaking against my teeth. Resigning myself, I ended up swallowing the bite almost whole, and I had to stop myself from gagging as the sloppy texture of the fungi slipped down the back of my throat. Wolv had warned us about the toxicity of some of the fungi in this forest, so I paced myself after my small bite, and decided to wait to see if I felt anything unusual before taking another.

As I continued walking south, the clouds above slowly drifted overhead, blocking my line of sight to the sun and diffusing its light into a muted grey. Having lost my only way of measuring the broad passing of time as well as direction, I continued walking in what I hoped was still southwards and didn't stop until the pinching feeling inside my cheeks returned as my body began to crave more water. I slowed myself to a stop and leaning against a tree, I listened hard to see if I could hear the sounds of the stream I'd been following the past day and a half. There were no sounds other than the gentle rustling of the branches above me. I considered the fistful of fungi I was still holding in my hand.

Their soft, gelatinous texture had to be due to water, right? Or at least some kind of liquid.

I'd no idea how long it had been since I'd eaten the smaller strip, but I'd felt none of the common issues with poisonous fungi, no shortness of breath, no tingling lips, no stomach cramps, even. Shrugging to myself, I ate the handful of fungi I'd collected, and happily only gagged once or twice at their awful texture. I'd hoped they had enough water in them to keep me hydrated, at least until I could find a stream. I was about to get moving again when I noticed something. On the ground, next to the tree I was leaning against was a small pitiful collection of burnt twigs. I crouched down and ran my fingers through the ashes. They were bone cold, the fire having long gone out, but someone had absolutely been here, probably camped here over night. I darted my eyes around the campsite, and sure enough there was a patch of disturbed foliage travelling south, kicked up pine needles and broken twigs on the ground.

Could this be Thain's trail? I thought to myself. Only one way to find out.

Tracking Thain was no easy job. Barrowheld had plenty of woods and forest for me to explore growing up, but as Eva rightly pointed out, my woodsmanship was effectively none existent. The past two weeks Wolv had been drilling us on how to track using various markers like waist height, broken twigs, or upturned foliage. But trying to find any of these signs out in the wild was incredibly slow going. The trail wasn't a continuous line I could follow. Instead all I got were various subtle hints that something had passed by the area; a scuff mark in a patch of mud, a thin branch with its fresh leaves still hanging loose, an uneven distribution of the brown pine needles on the forest floor. More than once I thought I'd lost the trail only to walk a few more miles and be fed another tantalising crumb of information. I tried to put myself in Thain's mindset and travel in the direction I thought he would have taken. It concerned me that since I'd picked up his trail, I hadn't seen a single water source nearby. The fungi had done the trick for me, and had somewhat sated my thirst, and appeased my stomach.

Had Thain found something similar? Or has he gone these past two days with no food or drink?

However misguided, I felt responsible for his safety and I couldn't bear the thought of Thain wandering around the forest lost, thirsty and hungry. I'd rather give up the trial then leave my friend alone in the woods.

The clouds above were growing dark, and sullen light was raining down from the canopy when I caught my first sense of drawing close to Thain. I was following a remarkably clear trail of footprints, left in the muddy remains of what I assumed was a seasonal river bed, when I heard the unmistakable sound of coughing coming from above the bank next to me. I smiled, relieved at having finally caught up with my friend.

"Ho there!" I called out to Thain. "You left me a clumsy trail, Thain!"

I heard rustling above me as my friend walked out of the undergrowth. A figure jumped down to join me in the dried-up river bed. It took me a moment for my brain to readjust. The man before me wasn't my friend.

"Well, not who I was expecting to see," Frennic said, drawing his knife from his sheath, giving me a lazy smile, "but a happy surprise for me."

"Frennic," I said slowly, my eyes drawn to the sharp glint of grey that he held at his waist, "what are you doing?"

He was still walking towards me slowly, knees bent a little, eyes fixated on my own.

"How many times can a man accept an insult, Kehlem, before he snaps?" He asked me, earnest voice in total contrast to the malevolence I could see burning bright in his green eyes.

"What are you talking about?" I demanded. My mind was racing. "Are you talking about the last fight?"

"I don't care how you tricked me, dog," he spat, all evenness from his tone gone. He was still advancing on me, knife drawn. "You Caserean rats are all the same. Why do they insist on letting you vermin into our country? Into my school."

He seemed to be talking to himself more than me. I started backing away, back the way I had come, not taking my eyes off of his own. I thought back to what Adléta had told me about Frennic.

"Adléta told me about you, you know?" I asked, trying to keep him talking while I tried to think of a way out of this. "I don't think you want to do this. You don't have anything to prove."

Frennic halted, shocked. "And what exactly did that bitch tell you?" He didn't wait for me to give him an answer. "She's a sad, pathetic little worm. Why should I give a fuck what she thinks of me," he snapped at me, flecks of spit sitting on the corner of his mouth. "Who the fuck do you think you are, coming to my country, stealing our magics, tainting our Aspect with your filth!" His voice rose into a scream, and there was a wild look in his eyes. "Your pathetic people were beaten to submission, whipped like the dogs you are!"

He pulled his arm up, and I caught a glimpse of his wrist as his sleeve pulled back. A glint of a gold ring bound against his wrist by leather straps. He darted into a pattern so quickly, I barely had a chance to react. I threw myself flat to the floor, as an intense heat blast over where my body had just been. Not wanting to give Frennic the chance to move again, I rolled forwards, and crawled on my knees. I pulled my own knife from its sheath and with blue flame continuing to burn above me, I stabbed the knife into Frennic's foot. The knife met a little resistance which I pushed through with my body weight and I felt it slide out through the other side, out through the sole of his foot. The flames above ceased as Frennic lost his concentration, and howled in pain. Before I could shift away, he booted me underneath the chin with his uninjured foot. My teeth slammed against each other and I tasted blood in my mouth. My mind went hazy as I fell onto my back from the force of the blow. I tried to stand but my mind was too fuddled. The world span around me and it was all I could to stop myself from throwing up.

Frennic pulled my knife out of his foot with a grunt, and tossed it aside, far out of my reach. He limped towards me, kicking my hands away from my side, and then knelt on each of my wrists, straddling my chest.

He bent close to my ear. "To think," he whispered, his hot, wet breath dripping poison into my ear, "the Aspect would bless a people as depraved, and useless as yours. You and your disgusting rent-boy friends."

I tried to struggle against his weight, but I was completely immobile. Even if his whole weight wasn't atop me, everything was spinning. Frennic sat back up onto my chest, and pulled out his knife again. He rested the point against his forefinger, and sat inspecting the knife, twisting it by its pommel.

"I'm told you were a physician, Kehlem," he said thoughtfully, still staring at the knife. "I studied anatomy a little you know," he said, and pressed the tip of the knife just below my ribs.

My ears were pounding, the forest suddenly fell quiet.

"Frennic," I pleaded quietly, "don't, please. You don't need to do this."

"Shhh," he said. And slowly, with deliberate patience, he pushed the knife into me. I let out a shrill scream as the point pierce my skin, pushing aside tissue and muscle. Pain radiated through my abdomen like liquid fire. Frennic kept pushing the knife deeper and further, each slow movement sending spasms of agony throughout my body. Sweat was pouring from my body and a hot, wet fluid spilled across my stomach and drenched my clothes as Frennic yanked the knife out. I let out another scream of pain. He considered the bloody knife once more, and now placed the point on the right side of my waist.

"One more for good luck, what do you say?" He asked, and once more plunged the knife into my body, twisting it slightly as it pushed in further.

My throat was bloody from screaming, and my body was ablaze in agony. Frennic looked down at me, disdain etched deep in his eyes. And without another word, he pushed himself off me, and limped up and out of the river bed.

I had no strength to move, and I could feel blood pooling around me from the first wound. I tried to lift my arm, to try and staunch the blood flow, but my arms were still numb from where Frennic had knelt on them.

There was a tingling in my lips, and the forest around me was drawing cold. My eyes felt heavy, and sleep promised me an escape from the pain that was ablaze within me.

27

Aspector

Prismatic translucent shades seeped around me, gliding frictionless in impossible angles. I was within myself, or without, neither above nor below, floating softly like fine silk on a coastal breeze. At first concern, the shades seemed to shift randomly, sliding this way or that, without rhyme nor reason. But with focus, a path blossomed before me. Not a path. A pattern. I watched the swirling colours obey the impossible current carrying it with its undertow, happy in the knowledge that I knew where the shade's journeys would end. The pattern was familiar to me. The essence around and within me pulsed, slow and loud. I rattled with the translucent shades, as they began to dart in a new, and alien pattern. The pulse came again, quicker, sharper this time. A third time the pulse hammered against me, falling slower than the last, but quicker than the first, as if whatever it was, was trying to readjust itself for my benefit. And it seemed to work. I recognised the pulse, or I recognised whatever the intent was behind the pulse. It spoke within me.

You….are…of….mine

Each word reverberated with great deliberation, as if the speaker was savouring the taste of each individual meaning. Eons stretched in the pauses between words.

Your what? I shot back, more out of instinct than out of actual deliberate intent.

...Mine... was all the essence around me had to send me back.

The shades around and within me slowed their alien pattern, and a third arrangement began. I felt a stinging sensation.

Felt? Can I feel things here?

It came again, muted, but sharp like a knife stabbing through pillow to reach flesh.

"..."

That sounds familiar, I thought trying to place the memory, chasing after the floating silk on the wind. My fingers caught the end, and with a sudden rush of vertigo, the prismatic colours shifted, darting away from me, and I fell backwards.

Pain like I'd never felt before was coursing through my body, each laborious heartbeat struggling against my failing body. I was cold, but had no energy to shiver, and the world was dark. I heard movement around me.

Frennic probably came back to finish me off, I mused, detached.

Another stinging sensation, across my cheek, followed by a horrible rhythmic pressure against my sternum.

"Come on, stay with me," a man's voice sobbed.

With great effort, I pried my eyes open, relieved to see a solid world around me, and Thain's face close to mine.

"Thain?" I said, confused.

"Oh!" Thain cried, seeing me stir. "You're alive!" His eyes were red and swollen, snot and tears pouring from his nose and eyes. "We need to get you back to the academy," he said quickly through gasps of tears. "I thought you were dead!"

I tried to shift myself so I could sit upwards, but the pain in my abdomen wouldn't allow it. A coldness crashed through me, the likes of which I'd never experienced before. There was a sense of dread building, pumping through my failing heart that I knew what was to come with a certainty.

I looked up at my sweet friend. "I'm not going anywhere Thain," I said quietly, trying not to upset him. "You should go, get back to the academy and tell them what happened."

"No!" He cried. "I'm not leaving you here!"

We both understood what was missing from that sentence. *To die alone.*

I grabbed his face with my hand, smearing my blood against his cheeks, and staining some of his white hair red. "It's ok Thain. I'm okay. Leave me." With a start I suddenly remembered what Frennic had said to me, 'Not who I'd been expecting to see'.

"Thain, listen to me," I said, suddenly urgent. I grunted as the effort sent spasms through my body. "Frennic was tracking you. We both were. You need to get back to the academy before he finds you and kills you."

Kills you *as well*. I corrected myself internally.

I could see the turmoil in my sweet friends' eyes as he knew he'd have to leave me. "Martyr fucking damn it Kehlem," he cried, hopeless. "Are there no patterns? What about the one you taught me, the one you used on Broch?"

I smiled sadly at him. "That was for treating his infection. I don't know a pattern to heal open wounds like this. I'd need a full pattern."

"Fuck Frennic, I'm not leaving you," Thain cried, but his voice was suddenly very quiet to my ear.

There was a peace I found in dying. All the struggles and concerns of my life some few hours ago fell away from me, meaningless. I thought of Eva and of course felt a longing within my failing heart, that I would never see her face again, but I took solace in the fact that in my dying, I probably eased her life significantly. She could live a life untroubled by me. Thain was holding my hand, and stroking my hair out of my eyes, quiet tears falling down his cheeks. It would be so easy just to close my eyes. To allow myself to sink into the encroaching darkness.

Colours shifting endless around me, and a single pulse that reverberated through my soul shook me. And there it was. That sudden understanding. The colours were shifting in a pattern. A huge, sprawling geometry of such beauty that it took what little of the breath I had away from me. With the last of the energy I had, I reached out, and once more touched the Aspect.

"What are you doing?" Thain asked, jumping up in surprise.

I ignored him and pictured in my mind's eye the patterns I'd been shown in the gliding essence. It felt different somehow. Whereas before I'd always felt my hand was being guided by a current, this time I was the ocean, driving forth ripples in the boundary, carving out my own pattern with which to command the Aspect. I finished this new, simple pattern and lay my hand on my chest, and felt a warmth against my thigh as my bronze tether directed energy to me. Like before with Broch's injury, I once again saw the pattern I'd just carved etched in red in my mind's eye, laid across the consciousness of my own body. I moved and flexed the pattern around my body, finding the wounds Frennic had inflicted. First, I stitched closed the wound in my waist, which had been largely superficial having only torn tissue, no organs or significant vessels damaged. The area itched as the pattern sent spiralling fractal repeats of itself into my torn flesh, repairing and re-joining asunder tissue. Content with that simple repair, I moved over to the more pressing issue. The first wound Frennic had gifted me was a lot worse. The wound had torn muscle and organ, and sliced open one of the minor arteries leading to my lower body. I could feel with each heartbeat the sliced vessel spilled my life essence out, draining me of warmth and energy. Once again, I encouraged the pattern around, stitching the vessel closed. It was going too slowly and the warmth of my tether was failing. Our water butt at the dormitory must be running out of energy. It wasn't enough.

After all that, I'm going to die anyway. I almost felt like laughing. Just before I cut my connection to the Aspect, resigning myself to my fate, there was a sudden warmth against my shoulder, and suddenly the pattern sprang back into life. The vessel finished its fusion, once more smooth and complete. The damage to my liver was thankfully minimal, and I knew that of all the organs it was fairly resilient, so I left that to heal naturally and focused on closing the skin and muscle shut. Again, I felt an itch as the wound closed, and with a slow, shaky breath I cut my connection to the Aspect, and opened my eyes.

Thain was stood over me, hand on my shoulder, smiling at me with a profound look of relief on his face. He was swaying slightly.

"You saved my life," I whispered, realising what he'd done. When my tether was failing, he'd offered himself as a source for the Aspect and I'd drained him healing myself.

He offered me a hand and I took it, pulling myself to my feet. I winced, clutching my abdomen, liver wound still open and painful. Thain pulled me into a tight embrace, and I could feel his body shaking as he shed quiet tears.

"I'd do it a hundred times if I needed, Kehlem."

"How did you find me?" I asked, shaking with relief and exhaustion.

"I was looking for a stream to drink from when I heard a scream from where I'd just left. I came running back to help." He said, through his tears.

Of course, he'd come running to help. Probably didn't even know it was me, and would have helped regardless.

"How did you do that?" Thain asked. "When did you learn that pattern?"

I pulled back from the embrace, and gripped Thain's shoulder, partly to comfort him, and partly to steady myself.

"I didn't learn it," I said, trying to piece together what had just happened. "I was shown it, I think." My voice was hesitant.

"Shown? By who? When?" Thain asked, confused. We started walking down the dried river bed together supporting each other's weight.

I took a deep breath. "The Aspect. I think the Aspect showed me."

As we walked I tried to explain to Thain what I had seen, the swirling, impossible colours, the words spoken to me without sound.

"I think I was dying, and for some reason the Aspect spoke to me. When you woke me, I felt like I knew what I needed to do."

"That doesn't make any sense Kehlem. The Aspect isn't a physical thing, it's not sentient. Why would a place try and save your life?" Thain asked, looking at me through the corner of his eye.

"I've no idea," I said honestly. Do I tell him the whole story? Will he think me mad? I took a steady breath. "It's not the first time I've seen it either." I braced myself, ready for his ridicule.

"When?" Thain asked gently, surprising me.

"Last night," I breathed. "I was trying to see if I could see Eva again, you know like I'd done before," I said, not meeting Thain's eyes. "But I had an idea to look for my father, at first there was nothing. But then I was surrounded by those prismatic colours once again, I think I was looking directly into the Aspect."

"But if you were looking for your father and you found the Aspect…" Thain trailed off, realising the implication that I'd been trying and failing to ignore all day.

"Then my father is most likely dead. And it was probably me that killed him. Themia lied to me." My voice sounded hollow, and strangely level as I spoke the horror of my revelation. A seething anger at the lies and betrayal at the hands of my father that I'd been holding within my gut for months now soured to shame and guilt.

We continued walking south, making painfully slow progress. Thain was exhausted from lending me his own energy and the pain in my abdomen was getting worse with each mile. I called a halt so I could rest a moment, and so we could regroup our thoughts.

"I think we should go back tonight," Thain said, beating me to it. "We should go back to the academy tonight, you can get some rest, and then we can go see the Primus in the morning. Explain to him what happened."

I hated to admit it but Thain was right. We had nothing left in our tethers, bronze or iron, and the thought of another night sleeping rough with no food, no drink was not a pleasant one. Not to mention Frennic was out there somewhere, probably still looking for Thain. I didn't have a great deal of confidence that either of us could fight him off in this state. It would mean forfeiting the trial and forfeiting any hope of getting my tether by year end. But I could see no other choice, no other option before me.

I looked at my friend. His skin had a grey pallor to it, and even stood still he was swaying gently, trying to keep himself up right. I pushed myself to my feet, holding my stomach. "You're right," I said. "Let's go back."

And so, we continued our trek south, traveling at a glacial pace. As the pain in my stomach got worse, so too did Thain's energy. More than once he stumbled, losing his footing and I had to pull him back to his feet, coaxing him into walking again. We had no idea how far away we were from the academy and all we could hope for was leaving the coverage of the forest before nightfall.

Mercifully by late afternoon we stumbled across a large, flat river, filled with clean and cold mountain water. Thain almost threw himself to the ground to quench a two-day old thirst, and I eased myself down to have my fill as well. I tried to wash some of the dried blood off of my clothes and stomach, but in the failing light it was impossible to tell if I was cleaning myself or just smearing more blood over my body. Our thirst replenished and some small amount of morale recovered, we decided to follow the river south, with a hope that it was the river that fed the lake in the grounds of the academy.

We walked for hours, following the meandering course of the river as it flowed between the trees, each step I took awakening a new pain within me. The hunger pains had returned, and played a symphony accompanying the pain in my abdomen.

Every so often, between the laborious periods of utter, dreadful silence, Thain and I spoke of hopeful things. Sweet things to take our minds out of the darkness they were readily sinking into. Exhausted though he was, Thain spoke most of all of Broch. He told me he loved him and the shape of his sharp smile, his relaxed demeanour. He spoke for hours about his quick wit, and his generosity, and spoke of a gentle aspect of his love that showed itself only to him. I think he mostly spoke of Broch for himself to give him the strength he needed to return to the academy, and I was happy to let him speak. Thain had drained himself, more than he was letting on when he let me tap into him for healing. I could never repay him for such a gift.

I'd been blindly listening to Thain's soliloquy, paying it little mind, which is why it took me a moment to process what Thain had just said.

"Lights," he repeated, grunting and pointing to the distance.

Lights? I followed his finger, trying to see what he was pointing at. Lights! I saw the unmistakable amber glow of lanterns and torches, shining out of windows and into the twilight of the night in the distance. The academy. I looked around, and realised to my surprise that we'd walked out of the forest, having left the tree line 100 or so yards ago. With flat ground, and an end to our hellish travel, we made steady progress, reaching the doors to the courtyard as the first stars were beginning to shine down.

There were few people walking around in the entrance hall, none of which paid myself or Thain the slightest bit of attention. Desperate to retreat to our dormitory, we made a beeline to our elevator, and climbed in, stumbling out into our fire-lit room.

Broch jumped up from the armchair he'd been reclining in when I stumbled out of the doorway, followed shortly by Thain.

"Thain? Kehlem? What are you two doing back? You're not supposed to be back until tomorrow," he said. walking over to us. "Kehlem? What the fuck happened to you?" he shouted, horrified as he noticed the dried blood on my ruined tunic.

Thain and I both pushed past him, and collapsed onto the two other armchairs, exhausted.

I wiped the crumbs from my face as I finished the last slice of buttered bread, revelling in the feeling of being fed, and comfortable. After Thain and I had collapsed on the armchairs, Broch disappeared downstairs, returning with a pile of bread and cheeses which he'd managed to talk his way into getting from the mess hall, despite it being out of hours. Thain and I had eaten greedily, tearing huge chunks of bread and stuffing them into our mouths. While we waited for Thain to finish his meal, I did my best to catch Broch up on what had happened in the forest, starting with Wolv dropping Thain and I the furthest away, and finishing with Thain rescuing me. As I told my story, Broch remained uncharacteristically quiet, although I noticed he was gripping the arms of his chair with a white-knuckle ferocity.

"So, let me get this straight," he said, after I finally finished. "the star Vin Irudur student tries to kill you, then goes hunting for your other Caserean friend, and your first thought is to tell the Primus?"

"What other choice do we have?" I demanded. "The Primus won't stand for two Aspector students trying to kill each other, he'll have to do something."

Broch rubbed his eyes. "You don't get it. You're too pig headed to see things for what they are." He sounded exasperated. "Someone must have helped him, someone must have helped Frennic. It's not a coincidence that the Hunter sent you and Thain into the deepest parts of the forest. You weren't supposed to make it out alive. And what's with that pattern you told me he did? There's no way he should have been able to shift that much energy with an iron tether. You've seen it yourself, yours broke in your Pattern Trial."

An image of gold flashed into my mind. "He didn't have an iron tether," I said slowly. "His was gold."

"Fuck me," Broch swore.

"Gold?" Thain asked, putting his bread down. "I didn't even know they made gold tethers."

"And unless you're a Foclir, you wouldn't," Broch said. "A gold tether is what they give to the first degree Foclir if there is an issue with their permanent tether. They're given when we have to perform maintenance on the great waterwheels."

"How would a student get their hands on one?" Thain asked.

"There's no way he got it on his own. The gold tethers are locked in a vault only the training monks can access."

The three of us sat back in silence as we realized the ramifications.

"So, what can we do?" I asked Broch.

"We need to leave. We need to try and get out of here. Someone in this place wants you both dead. Me as well most likely. There's nothing for us here."

"What about the permanent tethers?" Thain asked.

"What about them? We can make our own! Why do you think they control the tethers, and tie them all here?" Broch demanded. "It's so they can control you. Fuck them, and fuck their tethers. How do you think our countrymen of old Aspected? They certainly didn't rely on giant Vin Irudur waterwheels, and neither should we."

Thain and I looked at each other. Broch had a point.

"They'll send Hunter's after us. We'd be breaking the accords," I said.

"Better to die chasing freedom, then be killed in our sleep," Thain said quietly.

There was no arguing with that. "So, what's the plan?" I asked both of them.

"We rest tonight, lie low tomorrow, and then go down to Isale town tomorrow evening," Broch said. "I've enough money to purchase a horse and cart, we'll travel west up the border, and try and find a boat to take us across the Dravé. We'll take turns keeping watch tonight. I'll take the first shift, you two get some rest."

Too tired to argue, and my mind too full to think of a better plan, I retreated upstairs, with Thain following behind me. I collapsed into my bed.

"Hey, Kehlem?" Thain whispered to me.

"Yeah?"

"I'm sorry about your father."

And that was Thain all over. Exhausted as he was from the trial, having come to the aid of an unknown screaming man and then giving almost all his energy to save me, he continued to be more concerned with my wellbeing, giving little thought to the state he was in. I truly did not deserve such a good man as a friend.

He took my silence as all the answer he needed and continued. "If Themia lied to you, you don't know what else she didn't tell you. Don't blame yourself until you have all the facts."

It was too kind of a lie to tell myself, and I refused myself that comfort. My heart bled as I closed my eyes and let myself fall into exhausted sleep.

"Hey, it's your turn to keep watch." Thain's whispered voice woke me.

Somehow, I felt worse after a rest than I did before. My entire body was stiff, and it felt like every muscle in my legs had been pulled. With great effort I pulled myself out of bed, and hobbled down stairs into the dormitory. The morning sun was just beginning to rise, sending pale yellow light through our window, and I could see there was an early autumn haze swirling around the grounds. I dropped myself gently into an armchair, trying to avoid touching my tender abdomen.

I couldn't stop thinking about my father, about the Aspect and about Themia. It was like a puzzle with a single piece missing and I was doomed to miss the understanding until I found it. Had I killed my father when I'd first Aspected? If so then why wouldn't Themia had just told me? What was the point in lying? What was the meaning of what I'd heard in the Aspect? I was so lost in thought that I almost didn't notice the door of our dormitory open.

"Kehlem?" A voice called.

I looked up, alarmed that I'd let my guard do so easily, although relaxed when I noticed it was Kit.

"Oh, it's you, what are you doing here?"

Kit looked surprised to see me, which I suppose he was. For all he knew, I was supposed to be out in the forest still.

"I could ask you the same question. I was looking for Broch."

I ignored his first comment. "He's still asleep, you should come back later. How are you? You looked like hell the last time I saw you."

Kit's eyes wandered around the room, his gaze falling casually on the water butt we'd converted into a tether. With horror I realised the outside of the barrel was covered in condensation, the water held inside frozen solid after Thain and I drained it of energy yesterday. If Kit recognised it, he made no sign of noticing, and his gaze fell back to me. Thankfully I was still draped in my blanket, so I could hide the dried blood I still hadn't washed off myself.

"It's fine, I'll come back later," he said, distracted. He turned back to the door without a second look back.

That was odd, I thought. Why was Kit looking for Broch? Maybe to make amends finally? The sun had just risen enough to shine its warmth across my face, and still tired, I fell to the irresistible lull of sleep.

28

Fruits of labour

The sound of heavy footsteps hitting the wooden floor of the dormitory startled me awake, as I realised with dread that I'd slept when I was supposed to be keeping watch. Blinking out the exhaustion from my eyes, I caught the blurry form of a woman, resolving into the recognisable figure of Wolv strolling over to the water butt, with a hooded monk stood behind her. All feeling drained out of me, replaced with a hot, pulsing dread. They'd figured it out.

"Good work Do'Seer," Wolv said, pulling out the bronze inscribed plate from out of the icy water of the water barrel. Whether they'd noticed me or not, Wolv still hadn't looked over to me. I tried to get to my feet but everything ached. I was completely and absolutely drained. Still, my shuffling must have caught Wolv's attention.

"Restrain him," she said, still inspecting the bronze plate. The monk came striding over quickly and with a clumsy hand, bent both my arms behind my back, forcing me to bend double. With our only tether gone, and in such a weakened state, I had no choice but to comply. The position sent a furious pain shooting through my stomach from my damaged liver. Rough rope was tied against my wrists. As the pressure let off, I sat back up straight and caught a glimpse of the monk's hooded face. Blind fury shook me as I charged him.

"You bastard!" I spat at Kit, as he easily sidestepped my clumsy charge.

With my hands tied behind my back, I had nothing to stop me falling heavily and landing on my face.

"You sold us out!" I was screaming now, tasting blood in my throat. Was that why he came by earlier? To spy on the dormitory? Was that why he seemed so surprised to see me?

"We were friends!" I gasped, as he pulled my roughly back on to my feet.

"A Seer has no friends," he said, his voice barely a whisper. His hood had fallen in the struggle, and he refused to meet my gaze. The dark circles under his eyes stood out on his ashen face. He looked unwell, but his timid voice and refusal to meet my gaze just incensed me further, and I continued to struggle against his grip. The banging must have woken Thain and Broch, because they appeared down the spiral staircase. I tried to shout a warning to them, but Kit slammed his hand around my mouth, muffling me.

Thain's gaze fell on Wolv standing next to the barrel and to his credit, immediately drew the second Destructia pattern.

"I wouldn't finish that if I were you," Wolv said, her smile vicious. She held the bronze plate out in her palm so both Thain and Broch could see it.

Thain's shoulders slumped.

"Why don't you both come down here. The Primus would like a word."

With no other choice, my two friends joined me in the dormitory, where Wolv bound their hands behind their back like mine. They also gagged us, with a tight piece of rough linen which cut into the corner of my mouth. I tried to catch my two friend's gazes, to somehow communicate to them. All I could see in Thain's was a deep sadness and worry, whereas Broch's were burning with such a bright anger, it hurt to look at.

Kit and Wolv jostled the three of us roughly down the elevator, tying long rope connecting the five of us together so we had no choice but to be yanked out of the lift at the right floor. It was still early in the morning and the entrance hall was empty. I was at the head of our sad group, following Wolv's lead. All I could think of was what would happen next. Would they imprison us? Drug us? Would they send us away? We knew there would be risks to making our own tether, but we had no idea what the consequences would be for being discovered.

I was jolted out of my worry when instead of turning to the study hall, Wolv led us out and into the grounds of the academy.

I thought we were going to see the Primus?

The brisk wind caught my loose clothing and began to whip it around my body, pulling at my tangle of hair and snapping it into my eyes. I tried to crane my neck to clear my vision, struggling with my bound hands. As Wolv led us out of the courtyard, our destination became clear. By the head of the lake, stood beneath a lone tree, was a group of monks, and presumably the Primus as well. I could feel my heart pounding in my throat, tasting iron on my tongue. It was a struggle to keep my breathing in check.

Wolv came to a stop beneath the tree, and handed the rope holding the three of us to the monk standing next to the Primus. She pulled our bronze plate out of a pocket, and handed it over to the Primus who inspected it. We all stood in silence as he considered it. My heart hammered in my chest.

"Good work, Do'Seer Kit," the Primus said, handing the bronze plate back to Wolv. I heard a muffled grunt from behind me as my friends realised who their other captor was.

"What do you want us to do with them?" Wolv asked.

"Like I told you, we don't have space for three. I thought you said you'd handle the weaker one," he nodded his head over to Thain. "Besides, he looks spent. I doubt he'd be able to sustain himself for what we need. Keep the other two."

What does he mean 'keep'? My mind was screaming, but my legs were leadened. The Primus' blind gaze looked out to our group.

"I had such high hopes for you Kehlem. You would have made a fine Hunter for the Irudur empire. You will now watch and see what your efforts will have reaped." The Primus nodded to Wolv.

At his silent command, she quickly untied Broch and I from Thain, and dragged Thain away. Two monks came and held Broch and I still as we jostled and squirmed trying to break free. Thain's eyes were wide with panic, as Wolv dragged him towards the tree. Despite my gag, I started a wordless scream, unable to help or comfort my beloved friend. Next to me Broch started jumping, squirming this way and that, desperate to escape the iron grip of his captor but to no avail. Kit walked over to Wolv and Thain and pulled out a long coil of rope, which Wolv tied a loop in.

No no no no no no. My mind was blank, filled only with the horror of the scene before me. Broch fell to his knees, and I could hear him sobbing, his muffled mouth sending wordless pleading to anyone that would listen.

Thain stood still, his face a ghostly white, and his chest rising and falling like a small sparrow. His eyes darted between us and the rope. He looked very small and so frail in the shadow of the tree behind him.

This can't be happening, it's just a threat. They're trying to scare us.

Wolv threw one side of the rope over a thick branch of the tree, so that the looped end hung down from the branch, floating freely in the wind. Without any hesitation, she pulled the loop down, widening it to go over Thain's head and letting it rest against his pale neck. Thain's breathing seemed to slow and he looked at me, his eyes filled with terror and panic. Besides me Broch was still on the floor, his captor, holding his arms back, forcing him to watch. Despite his gag, his screaming was loud enough to drown out the sound of the blistering wind.

For as long as I live, I will never forget the sound of that wordless scream.

With a sharp tug, Wolv, Kit and another hooded monk, grabbed the other end of the rope, pulling it away from the tree. The loop around Thain's neck tightened, and he was pulled upwards, feet leaving the ground, flailing as his entire body's weight was held by the tightening rope against his neck. They held the rope steady, keeping his feet a meter or so off the ground. I watched in horror, unable to look away as my sweet, gentle friend writhed, and struggled for air. We were close enough to watch his face go from terror and slide right through to desperation as his body screamed for air. His arms were still tied behind his back, so all the movement he had was in his feet, which stamped vainly into empty air. The wind was still blowing, sending his body swaying like some kind of hideous fruit. His mouth was open, gulping slowly like a caught fish, begging for a breath that would not come. In horror I glanced over to where Wolv and Kit were still gripping the rope that was choking my friend. Wolv was watching with a look of disinterest, whilst Kit, the man I thought to be a friend, was staring at Thain's struggle with a grim determination, like he was forcing himself to watch, his hands white knuckled against the thick rope he held. I wanted to shout out to them. 'You've made your point. Drop my friend. Hang me instead.' But the gag just turned my supplications into wordless wails, and the monk behind me shoved my head roughly to watch Thain as he continued to swing from the rope.

The struggling of his legs slowed, each twist and twitch of his legs becoming slower and less powerful, until they ceased entirely. Even tied up, I saw his body fall limp, and a patch of damp appear on his trousers. The wind died down, and the swinging of his body slowed until he hung still. One of the monks hammered a stake into the ground, and tied off the other end of the rope, so my friend could hang lifeless from the tree, for all to see.

The screaming in my mind slowed and I forced myself to look at my dead friend. To see what I had done.

My friend was dead. And he'd taken a piece of me with him.

There was a sudden jolt at the back of my head, and the world turned black.

A splash of cold water fell onto my forehead, waking me from my slumber. I tried to sit up, but my hands and feet had been restrained against something. The cold I felt against my cheek, and the metallic tang in the air told me whatever I was tied to was probably some kind of metal.

There was little light wherever I was, but there was a darker shadow in the room, which moved towards me. I couldn't move, or even cry out in fear. A sudden hand on the back of my head, gripped and twisted the locks of my hair. It pulled my scalp tight, and when it had a firm grip, it pushed my face into the metal I was held against. Pressure and pain melded into one, and I grunted in agony. The unrelenting force continued, silent and uncaring. Tears of pain fled down my cheek, pooling and dripping into my open mouth. They mixed with the blood that was now pouring from my nose, as it was pushed against the unmoving metal. The pressure built, the hand pushing harder still and I let out a strangled cry as my nose popped. I gasped in blood and sweat, choking as it aspirated into my lungs. And as sudden as it started the pressure was gone, the invisible hand gripping my hair let go and I heard footsteps growing distant, followed by a door closing.

With the little range of movement, I had, I lifted my head, lying my face on its side, feeling the unmistakable chill of metal against my cheeks. My nose throbbed from where it had broken, and blood poured freely, dripping down the sloped surface, down towards my chest. It seemed like I'd been tied to some bulky piece of metal, possibly iron, with my arms wrapped around the sides, as if in an embrace. My legs had been bent, ankles tied together and all my weight was positioned solely on the trunk of my body, laid at a slight angle on the sloping chunk of metal.

How long had I been out? I tried to think back to my last memory, hands bound behind me, wind snapping at my loose clothing, a body hanging limp from a tree...

A light shone on the memory of Thain's look of terror as he was hoisted by naught but his neck up into the air, the dancing of his dying body trying to gasp for any relief. I let out a strangled sob. How could he be dead? It was my job to look after him.

A voice echoed out in the dark, dank room. "Kehlem? That you?"

"Broch?" I asked, my voice surprisingly dry and hoarse.

"Yeah," he groaned. "You tied up as well?"

"I am. Where are we?"

"Not sure. Somewhere inside the academy I think."

Not only was my friend dead, but my other one was trapped with me as well.

It's all my fault.

What could they want with us? I shivered with how casually and quickly they'd executed Thain. Like it was nothing. Martyr, if it was bad for me, how was Broch dealing with the loss of his love?

"Thain..." I whispered lamely. I couldn't finish my sentence. Even saying his name out loud brought with it a pain so severe it dwarfed the physical aches and throbbing I was currently enduring.

"Don't."

Broch's rebuke was so straight, so quick, it cracked against me like a whip.

"Broch I'm so sorry. It's my fault. I can't imagine what you're going through, I —"

"Just shut the fuck up Kehlem. You're right. It is your fault. I heard the Primus earlier, before you woke. They would never have been interested in Thain or me if it hadn't been for you. You shone like a fucking beacon to them, and like idiots we stood next to you, casting shadows far taller than they had any right to be. We both should have stayed way fucking clear."

I would have taken Frennic's stabbing again, the slow, brutal insertion of a sharp blade into my heart, than listen to my friend spit poisonous vitriol that I knew in my heart was true.

I swallowed my tears, not feeling worthy of self-pity. "I swear," I said, my voice shaking. "Whatever I can do, I will do it to get us out of here."

"Because of you, the sweetest man I ever loved, whose love I never fucking deserved is dead." Broch's words were sharp and deliberate. "If you ever let me loose, I swear I'll kill you myself."

29

The Altar

The passing of time was an incalculable entity chained in the dark. The only way I could mark its passing was by tracking the various routines of the monks, who were presumably our captors. In what I assumed was the morning, a monk would come and unchain Broch and I off of our metal throne, and chain us against the floor instead so we would eat, and drink. I eventually began to look forward to the sound of rattling keys coming down a distant corridor because it meant for a few steps, I could walk and stretch my aching joints if but for a moment. At first, I spent most of my time sleeping, fading in and out of consciousness as my body and mind tried to repair itself. Broch had remained silent since he threatened to kill me, leaving me with only my thoughts for company. At first, I thought of Thain, the looks of terror on his face, the way his skin paled as the rope tightened, and how the wind was able to blow his slight body with ease. It was like washing a fresh wound.

With only the Martyr knows how much time, the brutal images faded, replaced instead with memories of when we'd first met, him showing me around the academy. How he promised me he would help me earn my tether. In a way these hurt more, but they ignited a separate emotion, one that had been building since the day Themia had whisked me away. It was dark, and twisted, forged in the fires of my own self-hatred. A single, sharp blade of loathing for the Academy, for the monks, and for the empire which took everything away from me. I had nothing. Eva, Father and now Thain. All of them gone, all of them traced back to a single source. The Vin Irudur.

In my first weeks in my prison, that hatred sustained me, kept my mind occupied from the bleak despair which sat on my shoulder, waiting for me to give up.

My life was filled with monotony, in darkness I spent very little of my time fully awake, instead falling somewhere between sleep and wakefulness, mindlessly suspended between the two.

But now, now there was a new sound, waking me from my delirious stupor. Curiosity rippled through me for the first time in a long, awful time. It was a heavy, rolling sound.

Wheels?

I tried to twist my head so I could point my ear to where I thought the sound was coming from. My body complained, aching joints struggling to adjust to new angles, and open sores chafing against rough metal. I needn't have bothered the strain, as moments later a familiar crack of soft amber light creeped into our room. I slammed my eyes shut, not wanting to lose the only advantage of being kept in darkness; being able to see better in the dark than my captors. After I heard the door shut, I opened them again. Huddled around a tall dark object were various forms, busying themselves, and stood in the back, was a familiar outline.

"It's ready, Primus," one of the monk's whispered.

"You may leave us," The figure spoke back, voice ringing loudly through the dank room like a bell. Quiet shuffles left the room, leaving only the new object and the Primus. I saw his shadow grow, as he walked towards me.

"How are you enjoying the dark?" He called out.

Broch kept his silence, and so did I.

"You'll forgive me for not having any sympathy. I was blinded around your age, by the monks. I've lived most of my life in darkness."

His pompous voice was grating me, fanning the flames at the forge of my hatred. He walked past my line of vision, and a cold, wet cloth began wiping across my back.

"What is that?" I asked, my skin cringing away from his touch.

THE ALTAR

"Did you ever wonder, Kehlem, why there are so few Caserean Aspectors here at the academy?" he asked, ignoring me and continuing to wipe down my back. "I gave you every opportunity to succeed, I tempered the distaste of my fellow monks, and asked that you be taught with no interference. I had such high hopes for you, a Hunter, the likes of which the Irudur empire has never seen. And what do you give in return for my benevolence? You lie, cheat and steal away secrets that do not belong to you. Like all you Casereans, your rodent like greed always betrays your true nature, that of a conniving -" the cloth the Primus was using suddenly whipped against by back, cracking in the air with his fury, "dirty -" another *crack*, and a sharp pain against my stretched skin, "insidious race." He cracked the wet cloth a final time, leaving traces of stinging lines against my exposed back. I could hear him breathing heavily from the exertion. "You and yours were given a princely gift from the Aspect, one that you squandered, one that the Vin Irudur are due." His face came into view again suddenly, as he pulled out a small cylindrical shaped object, one that I couldn't make out in the gloom. He shook it slightly, and whatever it was inside the tube began to glow with a soft, bluish light. Plump and fat, it looked like an unholy mixture of maggot, lamprey and leech. The Primus' toothy grin was illuminated behind the steadily glowing bug. He stood back up, taking the dim glow with him. I heard the distinct 'pop' of a tube being uncorked, and the soft squelch of something landing on my back. I cried out in revulsion as I began to piece together what the now drying sticking solution on my back was for. Four more tubes were opened, the bugs landing on my back. I squirmed as they undulated across my skin, and then one by one, I felt a sharp sting, a piercing of my skin, and then a strange itching pressure next to the five or so wounds. The Primus stepped away and, in the gloom, I could see him repeating the same process with Broch, wiping his back down with the same sticky solution, and tipping five of the glowing maggots onto his back. The bugs continued to glow, and I watched in horror as they moved around Broch's back, seemingly finding the fleshiest parts, and suddenly almost in unison, bite down hard into his skin. The dim blue glow seemed to fade, and in a moment of confusion, I thought that the maggots had died, but then I spotted the skin around the wounds themselves began to glow slightly blue. They were burrowing. Almost as soon as the revelation hit, I began to feel the maggots within me begin to undulate and squirm, just underneath my skin, lifting, squeezing between my flesh. For the first time since I'd woken up chained, I thrashed against my bonds, trying desperately to get the bugs out of me. It was no use. All I managed was giving myself friction burns on my ankles and wrist.

Exhausted and light headed, I laid my head back down on the metal slab, feeling every wriggling sensation of the parasites within my skin.

The Primus stepped back into the centre of the room, next to the heavy object that had been wheeled in. Grabbing a rope tied to the object, he pulled, hoisting some kind of pendulum up to a joist, standing taller than shoulder height.

"May the Aspect sustain you, long enough so your body may serve some purpose for the empire," the Primus said. He unhitched a lever from the pendulum machine, and left the room. A sharp, mechanical ticking noise began to emanate from the machine. The pendulum waved in the air and with each sequential 'tick', line after line began to appear on the weight, lit from within by a self-sustaining red glow. The lines formed an intricate design which folded in on itself multiple times, and with its light, revealed the pendulum to be made of bronze, shaped into a squat cylinder. On the face of the weight that was directly opposed to the ground, a single, final pattern was illuminating. As the red glow spread on this final face, I noticed the metal chunk I'd been strapped to began to warm, as if intrinsically tied to the pendulum. A sense of dread enthralled me, but I could not look away, the pattern on the pendulum drawing itself towards an inevitable conclusion. The maggots in my back began to squirm, all in unison, pulsing to some invisible rhythm that throbbed through the heating metal mantle I was tied to. The pulsing was everywhere and all I could see was the pattern, glowing even when my eyes were closed. The ticking of the machine echoed around me. Both my hands, bound flat against the heating metal, sensed a shift, a change. Relief. The ineffable distance between our world and the Aspect, welcoming me away from the horrors with a comforting pull. I tried to embrace it, to reach out, but as my hands slipped through, the pulse of the room, the maggots and the pattern intensified. The same strangling lines of the pendulum's pattern wrapped themselves around my body, radiating out from where the maggots were burrowed in my flesh. With a slow, and irrefutable force, the pattern was forcing me into the in-between, to lie on the fabric that separated our world from the Aspect. The metal I was bound to began to unfold impossibly, stretching out, pulling my body with it, stretching me and guiding me into the in-between. Forced by the hideous pattern my entire body was enveloped into the in-between, no sight, no sound, with only the incessant pulsing of the parasites within my flesh to accompany me.

Wherever I was, time had no meaning, no concept. I floated in pointed agony, as power from the Aspect used me as a conduit to leach into the real world, the worms underneath my skin delighting on the feast of flesh and energy. Sleep and unconsciousness evaded me, but so too did settled thoughts, and for the third time in my life, a haze settled into my mind, as thoughts darted around my head, like fallen leaves caught in an autumn gust. My soul was stretched thin, cracks appearing in its extremities where energy from the Aspect began wearing away at my very being, exposing raw, fresh parts of my soul to the brutal and uncaring forces of this in-between void. Whatever the true purpose for the writhing maggots burrowed in the flesh of my back, they seemed to be the only thing anchoring me back in the real world, where I still felt the chill dank air of my prison. The ticking and pulsing of the pendulum machine continued to reverberate around me, through me. The pattern still wrapped around me, trapping me in this in-between. Occasionally, a thought-leaf would settle long enough for my mind to process its content. They often contained faces; a girl with raven hair and a sly smile, skin smelling like candle smoke and the dewy comfort of a grass bed in a clearing, a man with hair so blond it may as well have been white, with a smile that broke like a sunrise, and a woman with long flowing red hair tied back smartly. Each image pulsing a familiar, rhythmic pattern. All I had were their images, the thoughts being ripped away soon after they landed, too quickly for me to recall much else other than a feeling

THE SOUL'S ASPECT

of deep, soul-aching sadness. Occasionally a discordant pulse, opposite to the one that bound me, would erupt from out of the void. It hit me like a question, but one my mind was too broken, too confused to understand. Again, the new pattern would strike back at me, repeating the question, confused why I couldn't speak my own mother-tongue. Around me the ticking noise drew slower, the beat of the pattern that held me weakened and for the first time in eons, hands, physical hands made of flesh, blood and bone, touch skin. My skin. They gripped me, and pulled me out of the in-between, and like falling in a dream, my body shuddered as it found itself still chained, still bound to the heap of metal.

"......"

I heard words, but I was too confused, too tired to understand them, but the tone of them spoke 'revulsion'. I blinked out of reflex. That's right. I had eyes. I'd forgotten.

I moved my head slowly, feeling the sensation of cold metal against my cheek, and slowly, like water freezing and cracking open stone, my mind opened, letting me remember where I was. Who I was. I wish I didn't. With the memories came pain. I noticed that voice again, probably belonging to whoever pulled me out of wherever I just was. It was sobbing. I turned my head to the side, and saw a heap of a man, staring at his own hands, sitting on the floor. Stretching my body had caused the parasites to awake from their slumber and they began wiggling, pulsing beneath my skin, each little movement sending exquisite pain radiating deep into the tissue of my body.

I tried to speak, but only a dry gasping breath fell out of my mouth. But the sobbing man noticed regardless, his eyes were drawn to mine and held them for only a moment, before he broke his gaze away, and shuffled to his feet. That moment was all I needed for recognition to light a bonfire of hatred once more within me.

A water skin appeared by my lips, held by the man who made encouraging motions for me to drink. Parched, with bloody lips and aching mouth, I happily took the devil's drink, savouring each drop of the warm water as it flowed down my throat. Too quickly the waterskin was removed. The man crouched down so his swollen, bloodshot eyes were level with my own.

THE ALTAR

"I'm so sorry Kehlem. I'm so sorry," he whispered to me, eyes aching with a self-loathing I recognised within myself.

I wished I could spit poison at him. Vomit flames to engulf us both. "Why Kit?" was all I could manage, my voice crackling, sore from lack of use.

"I had no choice. The Abbot at the Eastern Garrison, he gave me a command. To befriend you, so I could keep an eye on you. I couldn't argue. Do you know what they do to apostate monks?"

I shouldn't have been surprised by the revelation. What was one more betrayal? And yet still, it hurt.

"Hang them?" I asked, hoping the monk could see all the hatred I held for him from my gaze alone.

"I didn't know they'd execute Thain!" he sobbed.

A sudden memory came to me, of Thain and Kit drinking together in the tavern in Isale in the first few weeks after arriving at the academy.

"It didn't stop you from pulling the rope though did it?" My voice was becoming stronger the more I used it.

"You gave me no choice! What did you think would happen if you made your own tether?" he demanded, but I knew he was deflecting. Killing Thain was haunting him, the same way it haunted me.

"Look around Kit. Do you think this is a fitting punishment?"

"I swear, I had no idea about this. I had no idea this was what they do to Caserean Aspectors." His gaze drifted to my back, and another look of revulsion crossed his face.

"And what is that Kit? What's the point of all of this?"

In the gloom I saw his shoulders slump.

"Vinnish Aspectors have always been a rare thing. While you Caserean prosper with a natural boon of born Aspectors, my people would go decades without a new Aspector being born."

"That doesn't make any sense," I said, interrupting him. "Look around the academy, everyone here is Vinnish!"

"You're not understanding," he said. "*Born* Aspectors."

The wriggling in my back intensified, pushing against my tight and swollen skin.

"Forty or so years ago, a Vin academic made a discovery. A new species of insect discovered in the northern jungles. The larva form of the insect showed a unique ability to consume energy directly from the Aspect. It was a huge discovery, the first demonstration of an animal outside of humans that can connect with the Aspect. Five or so years later, a monk discovered something new. By letting a larva feast and cocoon itself within an Aspector's flesh, the insect will absorb something, something yet unknown and indescribable from the Aspector. Giving the larva to a babe to eat, it gives them the same connection to the Aspect. The empire has been making Aspectors for almost four decades."

"So, the war?" I asked, stunned.

Kit nodded. "It wasn't for territory. It was for resources. A single Caserean Aspector can provide for around twenty or so larva."

How many people knew about this, I wondered. Did Themia know? Did she knowingly send me away to this torture?

"Why are you telling me this?" I demanded.

"There's no escape for you from this. The pendulum will keep you suspended. No man should die without knowing why." Kit's voice was little more than a whisper. He shuffled himself back onto his feet.

"Why are you here?" I asked, exhausted.

Kit pulled a pair of metal forceps from a satchel at his waist. "The Primus sent me to reap the first harvest."

He disappeared from view, and a cold hand braced itself against my back. My breathing quickened as I realised with horror what must come next. I cried out in pain as fingers squeezed the two sides of an open wound. Hot, radiating pain screamed into my flesh. I felt the unmistakable cold metal bite as the forceps entered the now open wound, exploring my ruined flesh, seeking out the insect's chrysalis. Every twist, every turn of the tool in my back sent uncontrollable racking sobs of pain out of me. Pain like I had never felt before bought me to the lowest level where I could only beg for Kit to kill me. I felt a tug, and sudden pressure. Something within the flesh of my back gave way, something hard and sharp. I heard a rattling sound as some heavy, hard material was deposited into a glass vial. The

THE ALTAR

forceps retreated from the wound, leaving the cold air to rush in, sending each exposed nerve into a cavorting dance of agony. Something hot and wet trickled down my back. My nose caught the unmistakable stench of flesh-rot. My breathing slowed as I tired from exhaustion and I blinked the sweat and tears from my eyes.

At least it was over. At least it was done.

Another pinch popped a closed scab on a lower portion of my back. Horror threatened me with madness, as I realised that there were four more chrysalis to collect.

The sound of Kit's footsteps trailed off down an unknown corridor, leaving Broch and I once again in silence. My back was an inflamed, seeping ruin, the larvae having burrowed deep into my tissue. I lay on the metal rock exhausted, sweat pooled around me, mixing in with whatever awful, smelly fluids were now flowing freely from the wounds left by the insects. I was grateful that Broch had remained unconscious through his procedure. It would have hurt me more than I can say to see my friend go through the same agony.

Before he had left, with his vile collection of bloody, engorged bugs, Kit had wound the pendulum back up again, not daring to look back at me as I stared vile poison at him.

As the echoes of Kit's footsteps quietened, the hateful tick of the pendulum began. Once more the room pulsed, the pattern on the pendulum growing until it was the only thing visible in the room. I resisted, pushing against the welcoming release of the Aspect, straining every sinew and fibre to resist. But I was a broken man. The longer I held, the greater the grip the pattern took of my body, wrapping ethereal vines around me, pushing me once more into the place between.

30

The Aspect

Once more adrift in an empty void, floating untethered and uncaring. Once more the Aspect touched my soul, but with no larvae to feed, it nourished me instead, healing the torn and tattered material of my being, calming the raging maelstrom of hatred until it was little more than a warm summer's breeze, which my thoughts floated gently atop. The pulse of the pendulum still gripped me, still reverberated through me with an undeniable rhythm. It told me *this is your place*. It spoke of helplessness and defeat.

How many Casereans had lived and died in this place? How many Vin Irudur Aspectors were created from the suffering of my people?

Again, the Aspect seemed to send its own pulses to me, discordant and syncopated to the pendulum. While I still couldn't understand their meaning, the pulses were now gentler, quiet and less disturbing. Instead of battering against my soul, they eased around me, supporting me, and little by little they settled underneath the pattern that bound me, growing up the trellis of my dying soul.

So quiet, and subtle was this Aspect's work, that by the time the pattern that bound me heard it, it was too late. My soul had been enwrapped by the Aspect, layering itself on me like a second skin, and with a single, star cracking pulse, it eviscerated the pendulum's hold on me.

Elation and confusion in equal measures flowed through me, as I floated

THE ASPECT

with no anchor in the space that lay between the Aspect and my own world.

"Come," a deep voice commanded, resonating through me.

I reached out, and felt a tear in the fabric of the Aspect. I moved towards it, pulled through with the pattern that had rescued me.

Sensations hit me, filling the absence that the void had left me with. Prismatic flowing colours seeped all around, gliding endlessly in countless patterns.

"Take a seat," the voice suggested.

I did so, without thinking, forgetting I had no physical body here, my own bruised and broken body left chained to the metal in the prison. And yet, here I was, seated. I looked around, surprised to notice hands, feet, legs and chest. Unchained, unbroken.

"It will be easier for you to listen, if you have control of something familiar," the voice said once more.

The sliding colours coalesced around me, forming solid ground which I could place my feet on. It was a meadow, with tall grass blowing in waves by a summer storm on the horizon. I was sitting on a simple stone bench on top of a rolling hill.

"Who are you?" I asked.

A large, black cat came padding up the hill, and stood at my feet staring deep into my eyes.

"Is that you?" I asked, uncertain.

"No, Kehlem," A familiar voice said behind me. "That's just a cat," the man laughed.

I spun around in my seat, and pulled the man into a tight embrace.

"Father!" I cried out, my face buried in his chest.

My father patted my head, smoothing my hair down. He eased out of my embrace, and sat next to me.

"What's going on?" I asked. "Where are we?"

My father reached down to the cat, which rubbed its head against his hand. "This is the Aspect, Kehlem. We brought you here, because there's somethings you need to know, if you're going to survive what comes next."

"I'm so sorry!" I cried out, my eyes wet with tears. "I didn't mean to hurt you, I had no idea what I was doing."

"It's ok Kehlem. It wasn't you that killed me."

My mind raced, trying to put the pieces together. "It was Themia wasn't it? She lied, she said you had escaped!" It was the only answer that made sense.

"She did lie, but it wasn't her that killed me," he said. "When you Aspected that day, you burnt through enough energy to kill yourself. In fact, you almost did die. They only way to stop the Aspect from taking you was to offer something else instead." My father smiled at me. "Me," he said simply.

A flood of guilt and confusion rushed through me.

The black cat jumped up onto my father's lap, circled around, and then lay itself down, demanding to be stroked.

"I'm an Aspector Kehlem, just like you. Before the war I learned the patterns of healing, and I even served in the war as a medic. It was there I met your mother for the second time, the first being at the University I told you about. She was the lecturing Aspector. Someone who I had admired from a distance. But war was the great leveller, and we were both young, too young to be facing the challenges we were, but that was the hand we were given. Unlike me though, she wanted to fight in the front lines. We had plans to wed, settle down when the war was over, but each month sent more Caserean casualties. There were rumours going around, of Caserean Aspectors being captured, taken alive for a purpose we didn't understand. Among the Aspectors in the Caserean army, there was a secret pact. We all swore that if it ever got to the point of surrender, we would kill ourselves instead of being taken. Well you know the story of Narrow-marsh. The bulk of our army got surrounded and true to their pact, the Aspectors immolated themselves, rather than fall to the hands of the Vin. Your mother being one of them."

"You were an Aspector?" I asked, stunned. "Wait, where were you at Narrow-marsh? How come you survived? And where was I at this point? The war was thirty years ago."

My father sighed, still petting the cat on his lap that was now gently purring.

THE ASPECT

"I saw the writing on the wall before the battle. I tried to talk your mother out of it, but she was too strong minded. Heartbroken, I left, I was halfway to Mercy when I heard the news of the surrender. As for you, well that's why you're here now.

"After I lost your mother, I felt a pain and loneliness I'd never known before. I'd lost both my parents at an early age, and since the day I first met your mother, I felt like there was a future for me, one with the family I had always longed for. And then it was all ripped away from me.

"I set a plan in motion, one that would take years of research and energy. But twenty years later, I figured it out. I called into the Aspect, spinning patterns that had been lost to the ages of time, and demanded for what should have been mine." Tears were streaking down my father's cheek, and he lifted his hand to cup my face. "And it gave me you. A miracle. A small, tiny babe. My own son. I moved to Barrowheld, started a new life and swore never to Aspect again. I knew if I Aspected it would only draw the Vin's attention to us. I couldn't lose anything else to the Vin. I kept myself numb with arrowwood, so I wouldn't be tempted."

I was breathless, staring at my father with horror as I began to realise what he was telling me. He sat watching me, tears flowing freely down his cheeks.

"So," I said slowly, "I have no mother? Am I even human?"

It was too much for one person to handle. My entire life, everything, has been one lie after another. Somehow knowing he'd given himself arrowwood made me feel angrier. He knew how it made me feel. He knew exactly what he was doing to me, and did so anyway.

"When the Aspect gave you to me, I know that a part of the woman I loved resided in you. I could just sense it. She is as much your mother as I will always be your father. You're made of flesh and bone like everyone else," Tema said. "The Aspect gives life to everything, you're as human as I was."

I just wanted to wake up. Leave this place. I'd rather be back in the prison than sat looking at my dead father's face any longer.

"So why am I here? Why tell me now?" I demanded, my voice suddenly sharp.

One of the cat's ears flickered in annoyance.

"Because of the nature of your birth, you have always had an unusually strong connection to the Aspect. You will have seen by now that you can grasp new patterns much easier than other Aspectors, perhaps you've even been able to intuit patterns by yourself. The Vin Irudur monks have been responsible for a lot of evil, but they are correct in some respects on the nature of the Aspect. It is itself a pattern, yet it continues to progress forward sustaining itself and us in the process. The Aspect is the ultimate destination for all living things, with Aspectors acting as the living embodiment of the will of the Aspect. What the Vin Irudur have been doing, it goes against the very nature of both our world and this. If they continue unchecked, they will forever change the one true pattern that the Aspect has been working towards for eons. It must be stopped. They need to be stopped."

Both my father, and the black cat were watching me intently.

I didn't notice it immediately, but something had changed in my father's demeanour. He was still sitting next to me, relaxed as if we were on an afternoon stroll through the woods, and yet, there was a tenseness to the air, like the whole world was holding its breath, a muscle pulled back, ready to run. Or strike.

"You want me to stop it?"

"I don't want anything Kehlem. If I got what I wanted, Eawain would still be alive, and you would be our true son. But you are as much the son of the Aspect, as you are of mine. If you don't do anything and you leave the Vins to continue unchecked, could you live with yourself? Knowing that by your inaction, the lives of your countrymen will continue to be subjugated?"

Thain's face flashed before my eyes. If there was something I could do, I had to do it.

"How can I stop the Vin, when I'm trapped in a prison, no tether, no freedom?"

"The tethers are a bastardisation, a weak solution for the crafted Vinnish Aspectors. A true born Aspector doesn't need to rely on such petty machinations. The Aspect is responsible for each living thing, all energy comes from the Aspect." Father looked up as the winds around us began to pick up, the sky darkened as the summer storm approached. "I tried to protect you from this Kehlem, when I should have trusted you. You'll always be my son."

The finality in his voice should have warned me. The winds whipped up around me, and before my eyes, my father vanished, fading into sliding prismatic colours. The meadow dripped away from me, until all that was left was the black cat, staring deep into my eyes.

I awoke back in the cell, still chained. The machine was still ticking, but having broken through its hold, it didn't seem to have an effect on me. It continued to tick, the pendulum swinging slowly from its rig. My body was feeling better than it had done in a long time, the aches and pains of my legs diminished to a quiet whisper, the oozing, inflamed wounds on my back apparently healed over. What's more, I felt strong again, not just physically but mentally as well. Since I'd been captured, and trapped in this place, it felt like the upper limits of my consciousness had retreated, pulling themselves away from my reality, leaving only the baser, animal parts to keep me alive. I'd subsisted in this place through anger and hatred alone, but no longer. My mind was waking up.

Memories of the Aspect floated up with my waking mind. All my life my father had lied to me, to everyone. How many people could he have helped if he'd never lied about being able to Aspect? He could have saved Job's leg, saved him so much pain. My mind skirted around the last revelation, one that felt too large, too incomprehensible to even explore.

I had no mother.

I wasn't born. I was made. What does that make me?

My heart was pounding, feeling hollow in my own chest. I knew I should feel different, that the revelation should have bought some clear understanding about my own true nature. Was I not a man of flesh and bone? Who'd loved, lost, bled and been broken? If I feel human, is that enough?

It was just one more legacy forced on me that I wanted no part of. And now the Aspect demands I stop the Vin. Once more I'd been thrust into a divot, that stretches out before me, the walls of each side too tall to surmount.

The only way is forward to follow the design that has been carved out for me. The choice taken straight from my hands.

I didn't want this. How can it be one person's responsibility to end an empire? Could I give up, let myself die here?

I thought of Thain's body hanging from the tree, lifeless and swaying gently in the wind. How many Aspectors had found themselves bound to these altars, kept alive only to have their essence stolen, consumed by parasites? Was I the only person who could change things?

If this is the path I must take, if all choice has been taken from me, then I won't do it for them. I'll do it for my friends.

31

The Square

Unbeknownst to my captors, I lay fully awake chained to the altar, planning and thinking about my escape. Father had told me it can be done and that I wouldn't need a tether. He'd said that the Aspect is responsible for each living thing, all energy comes from the Aspect. I wasn't sure what that meant exactly, but I had nothing but time to figure it out. Judging from how long my hair had gotten and the coarse hair I could feel on my face, I'd been trapped here for months, maybe even a year. It had already been hard to keep a track of the time but then they used that pendulum machine and time became meaningless.

As best I could judge, it had been less than a day since I had awoken and I hadn't seen a monk since, but something I had realised in that time was that the metallic 'tick, tick, tick' of the pendulum was quietening, slowing down. The barest ideas of a plan began to form and I lay quiet, waiting for my moment.

The sound of footsteps echoing through a corridor woke me from a gentle slumber. I'd been barely touching the deeper waters of sleep, just resting and biding my time. The door opened, and I heard a monk step into the room. I tensed and then untensed my muscles, laying still with my eyes closed. I would only have one chance at this.

In the gloom, I watched him walk over to Broch and begin unchaining him from the metal bench. He stirred barely and with a great deal of pity

THE SOUL'S ASPECT

I watched as he struggled into consciousness, pulled back from the in-between and into the real world. Taking advantage of his grogginess, the single, slight monk manhandled Broch's emaciated form off the bench, and half dragged, half supported him over to the floor where he chained his arms to a ring protruding out of the stonework. This was exactly what I'd been hoping for. They'd sent a monk down to clean the metal altars, and to feed the prisoners. Expecting us to be groggy and delirious, they'd only sent one. I closed my eyes, and let all the tension from my muscles go. I could only hope the monk wouldn't notice my miraculously healed back.

With my eyes closed, I felt the monk open the manacles binding my wrists, and then my ankles. It took every ounce of my self-control not to burst off the metal mount then and there, but I knew I needed to bide my time. I needed to surprise him. If he screamed, this would all be for nothing. After he unclasped the last manacle, he lifted my arm over his shoulder and tried to pull me off the block. I slid off, doing my best impression of a confused, and befuddled idiot, swaying with my weight on top of him. He grunted in surprise, expecting me to be light and thin. As soon as both my feet were on the floor, I twisted, grabbing his shoulders with both my hands for support. I may have been stronger than Broch, but I had been strapped to a bench for Martyr knows how long, and I needed to balance on something. He let out a startled cry as I stood myself up and I clumsily wrapped my hand against his mouth, cutting it short before it could draw any attention. Realising something was wrong, he started struggling against me, throwing wild elbows at my gut. I pulled him in closer to me, and held him so his back was against my chest, so I could hold his head still. He pushed hard against me, and threw my back against the metal rock I'd just been liberated from. Surprised I let him out of my grip and he fell to the floor dazed. He looked up at me, terrified. Knowing he was seconds away from crying out again, I threw myself heavily on top of him, hoping to drive any breath from him before he could shout. Before he could get control, and start hitting me again, I dashed his head against the flagstone floor, dazing him. The sound of his skull hitting the stone was a grim, sharp sound that woke me up from the violent haze I was in. I looked down, horrified at what I'd done, what I was doing. The monk's eyes were half lidded from the blow to the head and I could see he was no older than me. For all I knew he could be another orphan, tricked into servitude by the monks from a babe. I took a deep, shaking breath. It was him or me. I placed both my hands around his neck, gently at first, steeling myself. I needed to do it now. Now before anyone else came in. I squeezed my hands together, feeling the hardness of the rubbery cartilage beneath my hands bend and move, giving way to the strength of my grip. I could feel his heart beat beneath my skin, his eyes fluttering, fighting against the concussion I'd given him. A sickness rose in my stomach, but still I kept my grip, tightening it. His body started twitching and jumping as his mind tried to force it to fight back, but it was already too late. I could feel his movements become slower, his heartbeat slow, and I struggled with all my might not to think of Thain's slowing movements as he hung from the tree. I squeezed, gripping this poor boy's throat as tight as I could, just wanting it to end. After he stopped his kicking, I kept a hold for a few more seconds, and then let go, falling off his now dead body. I was breathing quickly, unable to take my eyes off of what I'd done. The nausea in my stomach rose, and a cold sweat hit my forehead, my legs giving way. I crumpled onto my front, and threw up bile, burning as it dripped from my lips.

It was him or me. I needed to tell myself that. *It was him or me.*

Slapping myself in the face, I tried to shock myself into action. Killing this boy would have done no good if I'm discovered now. I grabbed his wrists, and pulled him into a darker corner of the room. Hating myself for what I knew I had to do, I untied the long brown robe from his body, working quickly to not let my mind linger on what I was doing. With the waist rope untied, I gently lifted his corpse, and pulled the robe off his body, and lay him back down on the cold stone floor. It was too dark for even my eyes to make out what state this left him in, so I closed his eyes, gently draping both his arms across where I thought his chest was, trying to afford him some dignity in the horror I'd caused his last minutes to be. I stepped back out of the corner, still shaky on my feet, and pulled the dead boy's robes over my head, thankful that all the monk's robes were made to be loose fitting and long. I pulled the hood over my head, and tied the robe off at the waist. I strode over to where Broch was still tied to the wall, his eyes dropping as his mind fled in and out of consciousness.

"Hey," I whispered to him, "it's me."

His eyes barely fluttered in response.

"I don't know if you can hear me, or understand what's going on. I'm going to come back for you."

His head lolled to one side, eyes shut.

I continued regardless. "I'm going to try and escape now, and then I'll come back for you, once I can get you out safely. I swear it."

Drool pooled out of his mouth, which I wiped away. Up close I could see how much weight my friend had lost, his ribs painfully obvious through his thin skin. There was no situation I could think of where I could smuggle Broch's delirious form out of this place. I had to leave him, and hope that the Vins keep him alive long enough for me to rescue him when I had a better idea how. I pushed myself to my feet, and without a second look back, I strode, opened the heavy wooden door to my cell, and entered into the amber lit corridor.

Even these soft diffuse lights burned my eyes, accustomed as they were to the darkness. I put my hand out to the stone wall of the corridor to steady myself, the nausea returning. In the light, I could see how bruised and dirty my hands were, fingernails torn bloody from the fight, knuckles swollen from rubbing against the metal rock I'd been bound to. The sleeve of the arm against the wall had ridden up a little, revealing angry looking scars, from where the manacles had rubbed my skin bloody. Not wanting to linger, I stood back up straight, and pulled my hood down to cover my face in darkness. As I bent my head down, a strand of hair fell loose from behind my ear, having grown to shoulder length. I was about to tuck it back out of sight, when I realised with a shock, that my hair had turned a stark white. I stared at the lock of hair for a moment. It wasn't the fine, wispy blonde hair that Thain had, it was instead a bright, pure white, as if all colour had been drained from it.

Was any part of me unchanged?

I tucked the lock back out of sight, and shuffled slowly down the corridor, hoping I'd chosen the right direction. I walked as close to the wall as I could, hoping I could use it to lean on if the nausea I was feeling got any worse. As I walked I tried to figure out where I was. The air down here was still dank and stale, but the corridor walls had the same carvings on them that I'd seen in both the academy and the Eastern Garrison. Neither of which would be good places to try and escape from. The corridor seemed to be sloping upwards, to an exit I hoped. My heart was pounding in my chest, as I strained my ears trying to catch the sounds of anyone else coming my way. The robe would only protect me so far, with anything beyond a cursory glance showing I wasn't who I was supposed to be. The nerves tempered the fluttering joy in my heart at the hope of freedom that grew with each step taking me further away from the hellish dungeon. The air was slowly losing its stale qualities and new, long forgotten smells were beginning to flood the corridor. Fresh cold air, carrying with it the smells of hot, fresh bakery. My body's reaction to the smell was palpable. My mouth was salivating, my hollow stomach gurgling at the mere suggestion of food. But with the change in smell came a new issue. I heard voices. Quiet at first, but with each step, they grew louder. Changes in the lighting told me there was a small room up ahead on the right, the blackness around the entrance telling me the door was open. There was a metallic rattle and a laugh. Could that be armour? Weapons? There's no way I could take on armed guards, especially without knowing how to Aspect without a tether. On the other hand, if that was the guard room up ahead, that must mean the exit was close. If I walked quickly, and with purpose I had to hope they wouldn't notice me.

Stealing my nerve, I did my best imitation of a self-important monk, widening my stride so it would seem I was walking with a purpose. The door on the right was coming closer, and so too the voices within grew louder. A gentle curve in the corridor revealed a small set of stone stairs at the end of the corridor, ones I suspected would lead out of this hellish place. I was now almost level with the door, and my heart was beating loud enough that surely the guards must have heard it. I kept my hooded face straight, ignoring the urge to glance into the room, and continued my feigned confident stride past the doorway. There was no change to the patter of voices within the room. A wave of relief washed over me making my legs go weak. I slowed my stride down, still suffering a little in the light. The stairs were a few steps away from me and would lead me undoubted to freedom.

"Oi!"

A loud, male voice called behind me, echoing down the stone corridor. My body cringed, feet rooted in their spot. A cold wash of fear dripped down my spine. I heard the sound of the man's heavy footsteps walking towards me, my back still to him.

Had I forgotten to do something? Something each visitor to this place knew to do, one that a prisoner impersonating a monk he'd strangled moments earlier wouldn't know?

It was hard to stop myself from running. Just dashing for the door. But I knew if I did that then I'd have no chance to leave if the stairway didn't lead to an exit. Fighting my base instincts, I turned around, keeping my neck bent so the cowl kept my face in shade. I watched as the leather armoured chest of a man came into view, huffing slightly from the gentle slope he'd had to stride up.

"Well?" The guard demanded, voice gruff.

I kept silent, hoping that the monk I was impersonating had been similarly mute on his entrance.

"Oh, for pity's sake. Give me the damned keys," the guard said, his exasperated voice making it clear he thought he was dealing with a moron.

Of course, I thought to myself. I reached into my robe and pulled out the small ring of keys, careful to keep the sleeve of the robe hanging over my scars. The guard snatched them out of my hands.

"Fecking dolt," he muttered, and turned around, walking back to his guard room. I stood still, chest heaving as sweat poured down my neck. He was walking away. I turned quickly, and before the guard could remember some other thing I should have done, walked quickly to the stairs, climbed them and yanked open the door at the top.

THE SQUARE

Sounds, sights and smells washed over me like an ocean at high tide, threatening to knock me down, pushing me back through the doorway I'd just left. The sun was shining through a clear blue sky, low and bright but with little heat radiating from it. A chill wind was dancing around, tightening the skin on my face and threatening to push my hood down. I stood outside a nondescript wooden door, looking out into the familiar cobblestoned square of Isale. It was a market day, with wagons in row after row trying to flog their variety of assorted trinkets, the town's folk of Isale wandering around aimlessly pursuing the goods on offer. The sound of children's laughter tinkling like delicate breaking class could be heard atop the gentle, warm tenor of tradesmen's constant pleading and enticement. The smell of hot roasted chestnuts and caramel cinnamon nuts drifted through the square. Dotted around the square, I spotted a few familiar faces, students and Foclir who had descended from the academy to enjoy the festivities.

Blinking out the sensory overload, I hugged the edge of the market, trying to figure out what to do. There were so many people. I needed to leave Isale, get out and regroup, but how could I wander through the crowd? I spotted a group of monks who were wandering just as aimlessly as the townsfolk, probably on a day of leave from the festivities. My best hope would be to try and blend in, walk amongst the crowd, and try to exit through the other side of the square.

Head down, and walking slowly, I made my way into the press of the crowd. I needed to keep my head down, to make sure no one could glance at my face. My fair features and shock white hair would undoubtedly identify me as an intruder. From my vantage point, I could only make out tables of goods and only from the torso down of members of the crowd. I tried to think of the layout of the market, trying to float myself to where I thought the exit would be. I passed a stand of fresh cooked bread, where the tradesman was enraptured in a conversation with a young Vinnish woman holding a babe at her hip. The smell was intoxicating, and before I knew what I was doing, I'd let my hand fall casually to my side, and picked up a hot cinnamon bun. I kept walking, tearing small chunks off the sticky bun as I went, savouring my first taste of solid food in perhaps a year. As I continued to walk through the bustling market, I let myself relax a little. The market was so busy, there was no way anyone could spot me in the crowd, I was just another Seer monk enjoying the festivities. I let myself enjoy the smell of fresh, clean air washing against my skin. It replenished me, more than food, more than the light from the sun, and I revelled in the freedom it brought with it.

An errant shoulder bumped into my own, knocking my hood down.

"Excuse me," the offender grunted.

No. No no no no no. I knew that voice.

"Kehlem? Is that you?" Brin stood before me, his enormous frame a rock that parted the crowds. His deep voice seemed to boom around the square.

I snapped back into reality. Panic, true, heart hammering panic rose in me, an ocean of terror. "I don't know who you're talking about," I stammered, trying to pull my cowl back up.

"It is you!" Brin said. "I heard you'd left — what has happened to your hair?"

"Brin, please," I pleaded under my breath. "Please."

Something clicked behind Brin's eyes, some level of understanding of the situation I was in. "Do you need to get out of here?" he asked, finally keeping his voice low.

I nodded, relieved and beyond grateful.

"Follow me then, keep your head low."

I pulled my cowl down over my eyes, and stepped next to Brin as he turned around.

He wasn't moving. I looked up to see what the issue was, and then followed Brin's gaze. Running towards us were a group of monks.

"Run!" Brin yelled at me, pushing me in the opposite direction. As he did, with his free hand he tipped the table nearest the monks over, sending people scrambling and slowing the monks down. He then ran the opposite direction from me, back towards the academy, a few of the monks giving chase.

I jumped into action, pushing my way through the crowds that had pressed forwards to see what the commotion was. There was an alleyway between two shops just ahead, if I could just reach there, I could run free, maybe steal a horse from somewhere.

I kept my head low as I ran through the crowds, hoping to blend in, but at the cost of my vision, I collided head first with someone pushing the other way. Dazed, nauseous and with the world now spinning around me, I lost my footing and fell to the cobbled floor. Hands gripped me by the armpits, pulling me up.

A robed figure strode into view as I struggled between the grip of my unseen captors. "Kehlem?" He asked, lowering his own hood. "Is that you?"

I stayed silent, my face contorted with hatred as I looked at the face of the man who betrayed me, and executed my best friend. I tried to pull my arms out of the grip of my captors, but their hold was firm.

Kit turned to one of the cowled monk's next to him. "You, run up to the academy now. Tell them that Kehlem escaped, and that he's in our hands."

The monk turned on his heel and ran, running to the stone archway that opened up to the path up the mountain.

"How did you get out?" Kit asked, turning back to me.

I wasn't listening. My mind had tunnelled in, focusing on Kit's face. He was going to capture me. Send me back to that place. I'd never get out. They won't make the same mistake again.

In the distance I could see some Foclir looking at our group curiously, some of them making their way over to see what the commotion was. Most of the town's folk hadn't noticed something was amiss.

With my arms held firm, and no tether, I had no way of Aspecting, no way to escape.

Ignoring all the tension in our group, a large black cat began padding its way between the legs of the monks, occasionally meowing here and there, probably trying to entice some humans to give it food.

Time seemed to slow as memories from the Aspect came flooding back.

I don't need a tether. That's what my father had said. But how? All energy comes from the Aspect, he'd said.

What was it Themia had once told me? 'Energy was a currency'.

THE SOUL'S ASPECT

What if she was wrong? What if energy was the language?

The black cat had stopped at my feet, and was staring up at me, begging for food. I closed my eyes, and saw the slowly moving gliding colours once more. There was a pattern there, hidden amongst the sliding colours, one that called out to me. I opened my eyes, and the cat had gone. Kit was still staring at me. Quicker than I'd ever moved, I pulled myself to the ground, surprising my captors with the sudden movement, breaking myself out of their grip. Kit lunged at me, but I side stepped him easily. In a single, fluid motion, I grabbed the tear I'd found to the Aspect with both hands and drew the single, beautiful pattern I'd seen. As I finished, I sensed something new. My hands pushed through the usually ineffable membrane that separated the Aspect from the in-between, and I opened a small void, connecting me directly to the Aspect. Bright red lines appeared in the air from the pattern I'd traced. The wind in the square turned into a gale, and there were cries of dismay from the townsfolk as merchandise were thrown from tables by the wind. The monks around me shrank back, terrified of the apparition before them, as impossible light began flooding out from the voids I held in both hands. Connected to the Aspect, I found what it was I was looking for. A simple truth. Every living thing in this square came from the Aspect. Aspector or not, they were tied to it. The spirit that flowed through me, was the same that flowed through everyone else. All the hate, fear, and self-loathing burned bright, a star shining within my soul. This was true Aspecting. True power.

I focused on Kit, who had fallen to the floor and was staring up at me in horror. I knew what I needed to do. With both hands still gripping the Aspect, I pulled in as much energy as I could from around me, letting it sink, gravitate towards the voids I held in my hands. Like pulling heat from the lake or a fire, only this felt different, like I was pulling a thread that wove through everything. The winds slowed to a dead halt, and the sounds of the market faded to a complete silence. Connected as I was in the Aspect, I could hold as much energy as I liked. My body was a ship floating atop a surging sea. Like a puncture in the fabric of our reality, my hands held a globe of shifting colours, that were and were not made of light. Life and energy, spirit and power poured inwards collating and circulating into the voids I held. I looked down at Kit, his eyes wide with confusion and terror. In this moment, I felt no emotion. Just an odd, dispassionate appraisal of his cowardice. Kit had come to me while I was tied to a rock, bound and helpless. He had confessed his sins, asked for forgiveness when he knew there was no chance of me escaping, when he knew my death would come with certainty. When it was easy. And convenient for him. Now that I was free, his first thought was to call for his masters. I hated him almost as much as I loathed myself. I walked towards him, and crouched.

"No more," I said simply, and touched both my hands to his temple. He screamed in a language of pure pain and terror. I gripped his soul and tore it asunder from his mortal body. His screaming cut silent as I released my grip, sending his spirit into the Aspect.

I threw his lifeless body to the floor, his eyes smoking as blood pooled from his ears and nose. There was no joy to be felt at his violent removal from this world, only the pain and sadness he'd left behind.

I took a deep, shaking breath and pulled myself out of the Aspect, ready to fight my way out of the square.

Except there was just silence.

I looked around, and everybody; men, women, children, monks, students and Foclir. All of them were on the floor. Dead.

I spun around, eyes wide.

A hundred or so people. Dead. Blood was pouring from some people's corpses, pooling in the divots between the cobblestones, tracking the gentle rise and fall of the floor.

No. No no no no no.

My mind was a broken clock, the second hand forever stuck, ticking the same thought, unable to move on, to process what it was seeing.

No no no no no.

I was the epicentre of a disaster of my own making, the eye of death. Something hammered against the wall of my mind, banging its fists against the horror that has blocked off my consciousness. There was something important I was forgetting.

But what could be more important than this? The wind was starting to pick up again. A ribbon, tied into a small child's hair fluttered in the wind. The child was still gripping her mother's hand, who lay beside her. They both could be sleeping, the town struck by a sudden sleeping sickness, if it weren't for the abject stillness.

There is a difference between a living and dead person. One so obvious and strong that even people like my father who were without faith, struggled to explain it. An old farmer had died once, under our care. I was seven, and he'd come to us with a palsy that my father had tried to treat. He ended up staying with us for a week and in the process, he caught a mild cold, which turned into a wetness on his lungs. By the fifth day, he was sleeping more hours than waking, drinking only water. My father had encouraged me to attend the man with him. Death was a natural conclusion to life, he had said and not something we should shy away from. And so, my father and I had sat with the man as he took his last breath, and faded into oblivion. The thought of dying had terrified me, but I found I could not look away. I knew the farmer had died before my father had even checked his life signs. There was a sudden hollow, almost deflated essence to his whole body, as if his spirit was provided a vitality that was measurable and observable, and with it leaving to the unknowable, the body remained as little more than a collection of meat. A coincidence of flesh, sinew and cartilage.

That was the square. Everyone was dead. Their vitality vanished, removed leaving only meat, and silence.

The urgency was still crying out, muffled and unheard from my waking mind, as I drifted aimlessly through the silent square. I stepped over splayed arms, careful not to tread on fingers, wandering absently through the unmanned market stall, until I found myself facing the archway, the one that led back up to the academy.

The urgent thought banged harder, until it clanged the damn of madness loud enough to make it ring like a bell.

A monk had fled to the academy. They would be sending reinforcements. I heard shouting coming from one of the side streets. It sounded like men fighting. I needed to leave. I needed to leave while I still could.

THE SQUARE

My conscious mind had mostly retreated, still stuck, staccato ticking over images of the square. My body moved automatically. I grabbed items from the stalls around me. Blanket. Fleece roll. A set of simple clothes and cloak. A rucksack which I stuffed with some cooling loaves of bread. Twine. A single, sharp dagger.

The square was dead, a whole town left broken and ruined by my hand. I left the dread scene, fleeing the single high street and making for the long flat plains that would carry me away from my waking nightmare.

32

The road less trod

I walked for hours, one-foot treading ground in front of the other, the ground passing slowly beneath me, carrying me away from the burden of the town square. My mind was still adrift, floating on the tides of madness, surfacing only momentarily to attend to my mortal concerns, tearing small bite size pieces of bread from the food I'd pilfered from the market, my mouth chewing dry bread as I walked, making for the small copse of trees that littered the horizon. My body carried me away from the one road that travelled from the town, travelling through the gentle rolling fields, and away from any passing travellers coming to or from Isale. At some point, I must have stripped, and changed out of my stolen monk robes, and into the clothes I'd taken from the market, but I had no memory of stopping, no memory of pulling the robe over my head, its bloodied hem wet against my naked back. But then, I had little memory of anything that day. Just piecemeal snippets. The sound of a distant bird chirping forlorn into the cold winter air. The woollen cloak itching against my neck as I pulled it tight around me. A look of surprise permanently engraved on the face of a young man, his dead eyes reflecting the grey skies above him. Just snippets.

The sun was falling, and the cold was sharper now, like pins slowly pressing against every inch of exposed flesh. The silvery scars on my wrists and ankles ached especially, the freezing wind pulling the skin taut against bone.

I arrived at the small smattering of trees by true night-rise, relieved to find the small collection was enough to provide some small amount of shelter from the incessant wind. The road I had avoided all day curled and its apex touched the outskirts of my woods, so no fire could be lit to warm me tonight, lest I draw unwanted attention from nearby travellers. Finding a likely looking patch of gentle and soft ground, I wrapped my cloak around me tightly and lay myself down for the night. I hoped the cold uncaring night wouldn't take me in my sleep. I hoped it would.

"We can't trust them. Not anymore. Thadius is dead, how much more evidence of the corruption do you need?"

The familiar female voice whispered to my sleeping mind, and I woke up, startled. I sat bolt upright in the pitch black, twisting and turning to try and locate the source of the voice. Why did it sound so familiar? But there was no one. I was still truly alone.

"And what about Kehlem, then? I told him to trust the academy! If something happens to him it would be my fault!"

The haunting voice came once more, and now awake I realised it wasn't coming from around me. I was hearing it in my head. Eva. Her voice was once more reaching across the Aspect to me. And she sounded urgent. Worried.

What had happened? Had the Vin do something? In retaliation for what I had done?

My heart was racing. I jumped to my feet in a panic. Bone, muscle and skin complained in unison.

I couldn't think straight. My mind had been hiding from itself, but now it had been poked it was rearing like a bear waking from hibernation, swatting at anything and everything. Memories came rushing back; the look of terror on a young monk's face as I squeezed the life out of him, Kit's smoking eyes, Thain's legs stamping out in vain in thin air, desperately searching for a purchase to relieve the strain on his neck.

I couldn't breathe. Why can't I breathe? My lungs are too small. There's not enough air. I need to save Broch. I need to warn Eva, I need...

I fell to the ground, gasping for air as my heart hammered the anvil of my chest. I was on my hands and knees, tears pouring down my face. But then, there was a softness. A distraction. Soft fur rubbed against my forehead, and cheek, wet nose pushing against my own. A deep rumbling purr emitted from the creature beneath me, and the sound seemed to reverberate through my own body.

Stop. It said. *Breathe.* It said.

I did. And so, I did.

My breathing matched the rhythm of the purr. Deep, slow, shaking breaths. Gulping down the icy early morning air. Again. Again. Five minutes, an hour, a year later, my heart slowed. Slowed enough that I could sit back on my haunches. I could breathe again without worrying that the next wouldn't come. And there in front of me sat on its own haunches was a cat. Its green eyes collecting what little moonlight filtered through the barren branches above, shining out like candles into the night. It stared at me, and for a moment, I thought I saw something recognizable deep within its irises. A pattern of swirling green. But in a lazy blink, it had gone.

In my panic, I'd lost whatever connection I'd held that let me hear Eva. How had that happened? I must have been touching the Aspect in my sleep. Was that even possible? An icy shiver ran down my spine. I was losing control. Maybe I had already lost control.

Why hadn't my father warned me? Did he know what would happen?

I was freezing. Maybe I could start a fire? I pushed myself to my feet, and started feeling the ground for small twigs. The cat stayed rooted in its spot, and just followed me with its eyes. Once I had a pile big enough, I sat back down and reached out to feel for the Aspect. It was almost alarmingly easy. In the past, finding the Aspect took a moment, like leafing through a book for a familiar dogeared page, but now. Now it was instant. Like the Aspect was reaching back to me. As before in the square, my hand didn't rest on the surface, but instead was pulled straight through into the Aspect. There was power here. Real power, not just energy-lending. My hand was guided through a pattern, pulled this way and that by a current I did not understand. I started to panic. The cat was still watching me. I was stood back in the square, hopelessly pulling in the life and soul of all the innocent bystanders, an epicentre of death. I tried to close the connection, stop the pattern, but the current wouldn't relent. Like a riptide it tugged at my hand. With the fear of a trapped animal, who would sooner gnaw off their own limb then be captured, I yanked my hand, pulling it free from the Aspect. I was back on the cold forest floor, still surrounded by darkness, an unlit pile of twigs next to me. My heart was pounding, and I felt sick to my stomach, a cold sweat pouring from my forehead.

A deep, uneasy feeling that had been bubbling around beneath the surface for a while now began to push through, just enough to offer me a chilling thought.

If I wasn't in control of Aspecting, was the Aspect controlling me?

I wouldn't do it. I would sooner dose myself to the end of my days with arrowwood, then let myself be carried by the current of the Aspect once more.

I looked back at the cat, who was still considering me with his luminous eyes. Another memory from yesterday floated like beach wood to the surface.

"I know you," I said. "Have you been following me from the square?" I reached across the distance to run my fingers through its soft fur. At the mention of the square, images of corpses haunted my vision, but the cat's soft fur beneath my fingers grounded me, stopping me from losing my mind once more.

"I remember my friend had a cat once," I said, thinking fondly of Thain. "I shall call you Scarpi. I won't be sleeping again tonight. If you have a mind, we could travel together."

33

Winterwhail

My feet were bloody and raw. I'd lost count of the days since Isale. Maybe I'd forgotten on purpose. All I knew was walking, leaving behind death and pain. I needed to get to Mercy, get there before the Vins could take anything else from me. I'd diverted from the road some time ago, opting to travel west, deep into the forest. The food I'd pilfered from the market had long gone, and I was surviving off the small amounts of food I could forage from the woods.

Winter was upon us, and Scarpi and I were surely the only wild beasts out roaming the woods for many a mile, all other sensible animals asleep, burrowed underground waiting for spring. Since hearing Eva's voice through the Aspect, I had little else on my mind other than getting to Mercy. The only problem, other than the Hunters and trackers no doubt looking for my trail, was the ponderous river that separated Vin Irudur from Casere, a physical demarcation of countries. The Dravé bridge was out of the question, running straight through the eastern garrison, who I was sure by now had my description and were actively on the lookout. My best hope was to travel further inland, and cross the Dravé at a less perilous point. I was painfully aware however that each step taking me further west, I would have to make back up once I'd crossed the river to make it to Mercy.

My mind was a broken, pitiful being during this time and I would have gone quite mad were it not for Scarpi, who kept me company during the long days of walking, and the fitful nights of restless sleep. He would follow me underfoot, always keeping pace with me, and when I would rest my legs, I would often find myself talking to him as if he understood me. The way he watched me intently as I spoke made me sometimes think he could. I would tell him stories of my childhood, of Barrowheld, Eva and my father. After those stories were done, I spoke to him of Broch and Thain, these stories coming harder to me, and taking a physical toll on my soul the same way lancing an infection would.

Even in my muddled state, I had not forgotten Broch. Oh no. He haunted my dreams each night, every time I let myself think for more than a moment, there he was, still chained to the metal altar, still suffering as new bugs feasted on his essence. I had not forgotten my promise to free him. I had not forgotten, and yet, here I was walking west, each step taking me further away from Isale. From Broch.

When I had heard Eva, a piece of me awoke, jolted into action. I had purpose, something my floating mind desperately needed to latch on to. But another, deeper part of myself, the core of my being that I was sometimes too afraid to look at directly, knew the truth. I was relieved. Relieved to have a reason not to go back. Not to rescue my friend.

Because of me, the love of Broch's life was executed, hanged in front of us like a petty criminal and left to rot in the grounds of the academy. Broch had barely spoken during our time in that basement together, but what few words he had were so filled with loathing and hatred, I was grateful there was such loud silence between us since. He blamed me utterly for Thain's death, as did I, but to look at the truth, unbridled and manifested within a friend of my own, it was too much. And so, as I walked west, shivering and cold in the bleak winter, telling myself that I must stop harm befalling Eva, a small part of me, the truest and most shameful part, was relieved to be leaving Broch chained to that rock back in Isale.

Despite the cold, and despite my meagre resources, Scarpi and I made good progress. This was mostly due to us marching day and night. Sleep was not a relief for me. In fact, I would dread and shy away from it most days, taking it only when necessity demanded. I was a hunted man, and in every shadow that came with sleep lurked the faces of the people I'd killed. I'd see the faces of children and babes, mothers and fathers each of them watching me with accusatory dead eyes at the life I'd stripped away from them. But the longer I avoided sleep, the more likely these apparitions would appear as a waking nightmare, and I would catch glimpses of silent watchers in the shadows of the forest. A pair of dead eyes hiding behind the evergreen to my left, a pale face watching me beneath the waters of the spring I drank from. The worst would be the creaking, as I heard the sound of a heavy weight hanging from a hemp rope, twisting in the wind. When these visions plagued me, I would often fall to my knees, shutting my eyes and praying for the ghosts to leave. Panic, like I had never felt before, would rise up in my body like a wave and crash down over me so there was little that I could think of beyond fear. Unbidden, my body would respond - my heart a hammer and my chest the fluttering wings of a bird. The first few times this happened, I had no choice but to abide by the whims of my mind and body, and wait hours for the panic and fear to pass. With time however, Scarpi began to recognise the early signs, and occasionally would be able to bring me down. He'd distract me, nosing his head against my face, reminding me that there was a physical world I was still tethered to.

Snow was falling through the gaps in the canopy, the first I'd seen in years. It was fine and thin, but the heavy dark clouds ahead promised a flurry would be arriving soon after the soft vanguard. With it the snow brought a horrid chill, a wind that was strong enough to penetrate through the cover of the trees, pulling my skin uncomfortably taught and numbing the feeling in my fingers. Scarpi and I pushed through the wind and snow, our progress slowing to a glacial pace as visibility became poor from the thickening flurries. The forest floor became harder to walk on as the snow accumulated and before long, Scarpi was struggling to make any progress as the snow became taller than his shoulders.

"Come here," I called to him softly, and reached down, scooping him under his ribs, holding him close to my chest. He began purring deeply at being held, and despite the added weight, I found I quite enjoyed the warmth his fur gave to my hands as I held him close to my body.

Together we walked through the snow storm, my cloak heavy from frozen snow trailing on its hem. Thankfully the trees seemed to be opening up, so despite the poor visibility, we weren't in much risk of tripping over a stray root which had been buried beneath the fresh snow.

By what I assumed was midday, we were blessed with a cessation of the wind, as it slowed to a gentle gust. The snow stopped flying horizontally in a frenzy and was drifting down gently around us, like so many stars in a night sky. Curiously, now that the sound of wind through the trees had stopped, a new sound could be heard in the distance. A sound of running water. We had been crossing various streams for days now, but each of them had been small, trickling things, none so wide enough to make a sound significant enough to be heard before seen.

Could it finally be the Dravé?

Eager to find out and with Scarpi still held tight to my chest, I waded through the ankle-deep snow towards the source of the noise. As the noise grew louder, the landscape before us changed, trees giving way to flat ground, albeit smothered in perfect alabaster snow. Despite the heavy grey clouds above, the white of the ground was reflecting enough light that I found myself squinting, a tension behind my eyes starting to form. I waded through these snow fields for perhaps an hour, a walk which on a good day I probably could have done in half that time, but regardless of the expenditure, it was worth it.

I finished my trek, stood on the bank of a sluggish river, about a hundred yards wide. Peppered within its waters were large chunks of surface ice, floating gently, tugged by the current of the waters beneath. I'd finally arrived at the border to Casere. I set Scarpi down next to me as we studied the river. The waters were obviously freezing, not something I would survive swimming through. I'd need to find someone willing to ferry a penniless man across. Someone who the news of Isale had not yet reached.

With little plan of what else to do, I began following the path of the river, hoping maybe that we might find a spot where the river narrows. We walked for a few hours, and while the river never relented, I spotted something in the distance that was more enticing. Shelter.

THE SOUL'S ASPECT

In the distance, on the banks of the river stood a rickety fishing hut. The promise of shelter from snow and wind whispered to me, seduced me away from thoughts of crossing the river, and in a fever dream, I found myself pulled closer, despite my reasonable mind telling me to leave, to push forward. To get to Mercy.

Up close, I could see that the hut was nothing special. Probably just intended to provide shelter for fishermen during the day. It was raised on stilts, so presumably in the spring time when the banks of the river raised, it would be protected. Scarpi and I surveyed the exterior. The inside was dark, no smoke was coming from the chimney. Frost had settled on the multitudinous cobwebs that covered each nook and cranny of the exterior, giving the appearance of rigging that was structurally integral to the building.

Whoever used this hut had not been by in a while, I reasoned.

Before I could talk myself out of it, I climbed the steps and tried the door. It opened with a gentle creak of dry wood.

The inside was a simple affair. A small, unlit log stove sat in the corner. There was no furniture so to speak inside, beyond a single bed roll lying wall to wall, and various fishing paraphernalia propped up against the walls. A simple woven rug lay on the floor. I ushered Scarpi inside who slunk around the corners of the hut, sniffing the air. I closed the door behind us, blocking out most of the light, leaving us in the dim gloom as light filtered in through a single grimy window. I knelt beside the log burner, and to my unbridled delight, whoever had been last in here had the forethought to prepare a fire before they had left. Dry wood had been stored within the stove itself, probably to ensure it stayed dry. I continued to pat around in the dark around the stove, and yes, there on the top near the chimney was a battered tinderbox. I eagerly pulled out the larger pieces of dried wood from the stove, leaving the smaller pieces in place, and sprinkled some of the charcloth from the tinder box underneath the pile. With flint and steel, I showered sparks into the stove, and almost cried with joy as they caught, and beautiful, life giving flames spread through the kindling. I slowly fed it larger and larger pieces of wood, and then sat down in front of the stove, mesmerised by the dancing of the flames. To feel heat against my hands and face, warming a chill that had settled into my bones. It almost made me feel human again. Almost. At some point Scarpi had joined me, and had curled up into my lap as I absentmindedly stroked him to sleep. There was no food, or drink, but with fire and the promise of a sheltered rest, I fell into the deepest sleep of my life.

Tick, tick, tick, tick. The metallic clicking of the pendulum reverberated off of the wet stone walls. A man lay face down, chained to an irregular chunk of iron, which had been carved with intricate patterns. Both the man's wrists and ankles were chained to the metal, binding him like a hog on a spit. The skin of the man's back seemed to ripple occasionally, mounds of swollen, oozing flesh dotted irregularly against his sallow skin. The man's eyes were closed, but his lips moved slightly, as he whispered, barely above the volume of breathing, a steady mantra, matching the rhythm of the 'tick'. Like the insects in his back, his voice drove its way into the room, until all that could be heard, was his whispering voice: "murderer, murderer, murderer…".

My eyes flickered open as the familiar nightmare disturbed my sleep. I looked around, panicked for a moment, not recognising my surroundings. The fire in the stove had died down to just glowing embers. Scarpi and I lay in front of it. Recalling the events of yesterday, my heart slowed its slamming, and I took control of my breathing. I pushed myself so I sat against the wall, and rubbed the sleep out of my eye.

Little could be seen out of the grimy window opposite me, only a slowly lightening sky telling me morning was fast approaching. The Dravé still lay between us and Casere, and I would need to find a way to cross it. The weather did seem to be growing colder the past few days, and perhaps if I waited it out, the river would freeze entirely, just enough for Scarpi and I to cross. But how long would that take?

I lifted myself to my feet so I could peer out of the window, perhaps watch the sunrise before figuring out what my next move was. The snow was still thick on the ground, and it had bought with it a silence, deep and rich that can only be found during the depths of winter.

It didn't take long for the urges of nature to win the fight of wanting to stay warm, and I wrapped myself up in my now dry cloak, and headed outside to relieve myself. Snow had fallen in the night covering our footsteps from yesterday, smoothing them out into gentle rolls and divots. The morning was still, and not even the wind had awoken yet, and all that could be heard was the gentle slush of the sluggish river, accompanied by the occasional icy clash as two ice sheets collided with each other. For no reason other than an ingrained sense of modesty, I retreated to the treeline to relieve myself. I took the opportunity to gather some fresh, clean snow in a metal can I'd pilfered from the hut, in the hope of melting it for some fresh drinking water for Scarpi and I. But as I gathered snow from the ground, something caught my eye. There, just skirting the edge of the treeline, was a single set of footprints.

My heart stopped, and the can dropped from my fingers. They were fresh, no snow had covered them. They appeared to have come from the forest, towards the hut, and then back around the edge of the treeline.

It could be nothing, I thought to myself. Just a ranger. Or a fisherman, coming to see why smoke was coming from his hut.

Except it didn't feel right. The winter quiet suddenly felt too silent. Instead of a warm blanket of stillness, it felt like an indrawn breath, a taut bowstring. I darted back to the hut, cursing myself for being foolish enough to have lit a fire. If anyone had tracked me from Isale, I would have given them a shining beacon to where I was. Why had I walked so far from the hut? Scarpi would still be asleep. I needed to wake him and leave this place. Almost there.

I rounded the corner of the hut, ready to burst through the door, but an apparition stopped me in my tracks.

"Long time no see, Kehlem," Wolv said.

I kept my distance from her. She was standing at the top of the stairs, probably trying to sneak up on me while I had been sleeping. Though no weapon was drawn, she held her right hand on the pommel of her sword at her waist, and her left hand was at her side, two fingers pointed out from her fist.

"You're coming back with me," She said. It wasn't a question.

A wave of panic was rising in me. My one and only weapon, the knife I'd stolen, was still inside the hut. How could I be so stupid?

"You've been following me long?" I asked, stepping slowly away from the hut, trying to think of a way out.

"Since you escaped," She shrugged. "I'd been a few days behind on your trail, but you're a slow mover. I'd been hoping you would lead me to Broch, but ah well. Of course, it helps if you're thick enough to light a fire out in the open, miles away from the nearest village."

Lead her to Broch? What had happened to him? Had he managed to escape?

She said all of this so matter-of-factly. She wasn't even gloating. She was just explaining to her student exactly how badly he had fucked up.

I eyed the river behind me on impulse.

"Don't think about it Kehlem," She said, seeing my intent. "One slip into that water and you're dead. Look at you, there's no meat left on those bones. Do us both a favour and come quickly and quietly. If you do, I'll tell the Abbot. Maybe he'll give you a quick death."

She started walking down the stairs of the hut towards me. I had no choice. I was going to have to Aspect. It was that or be taken. I braced myself, ready to be taken by the tides of the pattern, when there was a loud crash. I looked up, startled. The window pane of the hut had smashed. For a second, I thought Wolv had done it, until I noticed she looked as surprised as I, and then I noticed at the foot of the hut, the soft black form of Scarpi.

Martyr bless that cat.

He darted towards me, and not wanting to waste the distraction, I joined him running, towards the bank of the river. I'd have to gamble on getting across on the fractured ice. The edge of the river was in sight, I could almost jump to reach it, but then a heavy impact hit my left calf. It caught me, sent my left leg sprawling, and I tipped forwards and slid face first down the bank of the river. Snow, mud and rocks rubbings painfully against my face. I span around, trying to see what had hit me. Wolv was walking towards me, still a distance behind, but her left hand was raised, a line of red light dissipating into the air behind her.

How had she done that? What was that?

Wolv smiled at my confusion. "There is so much that you don't, and will never, know about the Aspect. I always disagreed with the Primus. You would never have made a Hunter."

I got to my feet, my left ankle painfully twisted from the fall, and half-walked, half-hopped away from the hunter. I could hear her laughing behind me.

I tripped again, this time on a stray rock, no magical intervention needed. Wolv loomed over me. With a sudden, violent twist her, boot landed with a crunch into my side, my body flaring up in pain. She kicked me again and a third time, until I heard a sickening snapping noise.

I clutched my ribs, blinking the tears out of my eyes. I couldn't think straight for the pain.

She grabbed the front of my cloak, and picked me up bodily to my feet. I almost threw up from the pain. I could feel my ankle swelling, and each breath brought a sharp stabbing pain from the cracked ribs in my side. Appraising me for a moment, she lifted her gloved hand and backhanded me across the face so hard I saw stars and tasted ashes in my mouth.

"That's for not coming easily," She said.

I spat blood onto the ground, bent double from the aura of pain throbbing through me.

From behind me, a hissing noise pitched almost into a scream as Scarpi launched himself at Wolv, claws latching him into her woollen cloak.

"What the fu…" Wolv exclaimed, startled at the cat's ferocity, and tried to swat him away, but he was too quick. He clambered up her cloak and onto her back, scratching and biting at any piece of exposed flesh. Wolv furiously spun and twisted, trying to reach the cat who seemed always just out of reach.

It was now or never. Pushing past the pain, I not so much reached out, as plunged my hand into the Aspect. I watched, surprised to see that it didn't disappear as I thought it might, but instead my hand up to my wrist grew hazy, as if heat was shimmering around it.

Don't stop to think. Don't let it take you.

I pinched my fingers, holding onto a fibre of complete ineffability, and wove it into a pattern, one that combined the two Destructia patterns I knew better than the lines across the back of my own hand. Before I completed the final sweep of the pattern, I pulled my hand back out of the Aspect. With it, as if suspended in water, I held in my hand a marble of shifting colours. Sensing what I needed from him, Scarpi launched himself from Wolv's shoulders and back into safety behind me. In her struggle to rid herself of the cat, Wolv was now positioned between myself and the bank of the river. Her hair had come loose from its warrior plait, and harsh red lines drawn by Scarpi's claws covered her face. She looked up at me furious, and then surprised as she noticed what was floating in my hand.

I couldn't hold it any longer. I'd drawn the pattern, held the energy and then demanded the Aspect hold its form while Scarpi had gotten to safety. But it would wait no longer.

Wolv held her hand up, "Wai-"

Before she could say another word, I pushed the marble forward, palm flat out.

Brilliant, golden light erupted first, followed by a thunderclap of sound that threw me to my feet, and finally a scolding heat came last. All within the blink of an eye.

I blinked out the gold light which had seared itself into my eyes, and waited for the dizziness to pass. Everything hurt, from Wolv's beat down and from being thrown by my own working. I pushed myself slowly to my feet, eager to get away, in case Wolv had survived. But she was nowhere to be seen. Where she had stood, melting snow had been churned with the earth, but there was no sign of her, or her body. I looked to the river, wondering if she'd tripped, and fallen in. But it had frozen solid. From bank to bank, and as far as I could see mouth to source, it was solid ice. I had intended to use the river as a source, tie myself to it, but I had no control over how much energy I meant to draw. To freeze the entire river... It was a staggering amount of energy. It left me feeling empty, and disgusted, once more thinking about what I had done in the square. Even when I tried to control myself, I had no idea what I was doing.

I limped back to the hut, Scarpi in tow, to pick up my pack. I grabbed some useful things from the hut including the tinderbox and a thicker blanket that had been rolled and stored in the corner.

After taking the morning to clean my wounds, and having checked to see if Scarpi had been injured in his scrap, together we crossed the now frozen Dravé, feet finally back on Casere soil. Once on the other side of the river, we discovered what had happened to Wolv. Her crumpled form lay on the Casere bank of the Dravé, having been launched clear across the river. I refused to go near her to get a closer look, sickened once again by what I had done, but the smell of charred flesh lay thick and cloying in the air.

Scarpi and I walked throughout the day, trying to put as much distance between the Dravé and us. I struggled forwards, each step taking me further away from the horrors I'd caused, taking me closer to Eva. To Mercy.

34

Epilogue

A white stone archway rose above the man's head as he walked into civilization for the first time in months. At his feet, a black cat padded along the smooth flagstone floor, unnoticed by the masses. The smell of the rich sea air mingled with those of the market, as traders called out to passers-by to sample the spices and goods travelled here from far and exotic lands. Two- and three-story buildings rose up around him, and the man struggled to keep his steps even and measured as he fought against the ongoing sense of claustrophobia, unused as he was to not seeing the sky clear around him. As he walked deeper into the city, he pulled the hood of his cloak up, as he noticed more and more eyes catching glimpse of his white hair. He'd braided it back in anticipation, but amongst the masses he still stood out. He walked to the eastern parts of the city, the route familiar to him, keeping the ocean on his left. He ignored the couples, young and old who walked together hand in hand along the seafront, marvelling at the sea beneath them as the failing light of the sun sparkled on the crystal ocean. Even in the late afternoon, the city felt vibrant, alive, filled with people sitting outside taverns, enjoying the first glimmers of spring with an ale in hand after a long day of work. Somewhere music was being played by street performers, a tenor voice singing unheard lines, carrying only the hint of a melody across the distance.

Had the man been in a state of mind to notice, he would have seen the way guards' hands slipped to their belted weapons as he passed, the way they all seemed to look everywhere except him, and the tenseness that he left in his wake. But he wasn't in that state of mind. He had been thinking of but one thing, one person for so long now, that any reason, any logic or self-preservation was drowned out to make room for the single shining beacon left in his life.

The man spotted his destination, a tall unassuming house that stood overlooking the sea. Like its neighbours it was made of a smooth sandy coloured stone, with a small lantern held above its door. The sun had begun to set and blessed the city with a blood orange hue, as it sank into the sea.

The man came to a halt opposite the house. How many miles had he walked? How many years had it been? Would she recognise the man he was now, who he had become?

A nervousness rose in his chest, and his breathing quickened. For too long he had dreamt of this moment, and now with it within his reach he hesitated. A love so strong that it transcended the horrors his life had become. It had borne him on its wings to this place. Would she curse him? Would she love him still? Would she blame him for the life he would surely have to rip her from?

The cat beneath his feet mewed at the man, and he nodded to himself. He removed his hood, and stealing himself, strode to the door and banged heavily with his fist on the heavy oak planks.

An eternity passed before the door moved, inching slowly inwards as a familiar, yet new face greeted him with a spoken and unheard question. Her raven hair framed a face which had grown into a woman's, sharp and impossibly beautiful, yet her amber eyes remained the same, the ones he had loved within the candle-lit clearing a lifetime ago. Her lips moved once more, asking a question that was once again unheard, and the man responded with just a tear that fell down a sharp cheekbone.

A glimmer of recognition. A sudden white knuckled grip on the door frame, if only to keep herself from falling to the floor.

"Kehlem?" Eva asked, her voice hesitant, not believing the truth before her.

EPILOGUE

The man could only nod, all speech lost to him in this moment.

Eva cried, as she threw herself into Kehlem's arms, and the two of them sobbed into each other's shoulders. Overwhelmed by grief, love and pure unbridled joy they held each other close, speaking the words of their souls to each other, bathed in the warm light of the sunset.

Watching the couple from the shadows of an alleyway, a tall woman with red hair crumpled a note she held at her side, and tossed it to the floor. Nodding to herself, she walked towards the golden lit house, a promise of vengeance held tight in her grip.

Thank you for reading

If you enjoyed The Soul's Aspect, please consider leaving a review on Amazon and Goodreads. Positive reviews are the single most helpful way of ensuring indie books get noticed, and pick up traction. Thank you so much for your support.

Please reach out to me on Instagram if you want to chat books or have any questions!

The story continues in The Soul's Instruments.

About the Author

Mark is an indie fantasy author based in the UK. He lives with his wife and various pets, and is all together a jumbled bag of various hobbies dressed in an overcoat, pretending to be a human.

You can connect with me on:
- https://markholloway.xyz
- https://www.instagram.com/markholloway.author

Subscribe to my newsletter:
- http://eepurl.com/hKizOr

Also by Mark Holloway

The Soul's Instruments

Kehlem the Butcher. Hero. Villain. A pale ghost that haunts the empire, or righteous revenant of Casere. Titles thrust upon him that he had no desire to bear, charged by the Aspect itself to end the Vin Empire. And yet his only true desire is to get to Mercy before the empire, to salvage his only chance at redemption.

But change is coming. He can feel it in the crushing weight of his waking nightmares. See it in the uprisings in the empire. Hear it in the hushed rumours of assassinations.

The Aspect demands retribution. Balance. Where there was Order, now comes Chaos.

Long Live Chaos.

Printed in Great Britain
by Amazon